Jake stepped out into the middle of the street, barely registering the screams and gunfire, the dust and smoke. *Come on*, he thought, *show yourselves. Come and get me . . . kill me if you can.* He held the demon gun up high.

As if his death wish had suddenly been granted, he saw his target at last: One of the flying monsters swerved, its shadow-form making an impossible turn in midair. As it came back it fired down at people on horseback and on foot who were still firing their guns, blasting them apart with bolts of lightning.

Still it came on, straight down the middle of the street toward Jake, as if it had been searching for him alone. He could see lights covering its body—demon eyes glowing in the dark.

Come on, he thought, not even sure if he meant the demon or the demon gun. He stood his ground, holding his arm steady. People fled around and past him, clearing his line of fire. Suddenly the targeting arc shone above his wrist; he took aim, helping it find its mark.

The weapon fired with almost no recoil this time. The blue beam hit the flying monster like a bullet's trajectory made visible, before he even had time to blink. It struck the demon almost head-on; the explosion stunned his senses.

The demon tilted, wavered, and lost control, falling from the air even as it roared toward him, like it meant to take him down with it.

Jake ducked as the thing passed just over his head. He spun in his tracks and saw it hit the ground with a grinding crash, plowing a furrow into the packed dirt of the street, trailing fire and debris.

The other demons circling over the town suddenly vanished into the night, faster than they'd come. As they disappeared, a sound like the air exploding shattered windows along the street.

And then there was quiet, as deafening as the pandemonium of moments before.

COWBOYS
& ALIENS™

NOVELIZATION BY
Joan D. Vinge

Based on the Screenplay by Roberto Orci &
Alex Kurtzman & Damon Lindelof and
Mark Fergus & Hawk Ostby

Screen Story by Mark Fergus & Hawk Ostby
and Steve Oedekerk

Based on Platinum Studios'
Cowboys & Aliens by Scott Mitchell Rosenberg

TOR®

A TOM DOHERTY ASSOCIATES BOOK • NEW YORK

This is a work of fiction. All of the characters, organizations, and events portrayed in this novel are either products of the author's imagination or are used fictitiously.

COWBOYS & ALIENS

Copyright © 2011 Universal Studios and DreamWorks II Dist. Cowboys & Aliens TM & © Universal Studios and DreamWorks II Dist. Licensed by Universal Studios Licensing LLC.

A note to parents: Please consult www.filmratings.com for information regarding movie ratings in making viewing choices for children.

Edited by James Frenkel

A Tor Book
Published by Tom Doherty Associates, LLC
175 Fifth Avenue
New York, NY 10010

www.tor-forge.com

Tor® is a registered trademark of Tom Doherty Associates, LLC.

ISBN 978-0-7653-6826-3

First Edition: August 2011

Printed in the United States of America

0 9 8 7 6 5 4 3 2

To mamas who let their daughters grow up
playing "cowboys"
(and reading science fiction)

Especially mine:

Carol (Erwin) Dennison Ward
December 13, 1921 – March 17, 2010

I miss you, Mom.
—March 17, 2011—

ACKNOWLEDGMENTS

I'm much obliged to my steadfast and supportive publisher, Tom Doherty, and my editor, James Frenkel, at Tor Books, for giving me a shot at a real prize (the real prize is never the money); to Cindy Chang, Jennifer Epper, and Jennifer Sandberg, at NBC-Universal, and to the filmmakers, for helping this novelization to fulfill its potential by making possible creative decisions that don't affect the film, but very much enhanced this book.

I'm also obliged to Lawrence W. Cheek for his book *Nature's Extremes: Eight Seasons Shape a Southwestern Land*, an inspiring, lyrical portrait (both visual and in words) of the desert Southwest; as well as to James L. Haley, author of *Apaches: A History and Culture Portrait*, and Dody Fugate (et al.) at the Museum of Indian Arts and Culture, for their detailed and illuminating accounts of Apache society—as well as the mutually tragic history of the Apaches' interactions with "alien invaders" from their own planet. . . . And last but not least, once again, to my mom, for making me proud of the Native American heritage in our own family. The Erie nation may have been erased from history's map long ago, but its descendants remember.

—JDV

COWBOYS
& ALIENS™

"He wants a fight? Well, now he's got one."

—"Gunpowder and Lead" by
Miranda Lambert

*"All the lonely people—where do they
all come from?"*

—"Eleanor Rigby" by
Lennon and McCartney

"The universe is made of stories, not atoms."

—Muriel Rukeyser

1

Spring had come and gone in the desert lands of New Mexico Territory, with all the subtlety of an iron fist in a green velvet glove. For a few weeks rain fell, usually fretful, with frequent rainbows, and the land that had been bleached of color put on a cloak of verdant grass—in a good year, even a show of wildflowers. It was a thing of beauty for weary human eyes to behold.

But already the mantle of green was withering, laying bare the scarred, spectral face of the desert, its true face, amoral and pitiless.

There were some who found peace—or at least possibility—in the desert's truth: A man who had never seen any other place, or a man who never wanted to see someplace else again. Even a man who saw the chance to get rich, in a land where the treasures of the earth often lay right on the surface, marking the spot where veins of rich ore—silver, copper, and especially gold—lay waiting to be sucked dry like bone marrow.

A smart man on the road to a nearby destination—with a good horse and just enough food in his saddlebags, a canteen or two filled with water—might be glad it wasn't raining.

But the man on whom the sun shed light as it rose over the distant rim of a mesa didn't even have a pair of boots. From the heights of the sky, he was no more than a speck in an emptiness as vast as the sky itself, lying like a dead man in the middle of a dusty trail. His dust-colored pants were torn out at the knee, his tanned skin and short tawny hair caked with sweat and dirt. The large red stain on his torn Henley marked the place where something had left a deep wound, still fresh, in his side.

The man who might have been dead twitched and moaned softly, as the full-bore heat of a new day struck him. The unforgiving light of the sun shone in through his closed eyelids and reddened his skin like an open oven. Discomfort prodded him toward consciousness; he shifted again, growing more restless.

Abruptly the man sat up with a terrified gasp, like he'd been wakened out of a nightmare. He sat sucking in air as if he had been running all night, staring at the land around him with the empty eyes of someone who had no idea what he was doing there.

The buzzards that had been circling on the thermals overhead, watching him with more than casual interest, canted their wings and flew off, disappointed.

The man, dazzled by the light, never noticed, seeing the land around him in double vision. He kept blinking, until finally he knew—within a range of several thousand square miles—where he was. In the desert. *Lost in the desert.*

He stared at his bare feet, protruding like strange plants from the bottoms of his pants legs. *Where the hell were his boots?* And then he grimaced, abruptly aware of a sharp, deep pain in his right side. He covered it with his hands, leaning over.

That only made it worse. He sat up straight, taking his hands away. They were red and sticky.

. . . the hell? He looked down at his shirt, seeing the deep red stain; watched it blooming brighter as fresh blood oozed from its center. *A wound . . . bullet wound?* He pulled up his shirt, looked at the blood-caked gouge in his side. He made a face and pulled his shirt down over it again.

Nothing vital hit. He exhaled in relief. *Wasn't even bleeding bad, considering how bad it felt.* Wiping his hands in the sandy dirt, he took another long breath—consciously, cautiously, this time. *Lucky*, he thought, not wondering how he was so sure of that.

He looked at his hands again, as something out of place nudged him further into the reality that was *now*.

Around his left wrist he was wearing a wide, thick piece of metal. *A manacle*—? Too big to be a handcuff, it looked more like an iron . . . but it wasn't heavy enough.

He studied it, already sure that he'd never seen a shackle like this before. It was made from chunks of different-colored scraps of metal, somehow forged into a single band with a kind of precision that ought to be impossible.

Who the hell would make a thing like this? Even if it wasn't a shackle, it looked too much like one for his taste. And more to the point, what was it doing on *him*? Had it been put there by whoever had wounded him?

He'd been wounded, he was lost in the desert without a hat, or even boots. His feet were stone-bruised and cut like he'd come a long way; his right arm was scraped raw and the right leg of his pants had a hole in it big enough so that he could see the ugly bruise on his knee.

He must look the way he felt . . . and he felt like shit. But he couldn't have been lost out here that long, or he'd be dead.

He looked at the metal bracelet again, and a sudden reaction made his gut knot up—an emotion that went beyond confusion, beyond fear . . . closer to blind hatred than anything else he knew. He picked up a rock and hit the metal band with all his strength, hitting it again and again. Panic rose in him as the blows made no impression on it at all.

The metal was light, it should be soft—but it wasn't. Hitting it only made his hands, his arms, everything hurt more; the rock he'd been beating the thing with hadn't left a dent—not so much as a scratch—on its surface.

Cursing under his breath; he threw the rock away. He sat back, putting his hands over his knees, holding himself up and together. His throat was so parched he could barely swallow; his lips were cracked and his belly was tight with hunger. The weakness he felt was more than just blood loss—and yet, looking down at his arms, bare where he'd pushed up his sleeves, he could see that they weren't badly sunburned.

Why was he here? How had he gotten here? Where the hell was here? He couldn't seem to remember any of it. Closing his eyes against the glare, seeing nothing but darkness when he tried to look inside himself. He focused on shutting down his emotions, slowing his breathing, getting control of himself. *He needed to be under control; always ready, watching and waiting for the perfect moment or the wrong move. . . .*

At last he opened his eyes again, strikingly blue eyes that glinted like cut sapphire. He began to run his hands over his half-ruined clothes, searching his pants pockets for money, anything—

Nothing at all. At least he was on a track to somewhere . . . a long, unnaturally wide strip of packed dirt, running from one edge of nowhere to the other, hardly better than the bare ground between patches of rabbit bush and mesquite beside him.

In the far distance he could see the blue-gray, broken-toothed profile of a mountain range; in the nearer distance he saw the mesa over which the sun had just risen. On the other side of the trail there was a weather-etched cliff of reddish sandstone maybe thirty feet high. *At least there were no Apaches on top of it.* They'd be glad to make his day shorter, but a lot more painful.

He looked down again, this time searching every inch of the ground around him for anything at all that might have landed here with him. A spot of light caught his eye . . . something metal, half-buried in the dirt. Carefully, he picked it up, brushing the dust from it: A tintype, a portrait of a young woman. The picture was bent, battered around the edges, but not so much that he couldn't see her face clearly. She looked sweet and loving, with her dark hair mostly gathered up in back but partly free, long enough that it spilled down over her shoulders in deep, shining waves.

She was a total stranger. Why the hell was he carrying around a stranger's picture?

And yet. . . . He looked at her face again, the sweetness of her smile, her eyes that seemed to be gazing only at him with . . . love? For a moment his heart seemed to stop, along with his breath. He stared at the picture like a mountain lion looking down at a doe, ready to spring . . . and finding himself unexpectedly lost in the depths of her eyes.

Unnerved, he stuck the picture into his pants pocket. He wished he had someplace better to keep it . . . a hat. *Damn it, where was his hat?* This day figured to be long and hot, and it had only begun.

He stopped looking, stopped moving as he heard the sound of hoofbeats on the trail. Riders—in no hurry, but coming his way.

His hand went to his hip, before he could form a coherent thought about why; searching . . . His hand made a fist as it came up empty, and he realized his final loss: *his gun.* It was the only thing he could think of that was worth as much to him as his own life.

He looked at his hand and couldn't think of anything else to do with it . . . anything at all. Resigned, he sat staring at his bare feet, waiting for whatever happened next.

He didn't have to wait long. He didn't bother to look back as he heard the riders come over the hill: Three of them, he figured, from the sound.

He finally raised his head as the riders entered his line of sight, taking their measure as they circled around him and stopped their horses: three bearded men—tough, hard-looking men, dressed in typical dark, drab layers, with a black dog following them. Their clothes had a patina of dust on them, as if they'd been riding for a while. There was something about them, almost an echo, that told him they were family: a father and two sons, maybe. The grizzled older man had on a top hat; it made him look like an undertaker.

As the strangers closed in on him, the man saw a long, black-haired scalp hanging from the old man's saddle like a trophy. Another scalp hung from the saddle of one of the sons. By then the man sitting on the ground didn't need that much detail to know these three did more killing than burying.

The three riders stared down at him. At last the old man said, "We're riding toward Absolution. You know how far west we are?"

The man stared back at them, his eyes as empty as his mind was. *Absolution? Was that a place you could find on a map?* Or did the three of them figure if they rode far enough west, all their sins would be forgotten?

The three riders shifted impatiently in their saddles, waiting for an answer he couldn't give them.

"Maybe he's a dummy," one of the sons said.

The father got down from his horse. He was a walking weapons rack—holstered pistol, skinning knife on his belt, and a Winchester carbine slung at his back.

The man sitting in the dusty trail pushed himself to his feet uneasily as the father stopped in front of him and said, "Some reason you don't wanna answer my question, friend?"

The man didn't answer that one either, not sure if he even had enough spit left to let him speak. It didn't occur to him to ask for water, since it hadn't occurred to them to offer him any. He was too aware of the way the sons were positioning their horses around behind him, cutting him off almost casually as they edged in to get a better look at him.

"Look there," one of them said, "he's carrying iron on his wrist . . . and he's been shot."

The father glanced at the man's wrist, at the strange metal bracelet. His expression didn't seem to see anything strange about it. The man was completely surrounded now.

"Could be he broke out of the hoosegow," the other son said. "Might well be bounty money. . . ."

Bounty hunters. If the three of them hadn't been before, they were now. The old man pulled his carbine over his shoulder and cocked it, aiming it at the man as he took another step toward him.

"Not your lucky day, stranger," the father said, glancing down at the man's bootless feet, then up at his face again.

The man's expression had gone completely blank,

like his mind. He stood motionless, his hands down at his sides.

"Turn around real slow," the father said, "and start walking." The man didn't move, and the father took a few more steps, closing the space between them.

The man heard the black dog begin to growl, as if it sensed danger. He stayed where he was, not moving, with not even a flicker of doubt showing on his face. The carbine was now within inches of his chest.

"I said, start walkin'—" The rifle's barrel struck the man's chest.

Suddenly the man reacted like a striking snake. He grabbed the carbine's barrel; it fired as his left hand jerked it free from of the old man's grip. The shot went wild and the father fell back, but not before the man's right hand had snatched his knife from its belt sheath.

The man kept moving, swinging around with the knife, and drove it into the thigh of the closest son, clear to the hilt. The son fell off his horse with a howl of pain; the man slammed the carbine butt against the side of his head, breaking his neck.

The man flipped the carbine as he caught movement out of the corner of his eye; he swung back to see the father struggling upright, raising his drawn pistol. The man cocked the carbine again with barely time to aim, and fired. The bullet hit the father in the chest, and he went down like he wouldn't be getting up again.

The second son was already aiming his revolver. The man leaped, tackling him and dragging him out of the saddle. When the second son hit the ground, he still had the gun; before he could fire it, the man slammed his wrist down on a rock, and the pistol skittered out of reach. The son's hands went for the man's throat then; the man smashed the heel of his own hand into the son's nose, and felt things break and give way. He hit him in the face again and again . . . until at last his blind fury began to clear, and he realized he was hitting a man who was no longer trying to kill him . . . he was hitting a dead man.

He fell back from the body, dazed, gasping for breath. Slowly he forced himself to get to his knees, and then to his feet.

The man stood in the trail, alone again, the only human being left alive. The silence around him was almost deafening; all he heard was his own heart still beating. His eyes moved from body to body, then back to his bruised, aching hands. He stared at them. They were covered with blood again, but this time most of it was the blood of strangers.

He wiped his hands on his bloody shirt, staring at the carnage around him, even more stupefied by the fact that he was the one responsible for it.

Only a stone-cold killer could have done what he'd just done. *But he wasn't . . . couldn't be a killer . . . didn't* feel *like a killer. . . . He was only a . . . he was . . . Jesus God, what was he?* He couldn't remember. He couldn't remember anything at all about himself. He couldn't even remember his own name—

He pressed his hands against his head, trying to keep whatever was left of his mind from vanishing before he could get a grip on it.

The black dog trotted over and sat down in front

of him, as if it had recognized its new master. Frowning in disgust, the man turned away. His eyes went to the canteen hanging from the nearest horse's saddle. He reached out and took it from the saddle horn, uncorking it. *He was still alive. If he wanted to stay that way, he needed water, now.*

At least there was nobody left to kill; he was glad to let his instincts do whatever they wanted. His hands shook as he raised the canteen to his mouth. He drank, forcing himself to do it slowly, until he'd quenched his thirst. The dog lapped at the spillage that dripped off his chin.

The man went through the horse's saddlebags next, finding some beef jerky and hardtack, the only things there that interested him. He ate as he moved from horse to horse, collecting canteens and any other food he could find.

As his head cleared some, with his body feeling a little stronger, he faced the bodies of the three dead men again. He crouched down and went through their pockets, taking any money they had. *They wouldn't be needing that anymore, wherever they were now.* He stood up again, considering. He needed boots, he needed a hat . . . and some clothes that didn't have blood all over them.

The only dead man whose shirt didn't look worse than his did was the one with the broken neck. Their sizes matched well enough. He stripped the jacket, vest, and shirt off the body, threw away his own ruined Henley. He moved carefully as he put on his new clothes; the wound on his side had opened up again during of the fight.

As he buttoned the light-colored linen shirt, he saw fresh blood already soaking through the cloth. He tucked the shirt into his pants and put on the dark vest, hoping that would be enough to hide it. He almost tossed the coat aside, because the day was already too hot. But then he remembered he was in the desert. If he lived through the rest of today, by tonight he'd be getting damn cold.

The last man he'd killed was wearing leather stovepipe chaps that looked almost new. He took them and buckled them on to cover his torn pants. He sized the sole of the stranger's boot up against his foot; it was a decent match. He pushed his sore feet into the man's socks and boots, beginning to feel like at least he might pass for respectable now.

Hat, he thought. *If he died of sunstroke now, it would serve him right.* He picked up the hat he liked best and tried it on. It fit just right. He settled the brim low over his eyes, shielding them from the light and other people's curiosity.

He wondered exactly what other people he had in mind . . . suddenly he remembered the tintype he had found. Retrieving it from his pocket, he took off the hat and carefully wedged the picture into its crown. He resettled the hat on his head, satisfied.

But there was still one thing he needed: a gun.

He moved from body to body again, checking out the men's pistols. They all had decent-looking revolvers. *Good.* . . . He spun the cylinder of each one, rejected the first two because the movement wasn't smooth enough.

The third one was better: an army-surplus Smith and Wesson Schofield .45. Its cylinder moved like its owner had cared about his own life. *Better luck in the next one*, the man thought. The gun's grip felt easy, well-balanced in his hand.

He took the gun belt that came with it and buckled it on. Whoever he was, the pistol made him feel complete in a way he couldn't define.

Then he gazed out across the bleak, glaringly bright plain, feeling more like himself again. He realized that the thought was as completely out of context as he was, standing here in the middle of nowhere . . . and just as meaningless.

He checked over the three horses that stood grazing alongside the trail, waiting for riders who no longer had any use for them. They were all in good condition; he chose the only one without a scalp hanging from its saddle. He fastened the coat onto the back of the saddle, where a bedroll was already tied in place. He slapped the other two horses on the rumps and sent them galloping off down the road, trusting their intelligence to take them someplace better than this.

Still following his own instincts, he mounted the third horse and turned it in the direction the three men had been traveling. *Absolution*. He figured it had to be a town, and in that case, not impossibly far away. He touched the horse with his spurs. It set off at an easy lope, a pace his body didn't find unbearable.

As he started to ride away, the dog got up and followed him. He reined in, looking back at it. Some kind of herding dog, he guessed. Its fur was long and shaggy, mostly black, with a white ruff around its neck that made it look like it'd been born with a collar on.

Maybe it had, because whatever kind of dog it was, it didn't seem to have the sense to go off on its own, now that it was free. It looked back at him, panting with its tongue out, in that way dogs had that made them seem to be smiling.

He stared at it with the eyes of a cougar, passing judgment. Then he turned away again and rode on, not looking back.

The dog followed as he crested the next hill and rode into the valley beyond.

2

Absolution was just a place, not a state of mind. The man only had to ride for half a day to reach it.

Beyond the rise of one more hill, he saw the town waiting for him in the wide valley below. He saw cottonwood and willow trees, and some brighter greens that looked like they might be permanent—signs that the silver band of river running through the valley bottom was a reliable water source.

He was surprised by the number of buildings he could see lined up along Absolution's main street; a couple of cross streets branched off it like veins of ore. *Veins of gold:* A gold strike was the only thing he knew that could pull enough people together to build a town this size, in the middle of a godforsaken wasteland.

He slowed his horse to a walk well before he reached the town limits, giving himself more time to take in details about what he was riding into.

Absolution wasn't the town it had appeared to be from a distance. Even though it was well into afternoon now, the dusty main street was almost deserted. The buildings along it had been put up to last, but the paint on most of them was faded and peeling, blistered by the desert sun. More than one looked abandoned: Whoever had built this town in the first place had given up and left it awhile ago.

Another boom town gone bust, because the gold its founders thought would last forever had run out long before their expectations. It wasn't a ghost town yet, but the people who still lived here were only staying because they had no place better to go.

As far as he could tell, none of that had anything to do with him—except that an empty street in broad daylight made a stranger riding into town a lot more conspicuous.

Something, maybe long habit, told him he didn't want to be noticed, at least not until he'd remembered who he was. He pressed a hand to his wounded side, and then he turned the horse off the main track, circling around behind the row of buildings; looking for one that seemed to be occupied, preferably with an open back door.

To his surprise, he found what he was looking for without having to search for long. He dismounted behind a building with a fairly fresh coat of white paint on its clapboards; the back door was wide open to let in whatever breeze happened by.

He spotted a rain barrel under a downspout near the back steps—lidded against the heat, and still half full. His horse required a lot more water than he did;

anybody who forgot that might as well blow his own brains out, because he'd be dead soon enough anyway, along with his horse. The man let the horse drink, and then looped a rein over the railing of the steps to make sure it stayed there.

Definitely not expecting visitors, he thought as he climbed the steps and went in through the open door. It was only then that he noticed the damn dog had followed him all the way to town, as it appeared in the doorway behind him, gazing up at him with wide brown eyes and that mindless smile.

The realization struck him that the dog was just doing the same thing he'd been trying to do: survive, when its whole life had been pulled out from under it. *By him.* Resigned, he pointed at the floor. "Stay," he said. The dog sat down in the doorway and stayed there, satisfied.

The man took a longer look around, not able to tell what kind of place this was, but seeing what looked like a small kitchen ahead of him . . . and a bottle of whiskey sitting on a table beside the sink. The thought of that appealed to him, and he moved ahead cautiously.

"Hello—?" he called out, not too loudly, not wanting to be caught by surprise if somebody was in the next room, but not wanting to bring them running, either.

There was no answer, no sound of footsteps. Relaxing, he reached the table and the half-full bottle of whiskey sitting on it. He uncorked it and drank several long swallows, enjoying the burn.

The "water of life"—that was what "whiskey"

meant, according to Dolan. Right now he believed it. It didn't even bother him that he had no idea who Dolan was.

He set the bottle down with a satisfied sigh, and moved to the sink. Working the pump handle, he got the water flowing until he'd filled the bowl he found there. He plunged his hands into the cool water; it felt good on his bruised, abraded knuckles.

But he needed to clean himself up. He took off his hat and splashed the water on his face, rubbing off sweat and dust, before he did the same to his hands and arms. Leaning forward, he dumped the rest of the water over his head to rinse off his hair. He used the dry dishrag he found on the table to finish up the job.

Just doing that much left him feeling shaky and in more pain from his wound than he'd been when he arrived. He began to unbutton his vest. His wound still needed tending; even lifting a liquor bottle made the now-constant pain in his side worse. He pulled up his shirt and poured whiskey into the deep, bloody gash, clenching his teeth. The burn it set off in his wound felt familiar, but a hell of a lot less pleasant that the one in his throat and belly.

He took another long swig of whisky, set the bottle down on the table, reached for the cork . . . and froze in mid-motion, as he heard a rifle cocked behind him.

"Palms to heaven, friend," a voice said.

Slowly the man raised his hands.

*   *   *

PREACHER MEACHAM APPROACHED the stranger he'd found in his kitchen, drinking his whiskey, with considerable wariness. Few people came to call these days, and of those who did, none used the back door—or drank his whiskey without an invitation.

"Easy, now . . ." the man said, as Meacham pressed the muzzle of the rifle against the man's neck.

As Meacham removed the pistol from the stranger's holster, he felt more than saw the man's muscles grow taut and twitch. He realized that the man had *let* him take the pistol.

He took a deep breath, thanking God, as he stepped back again. "Turn around," he said.

The stranger turned around. Meacham saw the man sizing him up, the same way he was taking the man's measure; saw the intensely blue eyes catch on his graying hair and beard, his unremarkable clothing. Without his official preacher's hat and coat, he supposed he looked like any other townsman. The man looked up at him again.

His stare gave the blue eyes pause. He might be getting on in years, but those years had taught him a lot of lessons. Meacham was a man who'd seen a lot in his life, and done a lot, before he'd found God, or God had found him. The lessons he'd learned still showed in his eyes, proving that he hadn't forgotten any of them.

Looking the stranger over, he saw a man in his mid-thirties, a hard man whose gaze was as impenetrable as diamond. But most men who lived for long out here came to look like that. The clothes the man had on were mostly dark, and as unremarkable as his own, in these parts. It was only the telltale way he moved, or chose not to, that made Meacham suspect he was anything but ordinary.

But the man had surrendered his gun without a fight, and Meacham was sure he'd had a choice about that. He looked at the sizable blood stain on the man's light-colored shirt, which was untucked from his pants and dripping good whiskey on the floor.

"Been shot," the man said, as if it was all he could think to say.

Meacham forgave the stranger any whiskey he'd used for medicinal purposes. He wondered if the stranger had come here wanting more than a drink. From the look of him, he needed more than a drink. But the man didn't say anything else, just stood looking at Meacham like he'd decided at least that standing still hadn't been a mistake.

Out of the corner of his eye, Meacham saw a black dog, one he'd never seen before, sitting patiently just beyond the doorway. Most of the dog's body was still in sunlight, but it made no attempt to come further in out of the heat. Something about the way the dog sat reminded him of how the stranger now stood. His own tension eased just a little, but his curiosity only got stronger.

"Only two kinds of men get shot," Meacham observed, "criminals and victims." He carefully set the man's pistol down, well out of reach. "Well," he asked, when the man still said nothing, "which one are you?"

The man hesitated a moment before answering, as if he had to think about it. ". . . I don't know," he muttered finally.

Meacham heard truth in the man's voice. And for just a moment, as he'd said the words, the stranger's face had looked completely empty, lost . . . terrified. The man blinked, and the moment of vulnerability vanished. But Meacham had seen enough. *Lord have mercy*, he thought. *A truly lost soul.* "Got a name, brother?"

The man looked down. "Don't know that either."

Sympathy almost forced its way onto Meacham's face. But he'd lived too long to be scooped in that easily. "What *do* you know?"

The stranger looked up again, after a pause. "English," he said, deadpan.

Meacham raised his eyebrows, this time letting a faint smile show. But he still kept the rifle up, ensuring that the man kept his hands in the air. "Where'd you ride in from?" he asked.

The stranger glanced away. ". . . west."

"That's a big place," Meacham said mildly, "'. . . west.'"

The man ignored that, and Meacham nodded at the doorway he'd come through, indicating that the stranger should go through it, first.

Obediently the man stepped forward, pushed his way through the swinging door with his hands still up.

Meacham followed close behind, still carrying the rifle. "Take a seat."

The man looked around the large, high-ceilinged room, back at Meacham, with something like confusion. "This your place?" he asked.

The room was mostly shuttered, cooler but darker

than the kitchen, and Meacham remembered that it wasn't necessarily a familiar sight to most men's eyes. "Six days a week it is," he said, and this time he did smile. "On the seventh, it belongs to the Lord."

Comprehension dawned in the stranger's eyes, as he looked out over the rows of pews, back at the pulpit, and the large, plain cross hanging on the wall behind it. He sat down in a pew at the front; as he did, another stab of pain made his mouth thin. But his gaze followed Meacham, as the preacher moved toward a table at one side of the room, where the afternoon sun shone in through one of the few unshuttered windows.

The man's restless eyes went back to exploring the room with the frank curiosity of someone who couldn't remember the last time he'd seen the inside of a church.

In this case, Meacham realized, that could be literally true. He let down his guard another notch. "My name's Meacham," he said, by way of introduction. Quietly he laid the rifle on the table beside him. He noticed that the man picked up even that slight sound.

The stranger, glancing at Meacham, lowered his hands. His face stayed calm, his eyes showing only faint relief. He didn't move from his seat. Meacham turned his back as he went to the cupboard where he kept his assortment of medical supplies, and a spare bottle of whiskey. He brought the box and the whiskey back to the table.

"Woke up in the desert," the man said, volunteering information for the first time. "Like I dropped out of the sky."

Meacham looked up from sorting through the supplies. "Well now," he said, "I certainly recall one such story happening before . . . fella by the name of Lucifer."

The stranger blinked, as if he recognized that name, knew the story it belonged to. But there was nothing more to his reaction, as if hearing any name but his own seemed useless to him, and that one wasn't it.

"Come into the light," Meacham said, an invitation as much as an order. He wet his hands with the whiskey, and wiped them on a clean cloth. The man stood up, a little stiffly; something close to genuine relief showed in his eyes as he came toward the table, seeing Meacham's preparations.

Meacham took out a threaded needle and gestured for the man to sit on the table in the light. The stranger obeyed him, lying back and pulling up his shirt as if he knew what to expect.

Meacham gave the man a drink of whiskey from the bottle on the table, then took one himself. Sewing up a damaged human body wasn't like darning socks; it was one thing he never found to be a soothing activity. He lit a match and ran the needle through the flame to sterilize it, before he looked at the wound. His forehead furrowed, and he took another swig from the bottle. The man put up his hand, reaching for the whiskey again, but Meacham had already set it down. "Try'n hold still. . . ."

He ran the hot needle through the stranger's skin,

starting to stitch the sides of the wound together. The man's upraised hand knotted into a fist; his jaw clenched over a sound of pain. But then he held his body perfectly still and didn't make another sound as Meacham went on stitching him up.

It was a relief to work on a man with some self-control, Meacham thought. He was too used to patching up drunken victims of bar brawls, who generally wailed and thrashed like overgrown three-year-olds.

". . . mining town?" the stranger asked finally, his voice held under tight control, like his body. *Talking to take his mind off the pain, now,* Meacham thought, all the more convinced that some part of this man's brain knew things that maybe no one would want to remember.

"Yeah, that was the notion. Ore played out, like water sinking into sand . . . ," Meacham said, shaking his head. "No gold, no town. Most everyone moved on to the new diggings in the Mimbres Range." He stopped stitching, staring at the wound, as he realized he'd never really seen a bullet wound—any kind of wound—that looked like this before. "Odd wound," he said. "Looks . . . cauterized." That had to be the only reason the man hadn't passed out from blood loss somewhere on the trail. "This isn't a gun shot." He was certain of that now. "Where'd you get it?"

The stranger glared up at him, tight-lipped.

"Right: you don't remember." Meacham grimaced apologetically, and went on stitching. "Well, I can't absolve you of your sins if you don't recall 'em," he said, doing his best to keep on distracting the man as well. "That bein' said—" he met the stranger's eyes with a smile in his own, like sunlight reflecting in water, "whether you end up in Heaven or Hell, it's not God's plan . . . it's your own."

He looked down again and took two more stitches before he pulled the thread taut. He cut the thread with his teeth. "You just gotta remember what it is." He finished his sermon and glanced up at the man again. "Finger?"

The man obliged, putting his finger on the knot to hold it, while Meacham tied it off.

Meacham stood back, admiring his work. "Not too bad for a country preacher—"

A window exploded beside the church's front door; both men jumped. The sounds of gunfire and whooping and hollering came uninvited through the broken panes, destroying the peaceful refuge the church had been a moment before.

Meacham left the stranger sitting on the table like a startled cat, along with his medical supplies, as he ran to the front door and peered out. "Damnfool Dolarhyde kid, drunk again . . ." Meacham went out the front door without a backward glance.

The stranger got down off the table and stood listening to the commotion outside as he tucked in his shirt and re-buttoned his vest. Then he went through the door to the kitchen to fetch his hat—and his gun.

3

The late afternoon sun silhouetted Absolution's main street against a backdrop of red-gold, light filtered through dusty air. Long blue-violet shadows lay in graceful strokes across the ground, a promise that the days relentless heat would finally ease as the hours crept toward dusk.

But for once Meacham failed to appreciate God's artistry. His attention was already fixed on the riders heating things up a few doors away, in front of the Gold Leaf Saloon. He headed toward the trouble, hoping the Lord would grant him the tact, if not the saintly forbearance, to help keep any human beings from ending up like his window had.

He spotted Percy Dolarhyde, the Colonel's cocky hot-headed drunkard of a son, easily enough—always the center of attention, even though he was on foot, and the cowhands that worked for his father were sitting on their horses as they shouted and egged him on. They drank for free, and they drank a lot, when they were with Percy.

The only man there who wasn't drunk, or even smiling, was Nat Colorado, Woodrow Dolarhyde's half-Apache foreman. He was still a young man, but he was tough as saddle leather, and Meacham had never seen him smile. He'd been the Colonel's trusted right-hand man for as long as Meacham could remember, more like an older son than a stray Apache half-breed.

Everyone who knew the Colonel knew he hated Apaches with a vengeance, and as far as Meacham knew, Dolarhyde's trust was not something he'd ever given to any other man. Bearing the weight of that alone would be enough to make any man lose his smile.

But worse yet it meant Colorado was expected to play nursemaid to Percy whenever he went into town. So far he'd kept Percy from actually killing anybody, and anybody else from killing Percy. But that was all he was allowed to do.

Nat sat in a chair on the boardwalk, his feet up on the hitching rail while he watched Percy's antics. But a man would have to be blind not to realize there was nothing relaxed about him, or the way he held the rifle that rested in the crook of his arm. Even with the senior Dolarhyde's reputation, and Nat's own, there was no guarantee Percy's luck would last forever. . . .

Nat paid no mind to Meacham as he passed; all of his attention was fixed on Percy, his mouth set in its usual expressionless line. Meacham glanced back as he entered the crowd of cowhands and townsfolk, and caught a glimpse into Nat's eyes. He was startled when he didn't find resentment, disgust, or simply nothing at all there; the depths of Nat's eyes were dark wells of sorrow as he watched Percy.

The preacher looked away again, shaking his head. *Two lost souls in one day* . . . Either he was getting closer to God's own wisdom, or he'd been spending too much time in the sun.

Percy was amusing himself and the crowd this time by shooting holes in the saloon's elaborately painted sign. Percy was tall and brown-haired, a handsome boy—living proof that appearance was only skin-deep.

Meacham wondered whether Percy would be any different if he was sober. He'd never seen the boy completely sober. If Nat Colorado had it hard being trusted by Percy's father, Meacham figured that Percy probably had it harder, being the Colonel's only child.

Meacham tried to find a shred of compassion for the boy somewhere in his soul, and couldn't. Just because Percy was miserable didn't give him the right to act like a miserable bastard, taking it out on everyone he saw, any more than it gave anyone else that right. Either Percy would have to change until he was unrecognizable, or Meacham would . . . and that would be a miracle in itself.

He looked back as Charles Sorenson, the saloon's owner, came out through the bat-wing doors, wearing spectacles and an apron, shouting, "Hey, hey, Percy, what're you *doin*'?"

A lot of people besides Meacham called Percy a

bastard, and it wasn't due to an accident of birth. But unless they were as drunk as he was, they never did it to his face. No sane person ever called his father "the Colonel" within earshot either, because anyone who did wouldn't live to brag about it.

Everybody called Sorenson "Doc"—and he really was a doctor, who'd earned an M.D. at a medical school back east. He'd taught Meacham a lot about treating wounds, despite—or maybe because of—the fact that most of the men who needed tending had gotten that way in his saloon.

Out here, Doc was just a saloon keeper, and his name was a joke. He'd been born a fish out of water, here in the Territories where he'd grown up.

". . . little target practice, Doc!" Percy shouted, slurring. "Don't worry, ain't gonna wrinkle your dress!" Doc winced as Percy fired another bullet into the sign.

Percy laughed at the look on Doc's face as he tried and failed to hide how upset, and how scared of Percy, he was. Meacham felt his mouth pull down; he was filled with compassion for Doc, and an ungodly urge to bash Percy's head against the nearest hard object.

Doc's wife, Maria, came out of the saloon in his wake. It was mainly her cooking that still drew in customers from the town's small population, so that at least the Gold Leaf hadn't completely turned into an extension of Dolarhyde's petty empire, and Percy didn't drink them into bankruptcy. Maria's eyes were alive with both anger and concern—mostly concern for her husband's safety—as she tried to get him back inside, out of harm's way.

"*Stop*!" Doc was shouting, "There's roomers up-stairs!"

She caught him by the arm, forcing calm onto her own face as she tried to calm down her husband, but having to raise her voice just to make herself heard over him, "—*it's okay*. There's no one upstairs—"

"—Maria, *please*, go back inside—" Doc tried to shake her off.

She clung to him, "—*Mira*, he's *drunk*, just let him *be*—"

"—bad enough, he drinks for free, now he's gotta shoot up the place?" Doc shouted.

Percy spun around, looking up at Doc where he stood at the top of the saloon steps. Drunk or sober, Percy had his father's uncanny knack for hearing any-body who happened to badmouth him. "What was that, Doc? *What'd ya say?* Come over here and let's settle up what we owe." He beckoned Doc into the street, gesturing with his pistol.

Reluctantly, Doc started down the steps to where Percy was waiting. Maria held onto her best placating smile, even as she lost her grip on her husband's arm. "He didn't say anything! *Por favor, patrón*," she called to Percy. "What else can I get you and your men?"

But Percy had his eyes set on Doc, like a cat with a mouse hooked on its claw, and he wasn't about to let go. He shook his head, "No, *no*—I wanna hear what you said. You ungrateful for our business? Wasn't for my daddy's cattle, there'd be no coin goin' through this town! No meat on your tables, your doors'd be closed!"

"Don't mean no disrespect to your father, Percy,"

Doc said, realizing he'd crossed a dangerous line. But trying to backtrack, he only succeeded in stepping on the other foot of Percy's flimsy pride.

Percy swung at Doc's face, knocking off his spectacles; they landed in the dirt of the street. Doc's face reddened with fresh humiliation and anger as he stooped down to pick them up, before Percy had a chance to step on them.

Percy laughed and fired his gun. The bullet kicked up dust right beside Doc, who jerked back, startled, and sat down in the street. Doc never used or even carried a weapon, which was fine for a big-city doctor . . . but not for a saloon keeper. Even Percy knew Doc was as gun-shy as a nervous horse.

"You see his face?" Percy crowed. "He thought I was gonna blow his head off!"

Meacham stepped out of the crowd of onlookers and crouched down to help Doc find his glasses. Doc's body was trembling, not from fear but rage, as he got to his feet again and went back up the saloon steps to Maria's side. Gently, she led him inside through the batwing doors.

Meacham took a deep breath. "All right now, son," he said, amazed at the mildness of his own voice, "these people are scared enough of the damn Apaches without you shootin' your gun off."

Percy had planned to ignore the words; but then he turned back to Meacham with a wicked grin. "Know what, Preacher? You just gave me an idea. . . ." He looked around at his drunken crew, and at the townspeople who'd come out to gawk or frown at his one-man show.

"I know it ain't Sunday," Percy hollered out, "but what say we take up a collection for the poor man—" He took his hat off, flipped it over, holding it out like a collection plate. But his other hand still held his pistol, and he pointed it at the gathered townsfolk. "Who's got money? Greenbacks or silver, we won't pay no mind!"

At gunpoint, the suddenly helpless crowd was all too vulnerable. Folks began to toss their change into the hat as Percy circled around them, reciting like a Gospel sharp on Sunday, "Much obliged . . . much obliged. . . . Mighty Christian of ya . . . I'm sorry Doc's bad luck has to be taken out on you good people. . . ."

He stopped suddenly, eyeing the one person who made no move to give him anything. "Hey!" he shouted. "*You*, too."

Meacham suddenly realized that Percy was talking to the stranger he'd left in the church. The man had followed him, obviously, but Meacham had no idea how long he'd been standing there, casually leaning against a corner post of the covered walkway, just watching Percy like everyone else. *Or maybe not just like everyone else.*

The man stayed where he was—no surprise to Meacham—even when Percy moved toward him and pointed the gun at his face. The man never flinched, still surrounded by the unnerving calm that he'd worn like a second skin when Meacham caught him in the kitchen. "Watch where you point that thing," the man said to Percy. "Before you get hurt."

Nat Colorado's eyes were on the man now, too.

And this time, Meacham noticed, his expression was dead serious. Nat got to his feet, holding his rifle, watching the stranger like he might watch a rattlesnake suddenly coiled up in Percy's path. But then something changed subtly in his expression; he stared at the man with a deepening frown, doubt slowly turning into what looked like recognition.

Whatever it was he saw in the man's face, he didn't act on it, and any clues at all were lost on Percy.

Thoroughly riled now, Percy leaned in close to the stranger's ear and said, in a mock-whisper loud enough for everyone to hear, "I wanna give you the benefit of the doubt, 'cause maybe you don't know who I am—"

The man did move, then. His knee hit Percy in the balls, faster than anyone else could react.

Percy's eyes bulged and he doubled over, gasping, in too much pain even to scream.

The man turned away, moving through the crowd like water, and went on down the street. He walked past the small knot of deputies who stood outside the sheriff's office and jail, where they had been observing Percy's antics along with everybody else, just as ineffectually.

The sheriff was out of town—but even if he'd been here, it wouldn't have made much difference. Even the lawmen didn't make a move in Absolution without the Colonel's permission—at least not against his son.

Under the circumstances, they didn't say a word to the stranger, either.

But Percy had finally found his voice, and enough

self-control to raise his pistol. *"Hey! You!"* he shouted, his voice ragged. *"Turn around!"*

The man kept on walking, ignoring him. Meacham had never seen Percy this angry, and to his amazement, Percy's temper was still getting hotter. *"Hey!"* Percy screamed. *"I'm warning you!"* He fired a warning shot, aiming to the stranger's left.

One of the deputies cried out, clutching his shoulder, and slumped to the walkway's deck.

Meacham pushed through the crowd, hurrying toward the wounded man, his attention now solely on helping someone who really needed it.

"Whoa!" Percy said, in slurred surprise. "Where the hell'd he come from?" As he started toward the deputies, the townsfolk took the opportunity to get away from him, heading off in all directions.

WITH TIMING THAT might have been planned by God Himself, or maybe the Devil, Sheriff John Taggart and his chief deputy, Charlie Lyle, rode back into town through the scattering crowd of what appeared to be Absolution's entire population.

Taggart's seasoned eyes went directly to the center of the commotion: Percy Dolarhyde, as usual—drunk as a skunk and just about as pleasant to have around. Taggart exchanged glances with Lyle, who rolled his eyes and muttered a curse under his breath.

They'd been out all afternoon because somebody had found a couple of riderless horses wandering loose along the river. They'd seen the horses, established that they belonged to Wes Claibourne and one of his sons, either Luke or Mose. It had been impossible to follow their back trail for long, so he and Lyle had called it a day. Taggart had heard a lot of things about the Claibournes—about how they worked both sides of the law.

The scalps hanging from the Claibournes' saddles had only made it easier for the two of them to turn their backs on the whole matter: The scalps had been women's. If someone had beaten the Claibournes at their own game and left them for buzzard bait, he figured New Mexico Territory was probably better off for it.

But seeing Percy Dolarhyde in town and in trouble meant that their long, wasted day had just gotten a little longer. They rode on toward the sheriff's office.

"Damnation!" Lyle said suddenly. Taggart saw his other deputies huddled in a bunch, and one of them, Duffy, down on the walkway, bleeding. Preacher Meacham was already beside him—treating an injury, Taggart hoped, and not giving him last rites. The two men dismounted together, Taggart keeping hold of his shotgun.

"Grandpa! You're back!"

Taggart glanced up, hiding his concern as his twelve-year-old grandson, Emmett, came running to greet him. Taggart put an arm around the boy's shoulders, giving him a brief hug and the reins of the two horses, as Lyle went ahead to find out what had happened to Duffy. Whatever it was, he didn't want the boy witnessing too much, or thinking too much about it. "You go see to the horses, all right?" he said.

Emmett looked pleased to be given a man's job,

or what passed for one, to a boy. As he led the horses away, Taggart turned back to the real man's work, which too often involved bloodshed and possible death. "What happened here?"

Lyle's face said it was bad news; he nodded at Percy, who'd actually followed them as far as the entrance to the office. "He shot Duffy," Lyle said, keeping his voice low. "Just winged him," he added, as Taggart's face froze.

Taggart's expression turned grim clear to his eyes.

"It—it was a warning shot!" Percy was yelling. "It wasn't my fault! He came outta nowhere!" Percy pointed with his gun past Taggart and Lyle, at a stranger standing in the street. "He dry-gulched me! Tryin' to make me look like a fool!"

Percy had always done a perfectly good job of making an ass of himself without anybody's help, as far as Taggart was concerned. The man he'd pointed out was a stranger in town; but the stranger wasn't even trying to explain his version of the truth. He simply stood where he was, watching everything that went on, with an expression Taggart couldn't figure out.

Taggart wondered who he was. A man who stood up to Percy Dolarhyde and then just walked away from it wasn't your average stranger.

He looked back at Percy then, all too aware that his usual bunch of hangers-on, with Nat Colorado, too, were forming a circle around the boy now, on horseback.

"You crossed a line, Percy," Taggart said, loudly enough for all of them to hear. "You went and shot a deputy. I gotta lock you up."

The shotgun Taggart was holding was some comfort, but not much, as Nat Colorado turned his horse so that Nat was facing him directly. Nat's hand lingered above his holster; the look on his face was almost protective as he said, "Taggart, you know that's not a good idea."

Taggart knew Colorado had a job to do, and he'd do what he had to—anything he had to—for Percy Dolarhyde's father. He was a fast gun, a deadly shot, and half Apache. But Nat wasn't crazy; in fact he might just be the sanest person in the whole Dolarhyde outfit, and that included the Colonel.

Taggart understood Colorado's position right now, all too well. But he had a job to do, too, and Nat would just have to live with it.

"Nat, you know he drew blood on a lawman," Taggart said, glancing at Percy, his expression warning the other man off. "I don't have a choice—you get your crew outta here, now."

Nat looked back at Percy, and then at the stranger in the street. He looked down, considering, for a long moment. At last his hand dropped to his side, and he nodded to Taggart, letting the sheriff know he'd made his decision. He started to turn his horse away, a sign to the other men that they should do the same. The shooting had sobered them all up considerably.

"Nat, you son of a bitch!" Percy shouted. "Where you going? Don't even *think* about leavin' me!"

Nat turned back in his saddle. "I'll tell your father what happened today," he said, his voice expressionless. And then he rode away, taking the other men with him.

Taggart watched them ride off. He had mixed feelings—the only kind he ever seemed to have anymore. He took a deep breath, let it out. The trouble was under control for now. But when word reached the Colonel . . .

"Shit," he said to Lyle, who was still standing at his side. "That'll just bring more trouble." He turned to Percy, who was surrounded by deputies now, and no one else. Taggart gestured with his shotgun, and Percy finally handed over the pistol he was still holding. Two of the deputies helped Duffy onto his feet and into the office, as Lyle went back to haul Percy after them and lock him up.

"It was an accident!" Percy wailed. But this time nobody was listening.

Taggart walked out to where the stranger still stood, looking on. "John Taggart," he said, offering the man his hand.

The man shook it, meeting the sheriff's eyes directly. But he didn't give his own name; didn't say anything at all. Taggart noticed the metal bracelet the man wore on his left wrist, as it glinted like gunmetal in the late afternoon sunlight. He'd never seen anything like it, but something about it made his eyes skittish. And yet some part of his brain was starting to tell him the man looked familiar. . . .

The stranger turned and began to walk away down the street.

"Hey, mister—" Taggart called, before the stranger had taken more than a few steps. "I know you from someplace?"

The man turned back again and studied his face;

he looked as if he was trying to recall ever meeting Taggart before. Taggart's well-cultivated handlebar mustache usually made him hard to forget, even in a place where a lot of men tried to grow one as handsome. And then, there was always his badge.

The man shook his head. ". . . couldn't say." He shrugged and went on walking.

Taggart started back toward his jailhouse office, having nothing else left to keep him from facing the scene he knew he was going to find there.

THE WOMAN WHO had been watching them all, completely unnoticed for far longer than anyone suspected, slipped out of a sheltered spot between two buildings and began to follow the stranger.

As she moved past Taggart, he didn't even look at her, although she was also new in town, and a far more unusual stranger than the man without a name. Only the black dog that had come to Absolution along with the man she was following seemed to notice her. It accompanied her now as she moved slowly along the walkway, keeping her distance, but always keeping the man in sight.

4

The shadows of the cattle grazing in a field beside the river grew long as the sun set, bringing the blessed relief of an evening breeze.

The three Dolarhyde cowhands who sat around a campfire, sharing their evening meal, had spent the entire day searching for strays and found only two dozen. They'd driven them back here, to a place they weren't likely to wander away from during the night.

Ed and Little Mickey, who had worked for Dolarhyde longer than most, ate in silence as they watched the third man, Roy Murphy. Murphy was a new hand, and he'd been doing more drinking than eating, having brought a full bottle of rotgut home brew with him in his saddlebag. Ed and Little Mickey could tell already that Murphy wasn't going to work here much longer if he couldn't stay sober long enough to remember what a man did—and didn't do—when he worked for a mean-tempered hardass like Woodrow Dolarhyde.

Finally Ed said, "Take it easy on that Taos Lightning, Murphy—Mr. Dolarhyde don't like drinkin' on the job."

Roy glanced up over the nearly empty bottle, and the look on his face told Ed he'd just wasted his breath. "Don't give a rat's ass what the high-and-mighty Colonel don't like." His flushed face screwed up in mocking disgust. "Don't care how many Indians he sent under, neither."

Little Mickey snorted. "You sure flap them gums a lot when the boss ain't around."

Roy drained the dregs of the bottle. "I'd say it if he was here! Money makes you soft, boys . . . take it from me." He belched, and threw the empty bottle away. Ed heard it smash against a rock.

Ed glanced at Little Mickey, whose eyes said the same thing he was thinking: *Murphy wasn't gonna work out.* And unless he was luckier than he had any right to be, he wasn't even going to survive the experience.

Roy got to his feet somehow, and stumbled away down the embankment to the river to take a piss. Ed and Little Mickey went back to eating, content to let him go to hell in his own way.

Roy came to a wobbling stop at the river's edge, unfastened his fly, and leaned out over the water's edge to relieve himself.

A sound like the sky exploding knocked his brain sideways, as the air around him suddenly turned solid, and punched Roy into the water like a giant fist.

For what seemed like an eternity, he floundered in a watery cloud of bubbles and fright, until he burst through the river's surface again, gasping for breath, and then just gasping—

The sight and sounds up on the field he'd just left filled him with more fear than he'd felt half drowning: Blinding flashes like bolt after bolt of lightning struck the ground, out of a perfectly clear sky; things erupted in flames wherever they struck. Cones of bright blue light darted through the smoke from the burning field, moving so fast Roy couldn't tell where they were coming from or what they were doing . . . but he heard men shouting, and then screaming, as cows bawled in panic and pain.

Before he could finish absorbing the assault on his senses, the air and water and the riverbed he was standing on began to shake as *things* crested the hill— enormous things, the forms of which he couldn't make out as they shot toward him like flying bullets. *Flying* . . .

The water rooster-tailed around him as they skimmed the river just above his head. Roy yelled and ducked back underwater.

When he broke the surface again, out of breath, the river lay quiet, flowing as normally as it always had.

Coughing and wheezing, he waded ashore. He could only crawl, with his heart pounding fit to burst, as he struggled up the bank to the place where he'd left the others.

He finally managed to get up on his feet as he reached the top of the hill. He was instantly sorry he had, because the first thing he saw was a cottonwood tree, burning like a torch. His jaw went slack as he looked down again, and saw the charred carcass of a steer . . . and then another, and another . . . half a dozen dead animals lying in the field. Some of them looked like they'd exploded—entrails and legs and heads scattered, with nothing left to hold them together. The rest of the heard had vanished.

"Ed?" he called, his voice shaking. "Mickey—?"

But they were gone, like the cattle, as completely as if they'd never existed.

Roy's knees collapsed, and he sat down at the edge of the field, still gaping, until his brain had taken all it could. And then he passed out in the flattened grass.

BACK IN ABSOLUTION, in the hot, overcrowded jailhouse, Sheriff Taggart nursed a cup of room-temperature coffee, leaning against the wall alongside his other deputies as Lyle tried to finish patching up Duffy at his desk.

Duffy was wailing and squirming like a baby as Lyle struggled to tie off the bandages. Small wonder the preacher had gone home as soon as he'd determined that neither Duffy's body nor his soul were in any real danger. Adding to the general level of aggravation, Percy Dolarhyde was still all mouth, even locked in a cell in the back of the room.

Days like this made Taggart wish he'd gone deaf. He was getting old enough—hell, he was fifty-two—but he was blessed with the constitution of a man half his age, and on a good day he still felt like one. This hadn't been one of those days.

Percy Dolarhyde had ensured he'd have to stay up

most of the night, too—probably all of it. *God only knew if the prison wagon would get here before Wood-row Dolarhyde did, and what would happen, either way . . .*

Duffy gave another yelp, and Lyle half shouted, "Hold still, dammit, hold still—!"

Percy Dolarhyde hung onto the bars of his cell, sobering up now, but still more than halfway to drunk. "You know this is all your fault?" he said, glaring at Duffy. "Lettin' that stranger dry-gulch me—"

"Arrrgh, stooop—!" Duffy howled, as Lyle jerked the last of the bandage tight around his upper arm, and finally knotted it off.

Kids these days . . . no guts and no sense, Taggart thought, thinking not just about Percy, but about some of his own hired help. *Not that he could afford to be fussy, the way things were now in Absolution.*

He pushed away from the wall, too restless to stay still any longer. He thought briefly of his grandson, Emmett. Emmett was a good boy, and Taggart hoped he'd grow into a good man. But it was hard with the kind of job he had, to keep the boy from seeing or learning too much, too fast. He was vaguely surprised—and relieved—that Emmett hadn't shown up back here after he took care of the horses.

Taggart supposed Emmett had gone on home like he should have, and Juanita, the housekeeper, had fed him and put him to bed like usual. *Lord love her.* She was a good woman who'd raised seven children of her own. She'd taken good care of Emmett ever since Emmett's mother, Taggart's only child, had passed away. He was sure she'd take care of the boy even if something happened to his grandpa, one day. . . .

Taggart's face turned bleak again, his mood driving the regret and weariness from his eyes. He went to the gun rack and began pulling down shotguns and rifles, handing them out to the deputies. He was going to need all the men tonight, and they'd damn well better be armed to the teeth if they had to face Woodrow Dolarhyde and his crew.

Percy watched him from the cell, with too-knowing eyes. "Why don't you do yourself a favor and lemme go right now; we'll say this never happened. . . ."

"But it did happen." Taggart turned toward him, still holding a rifle, his stare more resigned than bitter. He turned back to Lyle, handing the rifle to him. In a low voice, he said, "Where's the wagon?"

"On its way—" Lyle said, his face showing Taggart his own mixed emotions. He began to pass out ammunition.

"We gotta get him out of here fast," Taggart muttered.

"What wagon?" Percy said loudly. *Nothing wrong with his hearing. . . .* "What wagon—!" he shouted.

Taggart finally looked at him again, keeping his own voice as matter-of-fact as he could. "We're taking you to the federal marshal in Santa Fe."

"Federal marshal?"

For the first time Taggart had the satisfaction of seeing a few simple words wipe the insufferable smile off that little cur's face.

"You done lost your mind?" Percy hollered, just as

loud, but whining now. "It ain't like I'm Jesse James! This might just cost you your miserable *life*. My daddy hears you put me in an iron coach, he'll kill ya—!"

"Percy, you wounded an officer of the law," Taggart repeated again, wondering if the significance of that would ever sink into Percy's brain, drunk or sober. "I don't have to—"

He broke off, stopping dead in front of the notice board papered with wanted posters and changes in the territorial laws. He pulled down a particular sheet, stared at it, speechless.

"But he's fine!" Percy waved a hand at Duffy, who frowned, oblivious to the fact that Taggart was no longer listening to him. "He's all fixed up! My balls hurt worse than his shoulder!"

"Sonofabitch. . . ." Taggart murmured, still staring at the poster. He looked up at his deputies; suddenly the Dolarhydes were the furthest thing from his mind.

DOC SORENSON SET down mugs of beer for two customers at a table. He set the mugs down harder than he should have, and foam slopped over the rims onto the well-scrubbed wood.

The two men looked up, surprised. He watched their surprise turn to amusement as they saw the anger still smoldering in his eyes, which the bent rims of his spectacles did nothing to hide.

"Can you put that on Percy's tab?" one of the men asked, looking at Doc like the soul of innocence. His buddy elbowed him, and they both snickered at the joke . . . laughing at *him*.

"Very funny," Doc said, his voice grating. He held out his hand. "Fifty cents," he said.

Across the room, Maria looked up as if she felt the pain behind his simmering frustration. She'd always seemed to know his moods better than he did, for as long as he'd known her. She was the reason he had come back here from the East; she was the reason he stayed here, in this land only an Apache could love.

She came toward him and he saw the concern in her luminous brown eyes. *God, she was so beautiful . . .* and not just because she had a beautiful face: It was her soul he'd always loved the most, looking out at him through those eyes. She was the only one who'd ever really seen him for who he was. "I can take over, *mi amor*," she said quietly. "Why don't you rest . . . ?"

Doc frowned, because right now her loving concern was the last thing he needed, after another humiliation at the hands of Percy Dolarhyde. He was a man, and in front of a bunch of strangers he didn't need a woman, even his wife—especially his wife— treating him like a weakling. "We got customers," he said. "I don't need any rest. What're you sayin'?"

Maria took her hand from his arm, took a step back from the look in his eyes. "Nothing," she protested, "just that I—"

"They made a fool out of me," Doc snapped, cutting her off. "You don't have to dress it up. Now the people got less confidence in me—in this *establish-ment*—!"

She shook her head, her long, midnight curls moving across her shoulders. "That's not true; I just didn't want you to get shot—"

"Well, I'm *fine*," he said angrily, only proving to both of them that he wasn't. There was no way he could explain it to a woman, how in this world a man's reputation for toughness was worth everything he had. His whole identity depended on the proof of his ability to survive, his ability to protect the people he loved and the things he called his own, with his skill . . . with a gun.

"Maybe we don't belong here," Maria whispered, looking down, blinking too much.

Impotent anger overwhelmed even his love for her—any emotion that would have let him understand what she was really saying. His self-disgust turned everything ugly, and made every word into a knife that cut them both. "You wanna leave?"

"How can you think that?" He could see the hurt in her eyes. "I followed you here because I'd follow you *any*where. *Esto es tu sueño*, your *dream*! Remember how happy we were when we first came?" She only moved closer to him, not further away . . . but every gesture she made only added to his feeling of failure.

"Don't you understand?" The truth burst out of him as if he'd shouted it. "I can't *protect* you! I can't even protect myself. . . ."

"You don't have to prove anything," Maria said

softly. "You're the bravest man I know." She leaned toward him and tried to kiss him.

He physically pushed her away. "I'm not a child." He turned toward the stairs that led to the upper level and began to climb them, disappearing into the darkness—angry at her, and this world they were trapped in . . . angry most of all at himself.

Maria watched him go, with the wounds his words had left in her heart still showing in her eyes. But the part of her mind that had not been stolen by sorrow registered another customer entering through the swinging doors. Hastily she pulled herself together, grateful for the composure her years of working in her parents' cantina had given her.

She turned back and saw the man who had ended Percy's reign of petty terror so effectively, without firing a shot, put his foot up on the rail and lean against the bar. A dog was following at his heels, and though he did nothing to acknowledge it, the dog lay down on the floor beside him.

Her smile became genuine as she approached the stranger to take his order.

"Steak," the man said.

Maria uncorked a bottle of their best rye, and poured him a shot. She set the open bottle on the bar and left it there. "I have a nice *pasole* today. On the house. For what you did." Still smiling, she turned away and went into the kitchen. Her mother had always made *pasole* with pork, but here everything was beef . . . Dolarhyde's beef. She would make sure there was plenty of steak in this man's stew, and put it in the biggest bowl she could find. He looked like a man who needed a good meal a lot more than he needed her gratitude.

THE MAN PICKED up the shot of whiskey and tossed it back. It slid down his throat like flaming honey . . . *this was the good stuff.* He was vaguely surprised by her generosity; he hadn't shut down Percy Dolarhyde for any other reason than because the little turd had stuck a big pistol in his face. He wasn't used to gratitude. But food and whiskey felt just fine.

If he had some food, maybe it would help him think straight. Or maybe enough liquor would make him go numb. Either one seemed like an improvement over the way he felt right now.

He leaned against the bar, resting on his arms. His eyes caught on the metal cuff he was still wearing. He stood staring down at it, watching the pattern of its colored metals change in the lamplight. *How? Where—? Who . . . ?* A thousand unanswered questions filled the empty space where a lifetime of memories from before today should have been.

He looked at the bottle of whiskey, wondering what it would really take to let him remember the past; or at least to let him forget today. . . .

He glanced up, into the mirror behind the bar, as someone else entered the saloon—a woman, all alone. The handful of other customers sitting around the room barely seemed to notice her, which struck him as odd. A woman who looked like that walking into a saloon alone would normally attract a lot of attention—particularly when she was wearing a gun belt over her dress.

Maybe it was the pistol that kept them from staring. . . . Her eyes flicked his way, but she didn't look like she had plans to use the gun on him. He looked down again and considered pouring himself another drink.

The woman took the place next to him at the otherwise empty bar.

He glanced at her out of the corner of his eye, mildly curious.

She was staring at him. He looked up at her, suddenly wondering if she knew him. Her eyes were the color of sage, ringed by darker green, and something about them was like a bottomless well. They caught his own, drawing him in until he felt like he was drowning. . . .

He broke her gaze with an effort, tried to focus on her face as a whole. Her expression was as unsmiling as a judge's, and yet her face was beautiful . . . *heartbreakingly beautiful.* . . .

Jesus Christ—what was he doing? She was a complete stranger . . . just like everybody else. And a woman was the last thing he wanted, or needed, right now. He looked away from her face, his gaze barely glancing off the rest of her as he let it fall away. Her dark hair hung free down her back like she'd never given it a second thought, and her pale, sand-colored dress covered her all the way up, and down to her practical boots. The dress had tiny flowers all over it. She would've blended into any background within a thousand miles of here. *Nothing unusual.*

The gun belt, on the other hand, was enough to make most men think twice about even approaching her. *Not the friendly type.* So why the hell was she standing there, staring at him?

"I know you?" he asked, finally.

The dog lying down beside him got up with a small whine and licked the woman's fingers.

"No," she said, looking at the dog with a faint smile. "But your dog likes me."

He turned back to the bar and poured himself another glass of whiskey. "You can have him," he said.

The woman made no response as he downed the second shot of rye. But she was still looking at him; he could feel her eyes.

"My name is Ella," she said, when he went on ignoring her.

He had no name to offer in return, and so he said nothing. As if she'd decided staring at him had been a mistake, or maybe for some other reason, her gaze moved to the metal cuff he wore. "Where did you get your bracelet?" She reached out and touched it. He let her, and saw the strange intensity come over her face as her fingers made contact with its surface.

He frowned, pulling his arm away, out of reach. "There something you know about me, lady?" He met her stare, ready for it this time—or at least he thought so.

Her gaze reached straight in through his, like she was trying to turn his soul inside out. But then the look on her face changed, and her gaze let him go.

"You don't remember anything . . . do you?" she

murmured, as if somehow she'd actually seen the truth.

The man turned away, looking down at the metal band, feeling his flesh crawl. This day had started like a bad dream, and now it had just gone beyond strange into something completely outside of his comprehension. "What do you *want*?" he asked, his voice actually getting away from him.

"I know you're looking for something. . . ." She hesitated, measuring his reaction. "So am I." The intensity now radiating from her made him want to take a step back.

He reached for the whiskey bottle and poured himself another drink. But as he raised the glass, his hand stopped in mid-motion. *Something was coming . . . danger.* He didn't know how he knew. But he knew—

"Move away," he muttered to Ella. Whatever showed on his face, she obeyed it.

Deliberately, he set the glass back on the bar. His hand moved down, closer to his holster, as he turned to face the entrance.

The saloon doors swung inward. Blocking the exit he saw Taggart—*Sheriff Taggart*—backed up by all his deputies. Taggart's grim stare was fixed on him; the barrels of shotguns and rifles shone in the light, all aimed his way.

"Need you to follow me to the office so we can have a little chat, fella," the sheriff said. The matter-of-factness of the words didn't match the way he held his gun, or how the deputies held theirs.

"No need." The man settled his hat more firmly on his head, pulling down the brim. "Moving on."

Apparently the sheriff didn't agree. He entered the saloon, making room for his deputies to spread out in a human barricade as they all started moving toward the man.

The man recognized Duffy, the one who'd been shot by Percy Dolarhyde, from the blood on his shirt front. Duffy was glaring at him like it'd been his fault, and holding a shotgun in the crook of his good arm.

They were all watching him with expressions as mixed as if they'd stumbled on a stick of dynamite with a burning fuse. *Why*—?

"Jake Lonergan," Taggart said, "you're under arrest."

Who the hell was Jake Lonergan? The name meant nothing to him. But the look in the sheriff's eyes said it ought to.

The man backed up against the bar. He looked at the sheriff again in disbelief; then he looked down at the floor, his empty eyes suddenly seeing nothing at all. *This was impossible. . . . The first town he'd come to, he'd walked straight into a trap? Was he really an outlaw, a wanted man, and he couldn't even remember that*—?

The sheriff and his men were slowly approaching from across the room; people who'd been sitting at the tables had already started to get up and back away. One of the deputies cocked his rifle.

"Wouldn't do that—" the man said, raising his head. The deputy who'd cocked his gun looked into the man's eyes, and his face turned pale. But Duffy only raised his shotgun to take better aim.

Christ, did the warrant say "dead or alive"—? The sheriff and his men were ready to use those weapons in a room full of innocent bystanders. Were they really that scared of Jake Lonergan? Or was "dead" just easier? *Damn it, he didn't want to hurt anybody. But he didn't want to die, either—*

The man's hand moved away from his gun; his glance went to the bottle of whiskey on the bar beside him, before he looked back at the sheriff's men.

The deputy named Lyle had gotten the closest, with his rifle raised to his shoulder, aimed at the man's chest.

Close enough ... The man caught the barrel of Lyle's gun with one hand, yanking it free as his other hand smashed the bottle of rye over Lyle's head. He flipped the rifle and shot Duffy in the leg. He punched the third deputy in the throat; the last one hit the faro table face first, and slid to the floor.

Only Taggart was left standing—his eyes clear and his rifle leveled.

The man grabbed the rifle's barrel, heedless, jerking it upward just as Taggart fired. The bullet lodged in the ceiling, and then the rifle was in the man's hands, and he was taking aim at somebody who'd just tried to kill him. His finger found the trigger and started to tighten—

"No—!" a boy's voice cried out.

The man's eyes flashed to the window. He saw a boy's anguished face: *the boy who'd come running*

out to greet the sheriff . . . and now was going to see
his grandpa shot dead by a total stranger—

The man eased his finger off the trigger. Slowly he
lowered the gun.

Taggart stared at him, astonishment replacing the
fear in his eyes.

"I don't want any trouble," the man said.

The butt of a pistol cracked against his head, and
his body dropped out from under him. He lay on the
floor, fighting to stay conscious as rushing blackness
began to smother his brain. He rolled onto his back,
and he saw Ella's face, blurring, her hand still holding the gun that she'd hit him with.

Taggart drew his own pistol, pinning the man in
place as effectively as if he'd put a foot on his neck.
He kicked the rifle aside, and leaned down to pull the
man's revolver from its holster. The man lying on
the floor looked toward his hat, lying overturned beside him, at the photo wedged inside the crown. . . . the
nameless woman smiling back at him with love. . . .

In a waking dream, she was smiling as he entered
the cabin, their refuge . . . as he took her into his arms
and kissed her . . . as he proudly dropped his saddle-
bags on the table . . .

No, don't . . . No—

. . . her smile disappearing as she saw the gold
spill out . . . as she turned to him, furious, and she
said, "No!" . . . and then . . .

No—

Then it all—

. . . a glass vase shattered . . . he heard a voice—
her voice?—screaming . . .

... the cabin ... the blinding light ... a maw of devouring darknes ... screaming ... pain ...

No ...

The image of her face blurred into patterns of light and darkness, and everything faded to black.

5

H e was dreaming . . . or was it—? . . . *the faces of demons, leering down at him . . . pain like the torture of the damned . . . screaming . . . human eyes gazing upward, white and opaque as milk-glass . . . a cavern, where nightmare shapes shifted all around him, things he couldn't even put a name to, flickering and fading like flame-shadows on the stone wall . . . on a cabin wall . . .*

. . . the wall, the ceiling, torn away . . . deafening noise and blinding light . . . a cabin, a cavern . . . the woman from his picture, her face filled with fear as she cried out, and he tried with all his strength—

But whatever he was trying to do or stop was lost, along with her face . . . as the whole world turned upside down, inside out . . . as it all changed. Light blinded him, blue light brighter than the sky, and the last thing he heard was her voice, screaming in terror . . .

* * *

THE MAN THE law called Jake Lonergan jolted awake, with screams still echoing inside his head. He squinted in the sudden brightness . . . only lamplight, not sunlight, this time.

Not blue light . . . He rubbed his eyes and groaned, rolling over. His face and hair were wet with something that didn't feel like water or smell like blood. Something slimy.

As things came into focus he made out a face looking down at him: Percy Dolarhyde's face. Percy spat on him, again.

That dung-eating maggot—Jake bolted upright, with murder in his eyes.

Percy dodged backward out of his reach, laughing at him from behind bars . . . the same kind of bars, Jake realized, that caged them both now. He wiped the spit off his face, swearing under his breath. As the rest of his senses began to come back, he remembered what had happened in the saloon to make him wake up here, and why his head hurt so much. . . . He touched the lump on the back of it, beside his ear; felt his hair matted with dried blood.

Ella. That woman, she'd knocked him out just as he'd. . . . *Damn her, that bitch, that* witch—

Jake wished he hadn't sat up so fast; his head left him feeling queasy from the change of position. Blinking more of reality into focus, he recognized the inside of a jailhouse.

Nobody official was in the sheriff's office right now; there was no one here at all but him and Percy.

"You're gonna burn, boy," Percy Dolarhyde said. His voice peeled Jake's nerves like a skinning knife. Percy was pressed up against the bars again, still wearing the same ugly sneer from Jake's memory. Jake had to look away from it, or be sick to his stomach.

But turning his head couldn't shut out Percy's voice, the diarrhea of taunting threats. "My daddy's comin' for me. He learned how to kill a man *slow* from the Apaches. I'm gonna watch you suffer a long, long—"

Without looking back at him, not even bothering to get up from the bunk, Jake stuck his arm through into the next cell, grabbed Percy, and slammed his damnfool skull into the iron bars, knocking him out cold.

Hell was other people. . . . Jake lay down on his bunk again, relieved to finally have peace and quiet so he could nurse his aching head. His body hurt almost as much, and he remembered his wounded side . . . remembered Preacher Meacham stitching it up . . . remembered everything back to the moment he'd come to, early this morning. Before that, nothing. Still. *Like he'd dropped out of the sky,* he'd said to the preacher.

He remembered what Meacham had said to him in reply: "*. . . another such story . . . fella by the name of Lucifer.*"

He stared at the bars of his cell. His name might as well be Lucifer, from the reception he'd gotten in this town. The sheriff claimed he was Jake Lonergan . . . and Jake Lonergan was a wanted man: *wanted dead or alive.* That meant the territorial government had put out a bounty on him—and up in Santa Fe they didn't pay bounties on dead men unless the law had declared they were of no use either way, to anybody but the Devil.

Jake Lonergan, in the law's opinion, was the kind of man who deserved to be shot down like a dog. Or, if taken alive, hung from a scaffold to choke away his final moments of life in agony and humiliation.

He sat up again, slowly this time. He crossed the cell with equal care and hung onto the bars, peering out into the sheriff's office. He spotted the wanted poster lying on Taggart's desk. With his body pressed up against the bars, he could only read the largest print from where he stood. But that was enough:

JAKE LONERGAN
WANTED: DEAD OR ALIVE
$1,000 REWARD

If you wanted a man dead, you put out a poster like that on him. If you wanted him dead a lot sooner, you offered a big reward. *But a $1,000 reward . . . ?* The territories were dirt poor; they didn't have the resources to spend that much on one man, no matter what kind of murdering lowlife bastard he was. Whatever Jake Lonergan had done, he must've woken up the wrong passenger when he did it . . . one with a whole lot of money and influence.

If he was really Jake Lonergan, with a thousand dollar bounty on his head, why the hell was he still alive?

Jake Lonergan. Jake Lonergan. "Jake Lonergan—"

He repeated the name out loud, saying it over and over, but it stirred nothing inside him.

Not his name, not his past . . . not his crimes. He didn't feel like a cold-blooded killer. But then, how could he explain what he'd done to the three men who'd tried to bushwhack him this morning . . . to the sheriff's men . . . to Percy.

He glanced over at Percy, sprawled on the floor in the next cell. Well, maybe that had just been doing the world a favor for a few hours.

This entire day seemed like one long nightmare, only with some of it worse than the rest . . . the part with the screaming, the undead faces, the pain . . . the bright-darkness, and sounds like nobody on earth had ever heard or made. . . .

But waking up from that had only left him trapped here: *Was this Hell?* He didn't know much about Hell, or Purgatory, any more than he really understood absolution.

Absolution was just a place. But somehow it had come to seem like Hell on Earth. "*Come into the light,*" the preacher had said; but he'd only meant to fix the wound in Jake's side.

Jake went back to the bunk and lay down again, shutting his eyes, blocking everything out. Even if he never opened them again, the darkness was the only hiding place he had, at least for now.

OUT ON THE Dolarhyde spread, the cowhands had taken Mr. Dolarhyde down to the river, to see for himself the mystery of the dead cattle. Torches lit the darkness of the same field where, not long before, a blazing cottonwood tree would have given them all the light they needed.

Woodrow Dolarhyde stood on the edge between light and darkness, staring down at the remains of a steer. His perpetual frown deepened, etching the bitter lines of his face into an even bleaker, more unforgiving mask.

If he hadn't known that was a cow before, he wouldn't have known what it was, now. . . . He kicked the carcass with his boot.

The men who'd ridden out here with him stole glances at him again; they were as skittish and wary as their horses right now, but not entirely for the same reasons. The horses were only animals; their senses told them things about this place no human could detect, told them to be afraid.

The men knew enough to be afraid of the unknown, too, but it was fear of the known—of him—that made them the most fretful now: his ruthless anger, his pitiless vengeance . . . his absolute control over everything and everyone that so much as touched his life. That was how he preferred things; that was how he intended to run things and keep things, forever—

He became aware again of the man's voice still whimpering and pleading, at the center of the torchlight: Roy Murphy, the only man left out of three, that some of his other men had found when they'd ridden out to check on things.

Just around dusk, he'd been told, the men had seen and heard unbelievable lights and sounds coming from clear out here by the river . . . things none of them could adequately describe. To hear them tell it, the strange phenomena had scared them shitless, even at that distance.

It hadn't scared them as much as he did, obviously, or they wouldn't have gone out to check on what'd happened.

When he'd ridden out himself to see what in hell the problem was, the men who'd been waiting there had still found only Roy Murphy, lying in the grass, reeking of alcohol—and half a dozen dead steers.

"*Please!*" Murphy's voice rose, intruding on Dolarhyde's thoughts again. "I didn't kill your cattle, Colonel Dolarhyde! You gotta believe—"

Dolarhyde raised his finger: the gesture was barely visible in the torchlight, but silence still fell at his signal. Dolarhyde was accustomed to prompt obedience—as well as to men who disappointed him.

What he was unaccustomed to was anything that made him doubt his own eyes and ears, or question his fixed view of the world. Right now, although he'd never admit it, he was confounded by the dead animals on the ground around him, and amazed almost to the point of amusement by the audacity of the lie that Roy Murphy had been swearing was true.

He moved closer to the place where two of his most reliable men, Greavey and Parker, had tied Murphy between two horses—his arms fastened to one horse's saddle, his legs to the other. The horses stood obediently, waiting, for now . . . but not for long.

Dolarhyde came close enough to look down into

Roy Murphy's wide, frightened eyes, letting the man have a good look into his own. "You only been riding for my brand what, 'bout two weeks?" he said. "You don't maybe know who you're dealing with, Roy. Nobody calls me 'Colonel.' Ones that did are mostly dead."

He paused, letting that sink in, satisfied when Roy's eyes got even wider and more desperate. "Now: You, Ed, Little Mickey was s'posed to be picking up strays. . . . How many you get?"

Roy strained just to form words. ". . . b-bout twenty-four, boss. . . ."

Dolarhyde's expression didn't change. "You say you weren't drinkin' . . . I can smell it on you. Don't you respect my rules, mister? What kinda man blows up other people's cows, and tells a bullshit story. . . . Couldn't do no better than that? Where's the other eighteen animals, Roy?" Roy shook his head. "It's like I said, there was a bright light. . . ."

"So there was these big 'lights,' you fall in the river; when you come up . . ." Dolarhyde's face twisted with disgust. "Two of my oldest hands was just 'disappeared.' And there's these, these exploded . . ." His voice trailed off as he looked again at the carcasses of the cattle lying all around him.

"There wasn't no storm tonight, no lightning. You don't respect me, do you. Otherwise you wouldn't lie to me . . . *would you?*" Dolarhyde drew a Bowie knife from his belt, letting the blade gleam in the torchlight, beautiful and deadly. "Funny thing about respect. When it's gone, it's all over; everything gets sideways. . . . I can't have that. Know what I'm saying, Roy?"

Murphy didn't even try to answer. But at the sight of the knife, piss stained his pants, and dripped onto the ground.

Dolarhyde's cold, scornful smile vanished abruptly as he turned away at the sound of riders approaching. He stood waiting, the knife still in his hand, as the men who had gone into town came riding out to find him. He searched their faces, looking for two in particular. He saw only one of them: Nat Colorado. His frown deepened again as he realized something serious must've happened for Nat to come looking for him clear out here.

Nat reined in in front of him and dismounted.

"Where's Percy?" Dolarhyde demanded.

Nat's glance went from his knife to his face. It was Dolarhyde's face that added a touch of fear to the respect in Nat's voice, as he said, "Taggart locked him up, boss."

Dolarhyde stiffened. "*Why?*" he rasped. "For *what*—? What the hell'd he do now?"

Nat forced the words out of a throat that didn't want to say them. "Shot a deputy."

"Goddammit!" Dolarhyde's fist tightened around the knife hilt.

The horses around them moved restlessly at the sound of his anger. The two that were tied to Roy Murphy, already stretching his entire body with every small movement, moved some more.

"He didn't kill him," Nat added, as if that might

bring Dolarhyde some sort of comfort, or cool his outrage.

"Who's Taggart think he *is*?" Dolarhyde's voice was enough to make Nat thank God that he wasn't Taggart. "He wouldn't have a job if . . . this is my town!"

Roy Murphy cried out in pain, as the two riderless horses stretched him almost enough to dislocate a limb, but Dolarhyde still ignored him. Confronting Nat, he said, "Now I gotta go in there, *reason* with him . . . cause of *your* failure to take care of my son. Didn't I tell you to watch my son—?"

Dolarhyde turned away abruptly with the knife in his hand, and in one stroke slashed through the rope tethering Murphy's feet.

Murphy's lower body slumped to the ground, and he breathed a sigh of relief. "Thank y—"

Dolarhyde slapped the rump of the horse Murphy was still tied to. It bolted away into the night, dragging a screaming Roy Murphy with it.

Dolarhyde put away the knife as he closed on Nat again. Nat glanced up at him, barely. Dolarhyde's fists were still knotted with anger; Nat's expression said he figured it was his turn. . . . Braced against the blow he expected was coming, Nat stared at the ground.

Dolarhyde studied his foreman, who stood gazing at the ground covered in dead cow parts as if he was afraid Dolarhyde had done that, and that he might be next.

Dolarhyde's fists unclenched. He looked at Nat a

moment longer. He shook his head. At last he turned on his heel and shouted, *"Everyone saddle up!"*

"Boss," Nat said, "we ought to bring some extra hands."

Dolarhyde stopped, turned back to look at him. "What for?" he said.

Nat took a deep breath. "You ain't gonna believe it . . . but I think Jake Lonergan's in town."

Dolarhyde's eyes narrowed, as if every other thing on his mind had suddenly ceased to exist. "What—?" he whispered.

"JAKE LONERGAN?"

Jake sat on the floor of his cell, his back resting against the back wall, staring into a void. He glanced up as the sheriff and his men finally re-entered the office, but it took his mind a long moment to realize someone had actually called his name—if that was his name. . . . He sat blinking, as Taggart stopped by his cell.

Jake still felt dazed, like his head hadn't recovered yet from Ella's blow . . . or he'd had too much whiskey on an empty stomach. *Or maybe it was just everything.* All it meant was that he was still sitting in a jail cell, trapped in what now passed for reality.

Sheriff Taggart turned the key in his cell door; for a moment, Jake's hope shot up.

It dropped into his boots again as he registered the way the armed deputies were flanking Taggart. Some of them appeared to be new recruits, but two men glared at him over their guns; they both looked like they had broken noses. Lyle's head was bandaged under his hat.

The sheriff looked into the next cell, where Percy Dolarhyde still lay unconscious on the floor. He looked back. "What happened to him?"

Jake glanced at Percy, back at Taggart again. "Couldn't say."

Lyle unlocked Percy's cell; he and another deputy dragged Percy out into the office, heading for the door. Taggart was holding a pair of manacles as he approached Jake. "Am I gonna need these?"

Jake glanced at the other deputies and their weapons; they kept their guns trained on him, but they were keeping their distance this time.

"No," he said, looking back at the sheriff again. He'd done enough damage for one day . . . and he didn't particularly want to end it riddled with bullet holes.

But either the sheriff had been watching his eyes move, or the question had been rhetorical, because Taggart came forward and put the irons on him anyway. He had a hard time with the left one, finding a place for it by the metal bracelet. He glanced at Jake with an odd look, and another look at the bracelet, before he backed away.

"What're the charges?" Jake finally remembered to ask.

Taggart picked up the wanted poster from his desk and began to read them off: "Arson, assault, mayhem, hijacking—says you robbed the bullion coach last month, with a gang of outlaws including Pat Dolan and Bull McCade, which makes you accessory to every law *they* broke. . . ."

"That it?" Jake said, almost relieved . . . almost amused. *A thousand dollars on his head, just for that?* The sheriff held the poster out so he could take a look. He glanced at the face on it: it looked like a prison picture, badly reprinted. *Was that him?* He realized he didn't even remember what he looked like, anymore . . . He read just above the picture, "SCOURGE A' THE TERRITORIES." *Yeah, right.* His mouth curled up at the edges.

"Murder," the sheriff added. "Whore outta Cottonwood Grove, next county over—name of Alice Wills."

Jake's smirk fell away, leaving his face stunned. *No. . . . That was impossible; it couldn't be true. He wouldn't hurt—*

Taggart took down Jake's hat from a hook on the wall, and removed the tintype of the woman from inside it. He held up the picture. The loving, gentle eyes found Jake's—or he found them, automatically, as she smiled, seemingly only for him.

"This her?" Taggart asked.

Jake gazed at the picture, feeling only confusion, a nameless grief, an inexplicable resentment at the question. "You say I killed this woman?"

Taggart shrugged. "You tell me."

Jake looked down, his eyes desolate. *How was he supposed to do that?* He didn't know whether he was a cold-blooded killer or not. He had no idea what he was really like, or capable of. He thought of the face on the wanted poster, a face with stark, angular planes, and the eyes of a man he wouldn't want to cross. The eyes of a man who'd kill you for saying the wrong thing, or maybe for no reason at all. *If he would actually kill a woman like that . . .*

He only knew that if he had to live his life this way much longer, he didn't give a damn if they hanged him—guilty or not—because he couldn't take much more of this.

The sheriff put the picture back inside the hat and tossed the hat to Jake. Jake caught it with cuffed hands. Looking up at Taggart, he said, "Why would I carry around a picture of a woman I murdered?"

Taggart only gave him a look that said anything Jake Lonergan, Scourge of the Territories, might do—even sparing his life—was beyond his comprehension. "That's for Santa Fe to sort out."

He opened the cell door, and gestured to Jake. "Now I'm puttin' you in that coach," he said. "I will treat you with respect, but make no mistake—if you try and escape, I *will* put a bullet in you."

Jake put on his hat and walked out of the cell. At gunpoint Taggart pushed him toward the front door, and through it into the shadowy lamplit night.

A coach stood outside the jail—an armored prison wagon with oak lattices barring the windows. Deputies lined the short path between the door of the jailhouse and the coach, their guns still trained on him.

A crowd of murmuring onlookers was gathered behind the deputies, staring at him. *Christ, didn't these people have anything better to do?* He supposed they didn't, in a place like this.

If he tried to make a break for it now, he'd never get through that crowd without someone getting hurt. It would probably end up being him; but now he really didn't feel like he wanted to hurt any more strangers on his way out of town.

Even before he got to the door of the prison wagon he heard Percy Dolarhyde, awake at last and already mouthing off. Resigned, he climbed into the coach just as Percy tried to stick his head out the open door, yelling at Taggart about how *it was an accident, they got no right sendin' him to the federal marshal*—

Jake shoved the little shit back into his seat so he could get past. Percy broke off his rant to call him a few choice names.

Jake observed the bruises that had streaked Percy's face with the colors of sunset, wherever his head had collided with the bars of his cell. Jake barely managed to keep the smile of satisfaction off his own face. A few bruises were probably the worst thing Percy would end up with, if half the threats he was blurting about his old man were true. On the other hand, Percy's face just might be the last amusing thing Jake Lonergan ever got to see. . . .

Jake sat down on the opposite bench and looked out the window on the far side of the coach. He didn't expect to find a friendly, or familiar face in the crowd that had spilled out into the street; didn't even know why part of him was searching for one. But then he caught a glimpse of Preacher Meacham, framed by the bars of the oak lattice. As their eyes met, Meacham's face filled with sympathy, and regret. His was the only one, but Jake appreciated it, for as long as it lasted.

He thought he saw Ella moving through the crowd near Meacham; he recognized the dog that had followed him all day still at her side, like it'd come to say goodbye. He looked back again as the sheriff said, "Gimme your wrist." Jake held out his hands. The sheriff unlocked the manacle on his left hand, freeing it—grabbed Percy's arm, and locked the iron around his wrist.

Sonofabitch—Jake thought.

He saw a tight grin come out of hiding under Taggart's mustache. "Best way to make a man stay put— chain him to his enemy."

Taggart showed the grin to Percy as he said, "You lovebirds have a nice trip, now." When he slammed the coach door he was actually smiling; the relief on his face made him look ten years younger. Jake heard the heavy lock being fastened.

"Are you tryin' to get me killed—?" Percy whined out the window.

OUTSIDE THE PRISON wagon Jake heard Taggart again, sounding abruptly exasperated, but not at him or Percy.

"What are you doin'?" Taggart said to somebody. "Go on home, go to bed."

A boy's voice answered: Taggart's grandson—Jake could just see him outside the window, hanging on his grandfather's arm.

"Please don't go."

Taggart shook the boy off, gently but firmly. "Have to, Emmett. It's my job."

"I don't like it here," Emmett's voice rose as he got more upset.

Jake watched Taggart's face, seeing sorrow, strain, regret, and love move across it. Taggart said, like he'd repeated it a hundred times before, "Your pa's gettin' things in order. When he does, he'll send for you."

"Been over a year . . ." Emmett said, his voice starting to get tremulous now.

A flicker of something crossed Taggart's face that told Jake the man was telling lies he was having trouble keeping up. He watched Taggart force a smile as he put a hand on the boy's shoulder. "Don't you worry, he will. And this is where your mama's buried—you know I can't leave my little girl. Now what would she say if she knew I let you stay up so late?" He began to turn the boy around, urging him back to wherever he should've been.

Jake was suddenly glad he hadn't had to kill the man; even if it meant he'd wound up in this fix.

He sighed and tried to settle into his seat, too bone-weary and disoriented to do anything but let the coach's wall hold him up. *It was a long ride to Santa Fe. He could worry about the end of it later. . . .* Right now his whole body ached—not just pain, but hunger gnawed at him too. *Damn, he never even got to eat that* pasole—He realized how little the pain or hunger had really bothered him, until now; like they were things he was used to enduring, to the point of ignoring them, for as long as he had to.

His right arm jerked up short as he leaned back. Percy sat sullenly at the far end of the other bench, pulling the chain taut, keeping him from sitting comfortably. Jake yanked on the manacles, and Percy fell off his seat.

That little pissant wasn't going to make what might be his last ride miserable, simply by existing. Jake gave Percy a long, meaningful stare, and then leaned back again, making himself as comfortable as he could; forcing Percy to adjust, if he wanted to stay conscious.

"Ah, shit. . . ." Percy muttered. He got back up onto the bench and didn't try anything more.

Jake folded his arms and looked toward the streetside window. He started, as he found the last person he'd expected, or wanted, to see there—Ella, the woman from the saloon, staring in at him.

. . . the hell? He frowned. *What was she, a bounty hunter—?* He started to turn his face away.

But that desperate, driven look was in her eyes again; the look that had seemed to see right through him earlier. . . . Unwillingly he turned back, not able to ignore her even now, even though he wanted to.

"Listen, I'm sorry—" she said, her fingers tightening over the window lattice until they whitened. He glanced at her face, "But I had no choice. I couldn't let you leave."

Jake grimaced, holding up his chained hand. "Well, I'm leaving now."

Jake heard Deputy Lyle shout, "Taggart!" in sudden warning.

Taggart looked away at something, and his face

turned as hard as stone. "Get inside now," he said to Emmett. The townsfolk who'd surrounded the prison wagon began to vanish too, clearing out the street.

As their voices faded, Jake heard the sound of riders, coming in fast. Percy sat up across from him, suddenly alert and expectant, and Jake's eyes hardened.

"I need you," Ella said. Looking back at her, he saw the truth in her eyes, but no more clue as to why.

"You got something to say, *say* it," he snapped at Ella, as he heard Taggart calling orders up to the wagon's driver.

"I need to know where you came from."

His eyes widened, just for a second. Then he muttered, "So do I—" and looked away.

"Step aside, miss," Taggart said, through the far window, and it was a sharp order, not a request. The deputies nearest Ella moved in to force her back from the coach onto the boardwalk.

Percy sniggered, grinning at him. "Oh it's *on* now. . . ."

Jake peered out the street-side window again, trying to see what had turned the whiny little shit back into a gloating monster, just as riders surrounded the coach, most of them carrying torches. Two men rode up close on either side, peering in.

Jake recognized one of them—the man the sheriff had called "Nat" while facing him down, when Nat had tried to intimidate him into letting Percy go. Jake didn't recognize the other man, until Percy yelled, "I knew you'd come for me, Pa!"

Dolarhyde.

6

Dolarhyde peered in at them, his jaw set. He looked old . . . but he wasn't as old as he looked; torchlight only deepened the unforgiving lines of his face. He looked damned intimidating, especially from where Jake sat now—ruthless and vindictive, used to getting his way, always. And rich—his bandana was made of patterned silk. Jake figured that explained a lot about Percy.

"*Shut up*," Dolarhyde snarled at Percy. "I'll deal with you later—"

Jake glanced at Percy with real understanding, but no compassion. Looking back at Dolarhyde, he found Dolarhyde looking at him with eyes that were the color of steel in the torchlight.

Dolarhyde looked away from Jake again, looking toward Taggart. "What's my boy doing chained to that outlaw?"

Glancing from window to window, Jake saw Taggart's whole body tense up. Taggart looked like he was set to stare down the Devil himself. His eyes hadn't been that cold even when he'd gone up against Jake in the saloon. Suddenly a lot of random things Jake had seen and heard this evening began to add up in his mind.

"You know I can't let him go," the sheriff said. "He shot a deputy."

Dolarhyde's expression eased a little, but his eyes lost none of their deadliness. "We can work this out, John," he said, with a casual arrogance that told Jake he was used to lording it over this town—that he thought everything in it, including the sheriff, belonged to him.

And then his voice turned lethal, and his eyes filled with pure hatred as they fixed on Jake again. "But I want that other fella—" Suddenly he could have been the Devil himself as he glared in at Jake and said, *"Where's my goddamn gold?"*

Oh, shit, Jake thought. *Not another one. . . .* He met Dolarhyde's hatred with complete incomprehension. ". . . who the hell're *you?*" he asked.

The hatred in Dolarhyde's eyes turned to fury. "Who the hell am *I?* Woodrow Dolarhyde. . . . I'm the man whose gold you stole off the bullion coach a month ago. Five year's worth of my hard work. Five thousand double eagles." His voice grated, *"I want it back."*

Jake glanced away at the sheriff and his men, looked at Dolarhyde and the riders behind him: They outnumbered the sheriff's men by two or three to one.

He met Dolarhyde's gaze, thinking fast. "Why

don't you get me outta here? We can talk about it."
He smiled, making it a dare.

He figured a man who'd looked at him the way
Dolarhyde had probably would torture him to death,
just like Percy'd said—for information he didn't have
a clue about. *Or he could try, anyway. . . .*

"All right, that's enough." Taggart's voice cut the
invisible cord of tension between them. He said to
Dolarhyde, "You can handle it with Judge Bristol.
I'm gonna escort Percy myself, make sure he's treated
fair."

"I ain't talkin' about him!" Dolarhyde snarled.
"Lonergan ain't worth nothing to me hangin' from a
rope. Either you give him to me now—" His voice lit
the fuse on an ultimatum. "Or I'll *take* him!"

"What about me?" Percy whined.

"*I said shut up, boy!*" Dolarhyde gestured with
the pistol that was suddenly in his hand.

The sheriff responded by letting his own hand drop
toward his holster. The deputies, following his lead,
turned their rifles on Dolarhyde.

"Turn your men around and *go home*, Woodrow," Taggart said. "You're not an outlaw."

"No, I am not," Dolarhyde responded, looking
indignant, although nothing Jake had seen proved
he had good reason. "But I *am* a man who'll protect
what's his."

Suddenly the metal bracelet on Jake's wrist lit up
with a patch of blue light . . . *blue light* . . . and began to make high beeping noises. *Now what—?* Jake
gripped the window lattice with his free hand, trying
to see more of the street.

Dolarhyde peered in at him, at the flashing bracelet; he looked as surprised as Jake felt. But behind him his men were beginning to mutter, turning their horses, looking away. Dolarhyde looked away, too, toward the end of the street, and his face said he was seeing something even stranger now.

Jake pressed his face against the window bars, straining to get a better look.

He could barely make out what they were all staring at: On the far side of a hill, something was glowing like a brushfire . . . except there was no hill, and the burning line was getting closer to town with every heartbeat. . . . Now it looked like an iron bar hurled out of a forge, still glowing red and gold.

"What the hell . . . ?" Dolarhyde muttered. He urged his horse away from the coach, riding to the head of his vigilante band like a military man.

Jake looked down at his unwanted bracelet: The light was flashing faster now. He felt his hands start to sweat as he looked out again and saw the wind rising, kicking up dust in the street, making the torches of Dolarhyde's men gutter. Across the street he saw Ella and the dog, watching the sky like everyone else. Ella didn't look frightened—she looked like she knew exactly what she was seeing and didn't like it. The dog began to bark. The riders in the street were struggling to keep their horses under control, as the animals wheeled and collided in panic.

The glowing band of light was almost at the edge of town when suddenly it vanished. Jake held his breath, gaping like everyone else. Percy was yammering panic-stricken questions, tugging on the chain, not able to see anything. Nothing he did even registered in Jake's mind now.

Jake remembered to take another breath, just as lightning out of nowhere split the sky over the buildings at street's end. An invisible storm swept down the street toward him, whirling the dust into choking clouds, shaking the ground and buildings with explosions like deep thunder. Bolts of lightning struck one building after another, starting fires everywhere.

A different kind of light—a brilliant actinic blue—dropped out of the sky in sweeping cones, rolling over the streets and buildings, illuminating clouds of dust and smoke; silhouetting the people and animals running blindly through the whirlwind, seeking escape where there wasn't any.

Streaks of darkness began to lick down through the cones of light like whips—no, bolas, with weighted strands at their ends spreading open like fingers. He saw them close around human bodies to jerk them off a horse's back or off the ground like lassoed steers.

But the bolas carried their helpless victims screaming into the sky, into . . . something.

Through the clouds of dust and the barred window, Jake couldn't make out what was up there in the night. The light on his metal bracelet was now glowing steadily.

The coach shuddered into abrupt motion as its brake gave way, and the horses hitched to it bolted. Whoever was up in the driver's seat obviously hadn't been expecting that, any more than he could've imagined anything else that was happening now.

The prison wagon careened out of control down the street and around a corner, and then slammed into a pile of debris from a fallen building. The coach landed on its side as the team of horses broke loose and galloped away into the night.

Jake shook himself out, cursing and shoving as he tried to keep Percy from giving him more bruises than he'd gotten in the last half a minute, while they'd been tossed around like dice. Nothing felt broken on him—yet—but if that jackass didn't quit hanging on the manacles, his wrist was going to snap.

"Stop pulling, and gimme your hand—!" Jake said, yanking Percy forward.

"—the hell for—?" Percy pulled away from him.

"—I can get us free!" Jake shouted. "*Gimme your damn hand!*"

Percy's face filled with sudden eagerness, and he stuck out his hand. Jake grabbed him by the wrist, and bent his fingers back until something snapped. Percy shrieked, in real agony this time, as Jake kicked him hard against the wall, forcing Percy's hand out of the cuff. Percy crumpled to the floor in the corner, sobbing and cursing.

Jake was free of Percy, but not of Percy's presence, and they were both still trapped in this goddamn prison. . . . He shouted for the coach's driver, but there was so much noise outside that he could hardly even hear himself. There was only one accessible door, now—and it was in the roof. If the driver didn't show soon to unlock it . . . he glanced back at Percy, his hand making a fist.

One of the circling cones of light struck the prison wagon; the light hovered overhead, filling the inside of the coach with cold brilliance through the window above their heads. Jake caught hold of the lattice, trying to see what could make such bright light, or where so much light could be coming from. The brightness was blinding; all he could see, gazing up, was blue light. *There was something about* blue light . . . *he remembered something*. . . .

As the light struck the flashing metal band on his wrist, the thing suddenly changed again. Jake let go of the lattice to stare at it, forgetting everything else, even Percy, who forgot to keep screaming.

As if it was answering the light from above, the band lit up in a pattern of brighter blue all over. He watched in disbelief as what had been solid metal stronger than stone unfurled like a mechanical plant, growing and changing as it wrapped itself further up his arm, forming a brace, and down around his hand where it fused into a single piece across his palm. Long, slender tubes emerged from its surface; every one of them shone like a lit candle, filled to overflowing with blue light.

Something flashed on in the air just above his wrist—a small arc of light, with strange markings inside it that changed as Jake moved his hand. It reminded him of something else . . . something familiar: *A gun sight. Like a gun sight from God.*

Suddenly he understood: *He knew a weapon*

when he saw one. And he knew what it was meant to do. . . . But how the hell did it—

"How'd you do that?" Percy's voice shook; he looked like somebody penned up with a mad dog.

Jake ignored him, watching the weapon shimmer as he moved his arm, shook it, tightened his fist experimentally. *How the hell did the thing work? What could it really do? If he could only get out of here—*

There was an explosion as the thing on his wrist blasted the rear wall of the iron-plated prison wagon to smithereens. The recoil knocked Jake back against the other end of the coach.

Swearing with shock and awe, he pulled himself upright, staring at the hole the weapon had just blown in the back of the wagon . . . smelling hope in the burning dust and wind. *Now he* was *free. . . .*

Percy stared at the hole, too, and cowered in his corner; he'd finally stopped making any sound at all. Jake moved past him toward the gaping hole in the coach, not even bothering to look back.

There was nothing outside that Jake could see except wreckage. He climbed through into the open, glancing around. Even when he was standing in the street, a free man, Absolution still looked like Hell on Earth. The blue spotlight had moved on, but everywhere he turned buildings were on fire. In the flickering light, he saw dead or injured people and horses lying on the ground all around him. The air was filled with choking smoke and dust, and the crazy lights circled overhead, searching for more victims.

Jake picked his way through the ruins of the building that had foundered the prison wagon, searching for the coach's driver. He found the man's body without much trouble. It lay where it had landed when the coach overturned.

It hadn't been a clean landing; but at least it'd been quick. Jake grimaced. *Sometimes that was the best you could hope for.*

And sometimes one man's death was another man's luck. He kneeled down, searching the driver's pockets until he found the one with a ring of keys in it. He unlocked the manacle that was still around his wrist; shook out his hand as the heavy shackles and chain dropped to the ground.

He'd gotten rid of Percy, and even gotten free of the coach on his own; but it would've taken a lot more time and effort than he could afford right now to get those damned irons off. He glanced at his other wrist, where the strange weapon was still open and glowing, almost like it was waiting, eager, to kill and destroy. Somehow he'd come to possess a weapon out of his worst nightmares; but he had no idea how it worked . . . and he didn't like that.

He took the driver's gun belt and cinched it around his waist; drew the pistol, checked it, and held onto it. With those shackles hanging from his gun hand, he couldn't have used any weapon he actually knew. A pistol could take care of almost any problem he ran into. Anything but Hell on Earth.

He looked at the strange weapon again: *but maybe this was exactly the thing that could . . .*

Horses suddenly emerged from the clouds of smoke and dust—with men on their backs, coming his way. The first human being Jake recognized was

Woodrow Dolarhyde—followed by the few of his men who were still fighting back against the invisible attackers, uselessly firing at targets they couldn't see. Jake glanced over his shoulder at the prison wagon, realizing that Dolarhyde must be looking for his son.

Or maybe not—

As Dolarhyde saw Jake standing by the coach, he dug in his spurs and charged at him like he meant to ride him down.

Jake took cover in the wreckage beside the coach, losing himself in the shadows. Looking out from there, he saw the blue lightning and fire circling around back over the town, heading his way. This time he could actually make out shadowy forms silhouetted against the night . . . *Demons?*

Demons out of Hell. That was all he could think of that could be so huge, with so much power . . . that could fly, darting back and forth after human victims like bats catching insects.

Demons . . . sucking people into the sky, and eating them alive.

Dolarhyde and his men pulled their horses up short, staring at the sky like he was. But then Dolarhyde dismounted, and started toward the coach with his pistol in his hand.

He stopped as he saw the hole Jake's weapon had blown in the back of the coach. He shouted Percy's name and ran forward again; Percy was still inside hiding like a frightened child. His voice answered faintly from inside. Dolarhyde holstered his gun and climbed through the hole into the prison wagon. Dolarhyde caught his son by the arms and dragged him out, as oblivious to Percy's cry of pain and protest as he seemed to be to the boy's broken hand. Watching from the shadows, Jake saw the old man shake his son, calling him a coward in front of all the riders who were still around him.

Dolarhyde raised his hand. Jake wondered whether it was a signal, or whether he was about to slap the kid, too.

He never got to find out, as a cone of blue light swept over the two of them, and a black rope dropped out of the sky, twining bola fingers around Percy, jerking him off his feet, into the air.

Jake saw Percy's terrified face, saw the boy fling his arms out to his father. Dolarhyde lunged after him, shouting his name. But the demons moved too fast; Percy disappeared into the night before his father could grab so much as his boot.

Jake saw Dolarhyde's face then, lit by the fires of destruction, as he lost his son to demons. He saw fury, dread . . . confusion . . . disbelief . . . as Dolarhyde stood staring up into the night, as stupefied by what had just happened as Jake had felt waking up in the desert.

Nat Colorado dismounted and ran to where Dolarhyde stood staring at the sky. Incredulous, Jake saw Nat actually put a steadying arm around the old man's shoulders, his face full of what looked like concern as he guided Dolarhyde out of the middle of the street, toward the relative shelter of the nearest building that was still in one piece. The rest of the Dolarhyde crew sat on their horses, watching and waiting.

Jake shook his head. *This was Hell on Earth, all right . . . he'd just seen both the Dolarhydes get exactly what they deserved.* He moved on, staying close to the cover of buildings until Dolarhyde's vigilantes were well behind him.

His instincts were telling him it was past time for him to find a horse and get the hell out of town—before he found out what it was, exactly, that *he* really deserved. But instead he kept walking toward the heart of the chaos . . . searching the sky, glancing down at the thing on his wrist: It was still a weapon, and the ring of glowing blue tubes reminded him again that it had only turned into one when the blue light hit it, while he'd been trapped in the coach.

Blue light. . . . Just the sight of it made his gut knot up; it filled him with raw hatred and a hunger for bloody vengeance he didn't understand.

And yet, some part of his mind realized now exactly what the weapon was telling him—and it wasn't something his instincts wanted to hear. *It was telling him not to go.* That he didn't need to run . . . that if those things were demons, he was a demon hunter, the only one in town. *That he wanted to do this—and what the hell did he have left to lose?*

He looked on along the firelit street, not seeing just dead horses, but seeing the human beings lying dead or injured everywhere around him—old and young, men, women, and children. Seeing the ones who were still alive fighting to stay that way, as demons tore their lives and homes apart.

He heard someone scream—saw the woman who'd given him free whiskey at the bar dragged from her husband's side by another bola. The demon-tongue snatched her up through a hole in the walkway roof, as Doc leaped after her and fell back, shouting, "Maria!"

"Jesus God!" He heard Preacher Meacham's voice; saw him standing in the street, holding a rifle and staring upward helplessly, blinded by a kind of light that had nothing at all to do with angels or Heaven.

Trying to see what really lay behind the light, Jake pushed himself to move, coughing as he inhaled more dust and smoke. He dodged panic-stricken citizens, hoping he didn't get hit by random gunfire. Runaway horses came at him out of nowhere, not even giving him time to catch one, only to dodge aside, before they were gone again.

He stepped onto the boardwalk and looked for another glimpse of the demons, but they were too well hidden by their powers over wind, earth, and fire as they continued to tear the town apart.

Just as he was getting close to the sheriff's office, a racketing noise made him look down: It sounded like something huge was ripping apart a picket fence. He leaped off the walkway into the street as he saw the walkway's floor planks rippling like piano keys, flying away into the clouds and light.

"Emmett!"

Jake recognized Sheriff Taggart's voice, just as he

spotted the jail. He saw Taggart lean down to haul his grandson up from the ground where the board-walk the boy had been hiding under had all been torn away.

"I told you to get inside!" Taggart shouted.

"I just wanted to see . . . What's *happening?*" Emmett cried.

"Stay by my side." Taggart lifted the boy to his feet and held onto his hand. "You're gonna be oka—"

A blue spotlight fell across them; a bola cord spun down, whipping around Taggart's body. It snapped taut and jerked him out of Emmett's grip, up into the blinding, blue-black night.

"Grandpa . . . !" Emmett stood alone and com-pletely vulnerable in the middle of the street, staring up at the sky as the light swept on, hunting more prey.

Oh, shit . . . Jake broke into a run, compelled by an urge he couldn't explain to get the boy out of harm's way. If the weapon on his wrist had only warned him, he could have nailed the demon before it got Taggart . . . but the damn gun wasn't working like he'd figured.

Ella suddenly crossed his line of sight as she ran to the boy and caught hold of him, pulling him back into a safe hiding place between two buildings. Jake heard the boy shouting, "They took him! Lemme *go!*" as she fought to keep him there.

Jake stopped, turning away again . . . relieved, startled, and furious all at once. *Goddamn it.* He glared up at the hallucination that had replaced the sky; his empty left hand made a fist. *Why wasn't this deadly piece of crap he wore doing the job it was meant to do? If he only knew how to use the demon-killer, instead of letting it use him—*

He realized suddenly that he was thinking about a gun, a piece of metal, like it was alive. But it had seemed alive, the way it opened up; and now it was acting like it had a mind of its own. However he'd gotten it—whether it had fallen out of the sky, or crawled out of the Pit—using him was exactly what the demon gun was doing.

Maybe it would only protect itself. But maybe that didn't really matter: To protect itself, it had to protect him. And here in the middle of Hell on Earth, he didn't much care what the weapon really wanted if it would just kill the demons that were destroying this town and slaughtering its people for no good reason. *Just because they could. Like the man whose face he'd seen on the wanted poster.*

He wasn't that man, wasn't a demon wearing human skin. He was a demon hunter. And even if he had to make himself into a human target, damn him if he didn't have the grit it took to take on these demons—

Blue lights and explosions were coming his way again; they didn't look to be moving quite as fast this time. The cones of light zigzagged from spot to spot, still hunting more victims; the demons harvested them like the Grim Reaper, cutting them off from their futile attempts to fight or run away, swallowing them up into unseen maws.

Jake walked out into the middle of the street, barely registering the screams and gunfire, the dust and smoke. *Come on*, he thought, *show yourselves. Come and get me . . . kill me if you can.* He held the demon gun up high.

As if his death wish had suddenly been granted, he saw his target at last: One of the flying monsters swerved, its shadow-form making an impossible turn in midair. As it came back it fired down at anyone on horseback or on foot who was still firing a gun, blasting them apart with bolts of lightning.

And still it came on, straight down the middle of the street toward Jake, as if it had been searching for him alone. He could see lights covering its body— demon eyes glowing in the dark.

Come on, he thought, not even sure if he meant the demon or the demon gun now. He stood his ground, holding his arm steady. People fled around and past him, clearing his line of fire. Suddenly the targeting arc shone above his wrist; he took aim, helping it find its mark.

The weapon fired with almost no recoil this time: The blue beam hit the flying monster like a bullet's trajectory made visible, before he even had time to blink. It struck the demon almost head-on; the explosion stunned his senses.

The demon tilted, wavered, and lost control, falling from the air even as it roared toward him, like it meant to take him down with it.

Jake ducked as the thing passed just over his head. He spun in his tracks and saw it hit the ground with a grinding crash, plowing a furrow into the packed dirt of the street, trailing fire and debris.

The other demons circling over the town suddenly vanished into the night, faster than they'd come. As they disappeared, a sound like the air exploding shattered windows along the street.

And then there was quiet, as deafening as the pandemonium of moments before.

Jake stood motionless in the wake of the downed demon, stunned by what he'd just seen and done. The weapon was still . . . alive, cocked, armed, loaded—? *What the hell did you call it, when a gun fired lightning?* The downed demon's eyes still glowed; the weapon seemed to be keeping watch to make sure its victim was really helpless.

Slowly he again became aware of the world beyond the demon and his gun—voices murmuring, people venturing back out into the street. He realized abruptly that Woodrow Dolarhyde had come to be standing beside him—no longer on horseback, not saying anything. Just . . . staring, like he was; at the downed demon, at the weapon on his wrist. At him. Dolarhyde still had a pistol in his hand, but he made no move to raise it.

Jake took a deep breath as he realized that a grudging truce held between them, for now; that for the moment, he was safe, at least from his own kind. An entire crowd had gathered around the two of them. Everyone there was staring at him and Dolarhyde as if they were huddled together around a fire on a freezing night.

He got the feeling all of them—even Dolarhyde— were expecting him to say something. He had no idea what. Finally, Dolarhyde asked, "What . . . *are* those things?"

Jake looked at him blankly. "Why're you asking me?"

7

Dolarhyde ventured a step toward Jake, pointing at the weapon on Jake's wrist. He bent his head at the monstrous thing lying in the street. "You shot it . . . with that *iron*. Where'd you get *it*? It was shooting the same kinda lights they were."

Jake was saved from having to answer by Doc Sorenson, who stumbled up to him, eyes still dazed. His expression told Jake that Doc was in worse shape, as far as understanding what had happened, than even he was. He remembered seeing Doc's wife pulled screaming into the sky.

"What the . . . hell was that?" Doc asked. His voice shook. "They got . . . Maria . . . they took my wife. . . ."

Emmett came up beside Doc, his eyes red, tears still running down his face. "They got my grandpa."

A sudden loud hissing from the fallen sky demon drove them all to abrupt silence again.

Jake turned on his heel to face it. The fallen demon's

glowing eyes had all gone dark; it looked deader than before. *But it was still a demon. . . .*

Abruptly the wrist weapon began to shut down. As Jake and Dolarhyde both watched, it retracted piece by piece into itself; Jake opened his hand reflexively as the metal band across his palm withdrew. The ring of slender tubes that fired light disappeared back into the patterned surface of an ornamental cuff. Within seconds, it was again only the damnedest shackle he'd ever seen.

Slowly Jake lifted his head, until his eyes met Dolarhyde's. He saw that whatever else Dolarhyde was feeling now—hatred or loss or shock or awe—there was a healthy dose of fear in his eyes, too, when he looked at Jake. Jake raised his head a little higher, his eyes cold.

But there was also a trace of respect in Dolarhyde's gaze now—an acknowledgement of Jake's nerve in facing down the demon. And under it, a darker awareness that whether the weapon belonged to Jake, or Jake belonged to the weapon, he wanted them on his side. . . .

Dolarhyde looked toward the demon, glanced back at Jake; his pistol was still in his hand. Jake nodded, and drew his own revolver. Slowly, warily, they made their way toward the thing.

As they walked, Jake subconsciously took note of how the other man moved; realizing as he did that there was a lot more to Woodrow Dolarhyde than just a mean-tempered son of a bitch with too much gold for his own good.

Dolarhyde was no coward, Jake had to give him that. In fact, Dolarhyde moved with the confidence of a man who'd spent a lifetime using weapons—all kinds of weapons—to kill all kinds of people. He just might be as dangerous as Jake himself had looked, reflected in Dolarhyde's eyes, or in the sheriff's.

But Jake felt sure Dolarhyde meant to keep the silent truce that held between them—at least for as long as he was useful to him. And by the time he wasn't, Jake figured to be long gone and far away from Woodrow Dolarhyde's revenge. . . .

They closed in on the flying demon where it lay, its nose half buried in the street, a wake of dirt and stones piled up around it. Even up close, there was nothing about it that resembled any creature Jake had ever seen, except maybe insects: a hornet's body, a dragonfly's wings . . . a dragonfly with a wingspan the length of a freight wagon, and five wings on each side. Dolarhyde glanced at the weapon on Jake's wrist again; so did Jake. It was still nothing but a shackle.

And the demon sure as hell looked dead; in fact it looked like its head had been nearly ripped off, as they approached its front end. In the flickering light of too many fires, they could see clear into its strange guts.

Except there wasn't really anything inside to see— nothing a human could recognize, at least. No blood, nothing torn . . . no human bodies . . . just an empty hole. The weapon on Jake's wrist didn't stir, as if whatever it really was meant to kill wasn't there anymore.

"You see anyone in there?" Doc called out. The

rest of the crowd had stayed where it was. "Is—is my wife in there?"

Neither of them answered, still peering into the mystery of the demon's shell, spellbound by the sight of it . . . like a cicada's husk, or an abandoned cocoon.

"*Hey—!*" Doc shouted.

"No, she's not here!" Dolarhyde answered irritably. *Neither was his son.* Looking at Jake, he asked, "Is it dead?"

Jake kicked it with his boot, not too hard. Its surface resisted with an odd *clunk.* "It's metal," he murmured, surprised. *A flying machine? An infernal killing machine . . .* He glanced at the weapon on his wrist again and holstered his pistol. Turning away, he started back to the others. Dolarhyde followed, his face brooding.

As they rejoined the small crowd of townsfolk and ranch hands, Emmett asked, "Is it demons?" as if he'd read Jake's mind. But he was asking Preacher Meacham, not Jake.

Apparently the preacher wasn't in the habit of having demons come to call. He tried two or three times to speak, before he said, "I don't know what it is . . . but it sure fits the description."

That was met with another long silence. At last Doc turned to the preacher, exasperated. "Well, what the hell does that mean? Jesus Christ, Preacher, *what the hell does that mean*: 'Demons'? Bible stuff? Talkin' about the Good Book? Hellfire, and all that—?" His voice rose, angry and resentful and grief-stricken.

"Calm down, Doc . . ." Meacham said, somehow keeping his own voice calm. "You're scarin' the boy."

"'Calm down'?" Doc half shouted. "You telling me a bunch of demons came and took my wife—took our people—and you want me to calm down?"

Jake glanced up, as behind Doc something blurred past on the rooftop, too fast for him to see it clearly. The demon gun on his wrist lit up, and everyone around him turned, their faces stricken, as he raised his arm. But the weapon didn't transform, even though Jake could hear heavy footsteps thudding as the demon bounded from rooftop to rooftop. It disappeared again before Jake could track it far enough even to get a clear look at it.

". . . What is it?" "Where'd it go?" "There!" "—No, there—" The crowd began to panic again, some of them drawing guns, firing at any place they thought it had been, or might be, while others pointed and shouted, seeing monsters everywhere.

A window shattered and wood splintered as the demon crashed through the side of a building. They all heard a woman's scream, and then a shotgun, fired twice; Jake saw the muzzle flashes through a window. Then a man screamed, as if something had ripped his gun away, and his arm with it. The sounds that came next were too hideous to be human, sounds only a demon could have made. Somebody's entrails splattered across the window glass.

People in the crowd cried out, or else turned away, sickened.

The unseen thing crashed out through another wall on the far side of the building, landing heavily in the alley behind it. Jake caught fleeting glimpses of a shadowy figure beyond the slats of a fence, but the darkness and the milling crowd kept him from seeing any real details. All he could tell was that it was huge, and it hadn't looked human. . . .

The demon's hulking, misshapen form disappeared from sight completely as it fled the town. Everyone had turned to watch it go, trying to see which way it was headed. Their muttered voices debated whether it was likely to come back.

The alarm signals on Jake's weapon shut down. The real demon, the thing that had shed the skin of the flying monster, had killed two more people and gotten clean away, and the weapon hadn't even let him try for a shot. *Why—?* Jake's hands made fists at his sides.

But as silence began to fall again, he realized that at least the thing's failure to act had reassured everyone else that they were finally safe. Jake watched them pull themselves back together, until at last he felt as relieved as they were. He only hoped the demon gun was right.

Deputy Lyle moved his head like he was shaking off a daze, and went to where Emmett was standing. "C'mon," he said quietly, "let's get you back inside." He led Emmett away, without glancing twice at Jake.

"How'd you do that?" Dolarhyde demanded finally, gesturing at the weapon on Jake's wrist.

Jake just stared at him, without even the words to explain how much he *didn't* know. "I got no idea," he said at last.

"*Do it again.*" An order, not a request.

Jake went on looking at him, as frustrated by Dolarhyde's failure to get the point as by his own failure to understand anything at all. *"I can't."*

"Where the hell did you *get* it?" Dolarhyde said, as if his brain couldn't absorb anything Jake told him . . . or, more likely, thought it was all lies.

Jake took a deep breath. "For the last goddamn time: I. Don't. *Remember*."

"What do you mean, 'You don't remember'?" Dolarhyde's glare would've flayed him alive, if it could have.

Jake would have hit him then, except that Nat Colorado's voice called out from a distance, "I found tracks!"

They followed his voice to a spot near where Jake had caught his last glimpse of the demon. Dolarhyde was carrying a shotgun now.

Nat Colorado was kneeling by a deep footprint— the print left by something big, massive, with talons on its inhumanly shaped foot.

Dolarhyde's men and the townspeople who were still following them gathered around the footprint, murmuring in subdued voices as the sight of it brought back their fear.

"What the hell is that?" Doc asked.

"Not like any tracks I've ever seen," Nat muttered. Jake figured that had to be an understatement. He remembered the final sounds he'd heard; the sight of entrails splattered on a window. . . .

"Whatever the hell they are, they're headed west with our kin," Dolarhyde said. He turned toward the handful of his men who'd survived. Raising his voice, he called out, "Find the horses! We're going after it before we lose the trail."

The men behind him traded dubious looks and reluctant glances. "I said move!" the Colonel snarled, and they did. Only Nat remained behind, a protective shadow to his boss, the way he'd been to his boss's son.

"Wait a minute," Doc protested. "What do you mean, you're goin' after them? What are you goin' *after*, pal? What the hell you plannin' to do?"

The man had a point, Jake decided. Now that he had time to think about it, taking on a whole hive full of demons, even with the weapon on his wrist, didn't appeal to him. He'd just survived Hell on Earth . . . and he hadn't lost anybody to the monsters. Instead, he'd gotten back his freedom.

Absolution was just a place, and he'd done all he could for its people—all he wanted to do, and most likely more than they deserved from him. He turned away quietly and began to walk toward the street.

"*Hey!*" Dolarhyde said.

Jake stopped and turned around as Dolarhyde started after him, because he didn't want to end up shot in the back now.

"Didn't you hear what I said?" Dolarhyde asked, as if Jake was as thick-headed as he was.

"I heard what you said." Jake met Dolarhyde's stare, his face expressionless. "I don't work for you."

"Did you hear what *I* said?" Doc protested, because as usual nobody was listening to him. "*What* exactly you got in mind!"

Dolarhyde went on ignoring him, all his attention

on Jake like a burning-glass. He pointed at the metal bracelet. "I need that thing. It's the only weapon that counts. And you *owe* me."

For something he didn't remember doing. Jake's face got more stubborn. "I don't see it that way."

Dolarhyde swung at him. Jake barely had time to react before Dolarhyde hit him in the jaw, making him stagger.

Jake couldn't believe Dolarhyde had moved that fast; he'd barely missed the full force of the blow. Any other man would've had a broken jaw.

Dirty bastard ... Jake lunged at Dolarhyde and punched him with all his strength, returning the favor. Dolarhyde reeled backward, but stayed on his feet somehow. Nat started forward, his hand on his revolver, but Dolarhyde's sharp gesture stopped him in his tracks.

Everything stopped then, and everyone. They watched as Jake began to back away, his gun drawn, his eyes never leaving Dolarhyde.

Glaring back at him, Dolarhyde finally muttered, "Let him go."

He was officially useless again. Their brief truce was over. Jake kept on moving away into the shadows, keeping to them until he could round a corner; until Dolarhyde and all the rest of Absolution's survivors were gone from his sight.

ELLA WATCHED JAKE go, standing unnoticed in the crowd. Her eyes clung to the spot where she'd last seen him, her face haunted by shadows of her own. As she glanced back at Woodrow Dolarhyde, her gaze filled with frustration and anger. Thanks to him she had lost the man *she* needed more than any of them did, again, to a fate as harsh as the land it ruled with a cruel, amoral fist.

Dolarhyde rejoined the others, his face set, his eyes still burning with hate. He searched out Nat, waiting at the edge of the crowd. "Start packin' the horses. We leave at dawn."

Nat nodded, and headed toward the street to pass along Dolarhyde's orders.

BY THE TIME Nat had reached the main street, Jake was no longer in sight—he was already headed out of town, on the first riderless horse he'd found. He rode east, toward the dawn, a free man.

A running man, fleeing demons . . . or a wanted man, riding straight toward them. Cottonwood Grove lay east of Absolution . . . Cottonwood Grove, where the sheriff had claimed Jake Lonergan killed a woman named Alice Wills.

"RECALL THE BOOK of Numbers: God commanded Moses into the promised land of Canaan . . ."

A new day began to fill the streets of Absolution with light, driving out the darkness, rekindling the spirits of its frightened, weary, grief-stricken people.

A crowd had gathered at the crossroads in the middle of town, where Preacher Meacham stood, wearing his official Sunday coat and hat. He offered his impromptu sermon to all who cared to listen—people who had come out just to hear him, drawn by need, and those working all around them, searching for more survivors, or just for what remained of their own belongings. His familiar voice comforted them and renewed the faith of most who heard him.

He spoke from his own heart as he looked out at their faces; his spirits rose as he saw them working side by side to clean up the wreckage of homes and stores, or help each other search for things they had lost—*lost, but waiting to be found,* he prayed.

Like Jake Lonergan, who had saved the town from demons last night with the otherworldly weapon on his wrist—and then ridden away like the devil was on his tail, after trading words and blows with the Colonel. . . .

Jake Lonergan: wanted, dead or alive. Damned if he did, damned if he didn't even remember. *God help him,* Meacham thought, with complete sincerity.

He saw Emmett, who had lost his grandfather—his only kin—helping a little girl pull her half-burned doll out of the rubble that had been her home. Meacham smiled at the sight. Emmett was trying to deal with his loss in the best way Meacham knew by helping others deal with their own loss.

". . . BUT MOSES SENT *his spies to survey the land, and they returned with fearful hearts . . . for they'd seen giants there, evil beings more powerful than they'd ever encountered. 'We won't survive against them', they said. . . ."*

Emmett wandered on down the street, seeing his life in a mirror . . . a broken mirror: This was his life, lying in ruins. He'd lost Grandpa, even *Abuela* Juanita . . . but somehow he was still here, although his own body didn't even feel real to him.

When he looked in the mirror, it was empty. He must have thought that same thing a hundred times over. But no matter how often he thought it, he couldn't really *feel* it; not yet. His mind and his body had gone numb, like they had when Mama died. He knew how much it would hurt when the numbness went away. . . . *What was he going to do then? What was he—*

He stopped suddenly, as he saw Preacher Meacham's Bible lying in the street, dusty and slightly singed, but miraculously intact. He picked it up and brushed it off, then turned and ran back up the street to where Preacher Meacham was speaking.

MEACHAM GLANCED DOWN, breaking off in midsentence as Emmett held his Bible out to him. He smiled for the first time since yesterday—which seemed like a hundred lifetimes ago, now—as he accepted the boy's offering, and realized that the answer to his one personal request to God had been "Yes." The smile he gave Emmett then was one that last night he could have sworn would never touch his face again until Judgment Day.

Seeing it, Emmett smiled, too, although only moments before, he'd been sure he'd never smile again. Resting his hand lightly on Emmett's shoulder, Meacham murmured, "Bless you, boy," as he felt his resolve double. God had not abandoned him, or these people.

"... *and for their faith, the spies were allowed into the promised land, where they stood tall against the giants, and were saved.*"

As he picked up the thread of his sermon, he glanced toward the Gold Leaf Saloon, where this morning Doc was engrossed in his true calling as a healer. All night Doc, aided by family members and volunteers, had been treating townsfolk who'd been seriously injured but were still alive. For one day, at least, the saloon had become a field hospital, and Doc could refocus his life for a time, without spending every moment grieving over Maria.

Doc glanced up from his work, hearing Meacham's words, looking out the window. His eyes met Meacham's, then looked past him at the sunrise. His face filled with certainty and purpose, things Meacham couldn't remember ever seeing there before. Maria might be missing, but with God's help or without it, Doc meant to get her back alive.

Meacham gave him a slight nod, and looked around where he stood. If he turned in one direction, he could see the infernal machinery of the demons. If he turned another way, he faced the rising sun.

Suddenly inspired, his thoughts became his own call to arms to the people working all around him. "If those creatures are proof of Hell," he said, pointing at the dead machine, "then they're also proof of God! He's testing our faith—so we're goin' after our kin. Thy will be done, Lord, and there's an amen behind it."

Still smiling, he turned back toward the church to begin preparing for the journey.

JAKE WAS ABLE to make better time as the new day brightened around him. He could leave the main trail now and head across open country, where he was less likely to meet anybody else who thought they knew him.

But as he topped another ridge, a sense he couldn't name ran its fingers up his spine, making the back of his neck prickle: the same thing he'd felt yesterday in the saloon, just before the sheriff and his men had come through the doors. . . .

He reined in his horse, looking over his shoulder: *He was being followed.* His hand went to his gun out of habit as he watched his back trail, waiting. *Had Dolarhyde changed his mind—?*

His mouth tightened as the rider who was following him came into view: only one person, a woman . . . *Ella.* He recognized her by her dress. The only concession she'd made to riding out alone into the desert was that she had a man's hat pulled down over her long dark hair, for protection from the sun. *That woman had to be crazy.* He wondered if she'd even brought a canteen with her.

It suddenly occurred to him that maybe she *did*

want the bounty on his head. A thousand dollars was enough to turn a lot of people crazy . . . with greed.

Frowning, Jake stayed where he was until he was sure she'd seen him, too. He watched as she headed up the slope toward him, and then he dismounted.

When Ella reached the top of the ridge, she found Jake's horse cropping grass in the scrub, riderless. Jake had disappeared. Her face fell as she searched the far slope of the hill, where Jake wasn't, either. She looked from side to side at the mesquite, sage, and creosote bush that turned the entire ridge into a maze.

The look on her face became one of despair; the obsessed light faded from her eyes. She gave a sigh that sounded more like a sob of exhaustion as she began to pull her horse around—

Jake's arm came out of nowhere; his hand caught the back of her gun belt and jerked her from the saddle. He slammed her to the ground and straddled her, pinning her arms, glaring down at her with the feral eyes of a hunter who'd been hunted almost to extinction. His voice was murderous as he said, "You come clean right now, or I *swear* I'll kill you."

Ella met his stare with eyes like a wall, her gaze filled with disgust and resentment. But then something changed, in the mind behind her eyes, until she wasn't even seeing him anymore. Her eyes filled with tears—tears that had nothing to do with the pain of the fall, or any threat of death. *"They took my people too,"* she said, and her voice shook with grief.

Jake blinked, and blinked again, as the unexpectedness of her reaction broke the spell of his fury.

Suddenly he could see her face clearly, as if he was seeing it for the first time. He let her go, moving aside, sitting back on his heels as she pushed herself up from the dry grass.

Her eyes were alive with memory, and the kind of loss that could only exist in someone whose entire reason for living had been torn away. "I've been looking for them a long time," she said, her voice growing steadier as she got her emotions back under control. "I know you can help me find them." Her strange gaze suddenly held him captive again, pleading with him to admit that he understood . . . as if she knew him better than he knew himself, or thought she did.

Yesterday in the bar her eyes had looked straight in through his own like they were open windows . . . and somehow she'd seen the truth: that he couldn't even remember his own name.

But she'd seen something more, too . . . lost in the darkness, afraid of the light, she'd seen her own soul reflected back at her in the eyes of a wild animal.

Pain like he'd swallowed broken glass cut him up inside. He couldn't tell her feelings from his own, suddenly, didn't know which ones were trying to make him answer, *Yes. I will. Anything. Because I know. . . .*

No! He turned away, breaking the bewitchment of her gaze, even though it took every shred of his willpower to push her out of his mind. He got to his feet, and jerked his horse's rein free from the shrub where it waited.

He was more sure than ever now that she was trying to manipulate him, that she wanted the weapon on his arm and nothing more, even if it killed him . . . just like Dolarhyde.

He didn't care who she was; it didn't matter how she'd done that to him. . . . It only mattered that she could.

"Stay away from me," he said, his voice like sleet. He barely glanced at her as he swung up into the saddle.

Ella got to her feet, holding out her hands as if she was actually begging him to listen. "*I can help you—*" she said.

Even with his back turned, he could feel her eyes, her whole body, reaching out to him. He touched his horse with his spurs, and headed away down the slope beyond the ridge. *Don't look back . . . ever.*

ELLA STOOD ALONE at the top of the ridge, her face stark with failure, watching Jake disappear until he was only a speck on the bleak rising plain, lost to her eyes among the distant rocks and desert scrub. He never looked back, even once.

How could she have been so wrong about him . . . about everything? The desperation inside her doubled. *How did these miserable people live with themselves, let alone each other? Why was she even here—?*

At last, drained by the unexpected intensity of her own emotions, and Jake's reaction to them, she made herself stop watching nothing at all disappear into a greater nothingness. *What was the matter with her . . . ?*

Turning away, she picked up her hat and got on her horse, and started back toward town. There was only one choice left to her now, and she didn't like it any more than she liked the people it involved.

8

In the middle of Absolution's main street, Woodrow Dolarhyde and the toughest, most reliable of his men—only half a dozen, not counting Nat— were checking over their weapons and the supplies on the pack mule. They were waiting now for any townspeople desperate enough, or with guts enough, to join the demon-hunting party.

Dolarhyde wasn't expecting much. Even his own men had balked, threatening to quit, after the rumors of what had happened out by the river, as well as in town, spread through the bunkhouse like a plague.

He was certain now that the two things were related—that his missing cattle and men had been sucked into the sky like the people in town last night. He couldn't fire his whole crew. He needed someone to tend the ranch and the cattle while he was gone. He'd finally offered a bounty to any man who'd ride out with him today; but still only six of them had taken him up on it.

Damn Jake Lonergan. That coward, that insolent piece of shit who'd taken the demon gun with him when he'd run away. . . .

A few—very few—of the townspeople were coming to join the hunting party at last. Dolarhyde's eyes fixed on Doc Sorenson: Doc already looked tired to the point of exhaustion as he mounted his horse; as if he hadn't even slept last night.

"Where the hell do you think you're going?" Dolarhyde asked, his voice as scathing as his stare. The damn fool was as scrawny as a kid, he couldn't use a gun, and he was blind as a bat without the spectacles he always wore.

"I'm coming with you," Doc said, as if Dolarhyde was the stupid one.

"You're dead weight." Dolarhyde nailed the other man with an unrelenting frown.

For once Doc met his stare and held it. "I'm dead weight? I'm a *doctor*. You *need* me. They took my wife, you hear me—?" There was something in his voice that Dolarhyde had never heard before, that forced him to listen, for once. And there was something about Doc that even the man himself seemed to have forgotten, until now—he actually was a doctor. It finally occurred to Dolarhyde that Doc might have been awake all night treating victims of the demons' attack.

"I stand just as much a chance as any one of you," Doc said, daring him to deny it. "You don't like that? Tough."

Doc went on staring back at him until Dolarhyde decided Doc must have lost his mind, along with his wife. *Well, it was no skin off his nose if Sorenson got himself killed.*

"Suit yourself." Dolarhyde rode on past, followed by Nat.

Looking at his own men again, Dolarhyde noticed the uneasy glances they were beginning to trade as they saw how few townspeople seemed intent on joining them. "Somebody got something to say?"

Greavey cleared his throat nervously. "What if . . . they're already dead, boss?"

Dolarhyde's face hardened. "They were roping people, you understand? It was a *roundup*—" How many times would he have to say it, before these dumb sons of bitches got the point? "If they'd wanted to kill them, they would've." He rode on, heading with Nat toward the place where they'd found the demon's footprint last night.

The rest of the ranch hands looked at one another again, unconvinced. Finally Greavey said, in a low, resentful voice, "You heard the Colonel." They mounted up at last, and began to follow Dolarhyde away.

EMMETT STOOD BY the entrance of the stables, his face solemn with determination, holding the reins of his saddled horse as he watched Mr. Dolarhyde and his men ride away. He looked back as they left, to see who besides Doc meant to go with them.

He saw Preacher Meacham ride up, and relief filled his eyes. The preacher had always treated him more like an adult than anybody else in town; and it was the preacher's words earlier this morning that had caused him to be standing here now.

The preacher was wearing a brown hat and coat, with a rifle slung over his shoulder, not his Sunday coat and hat. He didn't look in the least like a preacher; somehow his whole manner was different. For a moment Emmett had the strange feeling that he was seeing into the preacher's past. That was something Grandpa seemed to know about, but neither man had seen fit to talk about it to "just a boy." But still, if anybody in town would hear him out today, it'd be the preacher. . . .

The only other person who looked ready to go along for the ride was Charlie Lyle. Charlie was acting sheriff, now—which made this an official posse—as well as being the only deputy who was willing, or able, to go after Grandpa and the other kidnap victims. Emmett began to smile. Grandpa had always said Charlie was a man to ride the river with. He was also the closest thing to a big brother Emmett had ever had; Charlie would understand why he had to do this.

Charlie mounted up alongside the preacher, and Emmett started toward them, leading his horse. As he crossed the street, Jake Lonergan's black dog trotted out from between two buildings and headed toward him.

Emmett's solemn face broke into a smile as the dog came right up to him. He scratched its ears and patted its back, happy to see it had survived last night. The dog's tail waved like a flag, as if it had discovered a kindred soul, after a lifetime of searching. An outlaw's dog ... it must have had a lonely life. And now Jake Lonergan had gone off without it. The poor dog didn't even have him anymore.

"Come on, boy," Emmett said, with sudden inspiration. "You can come with me ... good boy. . . ."

Emmett looked up again to find the preacher and Charlie Lyle staring at him.

Meacham shook his head, before Emmett even had a chance to ask. "Can't come, son. Too dangerous."

Emmett's face filled with sudden defiance. How many times had Grandpa said that to him, before he rode out to do "man's work"—but it was Grandpa who'd gotten kidnapped by demons, not him. "I ain't stayin' with these folks." He shook his head at the town behind him. "Besides," he said, "how do you know it's safer *here*?"

Meacham looked at him, startled, and didn't answer, as if he couldn't think of anything that made more sense, even to him.

"Come on," Emmett insisted, catching his hesitation. "I'll water your horse, do whatever you say ... you're all I got now."

Meacham's expression said he surrendered, reluctantly; as if there was nothing to be done with the truth but accept it.

"I'll look after him on the ride," Charlie said. He smiled down at Emmett, and Emmett saw that he did understand: *Neither one of them was going on this journey just out of a sense of duty.* Charlie glanced at Meacham, his gaze agreeing that it wasn't right to leave the boy here alone, at a time like this.

Meacham sighed. "Go fill your canteen," he said to Emmett.

Emmett grinned, and climbed into his saddle, where a full canteen of water already hung from the saddle horn. He followed the others as they rode off after Dolarhyde's men, the dog trotting contentedly behind him.

As ELLA HAD expected, the posse tracking the escaped demon was already gone by the time she returned to Absolution. But a dozen horses heading off into the desert were a lot easier to track than a single demon; it wasn't long before she spotted a telltale cloud of dust, and not much longer before she began to make out the actual posse.

What had looked from a distance to be one group of men turned out to be two, subtly but deliberately riding separate from each other. She spotted Woodrow Dolarhyde and some of his ranch hands in the lead; the few townsfolk who had joined them rode clustered together in their wake. Interesting, although hardly surprising.

What was surprising to her, on first sight, was the particular group of townspeople who had elected to come on this demon hunt. That Deputy—for now, Sheriff—Lyle was here made reasonable sense to her; it was his job, his responsibility. But a preacher, a saloon-keeper, and a young boy didn't make any more sense to her than seeing the black dog—the one that had seemed to belong to Jake Lonergan—keeping pace alongside them.

But then she remembered that Doc had lost his wife, and Emmett his grandfather, to the aliens. Maybe the dog was just lonely: in this world of closed-off, solitary humans, even their animal companions suffered for their losses, their weaknesses.

And the preacher . . . the preacher was something else again. He didn't look in the least like a preacher, now; and from what she'd observed of him, he didn't behave like most preachers she'd met, either. He was the one she chose to approach, as she said, her voice respectful, "If it's all the same, I'd like to ride along too."

Meacham slowed his horse and glanced over at her. He didn't seem particularly disconcerted by her sudden appearance, or even by the fact that she was a woman. He looked down at her gun belt, up at her face again. Then he nodded, not seeming to find her request either surprising or unacceptable. "Your choice, miss," he said. He touched the brim of his hat politely, and rode on.

Ella fell in with the rest of the group, feeling a rare, wry smile touch her face. *A man of God*, she thought, *but one who seemed to be a firm believer in free will*. . . . The other townsfolk glanced sidelong at her. As she had suspected, they were all more taken aback by her presence, unexpected or otherwise. But with the preacher's blessing, and a twelve-year-old boy already among the volunteers, none of them said a word. And she already knew the dog liked her.

Ella sighed, feeling some of the fatigue flow out of

her weary body, along with a little of the stress. She took a sip from the canteen she had refilled in town, and let her thoughts flow out into the wide-open spaces around her.

To the people here, entering the desert was like riding off the edge of the world, she thought. She wasn't surprised that most of them had remained in town, after last night. Their fear of the unknown, as well as hard experience, had taught them to stay put unless they had no other choice. Except for the main trails, journeying here was riding off the map, into uncharted land.

Here there be monsters, it said on old maps, wherever there was uncharted land. Humans saw monsters that didn't exist everywhere. Perhaps imaginary monsters were everywhere in their world because they could never be certain what lay in the mind of another human. Every new person they met became a potential enemy. . . .

But this time, genuine monsters were exactly what they wanted to find. Almost everyone riding with her understood the very real dangers of the wilderness they were entering; or they thought they did. But they had no idea what they were up against when it came to the enemy they were tracking now . . . a danger their worst fears could barely measure up to.

She forced herself to stop dwelling on what was to come, and turned her thoughts outward again, trying to let her mind roam free while it still could.

Once humans had believed their world was as flat and simple as a flapjack. Looking toward the horizon, which seemed to lie on the edge of infinity, she couldn't see a trace of the Earth's curve . . . maybe that wasn't so hard to understand.

But the term "desert" didn't describe an empty void. The desert was a land as varied and beautiful as any she could imagine. The sky was like a faultless dome of deep turquoise blue; the sunlit air affected her like a drug, energizing her, heightening all her senses.

Gazing into the distance as they rode, she could see a dozen varied landforms, most of them supporting some kind of life. The mountains, lavender-gray in the distance, rose through forests of oak and juniper and piñon pine to snow-laden peaks where vast amounts of moisture were imprisoned in a desert too cold and inaccessible to support any life.

But closer in, mesas, rough hills, and rising plains caught enough moisture to show the subtle olive, gold, and evergreen of desert scrubland . . . creosote bush, sage, mesquite, yucca, and a multitude of other shrubs, grasses, and cacti. The land was home to birds, land animals, and insects of all kinds, though most of those hid from the sun by day.

Where the plains broke up into badlands, fantasies carved from stone by the hands of time and the extreme weather took her breath away. Somewhere out here, she was sure, there were even dunes of sand, an endless beach without an ocean.

The desert's many kinds of beauty had only one thing in common: a completely unsentimental disregard for any form of life, human or otherwise, that couldn't adapt to its implacable demands. Most humans took that far too personally: Here in this amazing, alien, terrible, and awe-inspiring place, death was like breathing . . . it simply *was*, like nature itself.

Everyone she'd met who had lived here long came to accept the land for what it was, each in his own fashion. They retuned their senses to its subtleties, and their lives to it demands. Some had been more successful than others.

She thought of Jake Lonergan, whose eyes were as deep and clear a blue as the heights of the desert sky . . . and just as remote: a man as spare and silent as the land—until he caught you by surprise, in an unguarded moment. Just like the desert. . . .

She refocused her attention on the other people around her. Every one of them was a complete contradiction in terms; yet in their souls they all longed for such similar things: such surprisingly simple, obvious things.

But solitude did strange things to anyone's mind. *No man was an island*, someone had written . . . but human beings all lived in a desert of their own making. Whether they huddled together in a town like Absolution or in a big city a thousand miles away, they were always clinging to the edge of survival, afraid of life, afraid of death, and doubting themselves and one another.

Their constant inner conflicts had made them fierce fighters, for better or worse . . . definitely for the better, this time. It meant their enemy would underestimate them. But without Jake Lonergan—without what he knew, and the weapon bound to that knowledge as inescapably as it was bound to his wrist—

she was afraid all the courage in the world wouldn't be enough to defeat these demons.

Jake. . . . She frowned, and forced herself to stop thinking. Human beings thought entirely too much, usually about themselves—and that might be their worst weakness of all.

JAKE TOPPED ANOTHER ridge, slowing his horse as he looked ahead. He saw a line of green in the distance: not just the usual underbrush, but actual trees, marking a river that probably ran all year, fed by the runoff from mountain snows.

He had been riding most of the night and half the day, and the water in the canteen that had come with his horse was low. Whether his horse's water sense or random chance had led him here, it was what they both needed, at least for now.

He started the horse down the long slope. It didn't require any urging as it picked its way through the scrub, heading for the river.

But as he rode down the hill into the profusion of green along the river's edge, Jake felt something shift inside his brain—as if he had ridden down this hill, into this exact spot, before . . . often. *As if he knew this place . . .*

As the horse reached the bottom of the incline, entering the grass dotted with wildflowers, Jake spotted the ruins of a small structure lying scattered over the ground—a section of roof, pieces of wood, stones from a chimney. . . .

His horse turned its nose toward the water. He forced its head back around, riding toward the part of the cabin that was still standing. As he approached, he saw that nearly half of the cabin's roof and walls had been torn away, by something that had hit it with the force of a tornado.

And yet, he knew no twister had done this. He wasn't sure how he knew . . . but now he was certain about one thing: *He had been here before.*

He dismounted and led the horse down to the riverside, tying it to a bush where it could reach the water and fresh grass. He drank the water that was left in his canteen and refilled it, obeying long habit . . . forcing himself to go through the routines of survival, as he tried to prepare himself for whatever part of his past he was about to rediscover.

Slowly he walked back toward the cabin, and stepped up onto the porch. Broken window glass crunched under his boots as he went in through the doorway, which no longer had a door.

Light streamed through gaps in the roof and walls as his eyes searched what remained of the room. Everything seemed to grow eerily silent and still, as if he had stepped through the doorway into another world, a dreamworld. And yet he was sure, somehow, that this was . . . had once been . . . the reality he was searching for. That once he had belonged *here*. . . .

Memory broke over him like a wave, dragging him under its surface. . . . *Fresh flowers, held in a woman's hand . . . the woman from his picture. Humming softly, she was arranging the flowers in a glass vase. The white paint on the cabinets in front of her was peeling; it looked like nobody had lived in this place for years before she'd come here, but that didn't seem to bother her. Wearing a pale summer dress patterned with tiny forget-me-nots, her dark, shining hair falling across her shoulders, she looked like the most contented woman in the world.*

She turned around, setting the vase of flowers on a table at the center of the room, as someone opened the door behind her. She looked up, a smile starting on her face.

And Jake stood waiting in the doorway . . . waiting to see her smile. As she saw him, her smile brightened the whole room—as if to her the sight of him was like water in the desert.

Jake felt himself start to smile in return, until he was grinning like a fool . . . a fool for love. . . . Alice.

"You're back," Alice said, with joy and relief in her eyes.

He crossed the room, took her into his arms and kissed her. And then he proudly slung the saddlebags he carried down on the table in front of her; letting the bags fall over, letting them fall over and open. Coins spilled out, a gleaming waterfall of gold.

But at the sight of them, Alice's smile fell away, and her eyes darkened as if a cloud had crossed the sun. . . .

Jake stumbled against the doorframe, as the present broke the surface of memory, and jerked him back into his *now*-reality like a hooked fish. He put one hand up to support himself, shaking his head.

What was that? Was the woman in his picture really Alice Wills, had he really known her . . . had he killed her, like Taggart claimed? *Why? He'd never hurt*

Alice, she'd . . . he'd. . . . What was it about seeing saddlebags full of gold that had made her lose her smile?

Something glinted on the far wall of the cabin, by the place where the chimney had once been. Jake crossed the room, to find a gold coin—a gold double eagle—embedded in the wood. He pulled it out, staring at it as impossible questions filled his head, where no answers existed anymore.

Sunlight glanced off the coin's surface as he turned it between his fingers. He laid it flat in his palm, where it shimmered like light on water. . . .

And suddenly, his mind plunged through the surface of the day, back into memory's dreamworld.

The cabin was vibrating like a tuning fork. The shaking floor made more coins spill from his saddlebags. The pile on the table began to slip and slide; they fell, ringing, onto the floor. The glass vase tumbled over and smashed.

"What's happening?" Alice cried, her eyes filled with terror.

Jake caught hold of her, pulling her away from the table, his own mind gone white with fear. An earthquake—? He dragged her with him until his back hit the cabin wall. She pressed against it, against him. He stared at the gold coins on the table, on the floor, as they began to distort, stretching and curving into impossible shapes: Either he was seeing things, or they were . . . melting. . . .

A window exploded, and then another. With a grinding wrench half the roof tore away, and the chimney collapsed, leaving them staring up into a blue sky that was suddenly made of blinding blue light.

Alice screamed, as a dark rope spun down out of the blue, and the bola at its end opened like a hand and wrapped inhuman fingers around her. It jerked her up, beyond his reach, before he could even catch her outstretched hands. . . .

Alice—!

Jake burst through the surface into the present, her name echoing in his head as if he had shouted it, and not just in a dream. . . . He found himself sitting on the floor, as if his legs had given out. Slowly he got to his feet, shaking off dead leaves and bits of glass.

Now he knew who the woman in the picture was . . . maybe even what they'd been doing here. She must have meant something special to him, for him to always carry her picture. *And he hadn't killed her—*

They'd taken her. The demons. . . . His hand covered the weapon on his wrist, as solid and cold as if it had never come to life last night, living only to destroy the metal monster, and whatever had controlled it.

Jake looked up through the hole in the roof at the perfectly normal blue sky. He didn't know everything yet, but he knew enough to understand what he had to do—even if he never remembered why. He had a gun for demons; and now he had a real reason for using it. . . .

It was time to go hunting.

THE MISMATCHED BAND of riders from Absolution followed the demon's tracks deeper into the desert, crossing the bed of a long-dry lake, where time had petrified the muddy bottom, turning it to stone that preserved every crack in its desiccated face, while more time had filled in each line with sand.

Beyond the ancient lake bed they entered another seemingly endless stretch of scrubland. There was no place to find shelter from the midday sun that bleached the land of color and sound; it drove the riders to silence as well, as they simply endured, like their horses, with no energy to spare. Time itself seemed to crawl; the horizon shimmered as if it was dissolving . . . as if even the laws of nature were unable to withstand the searing forge of light.

As the sun fell past its zenith at last they entered a rust- and bone-colored, crazy quilt of eroded sandstone. The demon's winding trail through the canyons and arroyos of the badlands offered them some small relief from the heat as the shadows gradually lengthened.

The storm clouds they had spotted on the far horizon soon after they left town had been growing steadily closer throughout the day; by nightfall rain would probably be drenching them.

Even now Ella could feel the moisture in the air increasing, weighing them down almost physically, like the noonday sun had seemed to evaporate their thoughts.

She rode silently, as usual, making herself all but invisible as she observed the interactions of the others, which grew more frequent, and more random, as their tension and then their boredom finally eroded into discomfort and bad humor.

Jed Parker, one of Dolarhyde's men, rode up alongside Doc with the look of a coyote hungry for a meal. Ella supposed wearily that any man who could stand to work for Woodrow Dolarhyde would have to be as unpleasant as he was.

"Don't even know why we're going," Parker said to Doc. "You know they're all dead."

Doc kept his eyes straight ahead, knowing that he was being toyed with, and trying with all his resolve not to let it get to him. "If they wanted to kill em, they would've," he said, repeating what Dolarhyde himself had told his men.

"Well, if the boss is right, and they was *ropin'* 'em . . . bet it's to *eat* 'em." Parker's grin turned nastier. "If it was me? I'd start with your wife."

Doc glanced over at Parker, his face betrayed by a flush of anger as he put on the most mocking imitation of a smile he could manage. "You gonna be like this the whole trip?" he said. "'Cause if y'are, we aren't gonna have a lotta long conversations. Why don't you sing a song or something, make yourself useful. . . ."

Parker spat tobacco juice and turned his horse away, riding back to rejoin the knot of other Dolarhyde men, who were now at the reluctant tail of the group, not in the lead any more.

Preacher Meacham glanced at Doc, with a look that said he knew exactly how powerless and humiliated Doc was feeling, though he struck Ella as the kind of man who had rarely been in the same position himself. "Give you a little friendly advice?"

Doc looked over at him.

"Get yourself a gun and learn how to shoot."

Doc opened his mouth as if he was going to reject the idea out of hand. But he closed it again, looking ahead toward the growing darkness. His expression turned thoughtful, and he didn't say anything more.

Ella was surprised to realize that she'd never seen Doc with a weapon. She had assumed he at least kept a shotgun behind the bar, like most saloon owners . . . but she'd never seen him use one. She had supposed that fear of the Dolarhydes was the reason, since it seemed to be why everyone else in Absolution behaved the way they did. *But no, there was something more—*

She put her hand on her own gun, feeling the weight of it where it rested against her leg. She had grown used to wearing it, to the point where she had almost forgotten it was there.

Another of Dolarhyde's men, Greavey, rode up alongside her, reminding her suddenly of why she had started wearing a gun, as well as a hat—for protection. Greavey smiled at her with a look that said he thought he was God's gift to women. "So . . ." he began, "what's a pretty lady like y—"

"I'm not here to breed," Ella said flatly, dismissing him with a glance and looking ahead again.

He looked down at her hand, which still rested on her gun. "Well, oh-kay," he muttered, and dropped back to rejoin his companions. She sighed, hoping they hadn't decided to make a game of targeting the townsfolk, one by one, for the rest of the afternoon.

She barely suppressed a look of annoyance as Dolarhyde himself rode up to her. He didn't ride with his men, or anyone else, now—he either stayed aloof from all of them, or rode ahead to consult with Nat, his chosen tracker.

But now he had decided to take Greavey's place, as if he'd also been keeping an eye on the interactions among the others, all while he kept his distance from them. At least he wore his usual sour expression; romance was undoubtedly the furthest thing from his mind.

"What're you doing here?" he asked. "Woman wandering alone through Apache country . . . nobody 'round seems to know who you are."

She looked at him; her eyes locked onto his. "The men call you 'Colonel' behind your back, but they're afraid to do it in front of you. Why?"

Dolarhyde's face turned ashen, as she calmly crossed defensive boundaries that he had never let anyone violate, ever.

She knew why the men called him 'Colonel,' and why the word caused him so much pain that he'd actually killed men who said it to his face. He was a Civil War veteran, still tortured by the kind of memories that had stolen all the love, all the meaning, from too many lives; including her own. They had a different name for it, here: They called it "soldier's heart."

"All right," Dolarhyde said, his expression like a clenched fist. "You don't wanna tell me? That's your business."

She went on staring at him, into him, unblinking, expecting him to say something, anything, that would explain why he'd made the choices he had. The way he lived his life now was so different from the path she had chosen that she could barely even relate to him. . . .

She stopped seeing him at all, as she suddenly realized why Jake had reacted the way he had: Because his response to exactly the kind of loss and horror she'd once known had been completely different, when she'd expected it to be the same. . . . *Why had she even imagined—*

Movement in the distance caught her eye, giving her an excuse to ignore Dolarhyde completely. Her mouth fell open as she recognized the man riding toward them.

Jake Lonergan had come back.

Dolarhyde saw the change that came over her, and turned his head to follow her gaze. "Well . . ." he muttered, more grateful for the distraction—for *this* distraction—than he sounded. "Look who grew a pair."

He turned his horse and rode off to intersect Jake, as if something about the other man drew him like iron to a lodestone.

JAKE DIDN'T EVEN glance at Ella, his eyes on Dolarhyde from the moment he found the posse of demon hunters. He watched Dolarhyde ride toward him, and then rein in his horse as he neared. Jake's face got a little more expressionless as he prepared himself for whatever reception he was going to get.

Dolarhyde gave an unpleasant laugh as Jake got close enough so each could see the other's eyes. Jake thought Dolarhyde looked a little relieved to be back in familiar territory, after riding next to Ella; back to reading something he understood in someone else's eyes . . . *something about death*.

"I see *you*—" Dolarhyde grinned, more like he was baring his teeth, "but I don't see my gold."

Something flickered behind Jake's stare. "What say we find those people, first," he said, and he didn't smile at all. "Then you can take your best shot at collecting."

Dolarhyde smirked, his eyes still poisonous. "Right now the reward on your head might be a more attractive proposition. Or I can put a bullet in your chest, and cut that thing off your arm."

Demons had kidnapped the man's son, but gold was still the first thing on his mind. It occurred to Jake that Dolarhyde might just be the Wrong Passenger he'd wakened up, when he'd robbed that bullion coach—the one who'd convinced the territorial government to put a thousand-dollar bounty on his head.

Spiteful bastard. Jake grinned back at him this time, his stare equally baleful. He nodded toward the waiting group of riders. "You know where to find me."

Doc gave out a pained sigh. "Can't we just be glad the guy with the big gun's back?"

For a moment longer the two men held each other's gaze. And then Jake slapped his reins across his horse's withers and rode past Dolarhyde to join the others, as if somehow, overnight, he'd outgrown staring contests. He rode on ahead; Ella and the townsfolk moved on with him, leaving Dolarhyde to maintain his own position, like God, an outsider looking in.

Acting Sheriff Lyle looked toward Jake with a

frown that couldn't quite convince his face he wasn't glad to see Jake Lonergan again, after last night. The boy Emmett just stared, until Jake looked at him, and then he glanced away.

Preacher Meacham offered Jake a grin that looked completely heartfelt. "Welcome back."

Jake looked at him for a long moment. "Lord works in mysterious ways," he said at last. His own mouth turned up as he looked at Meacham, whose smile somehow made him feel like he'd just been reunited with an old friend.

But he slowed his horse, letting Meacham and the others ride on ahead. Only Ella stayed by his side, with a faint grin on her face, as if she thought he was somebody else. Any kind of smile was the last thing he'd expected to get from her.

But her glance welcomed him, as sincerely as the preacher's had. "Much obliged to you, Mr. Lonergan," she said, as if their encounter just after dawn had never happened. She touched the brim of her hat.

Jake nodded politely, his smile turning wry. "Well, I ain't done nothin' yet."

Her own smile only warmed as she said, "I appreciate it, all the same."

They rode on in silence, side by side, toward the coming storm.

9

Dusk came early as the midsummer storm closed over their heads, lidding off the sky. Inside the purple, bruised fist of the clouds, lightning flickered, and thunder rolled—far away at first, but approaching fast. The horses grew restless, anticipating the rain that the humans saw like a deep blue fog blurring their view of the distance.

The demon's trail had woven through arroyos and stayed close to the base of cliffs when it could, as if it preferred the darkness and shadows to the sun.

So had the demon-hunters, until now. . . . But the stretch of broken lands that had offered them all some small relief from the afternoon's heat had finally come to an end. Up ahead the land opened out into a flat plain filled mostly with cactus and sparse clumps of dry grass—a place that looked to offer no shelter from the storm.

Jake could see it clearly from where he rode now,

a self-exiled scout on the crest of a ridge, while the others followed Nat Colorado's tracking. He figured it was just as well: *The storm looked to be a real toad-strangler;* they were going to half drown, wherever they were. But if they didn't get out of these twisting canyons, they'd all end up drowned, period.

Jake stopped his horse, and pulled loose the jacket the horse's former owner had tied on behind the saddle.

Just as he shrugged it on, pulling up the collar, sheet lightning lit up the entire sky. Pitchfork bolts struck peaks and mesas all around them, the crack of thunder following almost instantaneously. As if the clouds had been ripped open, rain poured down like Heaven's waterfall: The storm had found them, and within seconds everyone was drenched to the skin in water that felt as cold as the day had been hot.

The desert never did anything halfway. It would kill a man with thirst, or sweep him away in a flash flood, horse and all. The kind of rain that fell during a *chubasco* like this ran off the rocks and over the bone-hard crust of the earth in torrents that could flood an arroyo or narrow canyon in a matter of minutes. A few minutes more, and a ten-foot wall of water roaring down the dry wash would catch an unwary traveler with no warning at all.

High on the ridge, Jake smelled the reek of ozone and felt his skin prickle with static. Soothing his nervous horse, he counted himself lucky simply to be only half drowning.

He should have been more careful . . . even the high

ground was treacherous, here. But riding too long in the middle of a posse, especially one that included Dolarhyde and Ella, had gotten on his nerves.

In less than five minutes Nat turned to Dolarhyde down below with a fatalistic shrug. Water sluiced from his hat brim as he shook his head, "Rain's too heavy. Gonna wash the tracks away."

Dolarhyde's face turned grim; even knowing it was bound to happen, he glared at the sky as if he took the news as a personal affront.

All the riders began to head up the steep slope as runoff water poured down it, following Jake's silhouette to higher ground.

Jake watched them make their way up the hill toward him, and understood the rest without explanation. He rode on to the end of the bluff to look for any place at all that might offer them refuge from the storm and the oncoming night.

He shielded his eyes from the rain pouring off his hat and searched the distance. All he could see was the vast swath of blue-gray blurring to green-black that the plain below had become as the rain began to fall. He moved his horse to the very limit of the outcrop, dropping his gaze inward to scan the land closer to the foot of the ridge, not really expecting to find anything better.

But there was something . . . *something*—? He stood in his stirrups for a better look. *It couldn't be . . . but it was*. He raised one hand, both a signal and a warning to the others. As they gathered around him, he pointed, waiting for their reactions. He heard sudden gasps; he heard curses and murmurs of disbelief. *So he hadn't completely lost his mind, after all.*

There *was* a paddlewheel steamboat from the Mississippi River lying in the middle of the New Mexico desert. Upside down.

Like it'd been dropped from the sky . . .

Jake didn't say anything, wondering why the hell he'd felt so surprised, after everything he'd seen and been through the last couple of days. Nobody else said anything either, just sat staring, as the rain endlessly poured down on them.

Finally Doc said, "Don't know much about boats, but I'd say that ship's upside down."

"And it's five hundred miles from the nearest river that can hold it," Dolarhyde observed, as if they were discussing the weather. *Or maybe he was—* "C'mon, let's get out of the rain."

"I ain't goin' anywhere near it," Doc said.

Dolarhyde shrugged. "Suit yourself. Sleep in the rain."

Charlie Lyle nodded, and Dolarhyde led the way down the treacherous slope into the valley below, although even his own men again traded dubious looks as they followed him.

The others headed down the slope after them, one by one. Doc was the last to leave the bluff, but he came, just the same.

The inside of the riverboat was mostly dry; but that was about all anybody could say for it. Ella was the only one carrying matches that would still strike a light. The others groped in the lightning-lit near darkness until they found some splintered furniture, and began to turn chair legs into torches. They moved as a group, cautiously, through an obstacle course of broken wood, upended furniture, and shards of glass, until they arrived in what once must have been the Grand Ballroom.

Its chandelier lay in a glittering pyramid of crystal pendants, in what had been the middle of the hall. A large rattlesnake lay coiled on top of it, having found refuge here before they had.

One of Dolarhyde's men drew his pistol, and made short work of it. He grinned: *fresh meat for dinner*.

Jake glanced at the dead rattler, suddenly hungry enough to enjoy eating snake. There hadn't been any food in the saddlebags on his horse. But he'd starve before he'd beg a crumb from Dolarhyde, or anybody who worked for him. He looked at the rest of Dolarhyde's crew, watching their mixed reactions. *Maybe the preacher'd be decent enough to break bread with an outlaw.*

The people from town were trying to ignore the prospect of snake for dinner altogether. They busied themselves prying loose any candles left in the chandelier. Ella passed around lit candles, smiling as she handed one to Emmett and leaned down to pat the wet dog beside him. *That* dog. . . .

More light revealed more broken furniture, including upside-down gambling tables and the remains of a long buffet that had been laid out with a feast of elegantly prepared food. The ship hadn't been here long—although it had been here long enough for the food to turn rotten in the desert heat.

Jake was surprised that the smell wasn't worse. Rats, never picky eaters, frantically scrabbled away from the light, as people began to explore further.

Jake glanced across the room, just as pitchfork lightning erased every inch of shadow. The far wall was all windows—and every single one of them had been smashed in. That explained the fresh air.

He suddenly realized what else it meant: They hadn't found any people on this ship, alive or dead. Everyone had been taken . . . by the demons.

His mouth pulled back in a tight line. He didn't bother to mention the obvious to the others. Either they'd figured it out for themselves, or they hadn't; but none of them seemed to feel like talking about it any more than he did.

The others began to move on in small groups, searching for places that were more private, where they could dry out and bed down for the night.

Jake prowled the corridors alone, like a cat, unable to settle anywhere in spite of the fact that his body felt like it had been through more in the last two days than it had in his entire missing lifetime . . . though under the circumstances, he had no idea if that was true or not.

His mind had been through as much . . . at least as much . . . more. So much that he couldn't rest—afraid of thinking too long if he stopped moving, afraid of dreaming if he slept. *No rest for the wicked.* . . . At least not while his wide-awake life was enough to make him question his sanity, over and over.

He was aware that Ella had begun following him

as he explored, carrying a candle and keeping her distance. She hadn't seemed like she wanted to talk to him, and he didn't think she was afraid he'd bolt again if he got the chance, now that he was back of his own free will.

If she'd wanted a bedmate, she had her pick of them: it wasn't like that, either. *What the hell, then?* Was she lonely, afraid, feeling in need of protection . . . or did she think he was the one who needed watching over, like that orphaned boy or that fool dog? Maybe she was trying to figure him out. He wished her luck.

Whatever it was, if she wasn't talking, he wasn't about to ask. Let her follow him if she wanted to—at least then he could be sure of what one person here besides him was doing, all the time. . . .

Navigating by lightning-light, he passed dark halls like tunnels and more empty rooms full of breakage and spillage, until he paused as he reached the end of the main hall. It opened on a larger area, where he saw Doc, actually wearing a gun belt, and trying to fast-draw a revolver—starting the process backwards, which figured.

First you learned to hit your target, every time it counted. Then you worked on a fast draw, or any other move you had the skill for. He watched Doc fumble another draw; watched him try it again, with the same results. Doc took hold of the pistol and attempted to twirl it around his finger; it fell on his foot. Jake winced, not in empathy, and hoped the goddamned thing wasn't loaded.

He wondered why Doc was even trying to handle

a revolver, when it was obvious that he was terrified of guns.

And then he saw Meacham watching Doc's futile practice session, with Charlie Lyle observing beside him. Lyle's expression barely hid his dismay.

But Meacham flashed his good-natured grin at Doc, and said, "Occurred to me—you might do better with two hands. . . ." He held out his rifle.

The frustration and self-disgust on Doc's face eased. He holstered the pistol and gratefully took the rifle from Meacham.

Jake backed further into the shadows before he let the faintest trace of smile show on his face. Meacham was a good man, and a sharp one, when it came to figuring out what people needed. But it was clear he hadn't been a preacher forever, or even most of his life. *Good or evil . . . it's up to you, from now on.* Maybe that was the truth he'd found, when he found his vision of the Lord. Jake would've liked to swap stories with the man, if he'd had any stories that he could remember.

Ella had stopped when he did, and followed him down the next darkened corridor he chose. Up ahead he could see flame-shadows on the walls; somebody had built a small fire out of broken furniture.

He stopped at a point just before the firelight reached into the hallway, to see who it was. Dolarhyde and Nat were sitting across the fire from each other, both of them as silent as if they were all alone. The two men weren't camped out with the rest of Dolarhyde's crew; Dolarhyde sat, lost inside his own thoughts, as if even Nat wasn't present.

Dolarhyde was peeling an apple with his Bowie knife as he stared into the fire. He peeled the whole apple with one perfect spiral motion; his hands were so skillful he could've cut a man's heart out blindfolded.

Jake watched, equally silent, completely fascinated.

At last he turned around and headed back down the corridor. He nodded to Ella as he passed her, as if they were two restless spirits passing in the halls of a haunted house, and kept on walking. She said nothing, only turned to follow him again, still keeping her distance.

DOLARHYDE GLANCED UP as he felt something disturb his concentration. He watched Nat feed another stick of broken wood to the fire, studying his expression. "You fixin' to say something?"

Nat hesitated, glancing away into the shadows, before he was able to look back again and meet Dolarhyde's eyes. "I dunno, boss. What do you think—is there enough of us here?"

It was Dolarhyde's turn to hesitate, knowing the truth—knowing that Nat recognized it too, or he wouldn't have asked the question. He said quietly, "What else am I gonna do?"

Nat took a deep breath. "Maybe we should . . . notify the army. Get the cavalry involved."

Dolarhyde looked up as if he'd been spat on. "We're not turning this over to some West Pointer—" he said, his voice as bitter as alkali, "wait for 'em to get on the telegraph and ask Washington which hand to wipe with. I waited around for 'em at Antietam to tell me what to do. . . ."

He looked into the darkness that lay inside the flames, seeing the past that would never die . . . not like his men had died. They'd died, and died, in meaningless sacrifice, in the bloodiest attack on the bloodiest day of the bloodiest battle in all the history of the United States. They'd keep on dying, forever, in his memory. . . . "Lost four hundred and twenty-eight men. Over a goddamn cornfield."

He stared at the fire. It had been nearly thirteen years . . . but nothing, no amount of time, would ever burn away the memory of that terrible day, deafen him to the screams of the dying . . . ease the agony of the wounded, or the agony in his own soul, as his grief and self-loathing forced him to live through it again and again.

The law, the orders, the chains of command that had held him prisoner . . . his inability to disobey them, then, had forced him to commit the sin of cowardice: moral cowardice, in the face of all that was wrong; the worst sin he could imagine. He had let over four hundred good men die, men who had trusted him, who would have followed him into Hell itself. Who had.

"Might sound foolish . . ." Nat murmured, so softly Dolarhyde could barely make out the words. Looking back into his own memories, he smiled. "I always liked it when you used to tell those stories."

Dolarhyde blinked the darkness out of his eyes

and looked at Nat. There was a look on Nat's face now that he'd never seen before. He frowned slightly. "I don't remember telling you those stories."

Nat glanced up, looking almost guilty. "I'd listen when you'd tell 'em to Percy."

Dolarhyde stared at Nat for a long moment, seeing a different person sitting across from him than he had ever allowed himself to see before. For a moment the pain of the past receded, as the full implication of the younger man's words sank in, and he felt something stir inside him that he thought had died long ago.

But then he looked away, at the darkness surrounding them. "There was nothing I ever did worth liking."

"All the same . . ." Nat said, the smile grown quiet on his face, "I liked the stories."

Dolarhyde looked back into the fire, letting it immolate all traces of an emotion he didn't deserve, and never wanted to feel again. He said irritably, "They weren't for you, they were for my *son*."

Hearing it come out of his mouth, he looked down abruptly, so that he didn't have to see Nat's face. "Wish he'd listened . . ." he muttered. Wishing to himself that the son he'd likely die for had turned out to be half the man that Nat Colorado was. "Now go check on the horses."

Nat got up without a word and left the fire, seeming as glad to put an end to their conversation as Dolarhyde was.

Dolarhyde picked up his knife. He cut a slice from

the apple, chewed it without tasting anything as he stared at the flames again.

He heard stirring just beyond the firelight. He looked up with faint surprise to see Emmett, John Taggart's grandson. He had forgotten the boy had been there at all.

He studied Emmett's face, seeing the admiration in the boy's eyes as he gazed at the Bowie knife, along with plain hunger when he looked at the apple.

Dolarhyde cut a piece from the apple, keeping his eyes on the boy as he did it. He held the piece of apple out. "Here."

Emmett came forward and accepted it with a sudden smile. He sat down cross-legged beside the fire and began to eat, as Dolarhyde cut another slice for himself. Dolarhyde wasn't sure how he'd managed to invite the kid to dinner; but there wasn't much he could do about it now that he had. He handed Emmett another piece of apple. Emmett watched each time he cut a slice, with a fascination that was almost awe.

It occurred to Dolarhyde that the boy was the only one here without some kind of weapon. It made him think about what the boy was even doing here— then he remembered that Taggart had been taken by the demons, just like Percy.

Taggart had been a smart, fair man, Dolarhyde knew, and a good sheriff: The fact that Taggart hated everything he stood for—his total disregard for the law Taggart was sworn to uphold—and wasn't afraid to show it, only proved the man's integrity. He was tough enough to do dirty work when he had to, but still human enough to miss his only child, and try to keep his only grandchild shielded from the real ugliness of the world they lived in for as long as he could . . . whether that was a smart thing to do or not.

Dolarhyde looked at Emmett again: all alone, but as determined as any man to save the last of his family. Even if he had to fight demons with his bare hands . . . The boy suddenly reminded him of someone else, but he couldn't think who.

When they had finished the apple, Dolarhyde held up the knife. "You lookin' at this knife?" he asked Emmett. "You like this knife?"

Emmett nodded, his wide brown eyes as serious as they were surprised.

Dolarhyde flipped the knife and caught it by the blade, He held it out to the boy. Emmett took the knife from him, speechless.

"You look after that," Dolarhyde said, his voice stern. Emmett nodded, his eyes going even wider. Dolarhyde took the knife sheath from his belt and tossed it after the knife. Emmett held the knife, staring at it in wonder. He picked up the sheath and put the blade into it, very carefully, and fastened it to his belt. Then, still silent, but with amazement reflecting like firelight in his eyes, he got up again and moved off into the shadows beyond the pool of light.

Dolarhyde took a deep breath, relieved to have his solitude back. This time, at least, he hadn't been left feeling ashamed by the results of what he had done. Instead, he felt oddly satisfied. Remembering the way the boy's eyes had shone as he accepted the knife, Dolarhyde suddenly realized who it was that Emmett had reminded him of: another boy, named Nat Colorado—orphaned, unwanted, and all alone— when Dolarhyde had first brought him home.

A rifle shot rang out in the quiet, echoing through the ship, making him start and look up. But it wasn't followed by further noise, no shouting or screams. He sighed, and tossed another chair leg on the fire. *That damn fool Sorenson,* he thought. *Nothing but dead weight.*

DOC SORENSON LOWERED the rifle, his face tight with frustration as he looked at the bottle he'd been trying to hit, still sitting unscathed on the table. He ran his hands through his dirty hair, further disheveling what had, until last night, always been a carefully groomed and tonsored look.

"Treat her like a woman," Meacham said, adjusting the rifle in his grip. "Talk to her like one: 'You look beautiful, darlin', you're the most beautiful gun I ever seen'."

Doc raised the rifle to his shoulder again, not sure whether hearing a gun compared to a beautiful woman, or hearing the comparison come from the mouth of a preacher, was more disconcerting.

He hated killing, hated the kind of men who enjoyed it. His hands and eyes were trained to use a scalpel, to heal the injuries men like that inflicted, and his memory was filled with the names of medical terms, not the caliber numbers of bullets, or who made the best rifles. But if it meant saving his wife he'd learn to be a killer—even if it killed him.

"Align your sights now," Meacham repeated, going over the checklist again with saintly patience. "Don't pull the trigger, you squeeze it . . . gently."

Doc fired the rifle again; the sound deafened him, the gun kicked him in the shoulder, hard. He looked toward the table: the bottle was still intact. "Dammit," he muttered.

"Keep your hands steady," Meacham said, sounding like one of his instructors from medical school, now. "You can do it."

Doc cracked open the rifle's breech and reloaded it, fumbling with the bullets in his anger and frustration. "Maria was right . . . I ain't no gunfighter . . . ain't no saloon owner. . . ." *He was a doctor*. But here in the territories where he'd grown up, a genuine doctor was still as much of a freak as he'd been to his own family: a small, sickly boy growing up with a father and brothers who believed in an Old Testament God, and that what defined a man was his ability to beat down or shoot anyone who didn't believe the same.

They'd called him "Mama's Boy," because his mother had tried to protect him, along with herself . . . until finally the misery of her life had driven her to alcohol, and he'd lost her to sorrow and drink.

When she'd taken to spending more time at the cantina that Maria's family ran than at home, he'd taken a job there, to pay for her tequila; it had been the only thing he seemed able to do for her, by then, in return for a mother's love. Maria's family had become his real family, and Maria . . . *Maria*. . . .

"That woman's the only one who ever believed in me," he said, looking back at Meacham. After his mother died, he'd learned she had family—rich family—back east. They'd granted his mother's final wish and sent him to medical school, when they learned what had become of her. And Maria had waited for him, until he came home. . . .

But he'd come home only to discover that he couldn't make a living out here as a doctor. He couldn't take Maria back east, away from her family and everything she knew—he'd had a hard enough time with that himself. The way he talked and acted had made him stick out like a sore thumb. He wouldn't expose her gentle heart to the stares, the remarks—all the hard feelings left after the War, after too many wars—which even a Mexican wife would have attracted.

Maybe they should've gone to Santa Fe . . . but they hadn't had the money to start a new life together there. His memories of the cantina were good ones: a place where not just drunk cowhands, but actual families, had come to enjoy life and celebrate. He'd wanted to run a place like that—but the only place available was the Gold Leaf Saloon, in Absolution. . . . "All I wanted was to put her in some silk, y'know?" he said. "Give her a little buttermilk. Show her I could provide a better life . . ."

But he'd failed at that like he'd failed at everything else. "It's my fault she got took. If I hadn't brought her to that damn town . . ." He felt his voice beginning to shake. He struggled to keep control, to hold onto his belief in any future at all; barely holding it together, afraid that in another minute he'd—

"You're gonna get her back," Meacham said firmly. "Y'hear? You're settin' things right."

Doc looked up, needing to see something in the man's face that could make him believe. "So you . . . think she's still alive?"

Meacham grinned, his face brightening with belief. "Wouldn't be here, if I didn't have faith."

10

Jake's restless midnight wandering brought him at last to what must have been the private cabin of the riverboat's captain. Right now the middle of the room was occupied by a waterfall, maybe the biggest actual waterfall he'd ever seen: Rainwater poured in through a hole in the upside-down floor, gleaming like molten silver in the near-constant flicker of lightning; it flowed away like a river through another doorless opening.

Jake leaned against the wall outside the range of the waterfall's spray, staring up at the silver curtain, listening to the sound; realizing as he did how much worse his body felt than it had when he'd gotten here—sick to death of always moving, being driven by his own fear . . .

At least he was finally alone; even Ella had given up following him some while back, surrendering at last to boredom or fatigue. He took off his hat, removed the tintype of Alice from inside the crown, and looked down at her face. Without even realizing it he started to smile as she looked up at him, smiling.

Alice . . . God. Any woman who could make him feel glad he was alive, even when he felt like he did right now, just with her smile, was someone he had to find—to save, if he could—if only to find out what they'd really meant to each other.

If she was still alive. . . .

The pain in his side suddenly seared him like hot metal; his face tightened as he put Alice's picture back into his hat, controlling his movements with conscious effort. He righted a chair and set his hat on it, feeling something warm and wet soaking the side of his shirt. He unbuttoned his vest with clumsy fingers, untucked his shirt and saw fresh blood on it. *Shit.* The damn wound had pulled open. He unbuckled his gun belt and hung it over the chair back.

He took off his coat and vest, pulled the shirt up over his head, cursing under his breath. That wasn't a good sign, more blood. He should have paid the wound better heed—

Not having a bottle of whiskey with him to pour into the wound, he ducked into the falling water in the room's center. *Goddamn, it was freezing. . . .* He rubbed the wound clean as best he could with his hand, relieved to see that most of the stitching Meacham had done was still holding. He stepped out of the flood again, shivering, and shook the water from his hair. Blinking his eyes clear, he raised his head.

Ella was standing in the doorway, staring at his body.

Startled almost to embarrassment, he turned his back to her as he reached for his shirt. "You been standing there long?" he asked over his shoulder.

"Yes," Ella said, still fixing him with the unabashed stare.

He suddenly wondered if he'd been wrong about why she was following him. "Something you need—?"

"Does it hurt? she asked, glancing down. *Had she only been looking at the wound?*

"It's fine." His mouth thinned.

"They did that to you . . ."

Jake looked at the wound; up at her, stunned. *They . . . did she mean the demons? The wound . . . the strange weapon . . . his whole missing life: The demons had done that to him? How—? Unless . . . unless they'd taken him, along with Alice. But that meant. . . .*

Ella closed the space between them. He saw something raw and vulnerable in the way she looked at him now, as if she'd seen wounds like this before . . . seen a lot of them, maybe even felt that pain herself. *"They took my people, too,"* she'd said, and he realized now that she hadn't been lying just to use to him.

She put out her hand slowly, gently, and he let her fingers touch the wound; her fingers came away with blood on them.

Jake said nothing, pulling on his shirt. Ella moved away; crouched down to search the floor as if she'd dropped something. Finally she straightened up again, holding an intact bottle of liquor and an unused table napkin. She was now almost as drenched as he was, but she didn't seem to notice.

"Who's the woman in your picture?" Ella asked, as she poured liquor onto the cloth.

Jake glanced toward his hat; realized she really had seen everything he'd done, without him even suspecting she was there. He looked back again, with a slight head shake. "All I know is . . . she got taken when I did." *When I did. . . . They took me, too. Then how—? His* right hand covered the solid band of the weapon on his other wrist: the demon gun.

He must've escaped. But if he had . . . that meant Alice—

"So you're going to save her," Ella said softly, as if she assumed the woman was his lover.

"She's the only one who knows who I am," he said, refusing to let his mind or his voice take it any further, especially in the presence of another woman . . . *especially this one.*

He pulled his shirt up and Ella began to clean the wound, with the unflinching skill of someone who'd done it before. Jake held still, staring at the wall.

"You know who you are . . ." Ella said. "You just have to remember." She turned away, putting her foot up on a chair, and tore a long strip of cloth from her petticoat.

But did he even want to remember being Jake Lonergan: the outlaw, the killer; the kind of man who'd . . .

He swallowed the sudden, choking knot of shame that kept him from speaking. ". . . I can't . . ."

"Yes, you can," she said, her face filling with encouragement and belief. She pushed his shirt up again;

he held it as she began to wrap the strip of cloth around his waist, binding the wound to protect it.

But she couldn't imagine what kind of heartless bastard he must have been; what it would mean—

He didn't feel like Jake Lonergan. He didn't want to be the Devil in human form, or a gutless mudsill who'd run away and leave a woman like Alice to demons. . . .

He wanted to stay whoever he was now. Only human, free to start over . . . *just a man* . . . Ella's face was so close to his now, and her hands touching his skin were so warm. . . . He realized she'd taken off the jacket of her dress and left it somewhere to dry; she only had on a camisole, and her bare arms were circling his waist, her long dark hair falling across her shoulder. *He wouldn't be a man, if she didn't make him think about . . .*

. . . about Alice. He shut his eyes.

She finished tying the knot on his bandage and started to turn away, not looking up at him. He gripped her arm, gently but firmly. "Now you gotta tell me something," he said, making her meet his eyes this time, willing her to look at his face. *"Who did you lose?"*

Her eyes filled again with a pain so terrible that suddenly she had to fight to hold back her tears—the same look she'd given him just after dawn, when he'd caught her trying to follow him.

"Everyone who mattered to me—" she whispered.

Their eyes locked, and before he could stop it he was seeing double—*seeing two different people, each trapped inside their own loss and need, fate-bound to each other until they could become one, united to achieve a single impossible goal—*

The demon gun on Jake's wrist lit up and began to sound its alarm, shattering the fragile link between them.

"It's here," Ella said in a shaken voice, looking toward the doorway.

Jake grabbed his gun belt, and was out of the room before her.

EMMETT ROAMED THE dark corridors of the riverboat with the knife Mr. Dolarhyde had given him clutched firmly in his hand. He felt stronger and more confident right now than he had since before Ma had died, and Pa had . . . left him behind, over a year ago.

This morning, it had seemed like his whole world had ended . . . until he'd heard the final words of Preacher Meacham's sermon, and they had given him new hope, and inspiration. He'd vowed then to go after the demons too, and bring his grandfather home.

Grandpa was the bravest man Emmett knew, but that hadn't saved him from being taken away by those things. If he could rescue Grandpa, he could prove to him, to everybody—and especially to himself—that he was as much of a grown-up, just as strong and able to survive as anyone here . . . even Mr. Dolarhyde.

Today he'd ridden through the heat and dust and then the pouring rain without complaining, like all the other men. He'd helped them take care of the horses tonight, just like he'd promised, even though his legs had been so stiff he could hardly walk. And the respect he'd seen then in the eyes and smiles of the people he knew had made him feel sure he could do it again tomorrow, and keep on doing it for as long as he had to. . . .

Charlie Lyle and Preacher Meacham were sleeping now, and so was Doc Sorenson; the dog had wandered off somewhere a while ago. As far as Emmett knew, he was the only one on the ship who was still awake. He was too excited, too eager for tomorrow to arrive, to go to sleep, so he'd appointed himself their sentry, keeping watch while they rested, like a soldier from Mr. Dolarhyde's army days. . . .

He was making his way through the eerie, upside-down world of the engine room now. It was like exploring a cave: Strange machinery hung suspended from the ceiling, and more unfamiliar shapes rose up from the floor, all of it silhouetted by the constant lightning that threw long shadows like the hands of monsters across his path.

A faint scraping noise somewhere behind him made him shiver, with excitement or something darker. *Just a rat*, he told himself, and went on walking, a little faster.

This place really would've scared him if he hadn't had his knife. But he felt invulnerable as he watched its blade shine . . . even though he figured he'd need a little practice to get as good with it as Mr. Dolarhyde was. He wondered why Grandpa and Mr. Dolarhyde had never gotten along.

If he had looked back, he would have seen a piece of what he'd taken for fallen machinery detach from the solid mass of darkness and slowly unfold, until it loomed far above his head, more than seven feet tall.

Nothing Emmett had ever seen, no picture books of strange creatures from foreign lands, no tales of heroes who battled monsters—nothing in the darkest corners of his imagination—could have prepared him for the thing that turned to follow him now.

But at the last moment, it paused. It turned away and started off in another direction, as its inhuman senses registered signs no human would even have been aware of.

DOLARHYDE'S MEN HUDDLED around the campfire they'd made from the broken furniture they found in a salon as far from the Colonel as they could get, and with enough floor space for six tired, disgruntled cowhands to bed down.

They'd found a couple bottles of first-rate bourbon, too, which had made this place even more appealing. Drinking all the liquor had kept them awake longer than they'd intended, but it hadn't done anything for their mood. They still sat close to the warm light of the fire, their discontent only growing every time the bottle got passed around.

"What the hell're we doin' here?" Greavey said resentfully. He passed the bottle to Jed Parker, watched him take a swig. "We should be ridin' in the *opposite* direction of these things—"

"We do that, the old man's likely to shoot us himself," Parker muttered. "Only way outta this is—"

His thought went unfinished as a horde of panic-stricken rats came pouring into the room, scurrying around and over the men as they scrambled to their feet, cursing and kicking. The rats ran on, oblivious to human presence, fleeing something they found infinitely more terrifying. The men turned back, facing the door the rats had come in through.

A sudden bolt of lightning made the room as bright as day: Standing in front of them was the thing that had driven the rats into a frenzy . . . a monster that made all of their worst nightmares combined pale by comparison, as it towered above the men's heads. *A demon . . .*

They stood frozen a moment too long, too drunk even to act on their animal instinct to run away. And then the bottle of whiskey smashed on the floor, forgotten, as they went for their guns.

Before a single man could fire a single shot, the demon swung a forelimb the size of a small tree; its hide was as thick as armor plating, and its hand ended in razor-sharp slashing talons. The arm came down, ripping through flesh, snapping human bones as if they were bird legs. A man's scream of terror and pain began and ended, cut off in a gurgle and a fountain of blood, drowned out by sounds of inhuman frenzy.

More lightning flashed, as the other men finally ran like rats. They didn't stop until they were out in the storm, dragging horses and gear with them onto the plain, where—they hoped—they could tell if a demon was following them.

They saddled up in record time and rode away into the teeth of the storm, leaving behind the cursed riverboat that had offered them such dreadful sanctuary and everyone who was still in it . . . leaving the Colonel to fight all the demons he wanted, right there in the ship that had become a trap, a slaughterhouse, a morgue. . . .

EMMETT HEARD THE dog barking somewhere—barking and barking, like it had something cornered . . . or something had cornered it. Suddenly worried, he doubled back, toward the place where Charlie Lyle and the preacher were sleeping. He made the best speed he could, retracing the turns of his wandering path until he realized that the dog was somewhere nearby.

He followed the sound of barking down one corridor, and then another, until at last he found the room where the dog was. He found the black dog standing on a hill of piled-up furniture, its hackles standing on end, barking furiously at a darkened corner.

Emmett entered the room, holding his knife, trying to make out what the dog was barking at. "Easy, easy . . ." he murmured, coming up beside it. "What's wrong, boy?" The dog glanced toward him with a small querulous whine as he stroked its back. But then it looked away again, at whatever had been making it bark almost hysterically.

"Hello—?" Emmett called out uncertainly, peering into the shadows beyond the pile of furniture, trying to tell if anyone else was in the room. He heard a rustling, creaking noise, but no one answered.

Suddenly the dog growled, and sprang from the

pile of furniture into the darkness. Emmett heard a *thud,* and a yelp of pain.

"No!" Emmett started forward ... skidded to a stop, as the massive silhouette of something huge and indescribable began to take form out of the deeper darkness, and he realized—

Emmett darted back and crouched down behind the pile of furniture worming his way beneath it. He held his breath as the demon moved slowly past his hiding place, then paused, shifting what could have been a head from side to side as though it was searching for something ... for him. ...

But then it moved on, forcing its enormous bulk through the doorway as it went back out into the hall.

Emmett exhaled, a long quiet sigh of relief. He stayed where he was until the demon's heavy footsteps had faded away down the corridor.

He crawled out from under the furniture and got up, moving as softly as he could, his heart still pounding so loudly he was afraid the demon would hear it. "Dog—?" he called softly. "Hey, fella ... where are you, boy?" But there was no answer. Either the dog had escaped out of the other entrance to the room, or it ... it. ... He couldn't bring himself to search the cabin's darkened corners to find out.

He slipped out the other doorway, hoping the dog had gone that way too, but realizing that the most important thing right now was to find Charlie and Meacham, to warn everybody else.

He headed on down the corridor, afraid to go back the way he had come, fearful of running into the demon if he did. But he could barely remember the turns he'd made then; he realized he had no idea of where he was heading now in this dark maze. He could only go on searching until he found somebody, or at least something he recognized.

After a few more turns, Emmett suddenly found himself entering a vast open space—the Grand Ballroom, the first real room they'd entered, when they'd come onto the ship. He felt his confidence come back as he started out into the ballroom. From here he was sure he could find the way to where he and the others had bedded down for the night—

He froze in midstep as he heard a sound behind him in the hallway he had just come through; not a sound he recognized. He turned slowly, unwilling, to look back; choked off the cry that rose in his throat as he saw the demon.

The demon paused as it entered the room after him. Even though the near-constant sheet lightning in the clouds overhead made Emmett stand out clear as day, the thing didn't seem to see him as he backed up slowly, slowly, until he was pressed against the wall.

And then his foot bumped the fallen picture frame beside him. It crashed flat on the floor, its glass shattering loudly in the silence.

Before he could even gasp, the demon was looming over him, its enormous claw-fingered limbs sunk into the wall on either side of his body, blocking any escape.

Emmett opened his mouth to scream, but no sound would come out. What seemed to be the demon's head lowered toward his; slits in its protruding, reptilian face opened, revealing red, pupilless eyes like polished agates, peering down into his own with hideous fascination.

The thick, roughly plated hide on its chest split open, revealing a small set of glistening inner limbs protected beneath its outer skin. The limbs extended toward Emmett, and began to poke at his cheeks, nose, mouth . . . exploring his face with its fingers like a blind amphibian. Being touched by them was like being covered in worms, or the clinging toes of wet frogs, slippery and sticky all at once; they set off the nerve-endings in his face, until every muscle was twitching.

Sometime during the demon's exploration, Emmett began to cry helplessly. The Bowie knife dropped from his fingers and landed on the floor, forgotten. He was still crying as the demon's mouth slowly opened, and through his tears he saw its massive jaw unhinge like a snake's, until it opened even wider. Row after row of razor-sharp teeth lay waiting inside. The demon lowered its head above him—

The sound of a shot echoed throughout the room as Preacher Meacham fired his rifle. The demon's plated shoulder ripped open, spraying a gout of green blood. It screeched, the noise drilling into Emmett's ears.

"Get away from him!" Meacham shouted. He cocked the rifle and fired again. Another bullet struck home. The alien shrieked, and turned away from Emmett and toward Meacham.

As Meacham stopped to reload his gun, the demon leaped, soaring across the space between them, and drove one of its heavy claw-talons straight through the preacher's chest.

JAKE HAD FOLLOWED the sound of gunfire into the Ballroom, his demon weapon open and ready to fire— just in time to see the demon stab its arm through Meacham's chest.

He fired the demon-killing gun with an inarticulate cry of fury, and missed as the demon leaped aside. He ran forward, firing at it again, with nothing in his mind now except the need to see the monster dead.

The demon, escaped his second shot, leaping faster than Jake's eyes or arm could follow. It sprang away, up the wall, moving like some monstrous cockroach as it skittered back across the ceiling-floor, and vanished through a hole.

Jake reached the place where Meacham lay in a spreading pool of blood and crouched beside him while Ella crossed the room to Emmett.

The preacher's eyes opened and he looked up at Jake with that insufferably good-hearted smile, as if he was perfectly at peace, and glad to see him.

"Easy now . . ." Jake said, afraid even to lift the head of a man with a wound like that. "Don't move—" His first impulse was to call for Doc, but his eyes had already told him there was no point.

Emmett, held in Ella's arms, cried out, "Meacham!" and wept harder.

"It's okay, boy," Meacham murmured. "I'm going home. . . ."

Jake jerked his head at Ella, who was still clinging to the boy. "Get him outta here."

Ella nodded, and began to draw Emmett with her out of the room, neither of them wanting the boy to witness Meacham's dying moments.

Meacham glanced down at the demon gun on Jake's wrist; his eyes searched Jake's face. "Get our . . . people back," he murmured.

Jake nodded, meeting the preacher's gaze. "Stop talking," he said thickly, barely getting the words out without his voice breaking. *Why the hell couldn't the damned thing on his wrist have been for healing, not just killing—?*

Meacham caught the front of his shirt, pulling him closer. Jake's hand gripped the preacher's in a silent promise, as blood ran from the corner of Meacham's mouth, and the preacher began to gasp for air. Eye to eye with Jake, he whispered, "God don't care who you were, son . . . only what you *are*."

Jake pressed his lips together, blinking hard as the unexpected, unfamiliar burn of tears stung his eyes. Meacham's last breath bubbled out between his lips; his eyes closed, and his hand released Jake's shirt.

Jake crouched, strengthless, for a long moment by Meacham's side. He saw the cross the preacher always wore, now covered in blood, and his eyes filled with unholy rage—not against the symbol, or the faith it symbolized, or the man who'd worn it; but against the demon that had stolen the life of the man, and all he stood for . . . from him, from everyone here, from all the people of Absolution.

He put his hand on the demon gun. It had become dormant again, returned to its shackle-form as soon as the demon had disappeared.

Part of his helpless anger turned back on himself— and on the weapon—for his failure to reach Meacham in time, the weapon's failure to warn him in time. *"Chain a man to his worst enemy . . ."* Taggart had said. *"Best way to make him stay put."*

Jake got to his feet at last, cursing all creation as he walked away alone into the darkness.

BY THE NEXT morning the storm had passed. At least the rain had softened the ground enough so that Jake could dig a grave. He started before dawn, when there was barely enough light to see a shovel bite into the earth. His anger had been eating a hole in his gut as bad as the hole where his memory used to be. He almost felt like thanking God for the chance to dig a grave, as the hard physical labor burned away some of his useless frustration and kept his mind from thinking about anything at all. Almost.

By the time the others were stirring again, he had laid Meacham in his final resting place and driven a makeshift cross into the ground.

Ella came out of the ship, bringing him a cup of coffee and a tin plate piled high with real food; he accepted them with real gratitude. She looked from him to the grave with too much pain in her eyes; touched his shoulder, as if she was thanking him for something, too, and went back inside the ship. Jake ate alone, sitting on the ground.

He watched the others come out, finally, carrying saddlebags and blankets, reloading supplies onto the mule, saddling up horses. Doc had Meacham's rifle slung over his shoulder. Jake observed that their party was missing more people than just Meacham, and frowned as he remembered the screaming last night.

Emmett was wandering around the far perimeter of what was safe territory for now, looking for something, while Nat Colorado searched for the demon's tracks. Jake heard Emmett calling, "Dog? Come on, boy—!"

Dolarhyde, already impatient to be moving, shouted at Nat.

"Tracks turn north—" Nat answered from the rise where he was standing.

"Where's the rest of the boys?" Dolarhyde asked.

Nat came back down the hill, watching the ground, not looking Dolarhyde in the eye. He reached the bottom, his eyes still averted as he said, ". . . They ran off."

Jake wondered whether Nat actually couldn't look Dolarhyde in the eye because he was afraid of Dolarhyde's anger, or simply because he hated having to tell anybody news like that.

The hellfire look he knew too well was back on Dolarhyde's face; but underneath it, this time, he saw the real burn left by the stinging slap of abandonment. Dolarhyde mounted his horse, muttering, "Goddamn cowards. . . ."

Emmett returned, looking up anxiously as Dolarhyde settled himself in the saddle.

"Can't find the dog—" Emmett said, his eyes pleading for more time, as if he was certain Dolarhyde would actually understand.

Dolarhyde's mouth turned down. "Probably dead." He raised his hand, a signal to the others. "Let's go."

"He *ain't* dead!" Emmett shouted furiously, but Dolarhyde rode away without listening.

Ella and Charlie Lyle came up to the boy. Ella put her arm around him. "It's okay, he'll find us," she said, with that way she had of looking at someone that could make him believe she knew everything. "He'll be fine."

But Emmett wasn't fine with that, and the look on his face was only heartsick as he began to follow them toward the horses.

Doc glanced at Jake, at the dirt on his clothes and the fresh grave with its marker behind him. "Wait—" he called after Dolarhyde, "aren't we gonna say something?"

Dolarhyde looked back at him in disgust. "The only one who knew what to say's underground. Isn't it enough we wasted time burying him?" Dolarhyde's eyes struck Jake, as if Jake had made them wait. Jake's fists knotted at his sides, but he said nothing.

Doc glared at Dolarhyde, fresh grief and anger filling his face. "Shame on you," he said, as if he actually meant it like a curse. "Show some respect."

Dolarhyde only turned his horse's head and rode away, with Nat following silently behind him. Leaving behind regretful and apologetic looks, Ella, Charlie Lyle, and Emmett followed them, one by one.

Doc turned back to the grave, staring at it. Jake stepped up beside him, taking off his hat.

Doc gave him a fleeting smile. He stood a moment, then he bowed his head and closed his eyes. "Uh . . . Lord, if there is such a thing as a soul, he had a good one. Please protect him."

He raised his head again. Loss and empathy showed in his eyes as he looked back at Jake. "How was that?"

Jake nodded, more grateful than he knew how to express. The words had been good ones, and at least somebody besides him had borne witness to a man who had lived and died with a kind of courage that deserved everyone's respect. And God knew, Doc's eulogy was better than anything he could have said himself, if his life depended on it. "C'mon," he murmured, turning away toward their horses.

THE DEMON HUNTERS pushed on into the heart of the desert, only seven of them, now, but seven resolved never to turn back, never to yield to anything less than Death itself.

By the time the sun had been up for an hour, it was impossible to tell that last night the arid land had been flooded with rain. Red dust stirred by their horses' passage hung in the air like a blood-tinted shroud, with barely a breath of wind to carry it away.

Beyond the bleak plain where the riverboat lay, more broken stone and twisting canyons waited for them. All obvious traces of flash-flooding had vanished as they entered the labyrinth of stone, following the demon's random footprints through the time-jumbled remains of ancient sea bottom.

Eons of sandstone lay piled one age on another, or folded like strips of bacon, stained sunset red and purple-brown by pigments from iron and manganese, or showing a chalk-white underbelly of limestone, further broken by extrusions of hardened lava.

They'd ridden off the edge of the map the moment they'd set out; by now they could have ridden off the edge of the world, or wakened this morning to discover they were on another planet, given the alienness of the land around them.

But by now no one gave so much as a thought to the forces of nature that had etched the broken land into fangs of upthrust rock, or gouged it into deep, twisting arroyos and canyons. Every one of them was too preoccupied with memories of last night, with keeping on the trail of the demon, or simply making certain their horses didn't pull up lame or thrown a shoe on the stony, treacherous ground.

Jake rode alone again, keeping watch from the canyon's rim, staying away from the others, who followed Nat's tracking along the base of the canyon wall. The demon was clinging to the shade of any sheltering rocks or low ground it could find; and most of the hunters following it were glad enough to stay out of the sun when they could.

Jake preferred the solitary position, even if it gave him no relief from the heat. He wasn't sure, after last night, whether he still kept to the high ground because it kept him away from the others, or because it let him see more of what lay ahead. It felt familiar to him, which in a way was a comfort, and reason enough, given the mood he was in today.

After a few hours, he became aware that he was not the only rider who preferred the high ground. Searching the far rim of the canyon, he suddenly noticed three men . . . three Apaches . . . on horseback, holding the same pace, observing the progress of the group below . . . and no doubt him, too.

This had all been Apache land once; they preferred the mountains, but they knew the desert too, and how to live off it. They'd had the place all to themselves, until settlers from Mexico, and then the States, had come and tried to take it away from them, mainly because even this godforsaken ground had enough gold in it to make it worth their while.

In the end, the big bugs in Washington had had their way—they'd had the money, the guns and ammunition, plenty of time, and all the patience in the world, as long as other people were doing the fighting and dying for them.

The United States had taken this territory and the states around it in the war with Mexico, finishing off that deal with a hefty bribe called the Gadsden Purchase. Then they'd focused their attention on finishing the dirty business of wiping out the Apaches.

Now most Apaches in this part of the territories were on reservations, or they were dead—except for a few renegades like these, who were still too angry to give in and too savvy to get caught . . . still wanted, dead or alive.

The U.S. government claimed its victories were

"Manifest Destiny"—that God loved the United States so much He'd wanted its people to go on killing Indians and Mexicans until they got richer than anybody else.

Jake wondered who'd first scooped them into that pile of horseshit. Not that most people really needed convincing . . . just good excuses, when the only word they actually understood was "rich."

Nobody ever really owned the land, Jake thought, any more than they ever really had claim to another person's soul. . . . But he knew that was just his opinion, and for any person he could find who'd agree with him, there were a hundred others waiting to hang him for it, right now. The whole damned United States had nearly killed itself over the right to own someone else's life, back in the War.

And now demons were trying to claim this piece of Hell. It made as much sense to him as anything else. Maybe more.

Life wasn't one damn thing after another . . . it was one damn thing over and over. He wiped sweat off his forehead with his sleeve, glancing across at the Apaches again as he did.

Right now he felt like he had more in common with them than he did with his own people. But that didn't mean the Apaches wouldn't kill him just as dead—and everyone with him—if they got the chance. And it would likely take a lot longer, and be a lot more painful, than a bullet or a noose.

At last Jake saw the end of the canyon up ahead. He took a drink from his canteen, shrugged the tension out of his shoulders, and scanned the lay of the land beyond the canyon's mouth. Then he turned his horse's head, as if he'd simply spotted a place where he could get down off the rim, and went to tell the others the news.

DOWN BELOW, NAT called out to Dolarhyde, "I got him." The terrain had grown so rocky by the time they'd entered this canyon that they'd been going partly on guesswork, following the demon's general direction of travel.

Dolarhyde rode up to the spot where Nat had dismounted and was crouched down beside an imprint in a spot of sand. "Tracks are getting closer together. He's slowing down and heading for that canyon." Nat pointed across the rock-strewn plain ahead of them toward a gap in the wall of the mesa on the other side.

The plain in between was only the floor of a larger canyon . . . one of dozens, or more likely hundreds, that had carved the tablelands around them into a patternless maze. This small canyon, and the one waiting for them—and hundreds on hundreds of others—fed into the larger ones like funnels, waiting to draw the unwary into a labyrinth most travelers probably never get out of alive. "Good job," Dolarhyde said, relief easing his face just a little. "I thought we lost him."

Nat straightened up from his crouch. Out of habit his eyes scanned the heights around them; he spotted Jake riding down from the canyon rim . . . and the three warriors who had stopped their horses on the other side, waiting and watching. Nat murmured one more word. "Apache."

Dolarhyde gave him a brief nod. "I know. Been back there a while." He glanced out across the plain again, at the place they were headed for now. "They won't follow us into that canyon." It had once been a favorite trick of the Apaches to lure cavalry or troops into a canyon, using two or three of their own, on fast horses, for bait. They'd trap the poor fools in a crossfire and pick off every last man, if they could.

The army he had once belonged to hadn't been fighting Apaches for very long before the scouts, and even any officer who didn't have shit for brains, learned that trick, and then began to turn the tables on the Apaches. The Apaches didn't like that any more than the troops had; and Apaches caught on real fast. "Best not to mention it to the others," he said.

Nat nodded in silent agreement and remounted his horse, just as Ella rode forward to join them.

"I think we're being followed." Her voice was quiet and calm; she didn't glance back at the rest of the party.

Dolarhyde's frown deepened. He wondered again who this strange woman was, where she'd come from . . . how she seemed to know everything, and why she intruded on his personal territory in a way no sane man had ever dared to do. Most of all, he wondered why he didn't have the nerve to ask her for the answers. . . . He only said, sourly, "We know."

Jake reached the spot where the three of them sat on their horses, as the rest of the group began to catch up, ready to ride across the open plain. "Apaches," he said. "Best bet is that canyon." He pointed toward the exact place where Dolarhyde intended to go.

"What the hell do you know?" Dolarhyde dug in his spurs, riding on ahead as if Jake had deliberately insulted him.

Jake glared at his retreating back, wondering what the hell had put a burr under the old rip's saddle this time.

Ella moved into his line of sight and gave him a brief smile of pained empathy, and suddenly he thought he understood.

He looked back as the rest of the group caught up, not saying anything to anyone as he stole a last glance at the canyon's rim, where the three Apaches had stopped their horses.

11

The canyon on the far side of the plain was a box canyon, just like Jake had figured, seeing it from a height. He could see clear to the end of it from the entrance. He didn't see any obvious demons' nest, and they'd be safe enough from the Apaches.

He told himself there was nothing to worry about—at least until they found the demons. After spending much of last night thinking about what had happened to Meacham, and almost had happened to the kid, he figured the people the demons had taken were likely dead by now. Being realistic, he figured the demons would probably kill him, and everyone with him, too.

If that didn't bother the others, it didn't bother him. From everything he'd heard, he should have been dead a long time ago . . . *at least, long before he'd left Alice to demons.* If the others had come here wanting justice but willing to settle for revenge, then they must all have come to the same decision, no matter how they'd arrived at it. All he wanted now was a chance to send a few demons back to Hell personally, before he died—just to let the Devil know he was coming.

But a box canyon was a box canyon: a natural trap. He felt the odd prickling run up his spine, the sixth sense that kept telling him things he didn't want to hear. The fact that Dolarhyde kept searching the canyon rim just as intently as he was only increased his bad feeling.

Nat dismounted again, kneeling down by another demon track. "That way." He began to raise his arm.

Rifle shots echoed from the canyon walls; bullets fired from above pocked the ground all around them. The horses spooked, and so did most of the riders who suddenly were trying to control them; a couple had to pull leather just to keep from falling off.

Jake looked up at the men with rifles trained on them, who'd appeared out of nowhere to pin them in a perfect crossfire. *Not Apaches.* And there was only one other thing men like these could be.

One of the men up above shouted, "Hands in the air!"

Shit, Jake thought, slowly raising his hands with the rest.

Two riders were entering the canyon mouth now, holding their rifles trained on the group. *The perfect trap.* Jake stared at the two men riding toward him. One of them was Mexican, the other Anglo, both as hard-looking as the land itself.

His own expression felt stuck somewhere between frustration and disgust . . . disgust at himself, for not trusting his instincts; frustration because they'd been so close to finding the demons—

The two outlaws reined in, sizing up their catch. The Mexican said, "I say we just shoot 'em, and take their—" He broke off as he met Jake's stare. "Boss?" he said, incredulous.

Jake realized that both men were staring straight at him. They lowered their guns, their hostility turning to complete surprise. The Mexican who'd called him "boss" actually dismounted, looking nervous.

"What the hell you doin' back here, Lonergan?" the other man said. He stayed on his horse, only looking suspicious as he started toward Jake.

"Jesus, boss, Dolan's gonna *shit* when he sees you," the Mexican said. Looking past Jake at Dolarhyde and the rest, he added, "And who the hell are *they?*"

Now everybody was staring at him. *Oh, Christ. . . .* He could swear he'd never seen either of these men before, let alone been their leader. He had no idea what their names were. But they sure knew him: *Jake Lonergan—the Scourge of the Territories.*

The man still on his horse rode up alongside Jake, looking even more suspicious when Jake didn't say anything. "What's the matter, Lonergan? Cat got your—?"

Jake dropped his hands and smacked the man across the mouth, as hard as he could, knocking the words back down his throat. "Shut up!" he snarled, because it felt right. *If Jake Lonergan was wanted, dead or alive, then nobody from his gang—nobody at all—talked to him like that.* He was off the map for good, now. His instincts were all he had left to follow.

Now Ella and the others were staring at him. Dolarhyde looked at him with more disbelief than anyone; his eyes held a question that demanded an answer, one Jake couldn't give him out loud.

Jake gave him an urgent look, willing him to understand: *Just go with it.* He glanced back at the outlaws who'd confronted them. They were both looking at him like he was the Jake Lonergan they remembered, now. The man on the horse beside him mumbled, "Christ, Jake . . . you broke my *tooth.*" He put a hand over his bleeding mouth.

"Then keep your mouth shut," Jake said. "How many boys we got left?"

" 'Bout the same." The man shrugged.

Jake glanced at the sky, at the men still covering them from the ridge. "Still about, uh . . ."

"Thirty," the man said.

"That's right. Thirty. Good." Jake ransacked his empty brain for more questions, stalling for time and information. "Where's my stuff?"

The two men traded confused looks. "You took it with you," the man he'd smacked in the mouth mumbled.

Oh. "Damn right I did." Jake frowned at one and then the other. "Bring me to the camp. Time to get things straight."

The two men nodded, and the Mexican mounted up again. "Lonergan's back!" he shouted to the men on the cliffs. "Meet us at the camp!" The bushwhackers disappeared, as quickly as they'd showed. The two outlaws in the canyon rode off toward its mouth without looking back.

"This is your gang?" Dolarhyde finally asked, as if he had to confirm what he'd seen with his own eyes.

"So it seems," Jake said.

Doc leaned forward in his saddle, with a look that made Jake think of a possum trying to pass for a coyote. Jake swallowed a laugh, keeping a straight face as Doc muttered, "Listen, these guys look a bit lonely to me. I think it's time to call it a *noche*."

Jake glanced at Ella, back at Doc as he realized Doc was more likely thinking about death than dishonor.

But it was *his* gang. "We need every gun we can get," he said. He spurred his horse and rode away, leaving the rest of them to follow him, whether they liked it or not.

BACK IN CAMP, the rest of Jake's gang were getting ready to ride out, moving in and out of tents, rummaging in piles of boxes for supplies. Horses were being saddled, weapons from their full stockpile chosen, checked, loaded. Men filled gun belts with cartridges, and canteens with water from the seepage-fed pool at the foot of the canyon wall. A few rounds of extra ammunition for shotguns and rifles went into their saddlebags, or bandoliers.

Pat Dolan slung a rifle at his back, and turned impatiently to check on the progress of the others. "The coach is on its way and we best be sober for it." He strode through the camp, making sure everybody was prepared, and nobody who was riding out with him smelled too much like alcohol.

He paused by the man they all called Red, even though the color of his grizzled hair and beard was halfway to a memory at this point. Red had been a miner once, before most of the mines in the area had gone bust; he sat now on a crate of dynamite, surrounded by more of the same, as he rummaged in a barrel of rocks that gleamed with streaks of gold. "How's the haul, Red?"

"Gold from the Vulture Mine looks pretty rich." Red held out a chunk for his inspection.

Dolan nodded, glad to hear it, even though "rich" wasn't what it used to be. They'd had a long ride just to reach two mines that weren't played out or abandoned. It was the dynamite they'd been after; but the gold ore hadn't hurt anybody's morale. "How much dynamite we get?"

" 'Bout fifty sticks." Red nodded at the crates.

Dolan figured that should be more than enough to drop a good-sized rockslide in front of the overland mail coach, and blow open an ironbound Wells Fargo treasure box, if they had to . . . enough for two or three jobs, in fact. With this much dynamite, they could waylay a train, if the boys were of a mind to travel as far as the railroad line.

Times were hard; it might be worth the hard traveling. There wasn't a bank in Absolution with a vault worth robbing, anymore. The only man in the area who still had enough money to put in a bank was

Woodrow Dolarhyde, the owner of the only real ranch for a hundred miles. And he'd put all his money on the bullion coach, the one they'd robbed about a month ago . . . right before Jake up and left, taking most of Dolarhyde's gold with him, that no-good bastard.

Dolan glanced up the hill toward the only point of entry into their well-hidden camp, searching again for the men who'd gone to check out some strangers passing through. He wondered what in hell was taking them so—

"Dolan!"

He looked up again as he heard a familiar voice call out his name, and started toward the crest of the hill, where Bronc and Hunt were just now riding through the gap in an outcrop of sandstone so weathered it looked like bad teeth.

"'Bout time you got back!" Dolan said angrily. He saw blood and a bruise on Hunt's face. "What the hell happened to you—?"

Hunt nodded over his shoulder. "He did."

The rest of the gang behind him parted ranks, letting Jake Lonergan ride through. Dolan stared. He'd never expected to see Lonergan again, if they both lived as long as Methuselah. And following behind Jake was the damnedest ragtag bunch of. . . . *What the hell was that—his entire bloody clan?*

Dolan put his hands on his hips, near his gun belt, as he took it all in. "Well, shit," he said, an opinion that could've been an observation.

* * *

THE ENTIRE CAMP had fallen quiet around Dolan, every man in it staring at Jake.

Jake's eyes ran the gauntlet of accusing stares, realizing that the reaction to his return wasn't exactly the welcome he'd expected. At least the people with him kept their mouths shut; even Dolarhyde was smart enough for that.

Jake knew he'd heard Dolan's name before today—which meant either yesterday or the day before. He looked hard at Dolan, a black-haired Irishman in a derby that had seen better days. Dolan didn't look any more familiar than any of the others. But beside Dolan was a bearded man who stood nearly seven feet tall.

Suddenly Jake heard Taggart's voice in his mind, reading off the charges from his wanted poster.... There'd been two other names: *Pat Dolan, and Bull McCade*. The poster said they'd robbed the bullion coach with Jake Lonergan just last month.

He still couldn't recall a damn thing about robbing a coach. But face to face with his own gang, the circumstantial evidence had finally got so deep he had to admit he was up to his neck in it, or drown: *He was Jake Lonergan* . . . and now he was going to have to live up to his reputation.

Dolan must've taken charge after he'd . . . disappeared; and Dolan looked like by now he enjoyed being the big bug. He was the one Jake would have to face down . . . or take down, if it came to that. He looked like a surly son of a bitch, but Jake figured that came with the territory.

The man standing beside Dolan had to be Bull

McCade: He was big as a bull, and from the way he stood, probably Dolan's muscle. McCade wore a top hat, with a vest made of miscellaneous animal pelts over his shirt, and leather pants. Jake was glad Bull was standing downwind.

So Pat Dolan needed an enforcer, to keep order. . . .

He dismounted, watching Dolan the whole time, as prepared for anything as he could be. "You don't look happy to see me, Dolan," he said, sticking with the obvious.

"You got some balls, ridin' back here like nothin' ever happened." Dolan's face turned from wary to ugly before he'd finished the sentence. "*No, Lonergan—*" Dolan said, his voice dripping venom, "I *ain't* happy to see you."

Jake stopped moving, holding Dolan's stare as he tried to figure out how to get past bad blood he didn't even remember. "You'll get over it," the Scourge of the Territories said.

Jake turned away as if Dolan had ceased to exist, and looked toward the rest of the men. *If he was their leader, then he better start acting like it.* "Boys," he said, "grab your guns. We're ridin' out."

The rest of his gang stood glancing at one another in confusion, the way the two named Bronc and Hunt had, back in the canyon—like they didn't know what had just happened, or what was going on.

"But Jake . . ." Bronc said finally, speaking for all of them. "You . . . you said you didn't *wanna* be in charge no more."

Jake barely kept his own eyes from going wide in surprise. He glanced at Ella. *Maybe Doc had been right*. . . . He hated even thinking about it. He felt like he'd just put a noose around all their necks, and now his gang was trying to spring the trap door under them.

"—changed my mind." He lifted his head, and raised his voice. "So saddle the hell up!"

"They're not goin' anywhere with you." Dolan had blood in his eyes now. "We're fixin' to rob us a coach and that is exactly what we're gonna do."

Jake turned back, as something about the word "coach" set off alarms from his brain down to his boots. They'd robbed a coach just last month—the one with Dolarhyde's gold on it. It was too soon to hit the stage line again, especially after waylaying the bullion coach: The gang was still hotter than a whorehouse on nickel night. Dolan was going to get them all killed, or taken. *You never let your patterns become predictable, if you wanted to stay alive.* . . .

He frowned. The boys ought to have plenty of gold left. He wondered why the hell they were all still here, and not in Mexico, spending it.

The tension in the air was so thick now that it would have been easier to chew than to breathe. The people Jake had brought with him had dismounted when he did, and now they were surrounded again. Their looks were as surprised, but a lot more uneasy, than the looks on the faces of his gang.

Dolan moved toward Ella, getting way too close before he stopped. He looked her over with a mix of curiosity and contempt. "Are you her?" he asked.

"Am I who?" Ella stood her ground; her face was preternaturally calm.

"The whore Jake quit this gang for."

Jake's fists tightened as another piece of the puzzle that had been his life snapped into place. His eyes met Ella's as she glanced toward him—both of them realizing that Dolan thought she was the woman in his picture . . . *Alice*.

Dolan turned back to Jake, checking his reaction.

"Watch your mouth," Jake said, his voice cold.

Dolan smirked. "Or what? *I* run this outfit now." Intent on proving it, he called out, "Put your guns on the whore! He so much as twitches, blow her brains out her ear!"

At once, thirty guns were leveled at Ella's head, leaving no question in anybody's mind who the men of Jake's gang were loyal to now. Hunt stepped up to Jake and took his pistol. "Sorry," he said, smiling.

Jake glanced at the others he'd brought here along with Ella . . . outnumbered five-to-one, and completely outgunned. *Damn it—*

Jake looked back at Dolan as if he hadn't just had his own gun pointed at him. "Call her a whore again," he said, "it'll be the last thing you ever say."

Dolan laughed once. "You ain't in no position to make threats, boy. You're unarmed." He glanced up, nodding to the man who was standing beside Jake now. "Put him down, Bull."

Jake followed his glance, with barely time to react as a fist the size of a ham came at his face. It hit him, hard.

He staggered and fell flat on his back. The ground was as hard as Bull's fist. He struggled to raise his head, his eyes barely focusing. But still, he managed to push himself up onto his elbows, and then get to a sitting position. Dolarhyde and Nat Colorado were both wincing—probably the only two people who really knew how he felt, at the moment.

But Dolarhyde showed a faint smile as he saw Jake glance his way. "Got his hands full, here," he said to the others.

Doc quit attempting to stare down the six-footer beside him, and gave Dolarhyde the most fed-up look Jake had ever seen. "Wanna step in?"

Dolarhyde shook his head, his smile widening with spiteful amusement. "He's doing okay by himself."

Dolan strode up to Jake like the cock of the walk. "Where the hell's our gold?"

Gold. . . . That gold? Jake recalled the look on Alice's face as gold coins spilled out of his saddlebags onto the table, in his memory from the cabin . . . but not before he saw Dolarhyde's start at the mention of gold.

Jake managed to get his feet under him, and stood up. He spat blood as he looked back at Dolan, and grinned. "Don't remember."

Dolan nodded to Bull. Even ready for it, Jake couldn't move fast enough to dodge a fraction of the second blow. Bull hit him in the gut, and knocked him sprawling.

Jake retched and spat this time, a lot, before he could even lift his head.

His entire existence was turning into a blur of pain. He dragged the top half of his body up to a sitting position again, not even sure why he bothered. But this time, he glanced toward the others he'd put in this fix; ignoring Dolarhyde, looking for what showed in the eyes of Ella and Doc, Charlie and Emmett.

He saw fear, and helplessness, and anger—but not anger directed at him. No hatred for what he was, no disgust at what he'd done to them . . . only an empathy that was hard for him even to look at, let alone comprehend.

They would have helped him, if they had any choice; fought for him if there was any way they could . . . not because he had a gun for demons, but because they were good people, and he was . . . he. . . . He got up on his own, stood on his own two feet again, the pain fading into background noise as Dolan came toward him . . . because this wasn't finished yet.

Dolan looked at him in a way that suggested he was looking at raw meat. "Well," Dolan said, "I *do* remember you tellin' us you was leavin' us high and dry because of some woman—"

And Bull hit him in the chest, so hard that he flew off his feet.

He hit the ground, sliding, with the wind knocked out of him. He struggled to inhale, couldn't; his chest felt like he'd been nailed to the ground with a railroad spike. His lungs wouldn't even work. . . .

He felt his consciousness slipping, his mind falling through reality . . . *into his place of refuge.* . . .

. . . the rain ran like tears down the windowpane . . .
Alice's arms closed around him, her voice murmuring
in his ear. . . .

"It'd be a better life . . . clear your conscience. You
don't even sleep a full night anymore—"

. . . feeling her warmth against his skin, her long-
ing for him . . . for them to start fresh . . . like the
spring-green world where sweet rain fell, softening
the pitiless land. . . .

. . . sweet rain . . . he closed his eyes . . .

You're dreaming. Wake up—

. . . he opened his eyes to a sunbaked plain, where
life lay dying of thirst abandoned, like hope. . . . Soul-
less predator, hopeless prey: adapt or die. . . . The way
it had always been; would always be. . . .

"It ain't that simple."

"It is." *Alice's body twined with his, until they*
formed a lover's knot against the rain-streaked win-
dowpane. "We can leave all this behind, make peace
with our bad deeds—"

. . . And holding her, he could almost believe—

No, it's all a dream. Wake up—!

It had always been too late, for him. . . .

"Bad's all I was ever good at." *He shook his head.*

"You're wrong," *she whispered.* "I know you're a
good man."

. . . and as she kissed him . . .

. . . Jake woke up, lying on his back in the dirt. He
opened his eyes, blinking at the empty, sunburned
sky. *Lost.* . . .

. . . a good man . . . Alice, his lover, the only one

who'd ever believed in him. And he'd left her.... to them ...

"Alice ..." he whispered. He raised his head, and saw Ella. She was staring back at him with a look of grief on her face that made him hurt. The look said she knew exactly what part of him had been left aching and dizzy by a dream, a place physical pain couldn't reach. As if somehow she even saw through into his dreams, as he'd relived every moment of—

Pat Dolan's booted foot broke his contact with Ella's eyes, as Dolan stood over him, looking down. "Guess you just left out the part about taking our goddamned gold from that coach."

Oh, God— Jake let his head fall back. He caught a glimpse of the look on Dolarhyde's face now, heard Dolarhyde mutter, "... *my* gold. ..."

We're all alike, Jake thought. *Bastards ... demons. ...*

"So I'm gonna ask you one last time—" Dolan said, making him look up, "where's my gold?"

Bull caught Jake by the arm and pulled him up to his knees. Jake glared at Dolan, his hand tightened into a fist.

Dolan punched him in the face. Bull grabbed Jake's hair as his head flew back, and yanked him upright again. Dolan hit him again. Face to face, Dolan repeated, "One last time ... *where's my gold?*"

Jake looked up at him with eyes that saw only blurs of motion; his mouth and throat were full of blood. He coughed rackingly and sucked in a breath that sounded like a death rattle. He remembered Meacham, dying. . . .

Everyone who'd made the mistake of getting close to him was going to die . . . or they already had. And it was always his fault. Like the desert, that was all he'd ever been good at: making things die. . . .

". . . demons . . ." he mumbled.

"What's that?" Dolan shook him, refusing to let him fade away now.

"Demons stole your gold . . ." Jake gasped, forcing his battered mouth to form the words clearly, ". . . when you get to Hell you can ask for it back. . . ."

Dolan *tsk*ed at him, like he was a stubborn child. Bull let go of him, and he collapsed in the dirt again.

"That's the way you wanna do it—" Dolan looked back over his shoulder, and said, "Kill the whore."

Jake heard the gang cock their rifles, taking aim at Ella as he fought his own body for control; tried to make himself get up, hit somebody, do *something*— But his body wasn't listening anymore.

Instead, the demon-killer on his wrist suddenly came alive.

He blinked his eyes halfway clear, saw blue light on his arm—a lot of it—as the weapon opened up, wrapping itself around his wrist and hand like it was trying to drag him out of a pit.

An indescribable sensation spread up his arm, burning like invisible fire. The shockwave hit his brain, jolting him alert. It went on spreading through his whole body . . . almost as if he was a part of the weapon, and not just wearing it.

He sat up without realizing he had, and saw Dolan clearly—saw the disbelief on Dolan's face, and his hand dropping toward his pistol. Jake raised his arm without thinking; as the target covered Dolan, the demon gun fired.

The beam of blue light hit Dolan before his hand reached his holster, and punched him backwards. Dolan's body flew fifteen feet through the air before it hit the ground, stone dead.

Not for the first time, Jake found everyone in his vicinity staring at him. He staggered to his feet and stayed there, feeling stronger with every heartbeat. The bleeding had stopped; he knew he was in pain, but somehow he couldn't feel it.

He looked toward Dolan's body, what was left of it. "Told you not to call her that," he said hoarsely.

And then he turned, looking from stunned face to stunned face in the circle of his former gang—the men who'd watched as Dolan and Bull nearly beat him to death, who in another second would've killed Ella, without a trace of regret. . . . He kept turning until he faced the speechless Bull McCade. He kicked Bull in the balls, doubling him over. *"Everybody drop your guns—"*

Hunt laid down his own gun and handed Jake's back to him without hesitation. One by one, the others surrendered their weapons.

Jake grabbed his hat, all the while keeping his other arm high. With the demon gun still glowing on his wrist, he backed toward the handful of people he'd almost killed . . . and might yet, if his luck didn't hold. "Mount up," he said.

"—What—?" Dolarhyde said.

"On your horses—go! *Those things are close!*" Jake almost shouted, wondering what about the demon gun's alarm they still didn't understand.

This time they all moved, while he held the gang at bay.

He swung up onto his own horse. Pulling its head around, he led the others through the gap-toothed barrier of stone into the desert, leaving his old gang behind one more time.

12

Jake and the others rode like hell away from the outlaw camp, out across the plain, with no goal in mind except finding refuge from demons. His wrist weapon was still alive and targeting . . . something. *What did it expect him to do now?*

Jake heard Dolarhyde shout a warning behind him. He looked back, and saw his gang coming after them—not demons. It didn't surprise him that the gang was on their tail: he might as well be made of gold . . . their gold. *He'd crossed his own gang. He'd deserved that beating, and worse.* But for the sake of the others, he still hoped the demons found his gang before the gang could reach him. He glanced down at his wrist; the weapon was still fully open, ready to fire. *That wasn't right.* He looked ahead again, and suddenly realized why.

Jesus Christ, they were riding in the wrong direction.

He could see it coming now: A billowing sand

cloud on the horizon, moving inhumanly fast, coming their way. In the harsh light of day he could actually make out the forms of the killing machines, gleaming in the sunlit sky.

It was his turn to shout a warning: He pointed ahead, then waved at the others to turn back, as he pulled his own horse up just short enough so he could heel it around without falling. The others did the same; he saw their stricken faces as they realized they had no real choice left, and picked the lesser of two evils.

As they spurred their horses back toward the gang, Jake wondered what the boys would make of this. His former friends raised their rifles and started shooting. That figured. He guessed they thought he'd gone crazy—he couldn't blame them for that. Or maybe they just wanted him dead. Either way, he kept his head down and hoped to God nobody got hit before the gang figured out what was really happening.

He heard bullets whine past as the two groups of riders closed. They were well within rifle range now. He told himself it took more luck than skill for most men to hit any moving target smaller than a train from the back of a running horse; he hoped it was true . . . hoped it was his turn to get lucky. *Look up, you stupid sons of bitches—!*

The shooting stopped as the gang finally saw what was really coming after them. He was close enough by then to see the looks on their faces when they pulled their own horses up short, trying to turn tail before it was too late.

But it was already too late. The bola ropes began to spiral down through the sandstorm, striking random targets and snatching them up into the sky. Before his gang knew what'd hit them, they were losing members fast, as men were jerked, screaming, from their horses' backs. The few outlaws who still had working brains started shooting at the flyers. Jake already knew that was useless.

Charlie Lyle, riding close by Emmett's side, suddenly disappeared as he was taken by a rope that would have caught the boy.

"They're comin' back!" Dolarhyde shouted, looking up at the sky as the flyers that had passed over their heads made impossible turns in the air. "They're comin' back!" He yelled at the rest to spread out; his group actually listened, scattering in all directions.

Jake rode away after Ella, not about to lose her now. If they were followed, maybe he could get a clear shot at the flyer. The demon gun was ready to kill demons, or it wouldn't have changed . . . but he seemed to be the only human being it cared about. He didn't know anymore who owned who, but it wouldn't matter to him, if the goddamn thing would only do its dirty job.

One of the flyers swerved away from the main group, as if the demon in it was intentionally out to get Ella. Or him. *The demons owned the gun . . . maybe they wanted it back. Maybe it didn't want to go. . . .* That was something he could relate to.

He looked back, raising the weapon to take aim as the flyer closed with them. *Come on,* he thought. *Do it—!*

The gun obeyed him for once, and he saw the streak of blue light hit something on the infernal machine, saw the explosion. But at the same time the flyer fired a bola rope. The bola streaked toward Ella; she cried out as it jerked her into the air. Jake froze in mid-aim as he tried to fire again, afraid the blue lightning would hit Ella.

He'd hit the flyer with his first shot—but this time, that hadn't been enough to bring it down. He couldn't risk another shot, but if the thing got away from him now, Ella was as good as dead anyway. . . .

As he watched the flyer arc and soar away, he realized that it hadn't pulled her up inside; she was pinned underneath its wing. The demons knew he had the weapon; they'd had proof he knew how to use it. Whether the flyer was using her for protection or just carrying her off, there was no way he could keep shooting at it.

But the flyer wasn't even out of range yet—at least he'd slowed it down. And he was damned if he was going to leave Ella to them, now, like he'd left Alice. . . .

He dug in his spurs, desperate not to lose sight of the flyer. It was circling back toward the ragged cliffs they'd just escaped from, not speeding up, and steadily losing altitude as it headed for the entrance of a side canyon. *Maybe the demon gun had done a better job than he'd thought.*

But he couldn't follow it into the canyon; all its weapons seemed to be in its belly. The ropes would just trap him again, or the thing would fry him with a lightning bolt, like the demons had done to people in Absolution.

If he could only get above it—

He spotted a way up the slope to the top of the mesa and headed for it, hoping his horse was as sure-footed as it was fast.

It was. As he reached the top he saw the flyer not that far ahead, and barely below the rim of the side canyon. He sent the horse after it at a dead run, gaining on it, but knowing even the best horse couldn't keep this up for long; and if it stumbled. . . . *Didn't matter.* Only Ella mattered, only that flyer. All or nothing.

He was gaining ground faster—the flyer was still losing speed. As he began to close with it, he saw it waver and sink deeper into the canyon. It wasn't leading him back where it came from—he was sure of that, although he didn't know how. Whether its demon brain had figured to ambush him or only lead him away, Jake thought maybe it had just made a big miscalculation.

But then he realized he couldn't use the weapon to take it down from here, either; he had no idea even of how the flyers stayed in the air. If it went down like the other one, then Ella. . . .

Shit, what if it crashed anyway?

He was riding almost side by side with it, as if it was a moving train, when it dropped even lower: He was going to lose it no matter what. Unless. . . .

He'd robbed trains; he must have, he'd done everything else. This was like catching a moving train: *You didn't think about it, you just did it. A leap of faith. You knew you wouldn't fail, because failure meant you died.* He wasn't dead yet.

He kicked one foot free of its stirrup, letting his reflexes take it from there as he slung his leg over the saddle and braced himself, hanging on. The flyer was big, just like a train. It was following the canyon wall like it was on rails, because the canyon was narrow here. It was several feet below him, and flying through the air. . . . *Okay, not exactly like a train.*

He freed his other foot, his heart in his mouth. He must be crazy. He didn't know what was real anymore. *But if this wasn't all a dream, he hated how his body was going to feel in the morning.*

He was pushing off, leaping out into open air, falling. . . . He landed halfway onto the flyer's segmented body, and slid off onto the wings; barely caught a handhold and hung on before he slipped further, or fell through the space between two wings. The already damaged flyer shuddered and dropped even more with his added weight.

The wing surface he was clinging to abruptly tilted downward. It was as slick as hot ice; he lost his grip. His legs and body slid until he was halfway off the wing, his feet dangling in the space between, before his hands found something more and he dug his fingers in for a better hold.

His boots struck a stone and burned through a patch of gravel. The tilted flyer was dragging him now, at the speed of a running horse. Even knowing this had been his own damnfool choice this time didn't change the fact that he couldn't hold on much longer, couldn't pull himself back onto the wing. He was nearing the end of his endurance, and this time it really would kill him.

His raised his head, searching frantically for some way out, something he could reach for . . . saw a row of metal bands, along the front edge of the wing. He'd barely caught hold of two of them as he fell. He could see the ground rushing past in the space ahead of him; the sight made him sick. He looked away, saw the underbelly of the flyer . . . *he could see Ella.* His mouth opened, but he couldn't force any sound out.

But Ella had already seen him. She was conscious, she was alive . . . she was looking right at him, her eyes as wide as if he was the last person in the world she'd expected to try to save her. He saw her eyes change, filling with wonder. And then there was something else in them—as if he was the only man she'd ever needed to see . . . the only man she'd ever really wanted.

Ella . . . Alice. . . . *Never again.* Gritting his teeth, tightening his whole body, he pulled himself forward, reached up to grab a band nearer to the ship's body. He caught it, and reached up with his other hand. His feet were no longer dragging; everything got easier. He hooked one foot up onto the wing behind him, and managed to straighten his leg, got his other foot partway back onto the wing. He straightened out his body, reaching for the metal bands closest to the flyer's core.

The flyer's wings abruptly straightened to horizontal

again, and the flyer veered to avoid a collision with the canyon's wall.

Jake lost his hold. He slid down across the wings, barely managing to catch himself before he fell off the back edge. The wings began to tilt again as he hung on near the ends, halfway to death all over again. *What the hell?* Was the demon trying to shake him off?

No. Suddenly he understood: *It was like a see-saw.* He'd changed its position, just using his own weight.

From the place he'd fallen to, he could see the fear on Ella's face . . . he could see her bonds clearly, see where they were attached to the flyer's wing and body. *He had to reach the front wing; then maybe he could get her free.*

With fresh determination, he hauled himself back onto the wing, before his own weight had him eating dirt. He began to shift his body inward toward the flyer's core one more time, moving carefully, aiming toward a real goal now.

The wings and the core of the flyer were anything but plain pieces of metal, he realized. The whole thing looked like it was made from scrap metal, but whoever—whatever—had made it had cut the pieces like a gem cutter. And the flyer must have been forged in the fires of Hell itself, to make the welds so perfect. . . . He had no idea what it all meant, except that it reminded him of his demon gun—which was a hell of a lot more than it seemed on the surface.

He studied the point where the wing was attached to the flyer's body. *Like a hinge. . . .* That was something he knew, at least. And he could see now that the wing surface had plenty of handholds and footholds, as long as he didn't panic.

There were even gaps where he could see through to the underside . . . *all the way to the ground.* . . .

He looked up again, focusing on the bonds that held Ella: Not just the bola rope, now, but a long metal belt wrapped around her from her shoulders to her knees. One end was attached to the underside of the front wing, and the other to the underside of the second.

Damnation—how was he going to get her out of that? All he had that could take on a machine from Hell was the demon gun—and even if it obeyed him, he'd just end up killing them both. *But if he died, then the damned parasite on his wrist died with him . . . and it knew that.*

Maybe this wasn't impossible. Up ahead he saw the end of the canyon. He didn't know what lay beyond it, yet; all he could do was hope it would make for a better landing than the bedrock of the canyon floor.

He pulled himself forward, moving carefully, until he was halfway onto the front wing. There was a long gap in it, just wide enough for him to get an arm through . . . wide enough to see Ella's face looking up at him.

He looked into her eyes, willing her to see what lay behind his own: *Trust me.*

She nodded, and Jake aimed the demon gun.

They reached the canyon's end. Beyond it lay the true heart of the desert: a dune field, where wind-blown sand had piled up against the wall of the mesa.

The flyer was dropping still lower . . . much too low for his liking, along a wash that must have been cut through the dunes by flash flooding from the rain. There was no water down there now, though; nothing but. . . .

Looking ahead, he suddenly saw the impossible: At the far edge of the dunes, reflecting sky like a turquoise gem was a phantom lake: a pocket of runoff water, trapped behind a rock outcrop, not yet absorbed after yesterday's unwelcome downpour.

For the first time in his life Jake thanked God for something totally unexpected, and the inspiration that came with it.

He pushed himself back, edging around until he could get the weapon into position next to the place where the back of the metal belt holding Ella was attached to the second wing. The belt was attached to the ship by what looked like wire, maybe some kind of winch.

There was more than one way to use a weapon. . . .

He braced himself against the vibration of the ship, and concentrating on what he needed to do, he felt more than saw the demon gun open and fire. The juncture snapped, the belt uncoiled. He heard Ella's cry of surprise as the metal belt came loose and slithered off her. All that was left holding her under the wings was the bola cord, latched in two places. One more shot and she'd be free . . . or fall to her death.

He moved forward again until he could see her face. "Can you swim?" he shouted.

She looked up like he'd yelled total nonsense at her, but she nodded.

Jake braced his feet against the edge of a wing behind him and reached out for the hinge-joint at the top of the wing by Ella's head. He jammed his arm as far as it would go into the space between the wing and the body of the flyer, caught a solid protrusion with his hand, and pulled with all his strength, letting his weight shift outward toward the end of the wings.

The flyer veered toward the lake, its altitude dropping more.

"What are you doing?" Ella shouted, with more disbelief than fear in her voice, as the flyer screamed downward, the lake surface rising to meet them like the face of a mirror.

"Hold on!" Jake shouted back. He looked up again, trying to gauge the flyer's height above the water. When he guessed they were maybe twenty feet above the water's surface, he pushed his arm and the weapon through the opening on the forward wing, until he could line up the weapon and the latch that held the bola cord.

"Turn your head away!" he yelled. Taking aim, he focused his deadly control and every shred of his will on hitting a single, very small target. The demon gun fired again, severing the cord . . .

They fell free, plunging into the lake as the flyer hit the water's surface just beyond them and sank like a stone, sending up a fountain of spray.

Jake and Ella broke the water's surface, spitting and coughing, dazed and battered, but alive.

They swam, and then waded, to the shore and stumbled up the bank, holding onto each other for support. Jake was sure he had never felt this glad before just to still be breathing. He looked at Ella, found her looking back at him. He smiled, and so did she.

Her smile was the most beautiful thing he'd ever seen . . . and it was genuine. He'd never seen her show her real smile to anyone before, especially him—as if it was something she'd held back for too long, keeping it locked away inside her, until she finally found a reason to use it.

She'd saved it for him.

He thought of the way Alice had smiled, in the picture, in his memories from the cabin. But Alice was gone . . . *because of something he'd done.*

He looked down; looked up again. Ella was here, right in front of him, safe and alive and smiling like that at him. . . . *because of something he'd done.*

Suddenly he even believed what he'd seen in her eyes, only last night, in the abandoned riverboat: That together, they could do the impossible. He looked out across the lake, where the flyer and its demon had gone down for the last time. The surface was as smooth as glass again.

He covered his aching right elbow with his left hand, touching the spot where he'd flayed most of the skin off it as he bent the hinge on the flyer's wing. Now that they were safe on the ground, he could let himself feel the rest of it . . . feel giddy with vertigo, as he remembered the most impossible thing of all: "We . . . were . . . flying. . . ." His stomach lurched.

"Yeah," Ella murmured, so matter-of-factly that she might've done it before.

"I don't ever wanna do that again," he said, with utter conviction looking up at the sky.

He looked down at her again. As she looked back at him, she was still wearing the smile that made her glow. Her wet clothes clung to her body in a way he couldn't ignore. No matter if she carried a gun and lived for revenge, or talked like the nerviest man he'd ever met, she was a hell of a woman, and a beautiful one.

Her face was so close to his now, her lips close enough for a kiss. Her eyes filled with strange depths, with emotions he couldn't read . . . but he recognized the longing on her face; he could feel her whole body asking him to go ahead. . . .

He leaned in, more than willing, longing to take her up on it—

The shrill sound of his weapon's alarm jerked him up short. He turned to the lake as something broke its surface—something huge.

The demon rose from the water, towering over them, blocking the sun, more unbelievable and far more terrifying than his blurred impression from last night on the boat.

If the Devil had taken all the things humans feared or hated most, and squeezed them like a ball of clay into something that walked upright—a mockery of a human form—this was what would have come of it: roaches and maggots, snakes from the desert, sharks from the sea, covered in the thick, armored hide of a gator smeared with swamp slime.

Jesus, it was all—

The thing lunged forward with a speed his eyes couldn't believe, even as his mind flashed back to Meacham's death—

—nightmare—

The demon's limb shot toward him like a spear, its fingers ending in talons that could tear a man open like—

His demon gun opened and fired, point-blank. The beam of blue light blasted the demon back into the water; pieces of armored limb and body, entrails, blood as green as Jake's own was red, roiled the lake surface, transforming the serenity of blue into a pool of ghastly wreckage.

Jake stood staring at the water. His heartbeat felt like it was trying to crack his ribs, as the weapon on his wrist calmly retracted into silence.

And then he heard the sound behind him, a different sound entirely, too human, all too familiar—the liquid gasping of someone who'd just taken a fatal wound.

He spun around and saw Ella, lying in the sand with a gash on her forehead . . . and her chest covered in blood where the alien had run her through.

"—No—" Jake fell to his knees beside her. *This couldn't be happening to them, not now.* He put his arms around her, cradling her, carefully raising her head to help her breathe.

She looked up at him, her expression bewildered and filled with pain, as if some part of her mind could no more grasp what had just happened to her than his own could believe it.

He rocked her gently in his arms, smoothed a strand of dark hair back from her forehead . . . silently cursing the fickle God who had let Meacham die . . . the same God he had just thanked, for the first time in his life. *The only god who'd staked a claim on this wasteland was the one Apaches called Coyote, the Trickster. . . .*

"Ella," he said, his voice ragged with a kind of pain he'd never felt before. "*Ella*— C'mon, *talk to me*—"

Her eyelids fluttered as she struggled to focus on him. ". . . Don't worry . . ." she whispered. ". . . I'm gonna be okay."

Jake's memory showed him Meacham's wound, the same kind of wound. . . . He pushed the thought out of his mind, furious at himself. He caught the hem of her skirt, ripped a wide strip from it and bound up the wound. "We're gonna find Doc—"

"I'll be . . . all right—" Ella murmured, moving her head from side to side, "—just go—" *But she didn't understand. . . .*

Jake picked her up in his arms and staggered to his feet. Without the demon gun feeding him energy, or even his own adrenaline numbing his pain, giving him strength, he was still able to stand.

All he had left was the relentless perversity of his own will to survive. It had never saved anybody before but him; because he'd never cared about anybody but himself, until now. . . .

He was just like the demon gun on his wrist: *That bloodsucking piece of crap; no wonder it had gone with him.* His own life didn't mean anything, anymore . . . but it was all he had left that could save Ella.

He turned where he stood, his eyes searching the blinding surface of the dunes for any sign of the dry wash left by the floodwater, a path that would lead him back to the canyon they had come out of. Finally he made out the distant ridge, shimmering in the heat, that had to mark where they'd entered the dunes.

How far off was it? How fast had the demon's flyer been moving? No man could last long in this heat; and the floor of Hell must be paved with hot sand—it was hell to walk through.

Didn't matter. He couldn't afford to think about anything but Ella . . . saving Ella was all that mattered. He carried her along the shore until he found a low spot between the dunes where a few stunted shrubs and grasses struggled to survive, that at least looked like a path carved by water, not wind. He started walking.

Jake walked for a long time; although time had no real meaning here in the endless mirage of his existence. The ridge in the distance was getting closer—it had to be, he told himself, although it was impossible to tell how much closer, or even if it was true, through the shimmering scarves of heat that rose off the dunes.

He looked down at Ella, lying still in his arms, her face chalk white in spite of the burning sun. "*Hey,*" he said, giving her a gentle shake. "Stay with me."

Her eyes opened, closed lazily again . . . but before they did he saw something glimmer in them, the reflection of a memory, the uncanny gift that seemed to see into him as if his eyes were window glass. "You remember now . . ." she murmured, ". . . don't you. . . ."

Jake looked down again, startled. ". . . what?"

"The woman."

Jake raised his eyes, staring off into the distance as

his mind showed him all the puzzle pieces he had gathered: *Alice's picture, the cabin, his gang, the gold . . . Alice, holding him in her arms as she said,* "You're a good man. . . ." But they were only a part of a greater puzzle, and still he could barely guess what it looked like.

"Did you love her?" Ella whispered.

He kept his eyes on the horizon, as the void inside him refused to let him know even that much.

"You can tell me. . . ."

But he couldn't . . . he didn't know what was true. . . . He'd betrayed his gang over gold, and told himself he did it for love of her: Had that been nothing but a lie? He could still see the look on her face, when he showed her the gold. And in the end—had he really abandoned her to demons. . . ?

He looked down at Ella again, the emptiness inside him aching. "I guess I must've . . ." he said at last. *He knew she'd loved him. He knew he'd needed her . . . but was that the same thing?* He looked away into the distance again. "It's just . . . hard to see. . . ." He shook his head as sweat stung his eyes. "All I know is . . . I owe it to her to find her." *One way or the other, he owed her that—*

He stumbled as his boot caught in a tangle of ankle-high scrub; he kicked free of it and kept walking. There was actually some plant life—grass and shrubs—growing around him now, in red dirt, not just sand. *Almost there; almost to the canyon mouth—*

He sensed more than saw Ella open her eyes again . . . seeing everything, he was sure: Seeing him fading . . . how his beaten body kept trying to drag him down; how heat and thirst and exhaustion were trying to make his mind stray into even stranger dreams. Maybe she could even see the truth that would make her despise him. . . .

". . . It's not far . . ." he insisted, his voice scraping like sand in his throat, ". . . you hang in there . . . hang . . . in. . . . We're gonna be fine. . . ."

DOLARHYDE, NAT, DOC and Emmett—the last four members from the group of seven who had set out this morning—rode on along the stony floor of a canyon, between cliffs the color of bleached bones.

They kept their horses at a walk, preserving their animals' strength, although by this time Doc had no idea why they bothered. They had survived the pursuing outlaws and the demon raid, but they rode silently, as if they were heading to a funeral, every one of them far too aware of how much they had all lost.

Charlie Lyle, Ella, Jake . . . and Jake's weapon, their only real hope for defeating the demons on their own infernal terms—were all gone, which meant they had also lost any chance of rescuing their loved ones, and all the others who had been taken.

Dolarhyde had claimed he'd seen Ella taken by a flyer, and seen Jake follow it toward this canyon. But they'd been riding for hours, watching the shadow of the canyon's wall elongate as the sun dropped westward.

The shade hadn't brought them much relief, because the stone walls and canyon floor still radiated the heat of noon. The canyon seemed never-ending, and they still hadn't seen a trace of the demons' flyer, or any sign of Jake and Ella. He wondered how long they were going to keep pretending they might actually find them.

Doc raised his head, finally, from staring at his horse's dusty mane, the stony ground, for too long— trying to see Maria's face inside his mind . . . trying not to, because every time he did it only reminded him that he'd never see her again.

He glanced over at Nat Colorado, riding beside him. Nat's eyes were habitually scanning the ridgeline above them, and the sky; but Doc wasn't sure he was really seeing anything anymore, either.

"This plan wasn't very well thought out, was it?" Doc said, at last.

Nat lowered his eyes, but he looked straight ahead, to where Dolarhyde rode alone, trailed by Emmett. He didn't say anything.

"We lost?" Doc asked, because they seemed to be heading nowhere, without any reason or destination, now.

"We'll be all right," Nat said, with a slight twitch of his shoulders.

"How can you be so calm in all this?" Doc demanded. "I nearly messed my britches."

Nat glanced over at him finally, but without the expression Doc had been expecting. "You were good back there," he said. "Held your own with the gang. Rode hard just now." A faint smile formed on his lips, but his eyes were completely serious. "We survived a battle together. Look at you, you're a warrior now. Your wife won't even recognize you when you see her."

Doc's surprise fell back, dragged down by his memory. "If I see her. . . ."

Nat looked him directly in the eyes for the first time, as he said, "In Apache, there is no word for goodbye."

Doc let the words register, letting them seep into the cracked mirror of his faith, giving him back a glimpse of hope. He nodded to Nat, oddly comforted.

UP AHEAD, DOLARHYDE slowed his horse's pace just slightly, so that he dropped back alongside Emmett. His glance took in the boy's reddened eyes and runny nose. The boy had been crying for some time; he'd heard the sound of it, even though Emmett had been trying his best to hide the fact.

"What're you all bunched up about?" Dolarhyde asked.

Surprised and embarrassed, Emmett wiped his nose on his sleeve. ". . . I miss my grandpa," he said in a small voice.

And Charlie, and Meacham, and the dog, he might as well have added. Everyone, everything, that'd been a comfort to him. Dolarhyde remembered the last thing he'd said to the boy, about that damn dog, as they left the riverboat early this morning.

He regretted it now, just a little, as he studied the boy's face. For a moment his eyes looked through and beyond him, as if he was searching for some elusive solution to a question of battlefield strategy,

"I wasn't much older than you, back when this territory was Mexico," he said, at last. "Word come, Apaches were headed for a settlement outside Arivaca. My father wanted me to be a man, so he made me ride out with the garrison, banging on a drum." In those days the border hadn't mattered, when it came to fighting Apaches; the Mexicans hated them as much as the U.S. Army did.

His expression turned wry at the memory of himself, nothing but a wet-behind-the-ears kid. "Boy, was I scared—" He let his grin widen, so that Emmett saw it.

Emmett looked over at him in surprise, and then Dolarhyde saw a kind of relief settle over the boy, his face easing, his shoulders losing their tightness. Dolarhyde couldn't remember ever admitting to anyone, even his own son—especially his own son—that he'd once been a terrified child.

He didn't let himself wonder about it, only let his memory go on unwinding to its end. "So when we got to Arivaca—found the whole place burned to the ground. Then I saw a settler crawling from a cabin that caught fire . . . he was burnt bad—knew he was dyin'. All he could manage were two words—" Dolarhyde glanced down, into the eyes of the past. " 'Kill me.' "

Emmett stared at him. ". . . what'd you do?" he asked faintly.

Dolarhyde reached over and pulled the knife he'd

given Emmett from the boy's belt. "I took this very knife . . . and I slit his throat." He flipped the knife, caught it by the point, and held it out for Emmett to take back.

Emmett took the knife from him. For a long moment the boy stared at the knife, and then up at him, jarred by the history of the perfectly honed blade he'd been carrying like it was newly bought, untainted by any act of bloody violence, or even bloody mercy. . . . He put it back into its sheath, with the respect its history deserved.

Still acting on some deep impulse, no longer letting himself question anything he did, Dolarhyde put out his hand and let it rest reassuringly on the boy's shoulder. He said softly, "Now be a man."

Emmett looked up at his face, and Dolarhyde saw what he'd needed to see in the boy's eyes: Not that the fear had vanished from them, but that a sense of his own strength, the confidence to make his own choices in life, shone through it, until the fear no longer had the power to control him.

"Boss, look!" Nat's voice broke the spell that had held him, and Dolarhyde looked ahead again, squinting as a form began to emerge from the brightness. His eyes widened as he made out what Nat had seen: Shimmering like a mirage, Jake Lonergan was walking toward them, carrying Ella . . . stumbling out of the land's fever dream, back into their own reality.

13

Jake stumbled again on the stones of the canyon floor, somehow managing to stay on his feet, his lips cracked and bloody, his mouth too parched for words. He had to force himself to take in every painful breath of burning air, had to listen to a moan every time he let it out again . . . concentrating on the next breath, the next step. He couldn't let his heart, his lungs, his feet betray him, couldn't afford to fall, had to keep moving, for Ella's sake. *As long as he wasn't dead, he could keep moving. . . .*

But suddenly his barely functioning senses stopped him in his tracks, as his ears seemed to catch the sound of a human voice in the wind. *No . . . couldn't be. . . .*

His eyes were almost swollen shut, but he forced them open just enough to see search the way ahead. Wavering in the fluid, distorted distance, he thought he could make out four riders on horseback. . . . *Had to be a mirage . . . couldn't be . . .*

But the four were moving, riding toward him out of the zone of superheated air, until he could see them clearly—Dolarhyde, Doc, Nat and Emmett.

He bit his lip, filling his mouth with blood, and swallowed it. "H-he-here . . . we—we made it—" he told Ella. His legs collapsed as he let himself fall to his knees, still holding Ella protectively above the stony ground.

They'd done it. The others gathered around him; he could see amazement and urgent concern on their faces.

"Give her to me," Doc said, reaching out. He let Doc take Ella from his arms; his arms dropped strengthless to his sides. He sat back on the rocky ground, not registering the pain or heat, only relief.

Dolarhyde glanced up at the cliffs one more time, then kneeled beside him, offering his canteen.

"Her f-first—" Jake mumbled, trying to push it away. But Doc was already seeing to Ella, and Dolarhyde caught him by the jaw, raising his head to force a trickle of water into his mouth. Jake swallowed convulsively, and felt more water pour onto his tongue. He swallowed willingly this time; his hand groped for the canteen. Dolarhyde pushed his hand away, realizing what Jake couldn't, now; that too much water was as bad as none for a man in his state. Dolarhyde continued to feed him more, a sip at a time.

"Ella—?" Jake finally managed to ask, his arm shaking as he tried to reach out.

* * *

JAKE'S EYES WERE too sunblind to register the look that Doc gave to Dolarhyde then, filled with unspeakable grief and loss: the look that said, *Ella was gone.*

Dolarhyde turned away from Jake, as he took the full impact of the look, and ghosts stirred the dust of emotions that he hadn't known existed before that terrible day at Antietam . . . that he'd only known one other time, when his wife had died. He had buried them all, along with his wife, and sworn he would never let himself feel that kind of pain again.

But these two: Jake Lonergan—that defiant, treacherous son of a bitch, the first man Dolarhyde had actually hated in a long, long time; and Ella, a woman who could make his flesh creep just with her stare . . . seeing them like this. . . . *Why did seeing the two of them like this bring it all back—?*

Jake had taken down a demon flyer for the second time; he had to have done it again, or he wouldn't be here. But had he done it just to save Ella—?

Dolarhyde looked back at Jake, at the dazed anguish on Jake's face pleading with someone to give him an answer, the one he needed to hear, that would give him the strength to go on living. Not the Scourge of the Territories anymore. . . .

Right now Jake Lonergan was only a man in need, like too many Col. Woodrow Dolarhyde of the United States Army had seen for too many years: a wounded soldier who'd spent the last of his strength to pull a comrade from the battlefield, only to learn his friend had already died. . . . A soldier in a war that

Dolarhyde hadn't even acknowledged they'd been fighting, together, until now.

He put out his hands to support Jake, trying to get him to stand, to get him up off the burning ground, onto his own two feet again. They'd been in this canyon far too long; he'd let all of this go on for far too long. If the Apaches had. . . .

"—how is she?" Jake whispered, his swollen eyes searching, trying to find her face among the others around him, all of them gazing back at him with expressions he couldn't understand.

"She's gone," Dolarhyde said quietly.

Jake's body went rigid in his grip. "*She's not gone.*" Jake shook his head. "Lemme see her—"

Dolarhyde looked hard into Jake's eyes, forcing him to see, hear, accept reality. "*Jake . . .*" he said, insistent this time, "she's gone."

"Boss—" Nat said suddenly, urgently.

Dolarhyde looked up again at the cliffs, and saw his worst fear since they'd headed into this canyon, now realized: The Apaches who'd been scouting them this morning were back . . . and this time they'd brought friends. Apache warriors lined both sides of the canyon, rifles and drawn bows aimed downward.

The Apaches must have been trailing them, at a distance, all day. Even if they hadn't seen everything, they'd seen enough to know that the small group of people from town weren't bait for a trap, just easy targets.

Jake slumped back to the ground as Dolarhyde let him go and raised his hands along with the rest.

* * *

THE SUN HAD finally gone down on what had been the longest day of their lives for most of the survivors, by the time they reached the Apache camp. Doc knew they wouldn't have lived that long if Nat hadn't still been fluent enough in his native tongue to keep the warriors from killing them on the spot in the canyon.

Their unexpected arrival as prisoners of the war band turned the camp of about fifty or so Apache men, women, and children into what seemed to him like a subdued bedlam of barking dogs and murmured surprise.

Doc had no idea what the people around him were saying, but from the tone of their voices, they weren't happy to have visitors—at least not his kind. He kneeled on the ground beside Dolarhyde and Nat as they all had been forced to do, in the center of the camp by a large bonfire, where everybody could get a good look at them.

Jake had been dropped in the dirt beside him, barely conscious and mumbling in delirium. Doc clenched his bound hands—wanting to be allowed to treat him, knowing the shock of Ella's death had been the final blow to a man who had nearly sacrificed his own life to save hers. He told himself they were all as good as dead, anyway; maybe Jake was the lucky one.

Emmett had been dragged away from them when they first arrived, kicking and cursing. Doc could still see him, held back by the women and older boys, still struggling to break free, but with more desperation than defiance on his face now.

Nat had murmured to him that the tribe would adopt the boy. Doc had hoped as much. He knew that adoption of captive children was a long tradition with the Apaches. Growing up, he had heard a lot about Apaches, but unlike most people he'd actually listened to all of it, and not just to the horror stories.

The Apaches had adapted to life in this Land of Plenty of Nothing a long time ago, accepting what it gave them, and paying the price it demanded, unquestioningly. Adoption must be even more vital to them now, since their numbers had been decimated in wars with both the Mexican and U.S. armies, as well as endless hostile encounters with miners and settlers.

The United States and Mexico had fought each other often enough over this same territory, even while they both fought the Apaches. It struck him that his people and Maria's had had no more business claiming it than the Apaches would have had to try and claim the United States.

But that was the damn trouble with people . . . enough was never enough. He had told Meacham he couldn't enter a church in good faith anymore, because "Manifest Destiny" sounded too much like God telling the Hebrews to move into the land of the Canaanites, just because He said it was theirs now. Ever since the beginning of time, humans had used the name of God as a justification for their sins so easily, so often—as nothing more than an excuse to commit ungodly acts against each other. History seemed to him to repeat itself over and over, ever since Old Testament days. . . .

Meacham had understood, the way he'd understood so many things Doc had never expected a preacher would even have a clue about. . . . Maria might not have known exactly how he felt, but she understood *him*, and that was enough. If God didn't understand by now, it was too damn late. Demons would inherit the earth.

He missed Meacham . . . he missed Maria, more than he was going to miss his own life. He wondered why the Apaches didn't have a word for "goodbye." Maybe because they never got enough chances to say it to each other. . . .

Doc sighed, tired of kneeling, bending his head before God or a bunch of Apaches. He looked up to see the warriors who had collected their weapons handing them to Black Knife, the leader Nat had called a *nantan*—a chief.

In this case, Nat said Black Knife was also a kind of *sachem*, a word Doc had heard back east—one of the most highly regarded chiefs, even among other *nantan*s, of the scattered bands of "wild" Apaches still surviving off a reservation.

Black Knife was probably in his mid-forties, Doc figured. His eyes were keen and intelligent, and he carried himself with the confidence of a natural leader. Nothing else made him stand out in the gathering of warriors, except that his shirt was dyed red. All of the Apache men wore odd combinations of worn-looking traditional clothing and garments taken—one way or another—from their enemies.

Black Knife's unsmiling face gave away nothing at all as he studied the group of prisoners. He sat on a log, his rifle across his knees, and nodded at one of his warriors, who began to shout angrily in their direction. Doc wondered if the *nantan* was too high in rank even to speak directly to captive enemies.

Nat began to argue back, speaking for them all in Apache, since they couldn't speak for themselves anyway. Only Dolarhyde didn't seem to care whether anybody there understood him or not.

Doc knew Dolarhyde hated Apaches even more than he seemed to hate everyone in Absolution; but he didn't know the reason. He'd heard that Dolarhyde had fought them in the army, back before the Civil War. Maybe that had been enough. It suddenly struck Doc as peculiar that the only man Dolarhyde seemed to trust completely was Nat Colorado.

As the warrior finished with what Doc guessed were accusations, Nat began to translate them, while the warrior consulted with the chief. "He says this is all that's left of these bands, Western Apache, Chiricahua, and Mescalero—"

Doc was surprised. Those were different tribes, and even though they shared a common ancestry, it just proved how desperate they were that they'd willingly live together with strangers, even of their own kind. The people in this camp had banded together here for support, for survival. Not that there looked to be that many of them, even so . . .

. . . which only meant that they were under way too much stress: angrier . . . meaner.

"*Sonsabitches*—" Dolarhyde muttered looking toward the place where Emmett was being held.

"—they all came here, they lost people too—" Nat went on, ignoring his boss now, as Dolarhyde ignored everyone else.

"—who gives a *shit*—don't even listen to 'em, there's no reason, we're all *dead*—" Dolarhyde's eyes were locked on Black Knife, filled with the hatred that overflowed into his voice.

"—he says the *pindah-lickoyee*—the 'white-eyes enemy'—brought bad medicine to his people the last fifty years—diseases, plagues—" Nat didn't mention "extermination by the Army," but maybe he was being tactful. "And now we brought the Wind Walkers—that we burned their people."

In symbolic retaliation, a group of warriors brought forward Ella's body, and threw it into the fire at the center of camp.

"Noooo—!" Emmett screamed, as her body began to burn.

"—what—?" Doc said, in disbelief. "He thinks we did that? They're takin' our own people too! *Just tell 'em!*"

"Forget it," Dolarhyde snarled. "Ain't no reasoning with 'em."

Nat only stood staring, powerless, as Ella's body was thrown into the fire, and even Black Knife made no protest.

Doc remembered that the Apaches felt fear and

revulsion about handling the bodies of the dead—afraid of "ghost sickness," of being haunted by an undeparted soul. Even when they had to bury their own family members—especially then—sometimes they needed the help of a medicine man to recover from it; and they'd probably been doing too much of that, for a long time.

For them to do this with Ella's body meant anger and vengeance had driven them beyond their own beliefs, the way the demon attack had affected some people from Absolution.

Nat began to repeat Doc's words, translating his plea for understanding without so much at a glance at Dolarhyde.

But it was a losing debate. They were all suddenly grabbed and yanked upward by their hair, even Jake. Doc saw his eyelids flicker open, as the rough handling jarred him back to half-consciousness . . . to enough awareness that he suddenly realized Ella's body was lying in the fire, burning. "Stop—" Jake gasped, reaching out, but no one else was listening.

Black Knife stared at them, and Doc could see he was passing judgment on their fates.

"Kill us now," Dolarhyde shouted, his eyes blazing with hatred. "Get it done with!"

Doc wondered suddenly if Dolarhyde was trying to get them all killed . . . quickly. He realized what kind of things Dolarhyde must have seen firsthand all those years in the army—the thousand different ways the Apaches had of killing somebody slowly. How many soldiers and settlers had Dolarhyde seen who'd been made examples of . . . and what would that do to a man's mind?

Had he ever realized that most of the atrocities had been committed in retribution for lost loved ones—or that the torture only got worse as his troops, and settlers, killed more Apaches. . . ?

It struck Doc suddenly that maybe Dolarhyde, out of everyone here, was the most frightened of all.

A warrior hit Dolarhyde on the back of the head with his war club—not hard enough to kill him, but enough to stop his furious disrespect. Frowning, Black Knife nodded, and Nat's shoulders sagged, as he muttered, "Death."

Oh Jesus, Doc thought, *oh God, this was it*— A knife was pressed against his throat, as blades went against all their throats. He should be glad it was going to be a quick death, he knew that—but right now he just didn't feel very grateful. *Why couldn't they understand? If they could all band together. . . . Maria. . . .*

He heard Emmett crying mindlessly, *"Nonono—!"*, saw him fighting with all his strength to break free from the hands that held him back.

Doc felt the knife's edge bite into his skin, took his last glimpse at the others, before—

The funeral pyre in the center of the meeting space suddenly erupted in a blaze of light like exploding fireworks. The flames leaped upward with an enormous roar, turning from orange to green to white—

The pressure against Doc's throat disappeared as

the Apaches, even the warriors, backed away, staring at the flames.

And Ella emerged from the pyre, shrouded in a caul of fire and light. She walked toward the captives, toward Jake, and as the fire fell away from her she still radiated light, a blinding, angelic glow. . . .

An angel—? Doc thought.

No, it was really Ella . . . *but Ella wasn't human.* Doc's mind reeled, as the Apaches all around them began to kneel down, dropping their weapons, recognizing the spirit world for what it was, something that permeated all of reality—not separate, as his own people had always taught him to believe.

With every step away from the fire her glow faded, her skin returning to its flesh tone, her hair falling straight and dark down her back. When she finally stopped, standing directly before Jake, she appeared to be the Ella they'd all known, again. But alive.

As an entire village of strangers, and the handful of people who knew Ella—who thought they'd known her—went on staring at her in awe, Jake got to his knees on his own, raising his head; finally fully aware, and feeling saner than he ever remembered feeling, here in the middle of the impossible . . . as if the return of Ella's life had gifted him with the return of his own will to live. He didn't question it—beyond questioning anything, long since—but the empty place inside him, the place where a human heart should have been, felt suddenly, unexpectedly full.

Ella stood unmoving, with an expression on her

face that he'd never seen before, and couldn't understand. Jake struggled to his feet, never letting his eyes leave hers. He picked up a blanket from the ground and moved toward her, wrapped it gently around her, before he stepped back again.

"I'm sorry, "she said softly, as she looked at his expression; her eyes filled with gratitude and apology. "I couldn't tell you."

Jake swallowed, clearing his throat. "Are you one of them?" he asked hoarsely, his ragged voice barely more than a whisper. It was the only thought that would form in his mind: the one he least wanted to hear the answer to.

"No." Ella shook her head. "I'm from a different place—" She broke off, as she tried to find a way to explain it to him. "I took this form . . . so I could walk among you."

"You should have told me," Jake said, almost accusingly. *You made me believe. . . . You let me think you were dead.*

She glanced down. "I didn't know if I could heal this body. If I would wake up."

He stared at her, totally lost again, as words that made no sense at all to him echoed inside his brain.

Black Knife himself spoke then, gesturing toward a wikiup behind him.

"He invites you to sit in council—with him and the most respected of his people," Nat translated, his face and the words filled with a sense that they'd all just been profoundly honored. His voice was remarkably calm, for a man who'd had a knife at his own throat just minutes before—and then witnessed a miracle.

* * *

INSIDE THE WIKIUP, behind a makeshift screen of hides, Ella dressed in a borrowed man's shirt and pants, rolling up sleeves and cuffs, pulling on Emmett's extra pair of boots, all of which Jake had been allowed to fetch from the pile of their belongings.

The other men from the group had been permitted to join her and Jake in the meeting. They sat now around a small fire at the wikiup's center, along with Black Knife and a handful of men from the Apache camp. The townsfolk still looked as dazed as he'd been—except maybe Nat, who looked like it all made perfect sense to him.

And Ella, naturally, Jake thought, as she stepped out from behind the screen fully dressed, and with inhuman calm took the place that waited for her in the circle. *Inhuman.* Jake's mind repeated the word, but his eyes refused to believe it.

Black Knife and his warriors looked toward Ella with reverence and awe, a look they withheld when they glanced at the men who had come here with her.

When Ella had settled herself, Black Knife began to speak.

"He wants to know where are you from?" Nat translated.

Ella looked toward Black Knife, her face respectful, but with something in her eyes that Jake had grown too familiar with. She answered him in fluent Apache, gesturing at the stars above. Even in another language, Jake could hear the sadness in her voice as she spoke.

". . . the hell's she saying?" Dolarhyde muttered to Nat.

"That she comes from a place above the stars, another world," he answered, as if even that seemed perfectly reasonable.

Jake remembered her saying to him, *"They took my people too."* Her people . . . *Had she meant a whole world's people*—?

Everyone around the circle was silent for a moment, taking it in, in whatever terms they could accept.

"Another world? *What?*" Dolarhyde said, mockery filling the words. Jake frowned in irritation.

"—And that if we work together, we can get our people back."

"'Work' with them?" Dolarhyde repeated, his voice getting louder and more angry.

Black Knife glared at Dolarhyde, at the interruption. He spoke again, eyes on Dolarhyde, with anger filling his voice.

Nat looked toward his boss, his expression finally proving to Jake that he had nerve-endings after all. "The people here believe Ella was sent by White-Painted Woman. . . ."

"'White'—?" Dolarhyde began.

"White-*Painted* Woman," Nat repeated. "No one knows what she looks like—she went back beyond the sky with Yusn the Life-giver, long ago. But she was the mother of *all* people, Apache and white. They called Ella "*Sonseeahray*"—it means "Morning Star." They think she was sent here as a messenger, because what's happening now is different from anything that's ever happened to their people before. It's like . . . like the Virgin Mary or something, sending an angel. . . ."

Nat's face tightened with frustration, as Dolarhyde's eyes remained obstinately blank. Nat took a deep breath. "You—you shouldn't talk—"

"—Why the hell shouldn't I talk?" Dolarhyde demanded. "I got questions too—"

"—it's an insult," Nat said, his voice straining as he tried to make Dolarhyde understand. "A guest of the chief's must be invited to speak—"

"—oh, am I a *guest* now?" Dolarhyde snapped. "Or am I a *prisoner*? What the hell *am* I?"

Black Knife pointed at Dolarhyde, and the untranslated shouting match between them rose to a fever pitch.

"Hey! Enough!" Doc said, suddenly and loudly. "You're both big men, all right? Great warriors! Can we just listen to the woman tell her story? Or—whatever she is." His voice subsided as he glanced at Ella, his face reddening slightly. Black Knife, and even Dolarhyde, fell silent, looking away.

"What do they want?" Jake asked Ella, beginning to understand at last that the demons he'd been fighting weren't demons from Hell, any more than Ella was an angel. They were from someplace else entirely . . . other planets—like this one, only not—a concept so alien it made Hell seem familiar: *The demons were alien beings . . . like Ella, but not like her. Not like anything he could even relate to . . .*

"They want gold," she said. "It's as rare to them as it is to you."

Dolarhyde made a sound like choked-off laughter.

"Well, that's just—*ridiculous*," he said, not even making an effort to hide his scorn. "What're they gonna do, *buy* something?"

It occurred to Jake that buying something was probably just what he'd had in mind when he'd robbed the stage carrying Dolarhyde's gold. Why had the Mexicans come here in the first place; why had people from the States? Mostly they'd come to strike it rich. *On gold*. He glanced at the demon weapon, still closed around his wrist like a manacle.

He figured the only reason the newcomers had been able to kill off the people they found living here already was to call them "savages" not "people." He wondered what the aliens called humans. Wondering that didn't do anything to lift his spirits.

"Is Maria alive?" Doc asked Ella. "The others?"

Everyone there shared the same look, as Nat translated the question for Black Knife and the Apaches.

Ella looked down. "If they are, they won't be for long."

This time all their expressions froze, as a terrible chill seemed to fill the space around them. Even Dolarhyde had nothing to say to that.

"They're learning your weaknesses." Ella went on at last. "It's what they did to my people. First one ship came, then more. We fought back . . . but they were stronger. Only a few of us survived." The pain that always lay just below her surface rose into her eyes at the memory, before the urgency of the present drove it back. "I came here to stop them from doing it again. But we have to move quickly . . . before they leave and bring back others."

Black Knife then spoke to Ella; she glanced at Jake and the rest. "He says his men will follow me."

"Wait a minute, slow down—" Dolarhyde said, looking at Black Knife again. "What the hell you mean, you're gonna 'follow her'? Where you gonna go? What're you gonna do?"

Ella nodded toward Jake. "He's the only one who knows where they are." She turned to meet Jake's eyes. "You've been there."

Jake shook his head, as faces around the circle turned toward him. He struggled with the void where his memories had been, remembering why it existed . . . why he wasn't even sure he wanted to remember the truth, anymore.

"I couldn't even remember my *name*." He pointed at his head. "If it's in here? I can't get it out." But his frustration only grew as he realized just how much the aliens had really taken from him . . . even his chance to find them and pay them back.

Black Knife and his men murmured among themselves, before Black Knife looked at Jake, and spoke directly to him.

"They say they have medicine that will heal your memories," Nat translated. "There is a *di-yin* . . . a medicine man . . . here who is skilled in making it."

Jake glanced at him, suddenly feeling uneasy as he looked back at Black Knife. He wondered for a moment if they were really serious. Their faces said they were.

Apache medicine . . . that didn't exactly mean the same kind of thing Doc did. *He'd heard stories* . . . though he had no idea where, or when. All he could see right now was that it was the only choice left to him; and that he'd come so far beyond anything he'd thought he knew that turning back wasn't an option anymore.

Shoot, Jake, or give up the gun . . . He looked toward Ella again, and nodded.

14

Black Knife was a good host, once they were—at least for now—"guests" instead of prisoners. They were given food to eat, and enough water to wash it down with, as they waited for the *di-yin* to prepare whatever it was they expected Jake to swallow. Only Dolarhyde grumbled about what they were fed, but he ate it anyway.

Jake would have been happy to eat and drink Dolarhyde's share too, and anybody else's, by then. He forced himself to eat slowly, savoring every bite: Hunger made anything taste better. He was glad they'd fed him at all—the only stories he recalled about native medicine seemed to involve a lot of puking, therapeutic or otherwise. *If they'd let him eat, maybe this one wouldn't be so bad.*

By the time they'd finished, Jake felt some of his strength coming back to him, along with his sense of purpose: his vow to find Alice, if she was still alive—and to take his revenge, whether she was or not.

At last a handful of warriors led them across the camp to a wikiup set a little apart from the others. One of the Apache men led him and Ella toward the wikiup's entrance, while the rest held up their hands, keeping the others away, forcing them to wait outside. They traded concerned looks as Jake hesitated at the entrance and glanced back, before he entered what he finally understood was a kind of sacred space.

Inside, a small group of men and women sat in a circle. They included Black Knife and a solemn, graying man that Ella whispered was the *di-yin* who had prepared the medicine for Jake.

The Apaches sitting in the circle were chanting; it made Jake think of people singing in a church, though he didn't know why. Ella joined the circle, and signaled for him to sit beside her. He sat down cross-legged, feeling muscles in his legs pull painfully . . . feeling as odd as he would have felt sitting in a church on Sunday.

It had never occurred to him that Apaches had a real religion, or took it seriously. But then, he wasn't given to thinking about Apaches any more than he had to, or religion either.

He did think about Preacher Meacham; he wished Meacham could've been here, as he faced this. But Meacham's last request before he'd died had been, *"Get our people back."* Even God couldn't deny Jake was doing his best to honor that.

The *di-yin* picked up a small pot filled with some kind of liquid, and passed it to Black Knife, who passed it to the man sitting next to him, all of them still chanting.

The pot finally reached Jake's hands. He accepted it, staring at the bits of plant matter floating on the surface of the opaque brown liquid. He raised it closer to his face, sniffing. The smell was as unfamiliar as the look of it; instinctively he made a face, then glanced at Ella.

Her eyes were alive with hope and need—the need for him to do this, for all their sakes, and more. ". . . please," she murmured.

He glanced past her at the others; all around him he saw the same expression come over their faces . . . all of their hopes pinned on him.

Jake looked down again and shook his head—not in refusal, only astounded at his own foolhardiness. He took a deep breath, held it, and drank down the liquid in gulps until the pot was empty.

He felt an odd warmth in his throat and gut that was comfortingly like the burn of whiskey, even though the taste it left in his mouth was more like chewing tobacco combined with horse dung. *Could have been worse.*

Some of the Apaches sitting in the circle got to their feet and left the limited space within the wikiup, as Jake remained sitting next to Ella, wondering what came next. His body already felt like an old man's; otherwise, he was a little dizzy, that was all—maybe just his nerves.

Blankets covered the ground. Jake tried to relax, but his body reminded him with every breath that it'd had more abuse than any human being deserved already today. After a time, though, a strange calm began to settle over him, and gradually all his tension flowed away.

The light from the small fire pit at the center of the hut seemed brighter and brighter, breaking up into rainbows; he stared at it, hypnotized. All his senses seemed to be opening up: He heard the coyotes call-and-response somewhere out in the hills, as they sang love songs to the moon . . . smelled the mesquite wood smoke of the fire mixed with sage and damp creosote bush, as well as night-blooming plants he couldn't name, all carried to him on the cooling breeze. He could feel the ground solidly beneath him, through the woven texture of a wool blanket. . . .

Ella watched him intently, watching over him, like the handful of Apaches who had remained in the wikiup.

Jake felt his eyelids growing heavy with dream-sleep, vague images shifting like sand every time his eyes closed; he struggled to keep them open.

Ella put her arms around him, supporting him carefully as he lay back, too drowsy to sit any longer. his head was resting on her knees; she looked down at him, her face lit by firelight, by an ethereal light that seemed to be all the colors in existence at once. He smiled at her, feeling perfectly safe and content, as he saw not only reassurance but belief in her eyes.

A soft whirring filled his ears; he forced himself to open his eyes one last time, and saw the jewel-bright colors of a hummingbird as it darted above his face, glimmering in the firelight like a rainbow made solid.

He wondered vaguely what a hummingbird was doing here of all places, and after dark. . . .

It hovered over him in a zigzagging dance, as if it was inviting him to follow—somewhere, somehow, if he only could—before it disappeared again from his sight. He heard the Apaches around him murmuring to each other.

". . . a good sign . . ." Ella whispered. "They say it has come to be your spirit guide. . . ."

His eyesight blurred, unable to see where the bird had gone, or even make out Ella's face, as everything shifted out of focus. . . .

His blurring vision abruptly sharpened again . . . *and he saw Alice.*

Alice? How . . . where—? He saw her moving away from him through desert dunes, the wind whipping at her flowered dress, stirring up veils of sand around her. The billowing clouds of sand grew wilder, until he almost lost sight of her as she turned back one last time, and he saw her eyes gazing at him: at the only man she had ever loved, or ever would. . . .

". . . it's not your fault. . . ." she said.

"What—?" Jake called out the word, but he had no voice; no sound would come out of his mouth.

Ella stroked Jake's hair, soothing and reassuring him as he moved restlessly, his closed eyes following something, lost in a dreamworld. . . .

The sound of the wailing sand overwhelmed Jake's hearing as the swirling clouds obliterated his sight. He stumbled on through the dunes, searching for Alice.

". . . hello!" he shouted, suddenly able to hear himself speak; but there was no response.

Jake's eyes opened again, but he was seeing into another world now. Ella heard Jake whisper out loud, "... hello ..." and knew that the medicine dream had taken him completely. Placing her hands on his temples, she closed her eyes, her mind making contact, connecting, following his own as he moved deeper into the dream.

The sandstorm had blinded all Jake's senses; he couldn't see anything at all anymore, couldn't hear anything but Alice's voice, still echoing, "... it's not your fault. ..."

He turned where he stood, trying to follow the echoes to their source ... and all at once Alice was there again, moving toward him this time ... her beautiful eyes, her smile ... he put his arms around her, and they kissed ...

And as her lips found his, the world seemed to spin and tumble, sweeping them with it to another place entirely—one he knew. The long grass in front of the cabin ... whispering in the breeze as they lay back together on a sunny spring day, kissing, touching, making love ... losing themselves in the scent and feel of sun-warmed skin as they explored each others' bodies, lost inside each other's pleasure and joy. ...

Until at last, their shared passion spent, Alice drifted off to sleep, still held close in his arms. As he held her, watching over her blissful sleep, there was nothing more he could imagine wanting, or needing ... except for time to stop, so that they could stay like this forever: loved, cherished, safe and at peace, here in their hidden world.

... *He closed his own eyes, drifting away into deeper dreams ... deeper memories ...*

... *He rode down the hill, through the long grass toward the cabin ... saw Alice lying among the wildflowers outside their home, as if she had fallen asleep in the shade of a cottonwood tree on a warm afternoon. Only asleep ...*

But as he dismounted and approached her quietly, to wake her without startling her, he saw how her body lay ... saw something wrong about it. ...

He reached her side and saw that her eyes were wide open, unblinking ... her mouth open, in a soundless scream. ... No ... The skies overhead darkened with storm clouds, as he stood staring down in disbelief, and a flash of lightning shocked his eyes—

... *And suddenly he was standing inside the cabin, inside a memory he had already reclaimed, dropping the heavy saddlebags onto the table with a clatter of gold coins. ...*

But this time, the memory didn't stop as Alice's face fell, her eyes darkening—filling with anger, as she saw the waterfall of gleaming gold. She broke away as he tried to hold her in his arms, and said accusingly, "Where'd you get that?"

"Where do you think?" *Jake smirked, too full of his own twisted pride to see the warning signs of the storm—*

"Take it back," *Alice said flatly, folding her arms to shut him out.*

"Like hell—" *Jake started to frown.*

"—that's blood money—" *Alice's anger cut through his words.*

"—it's gonna buy us what we need," he insisted, his own voice rising, "I goddamned earned it—"

"—by robbin' and killin'!" Alice said furiously. "This ain't a clean break. Don't you understand—?"

But he had never understood, because he had never known anything else . . . there had never been anything in his life to compare it to, until now. And now, just when he'd begun to believe—

A deep rumbling filled the air, made the cabin floor tremble under their feet. More gold coins spilled from Jake's saddlebags, sliding, rolling off the table, transforming. . . .

And this time he knew why. But he was helpless to stop it . . .

In the wikiup, Jake broke out in a sweat and his body began to twitch, trying desperately to move. "—No—" His hand reached up like a drowning man's, but this time he was unable to break from the surface of his dream.

Ella's face contorted with grief as she shared his growing terror, his realization of what was about to happen, and that there was no escape—

An explosion shook the cabin, as part of its roof ripped away, and the stone chimney collapsed into a heap of rubble. Above them, a blindingly blue unnatural light blotted out the sky. . . .

And suddenly Alice was screaming, as she was pulled from Jake's arms up into the air. He lunged after her, but another bola closed its hand around him, jerking him off his feet. He saw the floor fall away, and then the cabin itself, as he was pulled up . . . up . . . disappearing into the depths of his darkest nightmare—

As it all changed, forever. . . .

. . . He was only dimly aware, this time, that the dream had changed, that he had gone somewhere else . . . somewhere dark and dank . . . a cave . . . where he stared up at the staccato flashing of a brilliant white light. Its hypnotic flickering held his conscious mind in stasis, the way the frigid, soulless embrace of the bola cord held his body . . . preventing thought, preventing movement. . . .

There were other people around him; their wide, empty eyes as opaque as white glass, reflecting the light that held them mesmerized. Their faces were as expressionless as the faces of the dead . . . the dead. . . .

. . . But Alice wasn't dead . . . he knew she wasn't. She was here somewhere, gazing up. . . . If he could only look at her instead, only see her, tell her he—

He wasn't dead. . . . He needed to remember . . . something . . . do something . . . it was important— But not now . . . not while the light held him with its rapture, like a moth drawn to a flame. . . .

. . . Until like a dream, more darkness followed the light . . . until he opened his eyes, suddenly, in shock, as he heard a woman's voice screaming in anguish, in agony—as if she'd been thrown into a fire. . . . He tried to turn his head to see what. . . .

As he moved, a flare of pain burned out all his senses—

His body went limp and stopped struggling, just as his senses came back in a rush.

But the sound of a woman screaming stopped, just as abruptly, and he lay in the daze of someone *who'd been painfully awakened but was somehow still dreaming. . . .*

He was flat on his back on a strange bed now—something between an operating table and a rack—and yet nothing more than a pair of metal bars was holding down his shoulders. But something was touching his head—the thing that had struck him blind with pain when he tried to move; that had left him even more physically helpless than before. . . .

. . . He lay motionless, afraid to move even a finger; paralyzed by his own fear. The hot breath of a wind that smelled of sulfur touched his exposed face, his hands and feet, but the table under him felt cold, as cold as the unnatural blue light that filled the inside of the vast—cavern?—a space so large he couldn't see its walls because . . . buildings? flumes? crates? telegraph wires? . . . forms that made no sense at all to him blocked his vision, most of them glowing with light that looked more like phosphorescence than lamps or flames.

The thing he lay on had glowing lights too . . . golden ones. Up close they looked like the rumpled surfaces of animal brains covered by glass . . . but as he tried at last to move his hand to touch one, pain drove through his head again like a bayonet.

His cry strangled in his throat as his hand fell back. . . . Weak with relief, his body surrendered completely to the bonds that held his mind. He could only open his eyes, only see as far as he could make them move, to one side or the other.

But maybe just that was enough. . . . At the limits

of his sight he could make out impossible forms—not human—moving as randomly as shadows, disappearing into strange, shifting clouds, emerging again, silhouetted by random cones of blue light. In the distance he thought he saw steaming pools, and streams glowing orange-red with the heat of whatever flowed in their beds ... lines of golden tears rising into ... inside of. ...

His mind finally surrendered, then: The only thing he'd ever seen that looked remotely like this was a painting of Hell. ...

There was a small table beside the one he was trapped on. Lying on it were more things he didn't recognize ... and things he thought maybe he did. Sick terror filled him, as he realized what things like that were meant for, what they could do to a helpless human body.

He looked away from it with effort, moving his eyes as far to the other side as he could. He realized then that there was another table like the one he lay on, beside his. And Alice. ... Alice? That was Alice, on the other table, gazing at the ceiling, not at him. ...

"... Alice ..." he gasped. His mouth and throat were as dry as if he hadn't had water for days. A band of red—a ribbon of blooming roses—circled the waistline of her flowered dress, as she lay the way he remembered her lying in the grass, outside their home ... not moving—not—

She couldn't move any more than he could; that was all. ... Her eyes were open—

"... Alice—!"

She didn't move, didn't glance toward him or even try to answer . . . She didn't even blink, only went on staring at nothing, her eyes wide and dark like a fear-stricken doe's. . . .

Jake called her name again, some part of his mind refusing to accept this final proof of their shared damnation. . . .

His eyes couldn't make sense of the monstrous shape that suddenly loomed over her. And yet somehow he knew what it was . . . a demon. That was a demon.

As it released the restraints from Alice's body, her face turned toward him at last . . . but when he saw her eyes, he realized she hadn't moved of her own free will. She stared through him at nothing, still without blinking, without moving, . . . without breathing.

That red band ringing her dress—he knew what it was now. It was blood. Alice was dead—

She was dead . . . lost to him forever . . . she'd been murdered, lying right there beside him, by monsters that could only have crawled out of Hell itself, to drag them into the Pit. . . . .

In the wikiup, Jake cried out, his voice raw with grief and rage, his body straining against the invisible bonds of nightmare. The tears that filled Ella's eyes spilled over and ran down her face, as the unfolding memory went on and on, as pitiless as the demons who held him captive inside his dream— too much like the demons buried deep in her own soul.

But she was unable to do anything to help him, even to comfort him. . . . It was all she could do to weep for him, with him, inside her own prison of memories. Because this was a path he had to walk alone, for all their sakes. . . .

Jake watched the golden brains under glass that ringed Alice's death bed begin to pulse and glow; her body shimmered like a mirage, glowing . . . disintegrating as he watched, into a pile of ash. The hot breath of the wind swept it away, like dust erasing her existence. . . . Alice. . . .

A long shadow fell across his tear-blurred eyes; he looked up, expecting what he would see as the demon who had just stolen Alice from life, and from him, body and soul, started toward the place where he lay. A kind of fear and revulsion he'd never known before filled him, smothering even his grief, as the reptile-skinned mockery of a face pushed toward him from the insectoid carapace that covered its skull. It stood over him, gazing down with red inhuman eyes, as if he was a fly trapped in its web, and it was considering which of his wings to tear off first.

And then its armored chest parted like a cabinet opening, revealing the extra set of manipulating arms hidden within the folds. The semi-translucent, sucker-tipped fingers of its hands began to pick through the selection of operating tools . . . things meant to torture and kill, never meant to heal. . . .

It brought up a long, slightly curved rod of silver metal. He saw a blue light appear at the tip of the rod, as if the demon held a lit candle, bring it toward his side. Trying to follow its track, he saw that his shirt had been pushed up; saw the marks that traced a pattern on his side and stomach.

Patterns were for cutting things out. . . . He clenched his jaw, his whole body trying to hold himself motionless, but was unable to keep from trembling as he was to stop anything else that was happening to him now.

The light-knife touched his side, burning through his flesh as it began its predesigned course toward cutting out his guts, one piece at a time. Jake cried out in pure agony, as his body convulsed uncontrollably, and one pain doubled another until he was blind and mindless, struggling to wrench himself free, his body fighting for its life.

Something gave way, releasing his left arm. He flung out his hand toward the instrument tray, frantically groping for something, anything, he could use as a weapon. He caught up a smooth metal rod like the one the demon held, pulled it to him and saw the tip catch fire with blue light.

The demon grabbed for his hand, too late. Jake was fast, and the cutter beam was like lightning; a streak of blue slashed the monster's face, burning a red furrow across it. The demon screeched and staggered out of his line of sight. Jake fell back onto the table, his arm coming down on a surface at its far side.

His hand landed on a piece of metal; he dropped the cutter as the hard, squared-off curves suddenly squirmed to life and clamped shut like a trap around his wrist. Panic-stricken, he tried to pull free; the metal band came with him, not trying to hold him down.

Jake wrenched himself loose from the table's restraints; half slid, half fell, off it onto the floor.

He stumbled to the table beside his, blinking his eyes clear; he ran his hand over the bed where Alice had been lying, as if somehow she might still be there, only invisible.... Nothing. Not even a trace of ash....

Alice was gone, as completely as if she had never existed. He could only believe that at least she'd been set free from this living Hell....

He turned away, forcing himself to move as a demon screeched and he glimpsed monstrous forms coming toward him through the fog. All he had left that he could save was his own life. *He had to run—get far away from here, and from what he'd seen— run until he reached a place where nothing could ever touch him again, not even memories....*

An explosion of blue lightning struck the wall ahead of him as he started for the nearest hollow in the wall that looked like a real opening, illuminating a maze of tunnels. He picked the only one that looked wrong—not shored up by timber or anything else he knew, but reinforced by struts like the ribs of a snake. They glowed in the blue light reflecting from behind him. He followed the metal-ribbed gullet on and on, because there was nothing left for him now but to keep running....

... Until at last he saw a different kind of light growing brighter up ahead: a light he knew, genuine daylight, not the cold deathly blue of an underworld filled with demons....

And then all at once he was outside, blinking in

the harsh brilliance of the desert sun. He staggered along the rough course of the arroyo that marked the entrance to the underworld, no longer feeling the pain in his side, the cuts and bruises as the ground punished his bare feet, as he tripped and fell down and got up again . . . no longer aware of anything at all but the need to get farther away. . . .

He made it to the end of the arroyo and out onto the flat plain beyond it, before he finally had to stop and catch his breath, so that he could run some more.

He looked back the way he had come, too far away now to see the hidden entrance he had come out of. Instead he saw the strange rock formation that loomed above it, rising out of the surrounding mesa . . . making an indelible fingerprint on the desert sky—

JAKE WOKE OUT of a nightmare . . . not sitting boot-less on the dusty track that led to Absolution, but in the fire-lit shelter of an Apache wikiup. . . . Waking this time with the final memories of the final days of his lost life intact, at last.

He hadn't left Alice to die . . . she'd already died, before he had escaped. He hadn't been such a craven bastard that he wouldn't even try to save her. He was certain now that he would have died trying; that he had never known how much he loved her, until those final moments, before he'd realized. . . . But . . . but—

". . . I brought the gold . . . in the house . . " At last he understood the whole truth, and its consequences.

". . . that's why she's dead." *It had been his fault, as surely as if he'd shot her.*

He became aware of Ella holding him, supporting him, her face wet with tears as she shared the kind of strength that only one survivor could give to another. "It's not your fault," she whispered, her arms closing around him more tightly.

He looked at her, and realized she was seeing the same thing in his own eyes now that he had seen once in hers, when he'd confronted her on that hill. . . .

He remembered that he'd left her there, with the look still in her eyes; turned his back and ridden off, abandoning her to her grief. That his only words to her then had been, *"Stay away from me."*

Yet she was still here with him, holding him, trying to bring him comfort.

"It's not your fault." Alice's ghost, speaking to him from a dream. . . .

He looked away, as far from comforted as he could ever imagine feeling.

And then he remembered something else. He looked back at Ella again, through her into the distance, as his eyes suddenly turned cold enough to make Hell itself freeze over.

"I know where they are. . . ." he said.

15

Jake slept through the night, so deeply that he
didn't even dream. But he woke at the first light of
dawn, like the stirring Apaches. No one else did, not
even Ella. Emmett had been given back to them finally, at Ella's request, and all of them were sleeping
like the dead. . . . Jake grimaced, and shook the image out of his head.

The need to follow the path he'd seen laid out in
his vision was too powerful to let him rest any longer; quietly he ducked out of the wikiup's entrance,
without waking the others.

He walked across the camp, forcing his stiff, sore
body to get moving, even though every step he took
felt worse than he'd been expecting. Children playing
fell silent and women stared at him; dogs growled
as they caught his scent. He tried not to look left or
right, until he reached the spot where some of the
Apache men were eating outside in the cool air of early
morning.

He stopped as they looked up into his sky-colored eyes, curious but wary, while he looked down at their bowls filled with whatever passed for breakfast here, unable to ask if he could share it. Finally one of them called out, in another direction, and one of the women brought him a food-filled dish. Jake nodded, and went away to eat alone.

Thanks to Ella, they all knew now that he could lead them to the place where the aliens were; they'd feed him and tolerate him until he did. But their looks made it plain that when his usefulness to them was done, he wouldn't be any more welcome here than he was anywhere else.

As Jake sat down in front of the wikiup and started to eat, Doc emerged from inside. Jake glanced up in surprise; he'd figured the first one up after him would be Ella, or maybe Dolarhyde. But then the hangover from his vision-dream, lingering in his brain like morning mist, gave him his answer to why Doc couldn't sleep: *Maria.*

Jake held out the bowl of food; Doc shook his head, with a faint smile of thanks. Rumpled and disheveled, with his sleeves pushed up and a stubble of beard, Doc looked more like one of Jake's old gang than like a doctor this morning. He'd even strapped on Meacham's gun belt.

Doc looked back at him with an equally critical eye. "Better let me give you a checkup before you ride out today, Jake," Doc said. "You look like a pile of used hay."

Jake stared at him, wondering what the hell kind of diagnosis that was. Doc just looked away, watching the sun rise. Jake sat beside him and went on eating, for once glad to have the company.

BEFORE THE SUN had gotten much higher, Jake led Dolarhyde and the remaining demon hunters, along with Black Knife, to the place he remembered from his dream. None of them had much to say as they rode.

Dolarhyde watched Jake's mind at work as he guided them by memory, instinct, and dead reckoning—matching the distant mountains to the ragged erosion lines of the mesa's rim as they backtracked along the valley.

Dolarhyde had to admit that Jake Lonergan was as sharp as a coyote, and a whole lot harder to kill . . . more like a cougar. Jake was also a far more complicated man than Dolarhyde would ever have given him credit for, before their mutual goal had forced them together. Dolarhyde had even begun to respect him, after what he'd seen yesterday when they'd found Jake carrying Ella back . . . although it galled him to admit that, even to himself.

But then, Dolarhyde figured a man like Lonergan would've been dead ten times over by now, if he wasn't all those things, and more . . . especially with a thousand-dollar bounty on his head.

At last Jake halted them near the place he had seen in his medicine dream—not taking them to the entrance itself, but to the top of a rocky rise nearby, where they could study the aliens' hideout without being seen.

They had actually been closer than they'd imagined to finding the stronghold of the demons from another world, before Jake's untimely reunion with his gang had made them lose the wounded one. The demon they'd followed all this way had still been trying to lose them before it reached its final destination, leading them off the track as the flyer had done to Jake.

But with Nat's skill they might've been standing here yesterday. Now they had the Apaches on their side—although Dolarhyde still wasn't convinced about how much that was worth. And it still meant almost another day lost, and another one of their group, Charlie Lyle, with it. He wondered how many more people, how many of their kin, had died in that underground torture chamber. . . .

He stared across the valley at the bizarre thing they'd taken for an odd rock formation, from a distance, until Jake had seen it up close in his dream. Now, with the indelibly changed view of their place in the universe that Ella had given them, Dolarhyde could see that the strange protrusion wasn't an eroded volcanic core, wasn't made of stone at all.

It was nothing like any natural object he'd seen: a mottled cylinder of the alien's strange metal, more like the weapon that Jake wore. . . . More like a tombstone, sunk into the earth: a burial marker for everybody on the planet Earth. He saw Jake look out over the rocks at the ship and then down into the canyon below it, his face haunted.

Ella crouched beside him, gazing at the tower, her expression showing the kind of unnerving focus Dolarhyde had seen on it the first time he'd met her.

At least now he halfway understood what had always seemed so damned strange about her. . . .

She'd come to Earth from someplace unbelievably far away, like a demon-hunting saint on loan from God. She was here for one reason, to stop the advance of the Devil's army that had destroyed her home . . . her whole world; hellbent on keeping the invaders from destroying another one. This was the culmination of her mission here, and her eyes shone with the knowledge that she hadn't come too late.

Dolarhyde took out his spyglass and peered through it, studying the alien monolith in clear detail. Even he couldn't scoff at the truth, anymore. "Jesus, Mary, an' Joseph . . ." he muttered, "how'd they . . . build something like that?"

"They came here in it," she pointed at the fortress-ship. "That's only the top . . . the rest is underground."

Dolarhyde looked back at her, incredulous.

"It's how they mine for gold." She looked him in the eye. He glanced down, remembering the bitter scorn of his comments last night, even after he'd seen her walk out of the fire, reborn. . . . He wondered how he could have been so blind, so short a time ago. He looked up again. "Can they see out of that thing?"

"It's hard for them to see in the daylight," Ella said. "They stay below ground, where it's dark."

She had barely finished the words when an alien flyer soared overhead, so low that they all instinctively crouched down.

Dolarhyde saw Jake look at his wrist. Jake's expression said he thought his demon gun should've warned him, or was afraid it would betray them somehow . . . as if he didn't trust his own weapon not to be as treacherous as the aliens who'd made it. Small wonder, Dolarhyde thought, after all he'd seen and been through in the aliens' stronghold.

But the flyer was already gone, before anyone had time to say anything. They watched in silence as it stopped dead in midair, hovering above the aliens' fortress-ship. Then it dropped vertically onto the top of the fortress, and disappeared as if it had been swallowed whole. Dolarhyde wondered whether it was returning with more captive humans.

"We'll never even get close," Doc said, shaking his head. "Those flying machines'll just pick us off before we get anywhere near it."

"There's another way underground—" Jake raised his head, peering down again into the valley below the mesa. "The same way I got out."

Dolarhyde's face turned grimmer, not because of Jake's words, but from memories of his own. "That's an impenetrable fort. We gotta draw those things out and fight 'em in the open, distract 'em so you can get inside with that arm gun and get our people out." But as he turned the words over in his mind, his frown only deepened.

"We have one advantage," Ella said, as she saw his uncertainty growing. Her voice hardened, "They underestimate you—you're like insects to them. They're not planning on defending themselves, so they'll be vulnerable."

Dolarhyde thought about the people who had come this far with him—only five of them left, loyal and alive . . . and one of those an untried boy. They were all the army he had, plus a handful of Apaches—and he trusted the Apaches about as much as he'd trust a handful of scorpions. He looked back at the alien tower, finally admitting the truth, even to himself. "We don't have the manpower or the ordinance."

Jake was staring intently at the tower; he looked down again at the open floor of the valley, the scarce amount of decent cover. "This is not gonna work," he said, more to himself than in agreement.

Black Knife spoke directly to Dolarhyde then, for the first time, and Nat translated: "He wants to use your spyglass."

Dolarhyde threw Black Knife a skeptical look, wondering how an ignorant savage even knew what a spyglass was, let alone how to use it. *Probably the same way the damned Apaches had learned to use rifles. . . .*

His hand tightened around the scope, as some part of him fought the idea of letting an Apache even touch it, never mind share it with him. *It had belonged to his father. . . .*

Black Knife stared back at him, his expression equally intense, almost a challenge, as if it was more about the principle of the thing—about what kind of man he was—than about the scope itself.

Dolarhyde glanced at Nat. The look in Nat's eyes was like the look Jake had shot him yesterday, when they'd confronted Jake's gang. "Generosity is considered a virtue . . ." Nat said, and Dolarhyde realized with a shock that he was talking about the Apaches.

He knew then that the real question in the chief's eyes was about trusting *him*: What kind of leader was he? That was a question he understood—backed up by the same kind of doubt. At least Black Knife had a human face, not an alien monster's . . . *even if this was a human being he'd never turn his back on.*

He wasn't so blind that he couldn't—by now—see the difference between an enemy who was only human and one that was inhuman. . . . His definition of "inhuman" had just undergone a sea change.

He held out the spyglass, letting Black Knife take it from him. There was reassurance, even a flicker of respect, on Black Knife's face as he accepted it, and Nat smiled fleetingly in relief.

Dolarhyde's expression turned grim again, but only because he figured the Apache leader's expression would be reflecting his own, once the other man got a close look at what they were up against.

Black Knife peered at the alien ship for a long moment, then scanned the rim of the slot canyon above the place where Jake had indicated the hidden entrance lay.

He spoke again, as he handed the spyglass back to Dolarhyde. "The Apaches are mountain warriors," Nat translated. "He says it's better to fight from high ground."

Dolarhyde stiffened. "Tell him he's a fool if he thinks he can shoot a few arrows from on high and hurt these things."

Nat hesitated, as if he was trying to think of a way to repeat that to Black Knife without it sounding like the insult it was.

Suddenly Emmett said, "Where's Jake—?"

The others turned, their eyes searching the rocks

around them. They found only one another. Looking out across the open plain of the valley again they saw Jake, on horseback, riding hell-for-leather away from them.

Ella looked stricken, and then her face filled with uncertainty; as if she'd thought she'd finally understood Jake and his tangled emotions, only to have him abandon her again . . . not knowing this time whether it was really forever.

". . . That son of a bitch. . . ." Dolarhyde muttered, surprised by the depth of his own disappointment. He wondered why the hell he'd ever begun to trust—let alone respect—thieving outlaw scum like Jake Lonergan.

Doc just looked tired as he asked, "What'd you say to him this time—?"

JAKE PUSHED HIS horse hard, counting on luck nearly as much as skill to keep them both from breaking their necks. Behind him the aliens' towering fortress-ship grew smaller and less threatening with every moment that passed. He'd needed to get as far from the aliens, and the posse intent on attacking them, as he could, before anyone realized he was gone.

Even now, he couldn't afford to slow his pace much more than he already had for his horse's sake; they could both rest when he reached the place he was headed—or his horse could, anyway. Time was running out—not just for the demon hunters, but for everybody: something he understood now better than any human being on Earth.

The others had to realize he was gone by now; they'd probably seen him riding away. *Running scared*, he figured the others were thinking, picturing the looks on their faces.

Running from an impossible situation. . . . And maybe they were right; but not for the reasons they figured. This time he was heading toward something too; a different kind of insane gamble, maybe, but one that might just turn a suicide attack into a fight they had half a chance of winning. . . .

THE REMAINING MEMBERS of Jake's gang—about two-thirds of them—who had survived the attack by the flying monsters were making plans of their own. Most of them were still nursing wounds, or sitting around listlessly—half drunk, or too dazed with disbelief to get past what had happened to them yesterday. There was only one thing they all agreed on . . . they wanted to get the hell out of this cursed place, to leave the whole damned territory, for someplace without flying monsters or Jake Lonergan.

Bronc was on his knees counting the gold they had left, with a half-smoked cigar between his teeth, as usual. Hunt sat by, moodily gnawing his thumbnail, not able to think of anything better he could be doing, especially while Bull McCade—their self-proclaimed new leader—was watching Bronc as well.

Bronc stopped counting and reached into his jacket pocket, looking for a match to relight the cigar, which tended to go out when he was concentrating on something else. He pulled out a match, struck it with his thumbnail. Nothing happened, and he swore, clenching the cigar tighter between his teeth.

Hunt tossed him a matchbox they'd acquired along with the dynamite they'd stolen from the Vulture Mine.

Bronc looked at the box: *Lucifer Safety Matches. Made in England. Strike on box only to light.* Those damned miners were too careful for their own good, Bronc thought. Like they'd expected they were gonna live forever. . . . He struck the match on the box, and re-lit his cigar again.

"Quit stalling—how much gold we got?" Bull said impatiently.

Annoyed, Bronc figured Bull's *cojones* were still hurting plenty, after that kick Jake had given him yesterday. He hoped so. "Okay—*calmate . . . como cincuenta pesados*—" he broke off, calculating, translating currencies. "A thousand dollars, maybe more."

Hunt pushed to his feet, restless and on edge, unable to achieve Bronc's level of patience even on his best day, which this definitely was not. "Just need to know how much of that is mine, and I'll be on my way."

"On your way?" Bull said, his voice turning ugly. "Dolan's dead, so I run this gang now." He looked at Hunt, trying to stare him down. "Gold goes where I go."

Hunt's gun was out, and pointed at Bull, faster than Bull could blink. "You might be in charge, but some of that gold is mine, fair. And after what we saw yesterday, I need it to get as far from here as I can go."

Bronc listened to the sounds of other pistols being drawn and cocked, as the men all around him heard the exchange, and saw Hunt pull his revolver. The men began to separate, taking one side or the other. Bronc glanced up, noticing the even split between them, aware that he was caught right in the middle of it.

"You're not going anywhere," Bull said to Hunt. In another moment, Bronc figured, that was going to be true: they'd all be dead.

Bronc got up, his own pistol drawn, siding with Hunt, breaking the tie as he pointed his pistol at Bull. "*Perdoname*. What's fair is fair."

Whether he was too stubborn or too stupid, Bull showed no signs of backing down. The rest of the men looked at one another, all of them already stressed to the breaking point—undecided, wavering. *No safety matches in this bunch,* Bronc thought, a little regretful.

The sound of a rider approaching the camp's entrance made him look away, out of habit. So did the others, then, turning their heads and their guns toward the opening in the rocks, suddenly united against an outside threat.

A lone rider came through the gap toward them, silhouetted by the sun, riding over the hill like he belonged there. He reined in his horse at the edge of camp and dismounted, walking toward them as if twenty men hadn't just aimed their guns at him all at once.

It was Jake. The last time Bronc had seen him, he was being pursued by one of the flying monsters. And yet somehow he'd escaped from them. Had he really killed one of the flying things with the strange weapon on his wrist, the one that had blown a hole you could crawl through in Dolan?

Jake's expression was unreadable, his face was still

a mess from the beating he'd gotten yesterday. Bronc could see that he was still wearing the weapon, too. *Shit*, Bronc thought. *Did he come back to save us—or to kill us all . . . ?*

JAKE WALKED INTO the camp where what was left of his gang stood with their guns pointed at him. But from the expressions on their faces this time, he got the feeling it wasn't personal. More likely, they'd been about to kill each other, after everything that'd happened yesterday.

A dog's soft bark made him glance to the side. It was the black dog he'd last seen the night they were attacked by the alien, in the stranded riverboat. It came up to him, wagging its tail in welcome.

Had that crazy dog trailed them all the way here? He laughed, not able to help himself, as he said, "Where you been—?" The dog only sat down, tail wagging, beside him.

"Jake? That really you?"

He glanced up at the sound of Hunt's voice and nodded, still smiling. The members of the gang began to holster their pistols, whatever they'd been arguing about forgotten.

Jake took a seat on a rock, as casually as if he'd just stopped by for a shot of whiskey. He glanced around, observing the disarray, the gold coins laid out on a tarp in neat stacks. "You boys thinking of taking a trip?"

"*Patrón*," Bronc said, "we're thinking of riding south. Remember the *playa* in Puerto Vallarta?"

"Yeah," Hunt nodded, his face relaxing. "Tequila, good fishing."

Jake shook his head. "Not far enough."

Hunt's smile of relief fell away, and his gaze grew hollow. "Jake, what the hell were those things?"

Jake shrugged. "Don't matter. They're gonna find us and they are going to wipe us out."

Hunt stared at him. ". . . the hell you saying?"

Jake looked from face to face among the men still left in the camp. "I'm saying you got a choice. You can drink your last few hours away on a beach—which is not a bad idea, by the way. . . ." He grinned fleetingly. "Or you can follow me, one last time."

The men glanced at each other, their faces turning uneasy again. He could practically hear their thoughts: *Follow him, after yesterday*—?

"Why the hell would we do that?" Bull said. He still stood like a man whose balls hurt, Jake noticed, with some satisfaction.

"Same reason you always have, Bull. . . ." Jake let the wry grin spread across his face again. "I'll make you rich."

Rich. That was a word they all understood. He saw the same strangely familiar look come over all their faces then—the look that said they'd follow him anywhere. His grin widened even more, because it felt so good.

DOC STOOD IN front of his makeshift shooting gallery, and took aim at the lined-up rocks and empty bottles his shots been hitting more and more frequently. It no longer struck him as an obscenity that the skills he had developed when he studied surgery were just as useful when aiming a gun, and keeping it on target.

Like it or not, in this world—in this universe—a human being sometimes needed both those things just to survive. If he had learned anything on this journey, it was the truth the preacher had known: that life was never simple; that his choices would never be easy. Sometimes even a gun could save lives, faster and more surely than any surgery he'd ever done.

He fired the last of his bullets, and heard the last of the bottles shatter. He smiled, satisfied with his progress, as he lowered the gun.

Emotions were what made a man want to become a healer, a saver of lives; but emotions had no place in the precise movements required when he performed surgery . . . or in the precision needed to fire a gun. Even if his feelings about using a gun would never be anything better than mixed, that didn't mean he couldn't hit a target if he really had to.

"Listen to me—!"

Emotions turning sour made him start back into the Apache camp, as he heard Dolarhyde's voice rising again. Dolarhyde's attempts to engage Black Knife in a discussion of military strategy weren't going very well. Dolarhyde was somebody who could definitely do with less emotion—the negative kind—in a situation like this. Even with Ella translating, and Black Knife's respect for her, the tone of Dolarhyde's words was all too obvious, no matter how tactful she was about translating them.

Every time Doc thought Dolarhyde was actually showing signs of progress as a human being, something would set him off again, like a bundle of explosives. It seemed like he'd been an Apache hater for too long to change now.

Jake's abrupt departure hadn't helped anyone's mood. But Dolarhyde's animosity toward the Apaches was plain bigotry, fear turned inside out, and that was something Doc had gotten a bellyful of, back East . . . for all his life, in fact. It had only made him more determined not to become the thing he hated, no matter what anyone said to him. *But if he hadn't had Maria and her family . . . would he ever have understood?*

Black Knife stopped speaking, as the Apaches who had gathered around them, listening and observing, turned to stare at Dolarhyde, at the tone of his voice.

"We can't just run around hooting and throwing spears at that damn thing!" Dolarhyde said, practically shouting into Ella's ear. "Tell him we gotta find a way to draw 'em out onto *open ground*, then surround 'em from all sides, *flank them*!"

Black Knife's answer to that sounded angry and final. The *nantan* got to his feet and put his hands on his hips, his stance delivering the same message to Dolarhyde as Ella's words, as she said, "He says yours is not the voice of wisdom; he won't let you lead his people."

As Doc finally sat down, joining the others, he glanced at Nat, who sat, with his usual stoic patience, at Dolarhyde's side. His face seemed much more readable to Doc now, since they'd spoken to each other— making meaningful human contact—yesterday.

Doc could tell from Nat's eyes that he was relieved Ella had taken over the job of translating, but his expression was now as unhappy as Ella's. Nat looked deeply conflicted, even if he was suffering in silence, as he listened to this exercise in misunderstanding. The two men he held in the highest regard seemed to be from worlds as different as the aliens in the metal fortress were different from human beings . . . except in this case Nat belonged, or had belonged, to both those worlds. If anyone here knew that it was possible for them to understand each other—if they really wanted to—it was him.

Doc wondered what had been going on in Nat's mind since they'd arrived here. He'd known Nat as long as he'd known Dolarhyde; knew that he was half Apache, and knew now that he spoke the language like he'd grown up with it. His boss hated Apaches . . . and yet Dolarhyde trusted Nat with his life, and Nat had always seemed more loyal to him than his own son was . . . and a hell of a lot more respectful.

But now Nat was sitting on the edge between two worlds; and fence-sitting was always a painful proposition.

Doc noticed Nat's mouth pressed into a thin line, the muscles in his face drawn taut, as if for once he was having real trouble ignoring his boss's temper . . . or the Apache chief's disdain.

Black Knife was done with speaking. He turned away, speaking to his sub-chiefs, until Doc wondered if everyone left in the group was going to wind up with a knife at their throats again.

As he thought it, Nat Colorado suddenly got up, turned to Black Knife, and shouted, "*Enough*!"

Doc froze. Everyone's eyes went to Nat, even the Apaches', every face there was as astonished as Doc's was.

Nat began speaking Apache, but this time the words were his own, and anybody there would have had to be deaf not to hear his frustration, or the insistence in his voice.

"What's he saying . . . ?" Dolarhyde murmured to Ella, his own anger forgotten as he watched his silent guardian finally stand up and speak his own mind.

Ella leaned closer, keeping her own voice low, "He says they have to open their eyes, to see in you what he's seen . . . that his parents were killed in the Mexican War, and you took him in when he was only a boy. . . ."

Ella's own expression began to change as the words she was speaking began to affect her—the revelation that two more human beings who had come from profoundly different pasts—different worlds—could share a bond of such deep loyalty and friendship that it made everything else they were, or had been, meaningless . . . a bond that she had never thought a man like Dolarhyde could even form. ". . . You gave his life a purpose, taught him how to take care of himself. Even though you didn't share the same blood."

Dolarhyde sat listening, blinking and blinking as the words reached him—his expression changing as his bitter mask began to fade, revealing the human being behind it; the face of a man who, for all his stubborn refusal of his own humanity, couldn't help being moved.

". . . and that you despise battle, but never run from it." Ella paused, looking at Dolarhyde with an expression she had never shown to him before, either. "That you are a great warrior, worthy of any fight."

Nat looked back at Dolarhyde, his own face filled with more real emotion than Doc had ever seen on it. Dolarhyde met his gaze; the space between them seemed to disappear into the silence. As they looked at each other, there was a connection so powerful it was almost tangible, needing no words to explain how much Nat's words meant to both of them.

At last Black Knife broke the silence, his words still challenging, although it was obvious that what Nat had just said had made an impression on him.

"He says, if you're such a great warrior, how come you don't have men to fight by your side?" Ella glanced down, as Dolarhyde's and Black Knife's eyes met . . . and this time Dolarhyde had no answer for the accusation.

A commotion on the other side of the camp saved the situation from deteriorating further. The group sitting in the council circle rose to their feet, looking in the same direction as the people in the camp.

With mixed emotions, they all saw Jake in the distance, topping the ridge that led down to the camp . . . inexplicably returning to them, apparently alone. But before any conclusions could take hold in anyone's mind, they saw that he wasn't really alone—following him was a band of almost two dozen men . . . Jake's gang, or what was left of them. And this time they followed their former leader willingly, not out for his blood.

If he had planned it himself, Dolarhyde couldn't have asked for better timing. The expressions on all the faces around him were changing, only for the better.

Dolarhyde had won his first victory.

Emmett ran forward to meet Jake and the riders, seeing only the black dog keeping pace with them— the friend he'd thought he'd lost forever, like so much else in his life.

The dog ran ahead down the slope to greet him, nearly knocking him over as he kneeled down to hug it, covering him with wet doggy kisses. "Hi, boy!" Emmett said, laughing for the first time that he or anyone else could remember.

As Jake dismounted, Emmett let go of the dog for long enough to reach out and hug him.

Jake felt as awkward as the boy looked happy— not used to hugs of affection, particularly not from a child, especially in front of his gang. But he couldn't seem to stop the smile that got out onto his face, even as he carefully pried the boy loose, murmuring, "Okay, kid. . . ." He sent the boy back to the dog, thinking they were a lot better suited to each other than either one of them was to him . . . but still feeling somehow lighter for seeing them reunited.

Jake moved on to Dolarhyde, the faint smile on his face turning into a confident grin, but not showing the least defiance, this time. The two men stood eye to eye, meeting for the first time as equals; each man seeing in the other's face the changes he had been through . . . the acceptance of more than a truce. For the first time they were meeting as true partners, not as enemies.

"I got an idea how to take out those flyers, and draw 'em out—" Jake said. He felt his smile widen, as he saw the look on Dolarhyde's face. "You ready to get your son back?"

"Hell, *yes*," Dolarhyde said, matching Jake's grin, and the look in his eyes.

Black Knife stood watching them, observing the others Jake had brought back with him—probably seeing the kind of *pindah-lickoyee* he hated most, short of the army: A gang of outlaws—reckless, short-fused saddle tramps and gunslingers, tough, hardened survivors, all too savvy in the ways of both the Apache, and their own people. . . .

Exactly the kind of men they needed with them right now, to face the coming battle.

Dolarhyde looked back at Black Knife in expectation, waiting, until at last Black Knife nodded, and their bargain was sealed.

16

The sound of drumming from the Apache camp, the voices of women chanting songs and calling out as their men danced, carried on the night air to the separate camp where Jake's men and the group from town had settled in for the night.

Hunt sat by one of the several small campfires, cleaning his gun as he discussed with Red and Bull the prospect of fighting the alien demons Jake had told them they'd be facing tomorrow, if they wanted their gold back . . . and a lot more of it besides. If he hadn't seen what he'd seen yesterday, with his own eyes—if nearly a third of the gang hadn't been kidnapped by flying monsters—he would have been sure Bull had knocked Jake's brains clean out of his head.

But he had seen what he'd seen . . . and so had everybody else. Even the Apaches. The demons not only wanted gold, they wanted people, to torture to death—and it didn't matter who. Jake had told them that even Ella, the woman the gang had nearly shot dead yesterday, was just one more survivor, who'd come looking for revenge. The woman Jake had left the gang for was dead: *The demons had killed her. . . .*

Bull passed him the bottle of whiskey they'd all been nursing with unusual restraint; he took another drink from it, just to steady his nerves. Nobody was drinking too much, tonight. Going up against the spawn of Hell half-drunk, or with a godawful hangover, didn't seem like a smart idea even to Bull.

At least Bull was more like the man Hunt remembered again, to his relief—and probably everyone else's—now that Bull was done trying to play follow-the-leader, and content to let Jake do the thinking for all of them.

Hunt glanced away at Bronc, who was giving the man Jake called "Doc" a fine-tuned lesson in how to aim a rifle. Bronc had ridden with Benito Juárez in Mexico—he was an educated man, probably even a respectable one, once. And although he'd never told Hunt how he'd ended up in a place like this, he was the only one in the gang who was smart and still honest enough to count their take from a robbery, and then divide it fairly, without a few guns pointed at his head.

It seemed to Hunt like *now* was a little late for Bronc to be trying to show some spectacles-wearing tenderfoot how to handle a gun. But Bronc never wasted his time trying to teach pigs to sing; he must figure the man had some kind of potential.

· Woodrow Dolarhyde walked by, like a general inspecting his troops the night before a battle. *Dolarhyde*. It was an unusual name, but Hunt had heard it before, back during the War. He looked up as the man passed.

"—Dolarhyde," he said.

DOLARHYDE STOPPED, TURNED to look back at the outlaw named Hunt.

"You the same Colonel Woodrow Dolarhyde who fought at Antietam?" Hunt asked.

Dolarhyde hesitated, looking down at Hunt, feeling an unaccustomed mix of emotions rise up in him. Now was the time when his bitterness and shame had always burst out of him as fury—

But he didn't even know Hunt. Hunt was only another veteran, another victim of soldier's heart who'd drifted west after the war, like too many others who'd lost everything that held any meaning for them in blood and smoke, in the endless years of killing or being killed.

The man wasn't a ghost, only a stranger, and curiosity was the only thing that showed on his face.

"Yes, I am," Dolarhyde said quietly, at last . . . realizing at last that after nearly thirteen years, there probably wasn't anybody left who hated him as much as he still hated himself.

Hunt nodded, his curiosity satisfied, and turned back to the fire as Dolarhyde walked on.

Dolarhyde kept walking, alone with his thoughts, until he passed beyond the firelight at the edge of their camp to a spot where he could just see the Apache camp.

He stood for a long moment watching the war

dance being performed there, trying to see what Nat had described to him: a sacred ceremony where the dance filled the warriors with life in the face of death; that sent their prayers for blessings and protection to God-as-they-knew-Him; that heated their blood for the coming battle, giving them the will and courage it took to win. . . . The dance would probably go on all night, until it was time to ride out in the morning.

Nat claimed that to the Apaches everything was sacred, everything was infused by the presence of Yusn, the Creator, and White-Painted Woman. To go into battle without performing the appropriate rituals and observing the proper traditions would be a disaster, and the result would be slaughter, without meaning or honor.

Slaughter. That was how he'd always seen war— the results of a battle with any enemy, but especially the Apaches, savages who he'd always figured had no God at all. Their ceremonies had looked as primitive to him as their weapons . . . until they'd gotten hold of rifles, anyway.

He remembered dignified army chaplains reading a prayer in front of lines of troops ready to go into battle, asking God's blessing and protection for the men—a prayer that had no more moved God to mercy than the agony of the wounded and dying had, once the fighting started.

The chaplain had always walked away again, without ever really seeing any of the very real men he'd just sent away to kill or be killed . . . especially not at the times when they'd needed to see him the most.

After Antietam, Dolarhyde had ceased to listen to the chaplains, ceased believing in any law of man or God, in anything but himself.

But if anything had proved to him that he controlled nothing in his own life, it had been seeing his only child snatched away by monsters. The alien demons had invaded his self-imposed exile from beyond the sky, to rob him of his illusions, along with Percy, leaving him stranded and empty . . . like that riverboat in the middle of the desert.

Dolarhyde wondered about the aliens in the metal fortress: what kind of ideas they had about God, whether they saw humans, or Ella's people, or any other—*sentient beings*, Ella called them—as nothing more than insects to crush, to eradicate.

Seeing Ella walk out of that fire, glowing like an angel, was as close to seeing Heaven as he ever expected to get; and yet even her people had been exterminated by these demons, these monsters . . . these alien *things*. He had no words left to describe "sentient beings" that lived only to destroy other people's lives, whose only god seemed to be gold.

But only yesterday, he'd laughed at Ella, saying, "*What're they gonna do? Buy something?*"

He suddenly recalled his first glimpse of Jake Lonergan, in that prison wagon, chained to Percy . . . remembered that he'd ignored his own son, too blind with hatred for the man who'd stolen his gold . . . *his gold* . . . not his son.

He'd been prepared to torture Lonergan until he gave up where he'd hidden it, and then kill him—simply for having the brass to challenge his non-existent control over the small piece of the world that he'd believed he owned.

He considered the painful irony of the truth: how Jake couldn't have told him anything if he'd wanted to; how the same aliens that'd kidnapped his son had taken the gold he'd cared so goddamn much more about away from Jake . . . and killed Jake's woman in front of his eyes.

Jake came up beside him, almost as if Dolarhyde had conjured him out of his own thoughts. For a moment they stood side by side, watching the Apache camp in the distance, each of them lost in memories. At last Dolarhyde said, "I knew you'd be back."

Jake cocked his head, looking at him in mild surprise, because there'd been nothing cynical inside the words, nothing accusing behind them . . . simply relief, and maybe even a little gratitude.

Dolarhyde turned away then, walking back into camp, content at last with the place his thoughts had led him to; ready to face tomorrow.

Jake stood a moment longer, watching Dolarhyde go. The edges of his mouth turned up as he said, to the air, "You're welcome." He left the place where they'd been standing too, because he wanted to find Ella, and Ella wasn't there.

EMMETT CROUCHED IN a pile of rocks, the dog lying down at his side, as he secretly watched the Apache war dance with wide-eyed fascination. He'd gone closer than anybody else had dared to get; thinking about the things he'd listened to Nat tell Mr. Dolarhyde about what the ceremony meant to the Apaches.

He wondered how Nat knew so much about Apaches, even how to speak their language, when all Emmett had ever known about him was that he worked for Mr. Dolarhyde, and Grandpa hated Mr. Dolarhyde. Emmett had never even spoken to Nat before. He'd never seen real Apaches before, either. It had never occurred to him how much Nat looked like an Apache . . . like he belonged to two worlds, or none; the way Emmett found himself feeling more and more, since his own world had started to fall apart, along with his family. . . .

But it was Nat who came up behind him, where he thought he'd hidden himself so well, and laid a hand lightly on his shoulder. Nat's voice was firm as he said, "Hey, Emmett, you shouldn't be here." The war dance was only for Apache eyes . . . even Nat had not been watching it, he realized.

Emmett looked up, half disappointed and half embarrassed. He couldn't tell what the expression on Nat's face was, as Nat glanced toward the Apaches. Emmett got up and shuffled away, the dog trotting behind him as he headed back into camp.

NAT WAS ABOUT to follow him, but he hesitated for just a moment, watching the warriors dance while the women chanted and called: an outsider looking on at a world to which he had once belonged, but never would again.

He lingered, watching, for a moment too long; just as he began to turn away, he realized that the *nantan*'s sharp eyes had spotted him standing there. Black Knife held his gaze for a long moment. Then, to Nat's surprise, Black Knife gestured for him to enter the camp, to come and take a seat by the fire.

Nat stood where he was for a long moment, overcome by emotions he had kept buried too deeply inside, for far too many years.... At last he started forward, crossing into the light of the Apache world, where a part of his soul had finally been granted acceptance again. Moving among his people, he sat down next to Black Knife.

Black Knife nodded to him; Nat saw in the chief's obsidian eyes both welcome and respect.

"You are a good Apache," Black Knife said. And with that, he rose to his feet and joined the dance, leaving Nat to share in a part of his past life that he'd never thought he would get the chance to reclaim.

AFTER WANDERING THROUGH the whole camp, and searching most of its perimeter, Jake found Ella at last. She was standing alone in the darkness at the top of a hill, gazing at the stars as if she were searching for her true home; a place that lay somewhere out there, like Heaven . . . a place that no longer existed.

Jake thought of the ruined cabin: the only real home he'd ever had, that no longer existed . . . the home he had shared with Alice . . . who no longer existed . . .

All he had ever wanted of Heaven . . . and he hadn't even realized it.

He tried not to think at all, as he stopped beside Ella and looked up at the stars. They were beautiful, out here in the desert. He must have lain awake at night and stared up at them for years, somehow he was sure of that, even though his memory of that time seemed to be gone for good.

But it had never occurred to him before that the stars were beautiful . . . any more than he could ever have imagined that someone like Ella might drop out of the sky one day like a wounded angel, as beautiful as the whole sea of stars . . . as beautiful inside as she was outside, whatever her true form was.

Even after all she'd been through—the loss and the hardships that had made her strong—life hadn't turned her bitter and hard; it had only filled her with more compassion.

She was like a guerrilla, a Juarista from another world, fighting in a battle she might never win . . . that might never end . . . but not just for revenge. Having lost her past, her world, everything but her life, she'd found a reason to go on living, in saving other worlds and their people . . . even his own people, who needed her help to save the world they all shared, however ungratefully.

When he'd been told she was dead, he hadn't known who or what she really was. Yet simply knowing her as a woman named Ella . . . when he'd believed she was gone, he'd felt like something inside him had died along with her; an emotion that had gone numb so long ago he hadn't realized he'd ever possessed it.

And then, seeing her walk out of the flames, reborn, shining like the Morning Star after a long dark night. *Coming directly toward him. . . .*

He remembered suddenly why he'd been looking for her, tonight: that the two of them had unfinished business left from that final moment standing heart to heart on the shore of the desert lake.

Ella looked down, away from the sky, and turned toward him as if she'd sensed his thoughts, or his emotions. "Just so you know," she said softly, and looked away as she said it, "I'm not going to be here for very long."

"None of us are here for very long. . . ." He met her gaze as she looked up again, his own eyes fearless. He took off his hat, like a gentleman, and kissed her. "Don't ever do that to me again," he murmured.

Her hands rose, catching his bruised face with the gentlest of fingers, holding it still, as she went on looking at him. He saw on her face the same kind of wonder and amazement he'd seen when she realized he was trying to save her from the flyer.

But this time her eyes said it was nothing but a kiss, only the briefest contact of his lips with hers, that she couldn't believe. He didn't understand that at all . . . even if his body had its own ideas, as his hands rose to take her into his arms.

Her hands dropped to her sides then, and closed over his own, tender but insistent as she moved his hands away; she gave a slight shake of her head. She glanced down, her own face as confused as his was, now. But one of her hands clung to his a moment longer; telling him that her body had its own opinions too, even if she wasn't ready to listen to them.

He smiled a little as he took a step back, understanding that much, at least.

As he began to turn away, Ella's hand reached out suddenly and caught his. He stopped; she let go. She didn't say anything, or even glance at him.

But she didn't have to. He stood quietly beside her, looking up at the Milky Way, the river of light connecting their separate worlds, their solitary lives, their destinies. Sensing her unspoken gratitude, all at once he became aware of his own, as he thought about lying sleepless, alone, staring up at the stars, at unreachable Heaven . . . tonight, of all nights, when tomorrow's dawn might bring the end of the world.

17

The scent of sage was strong in the dawn wind as Dolarhyde's motley troops assembled in two groups, side-by-side . . . together in their eagerness to go to war against a common enemy, but still uneasy with each other, not yet united in trust.

Dolarhyde sat on his horse, with Ella on one side of him and Jake on the other. As he looked back at the waiting riders, he realized he'd never seen a less disciplined, less likely looking group of fighting men in his life. But then, he'd never faced an enemy like this one before. . . . Somehow it struck him as fitting.

He looked past Ella at Black Knife, who waited at the head of his own band of warriors. Nat had explained to him that Black Knife's position as a high chief was due partly to his skill as a *di-yin* of war— not just a good fighter, but a kind of medicine man whose special gift from the spirit world gave him the insight to lead his men to victory in battles. *Battles against human enemies.*

The Apaches all wore a streak of war paint across their cheeks and the bridge of their nose, a Chiricahua pattern, although it was chalk-white instead of the usual red ochre. But then, not all the warriors were Chiricahuas: Maybe it was a new design, something that the survivors of different tribes had agreed on, a symbol of their united stand against the United States . . . or against the universe.

Dolarhyde glanced past Ella at Black Knife—and found the *nantan* looking back at him. He still had no real idea of how to read the Apache leader's face; but this time he got the odd feeling that Black Knife was thinking the same thing about him. He just hoped that today, Black Knife remembered who their real enemies were.

He turned back to Jake, who nodded. He raised his arm, a signal for all the riders to move out.

THE RIDE INTO hostile territory stirred an old familiar feeling in Jake . . . the feeling that he'd done the same thing far too many times before. This must have been what his old life had been like—riding out with the boys to waylay a stage, or rustle horses and cattle; something he figured the Apaches knew as much about as his gang did. It was almost reassuring.

Just the thought of real cavalry, riding in perfect lines, bristling with weapons, stirred something a lot more unpleasant. He wasn't sure if it was the way a troop of horse soldiers looked—like a stone wall topped with spikes—or more likely that they'd tried to nail his hide to their wall, one time too many.

This felt right . . . a bunch of misfit, need-driven outcasts. The only thing any of them really had in common, red or white, was the determination, and the skill, to survive against enemies who wanted to see them dead.

If they happened to save the whole goddamn world in the process, well . . . where would they be without it?

And knowing that the holier-than-thou, God-fearing folk who'd spat on them all their lives would end up owing their own lives to outlaws, Apaches and a woman from some other planet—even if no one in New Mexico Territory ever learned the truth—it would still let him have the last laugh, if someday the good people of the Territories finally put a noose around his neck.

THE RIDERS SLOWED as they reached the jagged crest of a final hill, and saw the aliens' fortress-ship, still sitting like a tombstone on the mesa's flat summit, now too close for comfort.

But comfort wasn't what they were here for. The two parallel groups of riders drew up together and sat staring at their target for a long moment as men muttered to one another in two different languages.

Dolarhyde's group and the Apaches glanced at each other a last time, acknowledging their mutual need, despite the fear of betrayal that lay just beneath the skin in every one of them.

Then they rode on down the slope, crossing the wide plain of the valley floor, where the land was already showing a trace of fresh green after the first thunderstorm of summer, transforming the pale dirt between the clumps of scrub. Every form of life in the desert fought back against annihilation with an unyielding perversity that could have been the definition of Life itself, as well as of Death.

When they reached the weather-eaten wall of the mesa on the far side, the riders stopped again at the foot of a talus slope below a protruding stone outcrop. The rubble and detritus had laid down a precarious path to the rim, identifying the spot where the two halves of the group had finally agreed that they would split up.

Leaving their horses at the base of the slope, Black Knife and his mountain fighters picked a trail up the steep scarp to higher ground, where they could surround the slot canyon that marked the aliens' hidden ground-level entrance, and fire down on the enemy as they emerged from their sunken fortress.

The two groups separated, with more than one uncertain backward glance, Dolarhyde led his men on around the foot of the outcrop, heading toward the only sufficient cover near the canyon's entrance, a timeworn ridge of granite that ran parallel to the mesa's foot, within sight of the arroyo Jake remembered. The outlaw cavalry would form up and reconnoiter from there, and they could keep watch for any aliens—or any surviving captives—as they came out.

* * *

NOW IT WAS Jake's turn to act. He dismounted, signaling to the hand-picked members of his gang that it was time to set the first part of their plan in motion. He led the five men across the open ground to the base of the cliff, all of them carrying haversacks slung over their shoulders as they scrambled up the eroded slope to the mesa's rim.

The protruding top of the alien ship threw a long, accusing shadow across their path as they pushed through the underbrush, moving cautiously over the flat ground of the mesa top until they reached the ship's base.

Jake paused for a moment, scanning the canyon rim across from them, until he caught a glimpse of Black Knife's warriors moving into position, fading into the land itself as they chose firing positions.

He was glad to see them there, even as they vanished into cover. He knew they saw him and his men too, reassuring them that Dolarhyde's part of the operation was proceeding as planned.

He glanced over his shoulder at the ridge where Ella, Dolarhyde and the rest were waiting their turn, waiting for a sign. . . . He saw a small spark of light, figured Dolarhyde was using that damned spyglass he was so fond of, watching everything that went on like a hawk.

Good thing he was using it against monsters that couldn't see in the daytime, and not the Apaches . . . or Jake Lonergan's gang. Jake tossed a salute at the ridge, just in case Dolarhyde was looking at him. He kept his smile to himself, letting his face go sober as he turned back to his work: *Time to get serious.*

Jake laid his gloved hands on the rough surface of the ship. Up close it looked to be the same strange-looking patchwork as his weapon and the flyers, except on an even larger scale---an odd fusion of different metals, with grooves and protrusions he couldn't imagine the reason for. There were circular patterns on the ship's hide, too, something he hadn't seen before—maybe some kind of hatches, or even weapons so large he didn't want to think about what they could do. As long as those openings stayed shut, they weren't his problem. . . .

He found the row of what looked like vents that rose in a convenient ladder almost to the top of the ship, where the flyer had landed yesterday. He hoped it would work like a ladder too, because the top was where they had to start—

Bronc and Hunt, the two munitions men he'd brought with him, stood ready to follow as Jake started to climb. Three other men from the gang kept watch below; though Jake hoped to God they wouldn't be seeing anything unusual.

The vents made it easy to find the handholds and footholds he needed; he climbed almost to the top of the fortress, where he could reach the highest row of the vents he'd marked as their target. Whether the vents were just for air, or for something else, he figured that as long as they were open to the outside, they were vulnerable . . . at least, they were on this world.

He'd seen one of the flyers land on top of the ship and disappear down inside. It figured the aliens must keep the flyers in some kind of stable, and it had to be a big space, given their size. He didn't know what else might be in there; he only hoped dynamite would be enough to blow it up. . . .

He'd noticed whole crates of the explosives back at Dolan's camp, where the boys had sat on it like it was furniture while they waited for a good time to use it. This was as good a time as any Jake could think of.

He gestured back at the men on the ground. Bronc and Hunt hung from the side of the ship below him. The men passed the first haversack filled with dynamite up to Hunt, who passed it to Bronc, who climbed nearer to where Jake was waiting, and handed it off to him.

Bronc and Hunt each took on a bag of their own, following Jake's lead as he pulled out bundled sticks of dynamite, laying them in vent after vent.

Bronc had been a Juarista and Hunt had been a sapper during the War. Along with Red, who was an ex-miner, they were the only three in the gang who'd been willing to admit they were familiar with dynamite, or anything else that exploded. Red was getting too old for this kind of action, but he'd spent last night bundling the individual sticks into efficient bombs, cutting fuse cord and setting fuses, doing as much of the preliminary work for them as he could.

Now, Jake and the others shoved the bundled dynamite as far down the throats of every vent as their arms would reach, and wove dangling ends into a few long braids that could be lit all at once, hopefully leaving them enough time to get away from their handiwork before it blew them up. The three men on the ground passed up the remaining bags, until they had turned as many ports as they could into time bombs.

Jake pulled a box of matches out of his second equipment bag, as the others finished doling out their explosives. He studied the label on top of the match box: *Lucifer Safety Matches*.

Hell if that wasn't a contradiction in terms. He glanced up at the sky, making sure again that no flyers were heading in. The sky was perfectly clear—not even a cloud.

He suddenly thought of Meacham, what seemed like a lifetime ago, telling him another story like his own "... *somebody who dropped out of the sky ... fella named Lucifer. ...*"

He'd always wondered why he'd heard matches called "lucifers"; always figured it was because lit ones stank like Hell due to the sulfur.

But an odd piece of lore popped into his head, then; the kind no preacher liked to talk about: Some people called the Morning Star "Lucifer" ... because the name meant "*Light-bringer*." He smiled faintly, wondering what Meacham would think if he saw what his fallen angel was up to now ... and he guessed that if Meacham was looking down from God's Heaven right now, he wouldn't mind a bit.

Jake pulled open the matchbox, and stared. There was exactly one match left in it. He gestured down at Bronc, mouthing, "What the hell—?" Bronc nodded in reassurance, and patted the bulging pocket of his coat. Jake struck the single match and lit a fuse-braid, and then another, and another before he had to let the match go out.

He looked down, expecting Bronc to have the full box of matches ready. Bronc was still struggling to get the box out of his pocket, one-handed, while he hung from a vent. The matchbox resisted like a mule . . . and then suddenly it slipped free and shot straight through his fingers, out into the air.

The men hanging from the side of the ship and waiting on the ground below all watched, stupefied, as the matches arced out and down, landing somewhere in the dense scrub around the ship's base.

"*¡Mierda!*" Bronc muttered, his teeth clenched around a half-smoked cigar.

His lit cigar—

As Bronc and the others looked toward Jake, their faces registering various shades of dread, Jake reached down, scowling, and jerked the cigar out of Bronc's mouth. He lit the rest of the fuse cords within his reach, and passed the cigar back, gesturing irritably at the others to get their asses moving and finish the job.

Bronc and Hunt lit the rest of the fuses as they went, and didn't hesitate from there.

Jake waited until both of them were down, and glanced up at the sky once more: *still clear*. He peered in through the opening in front of him, caught a glimpse of what he thought was a flyer's wing, and hoped he'd made the right decision, for the right reason, just once in his life.

"Jake!" Bronc called, in an urgent whisper.

Jake climbed down, making sure all the fuses were burning like they should. He dropped to the ground, wondering why the hell the others were still waiting for him. "Run—!" he whispered.

They all took off, dodging through the brush, running for their lives. The dynamite detonated, in a deafening series of explosions, before they reached the mesa's rim. A cloud of smoke and flame blew out of every vent, raining down bits of shrapnel. The men around him whooped in triumph.

The whoops turned into sudden loud cursing, as another explosion went off, deeper inside the ship, and another, and another, each larger than the one before, as if the dynamite had just been the primer for something much bigger and more volatile. They staggered and almost fell as the shockwaves hit them, barely keeping one another on their feet until the last explosion had passed.

Jake hesitated as they reached the rim of the mesa, as something made him look back, while the others went over the edge and down. He saw what he'd most needed to see, and been the most afraid of: *The aliens.* The circular patterns that ringed the base of the ship irised open, and masses of demons swarmed out, as if he'd just shot down a hornet's nest.

The demon gun came alive and armed itself in a flare of blue as Jake, suddenly frozen where he stood, watched them come. He couldn't think, couldn't move, even to raise his arm and fire at them. *There were so many . . . too many . . . demons.*

A beam of pure blue, like the one from his own weapon, blasted the brush beside him and set it blazing. Shaken out of his trance, Jake raised the gun and fired back, before he threw himself over the rim, sliding down, leaping from rock, to outcrop of stone, to slope, as agile as any Apache when his life depended on it.

The others were almost down to the ground; he

suddenly joined them, as another beam of light cut the rock out from under him, and he slid the rest of the way down on his back. He scrambled up, turned to fire back at the aliens that had reached the mesa's edge. He hit one, saw the others draw back, and bolted with the rest of his men, dodging through the brush, heading for the solid cover of the ridge where Dolarhyde was waiting.

More blue bolts of energy struck around them, from above and from ground level now, too—more aliens were coming out of the hidden entrance in the slot canyon. He stopped again, firing back, and went on running.

It was just what the Colonel had ordered. Except in all the planning, it had never really sunk into Jake's mind that this time he wouldn't be the only one with a demon gun.

The weapon's range was at least as good as any rifle he knew, and the damage it could do was a damn sight worse—lucky for Dolarhyde, and luckier for his crew, that sunlight made the aliens half blind: Otherwise none of his munitions team would have made it back alive, including him. He caught up with the others as they reached the rocky outcrop where the cavalry was waiting, and ducked around it, finally under cover.

He leaned against the warm wall of sheltering stone beside the others, trying to catch his breath, trying to prepare himself mentally for the next thing he knew he'd have to do. He only hoped it went as well as this had.

He glanced over at his munitions crew and grinned;

but he could see that knowing they'd succeeded, and lived to tell about it, was all the reward they needed. *But if they wanted bragging rights, nobody was ever gonna believe them. . . .*

"THEY'RE COMING OUT," Nat said, from the top of the rocks. He watched aliens pour into the slot canyon, coming out of the hidden entrance, or scrambling down the steep slope from the mesa. He saw their weapons, the explosions of blue light, as the Apaches on the canyon rim began to fire at them.

"Let's move—" Dolarhyde said, looking down at his contingent of volunteer cavalry; they began to mount up. Dolarhyde turned to Emmett, crouched at his other side. He handed the boy his spyglass. "Take this, go up where I showed you. If you see our people come out, you get up and wave your arms."

Emmett nodded, taking the telescope firmly from his hand, and slipping it inside his own shirt. Dolarhyde watched the boy climb higher among the rocks, the knife at his belt, the spyglass carefully protected, and the dog still following him like his own shadow, no matter where he went.

Nat was already on his horse as Dolarhyde and Ella finished their descent from the lookout point. The expression on his face was curiously like Emmett's as he met Dolarhyde's gaze: as if he would have saluted, if he'd dared—and meant it as a sign of respect. He nodded to them, before he turned his horse and rode away to join the rest of Jake's men, the riders Dolarhyde had assigned him to lead in a flanking attack.

Dolarhyde turned back as Jake and his munitions team made their way along the rocky wall toward him; he could see the satisfaction of a job well done on all their faces. Jake grinned, acknowledging the congratulations of his men, who were on their horses now, waiting to ride out with Dolarhyde. Bronc and the others were already glancing toward their own horses, ready to join the ranks. Jake put a hand on the shoulder of each man, before his nod sent them off to join the others.

He kept walking, past Doc, who glanced up with a wry grin from readying his medical kit and checking his guns—until he reached the place where Dolarhyde and Ella were waiting. "They're all yours," he said to Dolarhyde, gesturing toward the waiting canyon filled with aliens.

Dolarhyde smiled. "Good job." Jake returned the smile, before he looked toward Ella. *This was it.*

Ella had plaited her long hair into a braid down her back. She drew her pistol, checked it a last time, and holstered it again. Her eyes shone as she looked up at Jake; but nothing more unearthly than pride and resolve lay behind them now.

Jake glanced back at Dolarhyde. "If they're in there, we'll get 'em out."

"Godspeed," Dolarhyde said. He watched the two of them move away, heading back toward the slot canyon on their separate mission, aiming for the hidden entrance that led to all their greatest hopes and fears.

Then Dolarhyde mounted his waiting horse, steeling himself for the moment he'd thought would never come again. He raised his arm. "Let's go!"

A dozen horsemen followed him—the kind of men who'd follow him into Hell—as he rode out to war.

NAT COLORADO ARRIVED at the spot where his unit of riders waited, at the far end of the stone ridge—the other half of Jake Lonergan's outlaw gang, on their horses, ready and waiting. He studied the looks on their faces, faces like so many he'd seen all his adult life at the Dolarhyde ranch.

Except these men had something in their eyes the Dolarhyde hands never had—the same look that had been in the eyes of the Apache warriors he'd watched through the night. The fact that both groups were facing a kind of enemy that no one had ever faced before only added to their willingness to spit in the eye of destiny.

Whether their will to fight was born of courage, desperation, or just pure cussedness, they weren't the kind of men who'd throw down their weapons and yield to anyone . . . or anything . . . even if they faced the end of the world.

He felt strangely honored and proud that such men were willing to follow him into this of all battles. These men wouldn't falter, and he let them see in his eyes that neither would he. "You ready?" he said, not really a question. He turned his horse, and raised his arm, like Colonel Dolarhyde, and they followed him onto the field of battle.

* * *

THE FIRST WAVE of men entered Hell's front yard, led by Dolarhyde, all firing their weapons. Across the field Dolarhyde saw Nat leading his own men in the flanking maneuver, both sides closing in on the alien front with what should have been withering fire from rifles and pistols.

Up on the ridge, Black Knife and his men supplied covering fire again: bullets from rifles, and arrows from bows that could sink a shaft into a pine tree up to its fletching caught the aliens in a crossfire.

But nothing seemed to affect the enemy. The alien demons didn't fall like men, either to the crossfire from above, or to the guns of Dolarhyde's cavalry—their monstrous bodies were like a natural suit of armor.

The aliens might be mostly blind in daylight, but they weren't deaf, and they weren't stupid. As they recovered from the surprise of the humans' attack they began to strike back.

Dolarhyde saw one fire a weapon like the one Jake wore, blasting a man from his horse. Another man was dragged from his saddle, a third went down, horse and all, as an alien lunged at him from the side, seemingly from out of nowhere.

Suddenly they were losing men on all sides, everywhere—far more than they could afford. Dolarhyde shouted orders to his men, signaling the riders to fall back and regroup. As they closed ranks, Nat pulled his horse up beside Dolarhyde, his face tight with frustration as the two of them took stock. "They're not going down—"

"They will—" Dolarhyde said grimly, "—just keep at it."

He knew Meacham had made one of them bleed with just a rifle. The aliens might be wearing natural armor . . . but all armor had its weak spots. And he didn't believe Ella would have led them into this, if she hadn't had faith that they'd be intelligent and resourceful enough to find those spots.

The men around him were tense and angry now; but their eyes were on the enemy, and he knew that men like these were a long way from giving in to any enemy, even death itself.

He searched the steep slopes of the canyon walls, looking for the Apaches. *Damn them— It was obvious they were too high up to be effective against these things. Why the hell couldn't that Apache "diyin of war", Black Knife, figure it out—?* He glanced at Nat, and kept his thoughts to himself.

"Regroup!" he shouted. "Let's go—" They led the men forward again.

AMONG THE ROCKS just below the canyon's rim, Black Knife watched the *pindah* riders regroup and begin another attack. He signaled his warriors to start firing again, to give them cover, as he had promised. But from here neither rifles nor bows had any effect on the sky monsters.

"No good," one of his sub-chiefs said, looking over at him, echoing his thoughts. "We are not hurting them. Should we join the fight?" He looked down the cliff-face at the canyon floor.

Black Knife was silent as he weighed the cost of losing warriors his people couldn't afford to lose against his trust in the arrogant *pindah* he had given his word to. He meant to keep his word; but so far he had seen no signs that his own men's weapons would be any more effective at close range than the guns of the riders below. Finally he shook his head. "Hold your position—keep firing." He raised his own rifle again, and took aim.

JAKE AND ELLA entered the high-walled arroyo that led to the hidden entrance of the aliens' fortress, the one he remembered from his medicine-dream. Five aliens abruptly emerged from the tunnel openings. Jake and Ella pressed back into a hollow in the eroded wall. They stood motionless in the shadows as the aliens passed them by to join the others out on the battlefield.

After the aliens moved on, so did they. This time they made it all the way to the entrance.

Just as they reached it, two more aliens came out of the dark tunnel opening. Without even time for a conscious thought, Jake's weapon activated, and blasted them both before they could get the drop on him.

He glanced at Ella, both of them taking a deep breath as then they entered the tunnel together. The weapon's cold blue glow illuminated the metallic ribs that supported the tunnel walls, guiding them like a lantern back down the gullet of stone to the underworld, to a place Jake remembered now all too clearly. . . .

* * *

ABOVE THE SLOT canyon, two of Black Knife's warriors, hidden among the rocks, took aim and fired at the sky monsters far below with growing frustration, as no bullet or arrow seemed to penetrate the aliens' hides.

One touched the other's arm, silently nodding at the slope below them, where one of the monsters was now climbing upward. They retrained their weapons on the new target, as the unsuspecting enemy drew closer to their position.

But it was already too late—another alien dropped down on them from behind, its savage arms slashing and impaling, and they were dead before they could even cry out.

Far below, Hunt, Bronc and Bull found themselves unhorsed, unarmed, and bloody, pinned down behind a berm that ran along the canyon wall. Even lying flat on their bellies, the ridge of rubble and dirt in front of them barely kept them clear of the blue lightning from the aliens' weapons, or even friendly fire.

They'd already lost Red, when they first rode into the canyon. He'd been torn from his saddle by a demon's long-clawed arm, and even though they'd put enough lead into the monster to kill a dozen buffalo, the alien had torn Red to pieces in front of their eyes with its talons and massive jaws. The memory of that was something every one of them would take to his grave . . . although the way things were going, soon there wouldn't be enough left of any of them to bury.

They were lucky to still be alive now . . . but they were trapped with no way to fight back, or even escape from the ditch; they could only lie there and curse as they watched the aliens take more members of the gang out of Dolarhyde's dwindling troops. The aliens seemed to be invulnerable to human attack, and it was only a matter of time before one of those monsters got close enough to see them, or trip over them . . . either way, Hunt figured they'd all be dead before the day was out.

"*Diablo*—" Bronc muttered, his fists knotting, as another man—they couldn't see who—flew from his horse, torn almost in half by one swing of an alien's powerful, deadly arm. The dead man's rifle flew in an arc toward them, landing about fifteen feet out from where they lay.

Bronc leaped up from behind their scant cover and ran out onto the field, going after the rifle. He hadn't covered half the distance before a bullet meant for an alien hide caught him instead. He fell, clutching his leg.

"Bronc!" Hunt yelled. Bull's heavy hand caught him by the shoulder as he pushed up from their hiding place, and flattened him again behind the berm's shelter.

Bull shook his head: *No good.*

Hunt subsided under the pressure of Bull's hand, and stared at the ground.

But then Bull nudged him and pointed. Looking up, they saw the townsman Jake had called "Doc," on his own two feet in the middle of the battlefield, as he ran toward Bronc.

Opening the medical bag he carried, Doc bandaged Bronc's bleeding leg, so focused on his work that he never even flinched as the ground exploded around them. Finally Doc shouted, "I stopped the bleeding! Now take cover!"

Bronc half-scrambled, half-crawled back to the shelter of the berm. As Hunt slapped Bronc on the back, grinning in relief, he saw Doc pick up his own rifle and his medical kit, and dodge into the brush in search of other wounded men who needed his help.

"Well, knock me down with a straw," Bull muttered.

"I'll be damned. . . ." Hunt shook his head, glancing at Bronc's bandaged leg.

"Most likely," Bronc said, his grin pinching into a grimace of pain. "You won't be lonely there . . . but we won't be seeing that one." He nodded toward the place where Doc had disappeared into the smoke and chaos.

Hunt nodded, his face wry. He'd figured Jake called the man "Doc" because he was a useless, spectacles-wearing dead weight who couldn't even use a gun. But the man was really a doctor, and one with more guts than any field surgeon he'd seen during the War.

He looked out at the battleground again, thinking there was only man he really wanted to see more than Doc right now . . . Jake Lonergan, with that arm weapon of his, dealing with the aliens the way he'd taken out Dolan.

BUT JAKE WAS otherwise occupied.

He had no trouble leading Ella back along his escape route. With all his senses functioning normally, following the glowing meshwork of the alien's artificial tunnel was a cakewalk.

But as they pushed deeper into the labyrinth of tunnels, Jake began to make out a faint, blue glow ahead: the unnatural light of the hidden stronghold, welcoming him back to Hell, with the promise that this time . . .

"*No modo," as they said in Mexico*: No way out. . . .

Jake stumbled against the wall, thrown off-balance as his memories overwhelmed his sight.

Ella put a hand on his arm. He looked down at her, felt her sharing his fear, sharing everything he remembered . . . until he couldn't tell whether the fear in her eyes belonged to him, or was only a reflection of what lay in her own mind and heart. *But he saw her determination, too— never to surrender; not to lose her sanity, or her soul, to the enemy. . . .*

Jake straightened away from the wall, nodding. *No turning back.* He fixed his eyes and his resolve on what lay ahead. "This way—"

They followed the branch tunnel that opened on the vast underworld of the main cavern. Jake felt waves of dry heat washing over them, glimpsed the strange clouds, the sulfurous glow from the pits that filled the immense space with fog, making it impossible to tell how many aliens were still inside.

But before they reached the tunnel's end they came on a side cave, shut away from the main area by a wall of stone. Jake stopped at the entrance, looking in as the light falling across their path struck his eyes.

They'd already found what they'd come for. The captives taken by the alien flyers were all there, inside . . . the ones who hadn't been used yet for experiments, or food.

Jake swore under his breath. At first glance, it looked like the prisoners had all been hanged—their heads fallen back, their eyes open and staring, their bodies suspended from the ceiling by the same cords that had pulled them up into the flyers. But then he looked down and saw their feet still resting on the ground. *Not dead—or anyway, he didn't think so.*

Undead. He remembered, now: *Unable to speak, to move, to do anything but stare at—*

"Jake!" Ella caught his arm. "Don't look up at the light. Only look at the people. Get the people free . . . and hurry."

He nodded, not understanding what she meant about the light, but obeying without question. *Time was their enemy now, as much as the aliens were.* Ella headed for the far end of the cave, checking as she went to be sure they weren't surprised by anything non-human, while Jake moved toward the nearest captives.

The metal spider-fingers that had stolen the prisoners from their lives and loved ones still held them captive, in an obscene embrace that made him want to look away. He forced himself to stare at the prisoners' faces while he pried loose the clutching bola bands, trying to ignore how their eyes reflected the light like marbles made of milk-glass. . . .

Jake moved from one victim to the next, seeing Maria, Doc's wife . . . Percy Dolarhyde . . . Sheriff

Taggart, Charlie Lyle, and members of his gang . . . mixed in with two or three dozen strangers: towns-folk and Apaches, men, women, and children. He began to pull them free faster as he got the feel for how to do it; prying people from the grasping lifeless hands, one after another.

But even after he released them, the captives didn't come back to life; they still stood listlessly, their eyes wide open, gazing upward. He tried not to think about it, not to wonder what they were seeing . . . not to believe there was something familiar about those eyes, as he went on pulling them free. *Don't look up.* Ella had warned him about the light. She'd know how to help them, what to do next. . . . *Don't look.* It didn't matter what they were staring at, all that mattered was getting them free—

Dammit, they weren't dead—why didn't they react? He looked up, finally unable to face another pair of empty, undead eyes without seeing what it was that still held them all prisoner. Overhead he saw the source of the flickering white light, a formless, pulsing . . . thing, not any kind of lamp he'd ever seen. He counted two, three of them, clamped to the ceil-ing like the cocoons of some unimaginable insect . . . like glowing masses of . . . of. . . .

. . . *Like moths to a flame. . . . He remembered, now . . . himself, Alice . . . nothing he could do . . . nothing anyone could do, not even look at each other. . . . The living dead, imprisoned in a cold dank meat locker, where brilliant white light flickered like a frightened heartbeat, and they couldn't look away. . . . Nothing . . . he was nothing, an insect held captive*

*by a flame; unable to move . . . unable to think or
even—*

A gun went off; the light that held him mesmerized exploded and went out. Phosphorescent slime
fell from the ceiling in clumps and long glowing
strands, covering the floor below. Ella fired twice
more, putting out the other lights forever.

Jake shook his head, shaking off his stupefaction,
and looked back at her, grateful again. He wondered
how she'd known the secret of the light; forced himself to remember again that she wasn't human—
knowing he'd never really convince himself. Maybe
her people didn't react the same way. *They're learning your weaknesses, she'd said. . . .*

Jake looked at the captives again: Ella had already
started pulling off more harnesses, freeing other prisoners. Jake joined her again, freeing people, making
sure they got their balance . . . moving on, until they
were all standing on their own two feet, alive.

"Sheriff?" Jake stood face to face with Taggart,
who was still staring at nothing, like all the rest. He
figured seeing the Scourge of the Territories ought to
wake the man out of his trance as fast as anything.

But the sheriff only gazed blankly at him; as if
Taggart didn't even remember his own identity, let
alone Jake Lonergan's. *He looked like he'd dropped
out of the sky. . . .*

Jake suddenly realized that all the captives still
looked the same way, even after they'd been freed
from their bonds and the light.

Shit. How were they supposed to get these people

moving—? "How long they gonna be like this?" he asked Ella.

She only shook her head, as she moved from one freed captive to the next, placing her hands on their temples. "—each one is different. . . ."

An energy beam exploded against the wall that only half shielded them from the main cavern. Jake saw two aliens emerge from a cloud of vapor, running toward them; his demon gun came alive as another bolt of energy struck the wall.

"Go!" Ella shouted. "Hold them off while I get the others out."

He moved to the edge of the opening, positioning himself to give her covering fire. "You'd better hurry—"

Ella motioned to the group of captives. To Jake's amazement and relief they all followed her, disappearing after her into the tunnels. He wondered how the hell she did that kind of thing.

He didn't wonder long, as another energy strike cut a gouge in the wall just above his head. He ducked under better cover and raised his arm, taking aim: The weapon was ready to fire; to save him, or itself. *Do it*— he thought, and let the damned gun do what it seemed to enjoy the most—try to destroy its creators.

"CHARGE THE LEFT flank!"

Outside on the battlefield, Dolarhyde fought a holding action, trying to keep his remaining men alive and together in the midst of chaos, in the middle of more and more death and destruction. The explosions from the weapons the aliens used as handguns were worse than cannon fire, tearing up the already treacherous earth, endangering his shrinking force all the more.

"Rear rank, close up!" Looking back over his shoulder Dolarhyde didn't see the alien that came at him, and slammed sideways into his horse. Dolarhyde went down with the falling animal, barely managing to kick free of his stirrups before it crushed his leg. He landed hard on the ground beside his floundering mount, scrambled backward as the alien leaped toward him, stabbing its lethal claws into the ground where he'd just been. It lunged at him again, too fast—

Nat Colorado swerved his horse and charged the alien, pulling his rope from the saddle as he came. He spun out the loop at its end and dropped the lasso over the monster's head like he was bulldogging a steer. His horse stopped dead on his signal, already backing up while he pulled the rope taut. The alien screeched in fury as its striking talons missed Dolarhyde by inches.

But before Nat could hitch the rope tight around his saddle horn, the monster's taloned hand gripped the line between them and yanked him from the saddle. The alien was on him the minute he hit the ground; its fanged jaws opened, and it sank its teeth into his shoulder. Nat screamed in pain.

Dolarhyde emptied his pistol into the alien's body, all the bullets striking home, staggering it—but still it refused to go down. It turned toward him again, raising its massive arm.

A bullet struck the alien in the face, shattering its left eye—a direct hit, through a vulnerable spot. The alien toppled and crashed to the ground, finally taken down by the group attack.

Dolarhyde looked up, dazed, searching the canyon's slope for the shooter. He saw Doc perched in the rocks above him, Meacham's rifle still up against his shoulder after the surgical precision of his kill shot.

Doc glanced up at the sky, "Thank you for the steady hand, Preacher," he said, and smiled.

Dolarhyde got to his feet with a heavy sigh of relief. Turning back, he saw Nat lying on the ground, in a widening pool of red. "Doc!" he shouted. "Get down here!"

Dolarhyde kneeled by Nat's head, pulling off his coat to try and stop the bleeding. "Come on, boy—" he murmured, as Nat's eyes opened, looking up at him, "easy now, easy—don't move. . . ."

He wiped away enough blood to get a glimpse of the wound, and saw an artery spurting. He pressed his coat against it, trying to use the pressure of his hand to stanch the relentless blood.

Blood ran from Nat's mouth, and he began to choke. Dolarhyde cradled Nat's head on his knees, trying to help him catch his breath . . . recognizing all the signs he'd seen too many times before. *But not like this time, never like this*—

"Did we . . . get one?" Nat asked, his face unafraid, burning with the need to know.

Dolarhyde felt like his heart was being pulled out through his eyes. A thousand things it was too late to say crowded each other for space in his mind. He managed a weak smile. "Yeah," he said. "We got one." Looking up again, he shouted "*Doc*!"

"How bad is it?" Nat whispered. His eyes were glazing over with shock.

"You're gonna be alright. . . ." Dolarhyde laid a hand on Nat's forehead, stroking his hair the way he had long ago, when Nat was still a grieving boy whose nightmares woke them both. "I'm here with you." His voice barely held out for long enough to speak the words. He tried to control his expression, the only thing left in the universe that he had any control over—to keep it calm and reassuring, while Nat's lifeblood ran out through his fingers.

Nat looked up at him, and for a moment his eyes cleared as memory shone through. "I always dreamed . . . of riding into battle . . . with you."

Dolarhyde broke the knot of grief that kept him from words, finally able to say, only now, the one thing that he'd needed to say since forever. "I always dreamed of having a son like you."

Nat stared up at him, his face stunned, as if he couldn't believe he'd heard those words outside of a dream. Dolarhyde took his hand, held it tightly in his own. He felt Nat's hand close around it with the last of his strength. Dolarhyde held his adopted son's gaze, as he held his hand, willing him to believe.

Nat smiled up at him, and at last there was no trace of the lost soul that had been there behind his eyes through so many long years, when Dolarhyde had never been able to see it. Now there was only peace, as if this final moment of connection was all he had ever really wanted, or needed. "Go . . . get Percy. . . ." Nat whispered, and his eyes closed.

Dolarhyde kneeled on the earth, still holding Nat's body, although Nat was no longer there to realize it; unable to let him go. He wasn't certain why his own heart was still beating, when it seemed to him that it had taken a fatal wound along with his adopted son.

The fighting went on around him, but the sounds seemed far away, the world beyond touching him as he protected Nat . . . until he could bear to acknowledge at last that Nat's soul was gone from this field of battle, this world of pain and sorrow.

Doc was standing beside him as he looked up at last. Doc's face was filled with compassion, all that he could offer; because it had always been too late to do anything for a wound like that.

And beyond Doc, Dolarhyde saw Black Knife standing, with his warriors gathered around him. Black Knife raised his upturned palm to the sky, acknowledging Nat's passage to another plane.

Dolarhyde stared at him, as he saw the sorrow, the profound comprehension of his own loss, on the *nantan*'s face; emotions he never would have seen there—or been able to recognize if he had—before this moment.

The Apaches loved their children, too. Slowly Dolarhyde realized what had drawn the Apache leader and his warriors down onto the field of battle at last . . . and what it implied.

He laid Nat's head carefully on the ground, and

rose to his feet. Black Knife offered him a rifle. Dol-arhyde accepted it, with a nod. They mounted their horses, and rode back into battle.

This time, he knew, human beings would truly be fighting as a united force at last. The aliens weren't invulnerable; to be united was all they needed to be, now, to win this fight—

18

Ella led the freed captives to within sight of the tunnel entrance, where they had the genuine light of day to guide them to freedom. Keeping so many confused people moving in the same direction, the right direction, had taken longer than she'd expected. She glanced back, sensing no signs of pursuit, and still no trace of Jake.

"We have to keep going," she said again, to remind herself, as much as to make it clear to the others. She had given her word to the humans fighting and dying outside that the captives would be freed, and she would not go back on it. But that wasn't her final duty here. . . .

Sheriff Taggart looked at her this time as she spoke, and a trace of recognition showed in his eyes. "Do I know you?"

"Yes, Sheriff," she said, smiling her encouragement, "you know me. Emmett is waiting for you—your grandson."

Taggart's eyes showed real recognition, even concern, at the sound of his grandson's name. "Emmett—where's Emmett?"

Ella held his gaze, willing his mind to reach further, remember more: Remember who he was, what he had been, *remember his duty.* . . . "You have to get everyone out to the light, do you understand?" *To safety . . . remember your duty . . . to keep them all safe.* . . .

Taggart nodded, his eyes looking at her with genuine comprehension now. She stepped aside, as he began to act on his returning memories, taking her place as leader of the group as they all moved on toward the entrance, drawn toward the true meaning of the light at the end of the tunnel. . . .

JAKE FINALLY FINISHED off the second of the two aliens, and allowed himself to take a deep breath of relief. They'd been a damn sight harder to take down when they weren't caught by surprise: as fast as roaches, and as deadly with their light-weapon as he was.

He'd begun to think their own weapons protected them a lot better than his did, until he'd gotten lucky with his shots and hit a couple of vulnerable spots. He'd been even luckier that they hadn't hit any of his—he remembered what the weapon had done to Dolan.

Finishing the fight had driven him out of hiding, he suddenly noticed, and into the main cavern. He searched the space around him for movement, not seeing any other aliens. The weapon closed up again, as if it felt safe . . . but he knew better by now than to believe it was telling him everything.

The cavern could've held half the town of Absolution; he couldn't be sure the demons were all outside, through the clouds of steam or whatever it was that fogged the space around him. Its form was constantly shifting under cold blue lights or in bright-hot hellshine. All around him he saw the strange shapes of things he remembered from his dream, although he had no more clue as to what they were than he'd had when he first saw them.

It was hot in here, not cool, like caverns usually were. He realized this must be where the aliens' entire ore-smelting process went on, as they extracted gold from the stone they'd stripped out of the mesa's interior. He wondered if this place actually held their entire mining operation. It didn't look like any kind of mine he'd ever seen. *But then, he was probably being an ass to think it would—*

He looked up, and up, realizing the cavern was almost as high as it was wide and deep, although he couldn't really make out the ceiling. *Jesus God, they must have eaten out the whole inside of the mesa. How could anyone—anything—even do that . . . and where the hell had they put the tailings?*

He became aware of something suspended from the heights, filling the middle of the space all the way to the ground. His mind couldn't even begin to picture what it was, until he suddenly remembered Ella saying, *"The rest of the ship is underground."*

The real base of the ship: that had to be what it

was. The rest must be mining equipment, and supplies, and ways of dividing up the space. . . . He turned slowly where he stood, gazing around as his mind tried to hold onto a reality that kept trying to warp beyond recognition.

He saw and remembered the streams of golden tears rising in lines into the air . . . or were they falling? . . . as tall glowing cylinders crept along the walls, eating away at the stone—mining it. They were machines, like the flyer, moving as if they had minds of their own, although this time he couldn't see anyone—anything—even directing them. He moved closer to one, fascinated, feeling the heat that radiated from it as he watched the streaming tears of gold.

Was that real gold, being processed from the rocks? Or was it beads of heated light—some kind of bound lightning, like the blue beam from his weapon? The urge to put out his hand and touch a glowing strand, to find out what the golden tears really were, was almost irresistible. He resisted, remembering that either of those things would burn his hand off.

He turned suddenly to find Ella at his side. "What the hell are you doing back here?" he asked, surprised, worried, and caught off-guard as usual, as she found him gawking like a damn fool at the aliens' machine.

But she smiled at him, and her smile said she was more than relieved to find him in one piece; her glance reassured him that everything was all right—*the captives were free*. She looked at the mining machines, and her smile disappeared; she stared at them like he had, as if even she was horribly fascinated by something about them.

But then she turned away, gesturing at the ship. As if she expected he'd be smart enough to figure out what that was, she said, "When they realize what's going on, they'll pull up anchor and leave. We won't be able to hold them long."

Her face looked deadly serious again. She started away, leading him toward the ship. She holstered her gun as she walked and unbuckled her gun belt, handing it to him. "I need the bracelet. Take it off."

Jake took the gun belt from her, out of habit, without understanding what she'd just said. "What for?" he asked, as he cinched on the belt.

"I think I can use it to stop the ship from leaving."

He started, and glanced down at his wrist. "I can't get it off—" He touched the sleeping weapon with his hand.

"Yes you can," she said, with that way she had.

"How?" Jake asked.

"Same way you shoot it, with your mind." She was starting to look at him now like he was slow in the head.

He glanced at the metal cuff, thinking maybe she was right, since he'd never had any idea how it worked. The only time it had done what he'd wanted was when he freed Ella from the flyer. But that was . . . different. He'd never even known why the gun had latched onto him in the first place, any more than he'd understood the rest of it.

Unless the gun hadn't seen any difference between him and the aliens . . . him and a demon.

But he wasn't a demon; he was a human being— Maybe the thing had never understood him, either.

All he knew was that if Ella needed it, the gun was going to figure him out, right now— He stared at the weapon, thinking, *Get off me, you bloodsucking leech. I don't want you. I don't belong to you. . . . Goddammit, go to her . . . she needs you—!* Trying every possible order, demand, curse or threat that came into his mind. He tried to force his fingers under its edge, uselessly, as his frustration grew. "*This is not working.*"

"*Stop thinking.* Look at me." Ella's eyes met his, and their gazes locked; he felt her draw his mind into a place of almost ethereal calm.

She was the real Morning Star, come down out of the sky to save his world. . . . He remembered her as she walked out of the fire, glowing with unearthly light, walking toward him . . . remembered her standing on the hilltop, gazing up at the stars. . . .

"I told you, stop thinking," Ella said. He could have sworn her cheeks showed a faint blush.

"I'm not thinking!" he said. But how could he not think about her, when just looking at her made him weak in the knees, and not with fear. . . .

Alice had made him believe there might be more to him—something good, that made his existence here more than just a blight on the world. . . . *But Ella made him believe anything was possible . . . made him believe there might be something good in every human being, if they only had the chance to prove it—*

Ella pulled him into her arms and pressed her mouth against his in a kiss filled with frustration, desperation . . . *loneliness, as deep and vast as the space between the stars. . . .*

Jake's arms went around her and he kissed her back, the way he'd wanted to kiss her last night on the starry hill. He answered her with all the passion for life, the hunger for love, the human need that he'd buried under a pile of stones so deep he'd almost forgotten they had ever existed inside him. . . . Feeling the human warmth of her body, her lips on his, *her sudden aching hunger, impossible to separate from his own.* . . .

She kissed him then with all the longing of some-one who'd denied passion, need . . . any love that could touch her heart or soul too deeply . . . longer ago than he could imagine: terrified of her own vul-nerability after so much pain. . . .

She'd willingly abandoned herself when she be-came a warrior in a cause that was greater, more universal, more important than any individual's heart or mind, body or soul.

Until now, here, trapped in the paradox of this hu-man form she wore, with its brain so entangled with its body's needs, logic and emotion so intimately bound to each other that her struggle to reach the conflicted soul of one outcast human man had brought it all back to her—the true reason why she had chosen to fight, and what exactly it was that she had really been fighting for, for so long. . . .

Jake understood, with every fiber of his being, as the barrier between their separate minds vanished, and everything they were became one: *She couldn't go on, now, without letting him know, letting herself remember, the only emotion that had ever created something out of nothing, instead of tearing down all of existence . . . the one true thing that could make his people, and her own, into something more than the ruthless monsters they fought to save themselves from—*

I love you, Jake thought, and when she answered him he felt as if the universe itself reached through her, and touched him. . . .

There was an odd small *chik* as the demon gun's lock unset, as the aliens' manacle sprang open and dropped from his wrist, setting him free.

The moment outside of space and time ended: Ella's arms were no longer around him, and he had to let her go. The weapon lay on the floor like a lifeless piece of scrap metal.

Ella picked it up; she hesitated, looking at him again with an unearthly light still shining in her eyes, and the strangest, saddest, most joyful smile he'd ever seen. And then she turned and started away, circling the base of the ship, touching a deliberate sequence of different-colored metals on the weapon's seemingly dead surface as she moved.

Jake shook off his bedazzlement and followed her, scanning the shifting clouds around them, the shadowed crevices and blind corners, for anything more substantial than a shadow. For the smile she'd given him by that lake in the desert, he'd willingly led her back into Hell. For the way she'd left him feeling now, he'd willingly follow her beyond forever. . . .

A series of flashing lights appeared on the demons' weapon. Jake heard a faint rising whine like the sound of a distant engine struggling to pull an overloaded train— *Energy building up . . . in a weapon that fired energy like a bolt of lightning.*

He realized she meant for the thing to explode. He couldn't even imagine what would happen if something like that released all its energy at once; it would make being struck by lightning seem like spring rain.

"I have to go inside." Ella stopped, looking up at the side of the ship again. "It's the only way—if I get into its core I can stop them."

Jake looked up too, seeing some kind of open hatchway, and a dark tunnel that led God only knew where, into what kind of danger. "I'm coming with you."

"No." She shook her head. "This isn't my home, Jake. It isn't my destiny to stay."

He blinked, not understanding her sudden refusal. "I'm not letting you go up there alo—"

The energy beam from an alien weapon exploded the ground inches from their feet. They took cover behind an outcrop of rock by the base of the ship; more weapons-fire burst around them, pinning them there.

Jake peered through a crack in the rocks. He saw three aliens advancing on them. . . . The one in the lead had a red scar distorting its face.

That scar. . . . He remembered that scar, from his dream: He'd put that scar there, with the one of the aliens' own cutters. . . . *Alice—*

For a second, memory blinded him again. He forced his vision clear, vengeance and cold fury burning away the echoes of the past.

His eyes went to Ella again, trapped between impossible choices. He had no time to think about it, as Ella turned toward the side of the ship, reaching up to find handholds on its surface. She began to climb, her focus completely on the task she had come to accomplish, now, with the demon weapon she'd made into a stick of alien dynamite clutched tightly in her hand. He caught hold of her and boosted her up as far as he could toward the opening; with a quick scramble, she was inside.

"You *are* a good man," she murmured, looking down at him from the open hatchway. Her eyes, her mind, insisted that whatever he believed, whoever he'd been before, those words had always been the truth, and always would be. . . . "Goodbye, Jake."

She disappeared into the tunnel; the hatch began to close after her.

"No— *Wait*!" Jake reached up, gripping handholds to climb after her.

Another beam of blue light scarred the ship's side just above his hands, leaving him no choice: Ella had to do what she'd come here to do. He had to buy her the time to do it. He drew his revolver, and his finger pinned back the trigger.

He ran out into the demons' line of sight, getting them into his own sights at the same time, and fanned the revolver's hammer, not thinking, just reacting, letting his perfectly honed reflexes take over. He couldn't afford to fail her, or fail himself, now.

Against all the odds, he made a perfect five-shot run: The first bullet hit Red Scar in the neck and sent it stumbling back, screeching. The next two struck the second alien in the eyes, blinding it; two more hit the third one's temple.

Red Scar retreated into the steam; its eyes fixed him with an implacable stare. Jake met the red-eyed stare with his own unrelenting hatred before the demon disappeared from sight. He kept moving forward.

When Red Scar had vanished, Jake snapped open the barrel of his pistol, clearing shells out of the chamber, reloading all six chambers with mindless efficiency. No point in playing it safe now; if the gun went off, even by accident, he'd make sure it hit something besides himself. . . .

He closed in on the blinded alien where it lay thrashing on the ground, and took aim. The gunshot echoed as he put a slug through its head. The second one had managed to get up and away, but he was sure it wouldn't get far.

He moved on without stopping. He had no idea how many men he might've killed, in the lost years of his past . . . but right now, for Ella's sake, he'd just become the deadliest killer who'd ever lived. And the alien hunters had just become his prey. . . .

As Ella worked her way inward from the loading hatch, she listened to the sound of gunfire . . . a projectile gun, Jake's real weapon. The last image of him caught by her still-human eyes was a blur of motion as he drew the enemy away.

She could still reach him with her mind, hearing what he heard, seeing what he saw: Four more gunshots followed the first, faster than her own heartbeat, and she saw every bullet strike a vulnerable point with deadly accuracy: a lone man with an inefficient weapon actually halting three invaders, driving them back in confusion, killing them. . . .

She glimpsed at last what it was about this man that had made his own people fear him so much that they'd wanted him dead. And yet that same man had willingly offered himself as a moving target, going after the aliens with a vengeance driven not simply by hatred, or even righteous anger, but also by love, and need—the need to set her free to save his people from annihilation. . . .

His kiss still burned on her human lips; the memory of all that had passed between them in a moment that had seemed to stop time still stunned her mind and her human senses.

But far more, the epiphany of that moment had erased all doubt in her that her cause was just, that these people were worth saving . . . and that she still possessed the most precious part of her own soul.

She forced herself to stop following Jake with her mind as he disappeared into the clouds of steam, pursuing the two aliens that were still moving. She was running out of time to finish her own task—

The access would eventually lead her, unsuspected and unseen, to the ship's vulnerable core, where she could use the enemy's own weapon against them. Jake was risking his life for her, and for his people; she wasn't about to repay his final gift to her with failure.

*   *   *

THE BATTLEFIELD OUTSIDE had spread to fill the entire slot canyon, and threatened to spill out into the wider valley beyond.

Black Knife turned his horse toward the aliens, leading a group of mounted warriors across the open ground; banishing all thoughts of fighting like the *pindah*'s cavalry, because against this enemy, even the ways of his own people had not been enough. He led his people in this attack not simply as *nantan* but as a *di-yin* of war, one whose gift was meant to protect them and guide them to victory.

He had finally been given the sign he had been waiting for to commit his warriors completely to fight side by side with the white-eyes, and it had come in a way he had never expected—the death of Nat Colorado, the *pindah* leader's adopted son. The anguish of a white father's grief for his lost Apache son had been a far more profound sign from the gods than any he had ever witnessed . . . except when the dead woman's body emerged from the fire, not to bring ghost sickness upon them all, but instead returning to life, renewed, shining with the spirit of the Morning Star.

To witness two such things within so short a time could only mean that the gods meant for them to fight alongside the *pindah*, that these sky monsters were the greater threat to their existence, now and forever, unless the invaders could be stopped here.

He now carried a spear, a weapon used only for fighting close-in, carried only by the bravest of men— like the ones who rode with him now. His spear had been with him through many battles; bound to its tip was a bayonet taken from a soldier's gun. Only by getting that close could he even imagine bringing such creatures down. But he still did not see how they could kill so many of these things. . . .

The alien nearest them heard their approach and turned suddenly, raising a light-weapon aimed directly at Black Knife; he couldn't turn his horse fast enough to escape.

But then he saw the *pindah* leader, driving his own horse straight at the monster's turned back, as if he meant to ride right through it. The man and his horse slammed into the alien before it could fire, and Black Knife's own horse collided with it as it flew forward.

Both men were knocked from their horses by the collision, flying off in different directions as the alien went down with them.

But compared to the two men, the monster seemed barely to register the shock of the collision or its landing. It struggled to its feet again, turning its wrath and its enormous taloned arm toward the *pindah* to take its revenge.

Black Knife saw his spear lying nearby and caught it up. He ran at the sky monster and drove the point through its clawed hand, burying the spear deeply in the ground before the talons could be driven through the *pindah's* heart . . . repaying his blood debt to the man.

The sky monster writhed and struggled, trying to pull free, until suddenly another spear pierced it through the slit in its chest. The monster slumped to the ground, finally dead.

Black Knife looked up to see who—

The *pindah* leader jerked the spear he held out of the dead monster's chest, and looked at Black Knife. The man's blue eyes were no longer on fire with hatred for him, but shining with satisfaction. Their eyes met in understanding at last, and now Black Knife fully understood the will of the gods. The sky monsters were not impossible to defeat . . . but only if the *pindah* and his own warriors fought against their common enemy, as if they truly *were* one people. . . .

The warriors and the other *pindah* who had witnessed what they had done looked around at one another. Their own expressions were changing as they finally saw a monster die, and the reason for it; their desperation and helpless anger began to turn back into resolution and courage. They split up and rode away in twos and threes, working as one, to turn the battle against an enemy that had thought they had nothing to fear.

"GODDAMMIT," HUNT MUTTERED to the others still trapped with him behind the berm. "Look at that! There's enough of us—we gotta do something!" Because they'd been among the first riders into the canyon, they'd been among the first to lose their horses and weapons to the aliens Jake had tried to warn them about. For once, Jake's silver tongue had failed to do something justice. . . . *Or maybe they just plain hadn't believed him.*

"Do what?" Bronc said irritably, his hands pressing his injured leg. "We got nothin'." Bronc didn't even have a cigar on him, but he did have a point . . . and he had the wound to prove it. Any time one of them had tried to make a move—to grab a horse or even a rifle—he'd been targeted by an alien weapon, or nearly cut down by crossfire from guns and arrows. And every time the berm took another hit, or the brush around it was incinerated, they were left with less of the protection that was barely covering their asses.

There was an alien demon standing near them right now, not twenty feet away. Jake was right, these things couldn't see for shit. But there was nothing wrong with the demons' hearing. If they made a move on this lone empty-handed one, Hunt figured that would be the last move any of them made.

"I got an idea. . . ." Bull said. The others watched in sudden apprehension as he groped inside his shirt and pulled out a stick of dynamite.

"Where'd you get that?" Hunt asked, not asking what he'd been saving it for.

"Where d'you think?" Bull grinned as he fished in his shirt pocket, removing a piece of fuse cord and a match. He took out the knife he always carried in his boot. The others said nothing, afraid to speak, as Bull set the fuse and tied the stick of dynamite to his knife with extra cord. He struck the match against his stubbled cheek, and lit the fuse.

Before Hunt or Bronc could even form words, he was up out of the ditch, running at the alien. He leaped onto its back as it started to turn, and sank the knife into its neck, or what passed for one, beneath the carapace that shielded its head. He looked back at them in triumph—for the split second before the dynamite went off, and they both disappeared in a cloud of black smoke.

The others covered their heads as the explosion swept over the berm. When they raised their heads again, there was nothing recognizable left to see.

"*Vaya con Dios. . . .*" Bronc murmured, crossing himself. "*Idiota.*"

"Amen to that." Hunt pushed cautiously to his feet. "Come on," he said, offering Bronc a hand up. "Battle's not over yet—let's get in it. Ain't neither of us was born to die in bed. . . ."

EMMETT WATCHED THE battle spreading out below; his breath caught every time he saw a human fighter go down, or the hulking form of another alien monster. He'd read stories about heroes, about men like his grandpa—even stories about men who fought monsters.

But to see it with his own eyes: the men who fell covered in blood . . . to hear their cries of pain . . . the earsplitting sound of weapons-fire, the horrible screeching of the aliens; to smell the stench of black powder smoke and burning vegetation. . . . *It was nothing like the stories. Nothing at all.*

His eyes stung as he remembered the times his grandfather had ridden off with the deputies, leaving Emmett behind because it was too dangerous, saying that he was too young. Always trying to protect him from the truth . . . a truth too awful for a child to bear.

But did Grandpa really think he was such a kid

that he hadn't understood what words like that meant—that he didn't understand that one day his grandfather might not come home . . . that he'd be left all alone?

He'd rather have gone with him a hundred times, endured all the hardships, witnessed all the horrors, than to wait and wait at home, never knowing whether this would be the time Grandpa didn't come back—

Emmett didn't know if the tears that blurred his vision were from grief or from anger. He wiped his eyes clear and turned his head. As he did the dog, lying beside him, suddenly got to its feet and began to growl. Emmett lowered the spyglass, following the direction of its stare. *Oh, no*—

One of the aliens, searching just like he was, was climbing up the rocks below him.

Emmett stuffed the scope into his shirt and put his arms around the dog, trying to pull it back down. "Quiet!" he whispered frantically.

But the alien looked up at the sound and spotted them; it fired a light-weapon, shattering the boulder near Emmett as he and the dog scattered in different directions.

Emmett scrambled down the back of the ridge, searching for a place to hide. He saw a small, narrow cleft in the twisted mass of rocks and squeezed into it, pulling his feet up. Holding his breath in the sudden silence, he tried to tell if the alien had followed him. *Please God,* he thought, as memories from the riverboat filled his eyes to brimming again, *don't let it get me, please, please. . . .*

He cried out in surprise as the monster's face appeared right in front of him and tried to force its way in between the stones, its jaws snapping savagely.

Emmett shrank back against the rocks behind him, even as he realized the head was too big to force its way further in. He let out a sob of fear, more than relief, as images of being trapped in the riverboat overlaid his sight . . . *the demon that had almost killed him, but had killed Preacher Meacham instead.*

The alien's chest opened, and its rubbery secondary arms began to unfold, reaching into the crevice to grab him, and drag him out—

"Be a man," Mr. Dolarhyde had said to him. He'd been nothing but a scared kid the last time, forgetting he even had his knife; and because of that, the preacher had died trying to save him. . . .

Dammit, he'd been through this before. This time he was all alone . . . but he wasn't a helpless baby. This time he knew what he had to do—

As the grasping fingers caught in his clothing, his own hands dropped to the sheath on his belt and pulled out the Bowie knife. As the monster began to drag him from the crevice he launched himself at it, the cry in his throat turning to fury as his hands drove the knife into the exposed place between the alien's forearms.

The alien jerked back with a hideous shriek, dragging him with it.

And then it fell to its knees, its head drooping forward. Its arms released him, as it slowly toppled over backwards.

Emmett rolled off of it and crouched on the ground beside it, gasping with disbelief. The knife Mr. Dolarhyde had given him protruded from the alien's chest, driven in up to its hilt, with green blood seeping out around it. . . . The thing was dead; he'd killed it.

Emmett sat back, stunned, as the dog found him again, and began to lick his face.

BY THE TIME Emmett was back on his watchman's perch, he could see that something down on the field had changed, as profoundly as his own life just had up here in the rocks. The humans were gaining ground; Apaches and white men were fighting side by side, but in small groups now. He watched Black Knife and two other men taking on a single alien—saw one of the riders go down, as the second man leaped from his horse onto the alien's back, slamming a war club into its skull. As it fell, Black Knife thrust his spear through what passed for its heart.

All the aliens were beginning to fall back now, breaking away toward the shelter of their fortress-ship—scrabbling up the canyon side to reenter the ports above, because they were cut off from reaching the hidden entrance below. Shouts of victory from human throats reached Emmett's ears, another sound of battle he'd never heard before, but one that made him blink and smile.

He turned the spyglass toward the tunnel where he'd been waiting to see the human captives being led to freedom. *Still no sign of them.* . . . His smile fell away; he turned back to watch the battle.

* * *

DOWN ON THE field, Doc moved on from patching up another injured man. He pulled his pistol, cocking it, as he approached a wounded alien writhing in the dirt. He hesitated, thinking about life and death ... picturing Maria's face.... "Hold on," he said, looking down at the alien. "I wanted to give you something before you go—"

He fired his pistol into the thing twice, but it still thrashed on the ground, shrilling and screeching.

Standing well out if its reach, Doc smiled grimly. "Don't worry, plenty more where that came from—" Taking more care with his aim, he fired the pistol until the hammer clicked on the empty chamber, and the alien had stopped moving, for good.

"I got a perfect spot on my wall for you. . . ." He studied its hideous-looking head as he reloaded his pistol. A faint smile pulled at the corners of his mouth. "I'll bet you're probably handsome, for your kind, huh?"

He looked up, as an eerie deep thrumming filled the air, coming from the direction of the alien ship. *My God,* he thought. *It was getting ready to leave—*

DEEP INSIDE THE entrails of the alien ship, Ella stopped moving as she felt the vibration and heard the whine begin all around her, as the ship's departure sequence engaged, building up power. It was happening already: The ship was getting ready to leave.

So soon—? She had been afraid the humans fighting

outside would be overwhelmed by the sheer strength of their enemies and killed before they ever saw what they had to see. . . . That they had to stand and fight together—believe that their shared humanity outweighed their individual differences—or every one of them would die, alone. . . .

Jake— she thought, knowing that she couldn't reach him, couldn't touch his mind from here. But even with an entire world at stake, she couldn't stop this willful human body from thinking of one single man, or feeling torn by memories as she left him behind . . . afraid for his life, afraid he'd refuse to leave her . . . or that he'd never understand how much she loved him, with all the heart he had given back to her. . . .

To remember what love was. . . . He had been the one, at last, who'd given her what she needed to keep her strong, to keep her sane, to keep her from being consumed by the bitterness of her own revenge. The last man on Earth she would have expected to understand . . . the best man she would ever know . . . the one man she would hold in her memory, forever.

Now, for the sake of the greater good, for the sake of his life and the lives of all his people, she had to leave Jake behind, forget this human body with its human heart that loved him too . . . all too soon, forever. *Please, please, Jake, get out, get far away from here, while there's still time—*

She scrambled on, moving ever forward, closing in on the brilliant light source that was the ship's core.

* * *

DOLARHYDE RODE TOWARD the canyon mouth near the arroyo that led to Jake's secret entrance. *Still no one there*—no freed captives, no Ella or Jake. He looked toward the rocky outcrop where he'd stationed Emmett, not able to see him or hear anything beyond the ominous vibration that was coming from inside the mesa where the aliens' ship lay.

Just as he was about to call out, Emmett stood up on the ridge, waving his arms—the signal that the captives had finally all made it out of the cavern. "I see them!" Emmett hollered. "They went around the other side!"

"Percy?" Dolarhyde shouted.

"Yeah!" Emmett shouted back, and Dolarhyde almost thought he could see the boy's grin from here.

"What about Jake—and Ella?" Dolarhyde called. He saw the flash of the spyglass as Emmett raised it again to scan the gathering of captives.

"No!"

The relief vanished from Dolarhyde's face. He turned his horse and rode toward the arroyo with his rifle in his hand.

19

In the shadowed cavern, the alien that Jake had hit in the side of the head with two bullets still lived, still moved, barely. Green blood oozed down the side of its skull, its breath came in harsh gasps, as it searched . . . searching for . . .

Jake stepped out of a vapor-shrouded shadow directly behind it. He fired one shot through the side of its head as it tried to turn back; it dropped to the ground, unmoving.

Jake eased past the enormous body and went on, barely aware of the rising noise and vibration coming from the ship. He could only focus on Ella, somewhere inside it, and what she intended to do: *to finish her mission, to save a world of strangers . . . to give the demons another dose of payback.*

He thought about Alice, who'd only wanted to live in peace. His own mission wasn't complete yet, either; not until he found Red Scar. Not until he'd taken revenge for her . . . and killed his own personal demon—

INSIDE THE SHIP, Ella had reached the inner limits. She forced herself in through the opening to the most claustrophobic crawl space yet. Her human body shuddered as the intestine-like surface of the walls clung to it, afraid of suffocation, in what looked to be an impossible, impenetrable trap, with no way back, no way out. . . . *No other way but through,* she told it, as she forced it to continue wriggling and ripping through the gelatinous gut, into the belly of the beast. . . .

The ship's systems were still building up power, but she could tell by the sound that they hadn't committed a hundred percent of it to liftoff yet. They were probably still trying to suck in as much gold as possible—the riches they had stripped from a barren land, stolen from the people who struggled to survive there. Their greed—their insatiable, remorseless, predatory minds—would never think any other way, even as they were forced to flee by the very people they had wronged and underestimated so badly.

Like a monkey with its fist stuck in a candy jar. The peculiar image that human saying had put into her head had made her laugh the first time she'd heard it. Now it seemed all too appropriate. *The enemy had made that mistake before, and lost more than a handful of gold. . . .*

She held the flashing weapon clutched in a death-grip as she tore at the membranous barrier, as the gun's mindlessly quickening pulse of light and sound continued counting down to the moment, not far off now, when its self-destruct would trigger.

JAKE MOVED CAREFULLY around yet another blind corner in the maze of alien machinery beneath the keening, vibrating ship . . . and froze.

There in front of him were the two rack-like oper-ating tables from his dream, spotlit by a flood of harsh blue-white light.

Here—it was still here, the torture chamber, just as he'd seen it in his nightmares. . . .

He stumbled as his feet caught on something, and he looked down. He was standing in a pile of human belongings, a vast tangle of clothing stripped from the aliens' victims—from settlers, from Apaches . . . gunbelts, rifles, high moccasins and boots, dresses and jackets, shirts and pants . . . a hundred different gold-plated pocket watches, gold-colored spectacles and keys . . . children's toys.

His mind tried desperately, and failed, to keep re-ality and nightmare from merging . . . *as he saw himself pinned down, helpless, ready for dissec-tion . . . Alice, unmoving, staring through him, as the monster that had tortured her to death turned her mutilated body to ash . . . left to the wind, until no trace of her existence remained . . . while the demon moved on, to him. . . . A scalpel cutting him open, the blade of burning light. . . . A beam of light in his own hand, carving a gouge across the alien butcher's face....*

Oh, God.... He remembered his first sight of Red Scar this time, as he realized why it looked familiar: *How it had looked back at him like it remembered him, too....*

And he didn't have the demon gun anymore. He began to tremble, the way he had when he'd lain on the table; his nervous system felt like somebody had cut the telegraph wire to his brain. He couldn't look away from the tables, couldn't stop seeing double, seeing phantoms ... *Alice* ... *himself....*

No, no—stop it, he had to—

Everything in his sight tilted crazily as heavy arms seized him from behind, jerking him off his feet. Light and darkness smeared together as Red Scar lifted him into the air and slammed him down.

He landed on his back on the dissection table. Red Scar's taloned hands pinned him there. Jake struggled like a fish thrown onto dry land, until one of Red Scar's finger-claws came to rest across his throat, as its hand circled his head. One move, and his throat would be slit clear to his backbone. The alien was too big, a living weapon, impossibly strong ... there was nothing he could do.

No modo.... no way out....

Red Scar hovered over him, its pupilless red eyes gazing down into his, as if it could actually see the terror he couldn't control ... *God, as if it was enjoying this*—Fury pushed up through his fear, but it was no more use to him now than fear was, or pain.

He watched the alien's armored chest flaps retract,

saw the small instrument-using arms unfolding. The cold, clinging inhuman fingers began to poke and prod at him, trying to touch his open eyes, exploring his face and the rest of his body inch by inch. He whimpered like a child, his eyes shut tight—not even able to turn his face away, but ready to turn himself inside out, if it would only make those hideous maggot fingers stop *touching* him—

The feel of crawling, prodding fingers suddenly disappeared. He heard the click and clatter as Red Scar picked up something from the tray of torture instruments. One of the deft, translucent hands activated a light-beam dissecting tool, like the one that had cut a hole in his side . . . *like the one that had torn open Alice* . . . and guided it toward him, ready at last to finish what it had begun.

Jake cringed and shut his eyes tighter, holding his last breath—

"*Hey*," a man's voice said. A very familiar voice.

Jake opened his eyes, to see Red Scar's head rise as it looked away. Jake dared to lift his own head, just enough to see the barrel of a rifle . . . and Woodrow Dolarhyde standing behind it.

Red Scar swung around, aiming a blow at Dolarhyde. Dolarhyde dodged backward, colliding with the wall: he fired the gun even as he lost his balance and fell.

Red Scar screeched, staggering. Wounded but far from dead, it left Jake lying on his deathbed as it went after Dolarhyde.

Jake flung himself off the table the moment he was free, running for the rifle. He grabbed up the gun—*his old favorite, a lever-action Winchester '66.* He cocked and fired it once, twice, knocking Red Scar away from Dolarhyde before the alien could finish the job of killing him.

Red Scar reeled sideways and then backward as it tried to turn and face him, but Jake fired again, and again, driving Red Scar back toward a glowing river suspended impossibly in the air. The fluid poured into the alien ship's belly like whiskey from a bottomless bottle in a drunkard's dream. The river was well over Jake's head, but not Red Scar's. Red Scar hesitated as it felt the waves of heat radiating from whatever was flowing past.

Jake cocked the rifle, and fired the last bullet in the magazine. Red Scar crashed backward into the ribbon of fluid.

Whatever illusion held the fluid suspended, the impact of Red Scar's body shattered it. The stream burst free and poured down onto the alien's head, covering its body, as Red Scar fell shrieking to the floor.

Jake stood staring, as Red Scar thrashed and flailed, trapped in a lava-like flow of heavy, opaque . . . *Mother of God, it was gold. Pure, molten gold.*

The spoils of war—

Jake backed away, step by step, as the fluid metal crept slowly across the cavern floor. At the center of the lake Red Scar still struggled, frenzied; the shining crust on its armored limbs began to congeal, crippling its movements, as the iron-hearted flood of gold continued to engulf it.

Jake watched, his face impassive, as Red Scar

burst into flames. He listened to the alien's shrieks of agony without pleasure, without compassion . . . without feeling anything at all. He forced his gaze to stay fixed on the burning lake until it had consumed Red Scar completely . . . until there was no sign that the alien had ever existed except for a faint ripple of impurity, a ghost of the brand he had put on Red Scar's face.

The wages of sin. . . .

Bathed in hellshine, Lucifer the Lightbringer spat into the sea of gold. ". . . Go back to hell . . ." he muttered, and turned away.

Jake shook the burning brilliance out of his eyes and the nightmare haze out of his brain as he started back to where Dolarhyde was still struggling to get his feet under him. Jake's body was no longer trembling, but now the ground underneath his feet was. He helped Dolarhyde get up, but the shaking around them had gotten worse, fast. Dolarhyde put a hand against the wall to keep his balance. "Old man—" Jake said, with a trace of a wicked grin.

Dolarhyde gave him a dirty look, and then gestured toward the ship. "Where's Ella?"

Jake looked up, suddenly realizing how close the ship must be to making its emergency departure. The strange machinery, flumes, supports, were withdrawing into it or falling away as the hatches sealed up one by one. The ship itself was beginning to vibrate, like it was more than ready to tear itself free of the earth—only waiting for the signal.

But Ella still hadn't come out. Why—?

"We gotta move," Dolarhyde said.

Jake shook his head, still gazing at the ship. "Not without Ella."

Rocks and rubble were sliding down the walls; the ceiling began to drop chunks of stone all around them.

"Jake!" Dolarhyde said, as more chunks of stone fell to the floor between them and the ship. *"We're outta time."*

Jake resisted as Dolarhyde tried to get him moving, trapped by another impossible choice, like the one he'd faced when Ella had gone into the ship. *He'd had to cover her, then; that had made his choice for him. But this time—*

This time Dolarhyde made the choice. "I said move—!" He shoved Jake into motion. They headed toward the tunnels as a piece of ceiling the size of a horse hit the ground behind them, landing between them and the ship.

Jake glanced over his shoulder. *No turning back.* Ella had tried to tell him that . . . maybe she'd been trying to tell him all along: that she never intended to come out of the ship alive; never intended to stay with him, even for a little while . . . or to let him follow her as she faced whatever happened next.

Damned if he did, damned if he didn't. Jake nodded to Dolarhyde as they reached the tunnel entrance, and they began to run.

OUTSIDE, HUMANS WERE fleeing from the slot canyon on foot and on horseback as if they were trying to escape the worst earthquake they'd ever known, as the ground shook and the mesa walls began to crumble.

As Jake and Dolarhyde ran toward the light of day, the alien ship's thrusters fired deep inside the mesa, releasing waves of energy that sent a cloud of heat and pulverized rock roaring through the mine shafts after them.

They came out of the entrance a bare second before the choking cloud of fumes and dust caught up to them as it blew on out the entrance. It hurled them aside, shaken but alive, to stagger up and go on running along the steep-walled arroyo.

Behind them, the full force of the alien ship's power blasted the tunnel entrance wide open, but they didn't look back.

They only stopped running when they had reached the arroyo's end. Dolarhyde stumbled to a stop first, and leaned forward, his hands on his knees as he gasped for breath.

Jake stopped beside him, turning to watch as the side of the mesa avalanched down into the arroyo, burying the tunnel opening in broken rock, blocking the entrance to the underworld.

The shouts and cries of other survivors rang dimly in his ears. Dolarhyde nudged him, pointing.

Jake looked up, just in time to see that the thing they had all sacrificed, fought, and died to keep from happening, was happening in spite of everything they could do: The alien ship tore itself free from the underworld, the mesa imploding beneath it as it escaped the Earth's grasp and streaked into the sky, rising up and up. . . .

"No—" Dolarhyde whispered.

Not after all they'd done, all they'd lost. . . . It couldn't be getting away from them now.

Jake stared up at the sky along with Dolarhyde, and everyone else who was left alive—all of them watching the alien ship grow smaller with every second that passed . . . *getting away.*

Ella . . . they must have found her, caught her, stopped her. . . . He should have been with her. Why, Ella—?

Ella. . . .

ELLA HAD FOUGHT her way at last to the alien ship's heart, the power core. She had felt the ship's thrusters fire, endured the vibration that threatened to tear the ship and her body apart as it fought its way free from the burial place where it had hidden from human eyes. Now, she knew, it was already climbing, higher and faster all the time; too soon it would be out of Earth's gravity well, and able to engage its hyperlight drive.

But not soon enough. Her lips thinned, her eyes closed for a long moment, in a prayer of resolve. Simple survival had never been enough; death was nothing at all. . . . To keep what had happened to her and her people from happening anywhere else, ever again, had always been her only choice.

She waited with a patience that, this one time, was more resigned than serene as the countdown sequence on her weapon dropped into single digits. Her human body still resisted her with emotions all its own, its instincts so interwoven with its higher mind that they were inseparable: dreading the unknown . . . still praying, if not for survival, at least to be remembered, by someone, with love. . . .

Ella said a prayer of her own, then: that she would never forget what she had learned here from her existence as a human woman on the planet Earth—the thing that made even a single fragile life-thread important. . . .

Jake. Goodbye, Jake—

As the countdown on her weapon zeroed out, she let go, falling into the core. The weapon detonated, and everything went white . . . stealing her vision, her form, her thoughts, as all that she was became one with the blinding chain reaction in the core, and she blew the ship into stardust. . . .

THE ALIEN SHIP exploded in mid-air: The sky lit up with a fireball that outshone the sun, and then an invisible wall of sound seemed to crack the sky and earth apart—

For an endless moment the entire sky went white with blinding remnants of the explosion . . . and then slowly it faded, bit by bit, until it was gone . . . all of it. The sky was a deep blue, cloudless dome once again; the sun was back in its rightful place as the only star that mattered.

And Ella. . . .

Jake bowed his head and turned away, not wanting Dolarhyde to see the kind of pain that had hold of him now. But he felt Dolarhyde's hand come to rest on his shoulder; steadying him, supporting him . . . comforting him, as if somehow Woodrow Dolarhyde knew exactly what kind of pain he was feeling.

It finally occurred to Jake to wonder what Dolarhyde had been doing there in the aliens' underworld, after all the captives had been freed. It struck him that the only reason Dolarhyde could possibly have had for going in was because he, and Ella, still hadn't come out. . . . *That Dolarhyde had gone in there meaning to save his life.*

As Jake and Dolarhyde stood side by side, looking up again in silent amazement along with everyone else who had survived the end of the world, something began to patter down on their hats like falling rain. Something was falling out of the sky that . . . glittered. Jake held out his hand, and watched it begin to fill with gold dust.

He looked over at Dolarhyde, who was beginning to gleam faintly in the sunlight; looked down at his own clothes, as he dusted off his gold-covered hand on his chaps. He realized that without a coat, Dolarhyde looked too much like him—dark vest and pants, pale shirt, his hat covered in dirt and blood . . . and gold dust. *They could have been brothers.*

Suddenly Jake started to laugh. He doubled over with laughter, laughing until tears spilled out of his eyes and fell onto the dry ground like rain, vanishing into the dust, as all tears of laughter—of loss, of grief and pain—always did, here in the desert.

Tears were still running down his face as he finally raised his head again; but his eyes were as empty as the sky, and his face was as bleak as the desert.

Dolarhyde was staring at him like he'd actually gone crazy. *Maybe he finally had . . . but after a day like this, he dared anybody to tell him who was sane, and who wasn't.*

He took a long, shaky breath, wiping his face on his sleeve, getting a chokehold on his emotions as he slowly leaned down to pick up Dolarhyde's rifle. Some compulsion as natural to him by now as breathing had kept him holding on to it, through everything. He held it out to Dolarhyde. "Good gun," he said, only now aware of the peculiar form of decoration on its stock.

It looked like an Apache gun. The Apaches liked the Winchester '66 too, so much that they had their own name for it: They called it "Yellow Boy," because its receiver was the color of gold.

Dolarhyde only shook his head. "Thank Black Knife, if you see him. . . ."

Jake gave him a twist of a grin, to match his own.

Jake and Dolarhyde walked out of the arroyo side by side, into the valley and toward the ridge where most of the survivors were gathered now.

The group of captives Jake and Ella had freed still stood huddled together, looking hopeful but uncertain, as the survivors of the battle approached—whites and Apaches together, their faces filled with the same hope and longing, as they searched for loved ones they'd lost.

Jake saw Doc start to run forward as he spotted Maria, and the light in his eyes as she stumbled toward him, tears streaming down her cheeks. He put his arms around her, kissing the tears from every inch of her face.

Emmett pushed through the crowd, calling out, "Grandpa!" He ran to his grandfather, hugging him. A tremor of recognition and confusion flickered across Sheriff Taggart's face, as Emmett looked up at him, saying, "You're alive! . . . It's me!"

"Reb-Rebecca?" Taggart said, uncertainly.

"No . . ." Emmett said, glancing down. "She's gone, Grandpa."

Taggart blinked, as if some elusive memory had blown into his eyes, like smoke.

Emmett's own face changed, touched by an understanding he wouldn't have found inside himself only a week before. He smiled, gently, as he said, "We still got each other." He took his grandfather's hand in his. "And I'm lookin' out for ya."

Taggart glanced down at his hand, held tightly inside the boy's, not yet fully comprehending, but . . . somehow . . . accepting. His smile filled with a kind of wonder as he looked at Emmett's face again. "Emmett," he said. "You're all grown up."

Dolarhyde moved away from Jake as he saw Black Knife coming toward him. They stood facing each other silently for a long moment . . . and then the *nantan* offered his arm in a gesture of friendship.

Just for a moment, Dolarhyde hesitated. Then he reached out and gripped it, as if at last his heart, and not just his mind, fully understood the distinction between the word "human," and the word "monster." At least he'd never forget now what "father" meant, and "loss," and "grief"—and that they were things as much a part of every human being—every one—as life itself.

His eyes glanced past Black Knife's shoulder, as he suddenly spotted the one face that he had needed to see: *Percy.*

With a nod to Black Knife, he headed toward the spot where his son Percy moved uncertainly though the crowd, searching. . . .

Dolarhyde stopped in front of him. Percy looked up at his father's face, his own face furrowing with concentration, as if he knew that he remembered this man from somewhere—somehow, if only. . . .

"Don't you remember me, boy?" Dolarhyde asked softly, his expression somber with concern and uncertainty.

Percy only blinked, as if the memory still wouldn't come to him.

Dolarhyde's eyes filled with emotion, until Jake wondered if Dolarhyde was actually capable of shedding tears. But he didn't need to, because the look itself had more of grief and joy and everything in between than any tears could express. His voice catching in his throat, Dolarhyde said, "I'm your father."

Percy's frown of concentration faded, and he . . . smiled. It held only the barest trace of recognition, but it was so innocent, so content, that it could have been the smile of a small boy, full of unquestioning trust.

Dolarhyde put an arm around Percy's shoulders,

drawing him away through the crowd. "Come on, son," he murmured, "let's go home."

JAKE DRIFTED AWAY from the spot where the re-unions were taking place, since there was no one left for him to find, and nobody who'd been looking to find him. Not here, at least.

He saw the members of his former gang—the ones who'd survived, the ones who'd been rescued—holding their own private celebration, as the last of the gold dust still rained down around them. Some of the boys were carefully picking up nugget-sized dollops of gold that had congealed as they hit the ground. He saw the members of his munitions team, collecting their reward along with the rest—all still alive. Jake felt oddly relieved.

Well, at least he'd kept his promise to them ... he'd made them rich. Some of the gang glanced up as he passed; they whooped or called out his name, grinning.

He smiled and kept moving, until he was finally alone. And then he looked up at the sky again. Squinting against the glare, he thought he could still make out faint traces of the dissipated explosion, like sun-dogs, a kind of rainbow haze. He let his grief, his loss, out onto his face at last, where no-body could witness it except the sky.

Ella had been on that ship ... she'd kept her prom-ise: *Never again.* She'd been a selfless warrior ... but not a soulless one ... in a no-holds-barred struggle against her people's, and his people's, worst enemy, never allowing herself to think about her own safety, her own needs . . . or his.

Except in that timeless moment when they'd kissed, and he'd felt her passion, her terrible loneliness, her unanswered need, answering his . . . the truth about everything. . . .

He looked down again, the ache inside him somehow only made worse for remembering it. Worst of all, he knew he didn't even have the right to feel angry that she'd left him, to feel bitter because she'd left him like this—to feel any kind of emotion at all that would help him stop hurting, for her, for himself . . . or to stop wanting the impossible.

He looked out across the desert that stretched away on all sides, only meeting up with the sky at last on what looked to be the edge of forever. The desert was all he had left; maybe all he'd ever been meant to have. A place where, if he could get far enough away, he couldn't hurt anybody but himself.

You're a good man. He suddenly remembered Alice's words, in a dream . . . remembered that Ella's last words to him had been the same ones.

A good man. He looked up at the sky again, wondering if that could possibly be true.

20

Word spread faster than locusts could strip a
wheat field: *Gold had come back to Absolution.* It'd come raining down from the desert sky, miraculously, in the middle of a cloudless day, according
to some accounts.

The last half of that news had given everybody
who heard it a good laugh; the first half had started
them packing their bags, or their mules.

The streets of the town were already beginning to
come alive with wagons and horses and people—
not just Dolarhyde's cowhands anymore, but faces
both old and new: prospectors who'd pitched their
tents at the edge of town, coming in to buy supplies
for their personal plans to strike it rich, and people
who were there to open or reopen stores and other
establishments prepared to sell them anything they
could afford.

The Gold Leaf Saloon was alive and kicking—
kicking up heels, anyway, in the middle of the

afternoon. The new piano player deftly played "Lorena"—Doc and Maria's personal favorite—one more time, as they danced together, rejoicing in life. The tables were already mostly filled with hungry customers who'd come for Maria's home cooking, but later the bar would be crowded with drinkers.

Bronc and Hunt, newly arrived, stood at the bar with a bag of gold nuggets sitting on the counter in front of them, ready to start the evening early.

It was Hunt's turn to buy the drinks, but he didn't mind—he couldn't help feeling good-natured as he looked at the reminder of his personal fortune, one of the many bags of gold each gang member had managed to collect and stash away before anyone from outside even arrived.

He grinned as he watched Doc dancing with his wife. She was one of the most beautiful women he'd ever seen; wearing a new deep-red silk dress; she looked like a rose in bloom. But after so long in the desert, Hunt was a thirsty man. "How many more songs we gotta sit through before we can get a drink?" he called out, as "Lorena" came to an end again.

Doc grinned back at him. "Simmer down, Hot Sauce," he said. "Just happy to see my wife—I'm coming." Before he broke away, Maria gave him a kiss that made Hunt's eyebrows rise; he heard Bronc laugh appreciatively beside him.

Still smiling, Doc moved behind the bar and got out a bottle of his best whiskey to pour the two men a round. "*Muy amable,*" Bronc said, and Doc nodded. It occurred to Hunt that Bronc had the best manners he'd ever seen, for somebody whose name meant "rowdy."

Hunt raised his glass to Doc, and took a gulp. *Nectar of the gods . . .* he thought, and sighed. Maybe he'd die in bed yet.

DOC NOTICED THAT a couple of other familiar faces had arrived at the bar. He left Bronc and Hunt to their bottle and moved on down the bar to find out what the unlikely duo of Emmett, the sheriff's grandson, and Percy Dolarhyde wanted. Doc realized he hadn't seen Percy acting drunk, loud, or obnoxious once since they'd all returned to Absolution—in fact, he'd hardly seen him at all. Percy wasn't even wearing a gun anymore.

"A drink for me and my friend?" Percy said, in a perfectly sociable voice, as he nodded at Emmett.

Doc looked at them, dubious. "Isn't your friend a little young to be standing at the bar?"

"Not after what he's been through." Percy said, with a small grin, and added, "Two sarsaparillas."

As Doc reached for the bottle of non-alcoholic root beer, Percy reached into his pocket and pulled out a small wad of money. He laid it on the bar, pushing it toward Doc, meeting his stare as he said, "And this should take care of any outstanding debts." He glanced down. "And I thank you for your patience."

As he raised his head again, Doc gave him back a smile of appreciation, keeping his amazement to himself. *Will wonders never cease,* he thought. Percy

Dolarhyde really was a new man, a different man, since his encounter with the aliens.

Well, he wasn't the only one. . . . Doc poured their drinks with a flourish, while Emmett beamed at being treated like an adult.

Just then, Woodrow Dolarhyde pushed open the bat-wing doors, carrying ledgers under one arm, and called out, "*Percy.*"

Everything stopped: the music, the talking, the laughter. Everyone's eyes were fixed on Dolarhyde, out of either habit or curiosity.

"Coming, Pa," Percy said. He left the bar, leaving the drinks to Emmett, and walked toward the entrance where his father was waiting. Everyone else was waiting too; a few of them were even holding their breath.

DOLARHYDE GLANCED AROUND the room, taking in the anxious expressions, the silence. . . . Until finally he just laughed and said, "Next round's on the Dolarhydes."

The held silence broke into good-natured shouting as customers raised their glasses to him. Dolarhyde went back outside, relieved and satisfied, with Percy following willingly.

Dolarhyde walked with his son along the newly rebuilt boardwalk, passing a handful of locals who nodded and tipped their hats in gratitude. Because he'd paid for repairs and willingly loaned out money, the destruction the aliens' attack had done to the town was beginning to heal, and the spirits of its people were healing, too.

Dolarhyde smiled in acknowledgment, secretly amazed at how good it made a man feel to use his money for the greater good—to begin repaying some of the debt his soul owed for wreaking so much havoc in so many lives. He couldn't even recall why the hell he'd begun hoarding all that money in the first place. It was cold and hard and dead; and he had as much of it as he'd ever need, easily five times over.

He looked back at Percy, remembering what Preacher Meacham had dared, once, to preach at him about: that people . . . people like his own son, or Nat . . . were what he should've been paying heed to, because they were irreplaceable, unlike his gold.

He considered for a fleeting moment how it had been before . . . what he would have done to anyone who'd touched so much as one double-eagle of it . . . what he'd planned to do to Jake Lonergan, who'd ended up saving his son. Did the hunger for gold turn someone into a monster . . . or was the monster always there, waiting like a scavenger to gnaw at a man's soul, when something better had died . . . ?

Dolarhyde refocused his thoughts as Percy noticed his long silence and gave him a concerned look. He put on a smile again, and picked up the thread of what he'd meant to talk about—the kinds of things a rancher's son, and heir to his business, needed to know; things that he'd never thought about before, when he'd thought he'd never need anyone but himself.

"Real soon, a lot more people're gonna be hearing

about the gold." He gestured at the activity in the street. "Won't be long before there's a railroad spur in here—gonna change the entire nature of the business. People who make money'll be feeding cattle, not running 'em."

Percy nodded, alert and intent, taking it all in with an eagerness Dolarhyde knew came as much from the fact that he'd finally included his son in his life, as from the boy's real, and surprising, intelligence. *But then, he really shouldn't have been surprised about that.*

Dolarhyde handed the armload of ledgers to Percy. "Get these ledgers to the bank, tell 'em I need some new checks printed up."

Percy stopped in mid-motion, about to step into the street. He looked down, his smile and alertness abruptly falling away into resignation.

Dolarhyde was taken aback, seeing his son's face fall. "Tell the banker I want them to read, 'Dolarhyde and Son'," he added. He paused, as his son's face brightened again, like the sun coming out from behind clouds. Dolarhyde was suddenly reminded of his wife—Percy's mother. "That okay with you?" he asked, with a smile that invited his son to speak his own mind; feeling, for the first time, that he'd finally begun learning to be a father.

"Yes." Percy's smile widened. "Yes, sir." He moved off, carrying the ledgers as proudly as he should, when someday the Dolarhyde land, and everything on it, would be his heritage. He'd turned into a better son and heir than Dolarhyde had ever imagined . . .

than he had ever deserved, until he'd become a better father.

Dolarhyde walked on, approaching the sheriff's office. Taggart was sitting in a chair with his legs stretched out, relaxing, but keeping an eye on the street. He and Charlie Lyle were back to the men they'd been before the aliens had taken them . . . except that now Taggart actually seemed to be enjoying life. The black dog that had followed Jake Lonergan to town, and trailed them throughout their long journey into the wilderness, was lying at his side.

"John." Dolarhyde greeted him with a nod.

"Woodrow." Taggart looked up at him, looked out at the street again. "Our town's about to get a whole lot bigger."

"Hope that won't be a problem for you, Sheriff." Dolarhyde glanced out at the street, the number of people passing by. *Change was never easy.* . . . He looked back at Taggart. "This is your town—and if it wasn't before, it sure is now."

Taggart reached down to scratch the dog's ears. When he looked up, he was wearing the first genuine smile Dolarhyde had ever seen on his face.

The two of them looked up together as one of the riders passing by on the street reined in his horse in front of the jail. Jake Lonergan sat looking down at them, as if he'd just happened past by chance, but studying their faces as though he wanted to be sure he remembered them, if they ever met again. His saddlebags were packed for a long journey; two canteens hung from his saddle horn.

Other than that, he appeared to be leaving town the same way he'd arrived—on what had been a stranger's horse, with only the clothes on his back. The dog wagged its tail at the sight of him, but made no move to get up.

JAKE TOOK HIS hat from the saddle horn and put it on as Dolarhyde stepped forward and looked back at him.

"You were gonna leave without saying goodbye?" he asked. His smile showed a mocking trace of the Dolarhyde Jake remembered, making the words a challenge. But there was something in his eyes that surprised Jake—as if his leaving without saying a word would have hurt the man a lot more than losing a small fortune in gold ever had.

Jake shrugged. "Still a wanted man," he pointed out. Dolarhyde and the sheriff might act like they'd forgotten that, but he could never afford to.

He'd drunk too much whiskey, eaten plenty of good food, and had enough sleep to last him a couple of months . . . and he'd spent more time by himself, thinking, than he'd intended. He figured he'd had about as much of Absolution as he could survive.

This town was filling up with too many strangers—and he'd met all the strangers who wanted to kill him on sight that he ever wanted to. Although with a thousand-dollar bounty on his head, that problem wasn't likely to go away, even if he rode to the end of forever.

Dolarhyde raised his eyebrows. "I swear I saw

Jake Lonergan die in those caves," he said, turning to Taggart. "Isn't that right, Sheriff?"

Taggart smiled and pulled his hat lower over his eyes, as if the sun was getting into them. "Damn shame we couldn't hang him ourselves."

Dolarhyde looked back at Jake's stunned face, and this time he smiled like he meant it. "Man has a right to start fresh." His mouth twitched, and his smile widened. "And I got my gold back."

Jake glanced at Taggart, sitting with his chair propped against the wall. He looked back at Dolarhyde, who was standing there like he'd just come into town to take a stroll.

"That what you're doing?" Jake asked, his mouth turning up. "Get a rocking chair, sit out front while someone polishes your boots?"

"You want the job?" Dolarhyde grinned.

Still quick on the draw. Jake grinned back, settling his hat more firmly on his head in answer.

"I could always use a gun like you around," Dolarhyde said, and this time Jake saw that he was only half joking.

Jake kept his grin. "Yeah, you could," he said.

Dolarhyde laughed as Jake began to turn his horse away into the street again, heading for the trail out of town.

"Jake," Dolarhyde said.

Jake stopped, shifting in his saddle to look back.

"She's in a better place."

Jake stared at him for a long moment. Surprise, loss, and finally understanding filled his eyes, as he looked down at Dolarhyde's expression.

"Take care of yourself," Dolarhyde said, and smiled at him.

Jake nodded, his own smile genuine and complete at last. He lifted his hand to touch his hat . . . almost a salute. "Be seeing you around," he said, "Colonel."

Dolarhyde took it without even flinching; one more demon that he'd laid to rest, on their journey to the end of the world and back. He tipped his hat in return. He stood beside the sheriff, both men watching Jake ride out of their lives, until he disappeared into the mirage of the day.

JAKE APPROACHED THE ruined cabin that marked the end of his former life . . . and Alice's. He entered through the splintered doorway and laid the small bouquet of fresh flowers he had picked down by the river on the table. He took off his hat.

And then he bowed his head and closed his eyes. He wanted to pray, but he didn't know how. . . . He wanted to ask her forgiveness . . . but she had forgiven him already. He would have told her, *I love you*; but all he could do now was hope he'd had the sense to tell her that before . . . before it was too late.

And taking her in his arms, he would have asked her to marry him. . . .

But all those moments had been torn away from him, as surely as she had . . . *had been*. . . .

His memory refused to carry it any further. He had come to say goodbye. That was all.

He turned away, not letting his gaze linger anywhere as he went back out through the doorway.

He'd never even had this much of a chance to say goodbye to Ella. . . . He looked up at the sky.

Ella. . . . Even if she had never really been his to love, to spend a lifetime with, or even one night, enough time so that he could have let her know how much—

But then he remembered how she'd kissed him, there in the underworld. Maybe, in that one moment, they'd shared with each other everything they'd needed to know. . . .

She'd always seemed to know his deepest thoughts, sense the feelings he'd never even recognized in himself, in a way that was . . . *that wasn't human,* he realized at last. And in that moment outside any reality he'd known before, or would ever know again, she'd finally let him into her own mind, her own heart. One moment that had seemed to last a lifetime . . . that would have to last for a lifetime.

It made him wish, just for a moment, that humans could see into each other's minds and hearts, the way she'd done with him, with everyone around her. But what would that change about humans? They'd just use it all wrong, like they got everything else wrong.

He thought about Dolarhyde and Taggart, back in Absolution; remembered how Ella had made him believe that there might be something better in everyone.

But he didn't envy those two, or the town . . . or the last of the free Apaches, once gold fever really took hold of this place.

What the hell was wrong with human beings? Had they even deserved Ella's sacrifice? In their hearts they wanted to be like angels ... but one wrong move, and demon was too good a word for what a man could become.

But Ella had believed in him. He thought about the last moment before she'd left him forever—how he'd held her in his arms and let himself kiss her with all his heart and soul and mind, feel the warmth of her human body, her human heart beating against his ... just to get that damned shackle off his wrist for her.

He remembered then that when she'd kissed him, he'd known she was giving him—of all people—all the love she'd been afraid to feel, maybe for more human lifetimes than he could imagine, after losing more than anyone he'd ever known. She'd given him her heart to hold, for as long as he lived, and with it the unforgettable memory of everything she was. . . .

Morning Star: Sonseeahray ... Ella, who'd lived like a selfless avenging angel, fighting a war against demons over the right to destroy worlds—never allowed to feel the warmth, the comfort, the passion of the love that had made her choose to be who she'd become. She'd denied even the need for love until she'd begun to doubt the very reason for her existence. . . .

Until she'd found another Morning Star: Jake Lonergan ... *Lucifer*, who'd been thrown out of Heaven, God only knew why ... no longer loved, no longer wanted by anyone, dead or alive.

And yet it had been something about him, when he kissed her, finally acknowledging possession of his own lost soul, that had given her the key to set herself free, even for one moment—enough time for one kiss to fill his body and soul until all his senses sang. The kind of love he'd felt for her then was enough to break any man's heart. . . .

He closed his eyes, holding on to the memory of that moment, the way he'd wanted to go on holding her in his arms. He knew he had to leave here, get going, out into the wide open spaces of the rest of his life. Ella would expect him to—not to waste the gift he'd been given, not to throw his life away again.

But bad was all he'd ever been good at. . . .

". . . Jake. . . ." He thought he heard the barest whisper of his name, of Ella's voice, carried on the wind. His eyes opened. He turned, looking behind him, all around— *Nothing.*

Instead he heard a soft humming noise, above his head, shifting from ear to ear impossibly. His eyes finally found the source—a hummingbird, its colors shining like a rainbow in sunlight, dancing on the wind along trailing vines of wild honeysuckle . . . moving toward him.

He stepped forward, but it still hovered in front of his eyes, unafraid, almost as if it was looking into them the way she had . . . reflecting the countless emotions that passed and collided in a moment: the pain, the anger, the stubborn defiance . . . the decency and honor that Meacham had somehow seen inside a man with the Devil in his eyes . . . the love that Alice, and then Ella, had proved even he was capable of feeling . . .

And finally, the self-respect their belief had forced on him, as he'd come to realize that the faith they'd had in him was actually justified. . . . That he might actually deserve to live, after all; that he hadn't been born just to add to the sum total of human misery. . . .

That it wasn't a sin for him to be glad to be alive. All he needed, now, was the kind of courage it took to find out what he was really meant to do. . . .

The hummingbird darted away, came back, danced away again, almost as if it was inviting him to play a game of tag with the future: calling him into a new game, one he'd never played before . . . never knowing if the rules would be fair or foul, only knowing that there was still hope and there would always be new possibilities, because life was always changing. That it had changed already, if he was only willing to believe it.

He looked into the hummingbird's bright-dark eyes again for a long moment, before he turned where he stood, gazing at the distance where the sky reached down to touch the earth . . . a horizon without limits, only the promise of places he'd never seen. No black-and-white, no absolute right that he would always be on the wrong side of: He looked up into the sky's deep and perfect blue, which had always seemed so far away, so far above him—unreachable.

He glanced down at his wrist, at the spot where the demon gun had shackled him to his past—until Ella had kissed him. He raised his head again, to see the hummingbird flying off into the distance, vanishing almost before his eyes could see which way it went . . . realizing that he truly was free to choose his own path, at last.

Jake started toward his waiting horse, turning his

back on the lost years he was no longer chained to. The vividness of the few memories he did have would fade in time, just enough so that someday he could recall them without his eyes burning. . . .

He glanced up at the sky again, at the secret that lay hidden within the blue. It no longer seemed unfathomable to him . . . any more than the true meaning of freedom. A faint grin touched his face as he reached his horse, as if the universe had just whispered in his ear. He mounted up and rode away; no longer looking back, or needing to, as he followed his spirit guide into the future.

A WOMAN'S FIGURE, silhouetted by the sky, stood gazing down into the canyon from a cliff high above, invisible to any eyes that might have looked up from below. She watched as Jake rode away, her body haloed in rainbow light by the brilliant afternoon sun. She stood without moving, still looking after him until Jake was long gone from her sight. Jake hadn't seen her, and she was sure that he never would again.

But if he had, he would have seen her smiling.

FINIS

ABOUT THE AUTHOR

JOAN D. VINGE is the author of *The Snow Queen*, which won the Hugo Award for Best SF Novel, and its sequels *World's End, The Summer Queen* (a Hugo Award finalist), and *Tangled Up in Blue*, as well as three novels about the character Cat—*Psion, Catspaw*, and *Dreamfall*, and the novel *Heaven Chronicles*. She also has written a number of shorter works, and her stories, including her Hugo Award–winning novelette, "Eyes of Amber," have appeared in major SF magazines and anthologies. Her short fiction has been collected in two books, *Eyes of Amber* and *Phoenix in the Ashes*. Ms. Vinge is also the author of a number of film adaptations, including novelizations such as *Ladyhawke, Mad Max Beyond Thunderdome, Willow*, and the film *Lost in Space*, as well as *The Return of the Jedi Storybook*, which was a huge bestseller.

She also is the author of *The Random House Book of Greek Myths*, a book for young readers, with illustrations by Oren Sherman; and for several years was the manga and anime critic for the anthology series The Year's Best Fantasy and Horror, edited by Ellen Datlow and Kelly Link & Gavin Grant. She is currently working on *Ladysmith*, the first in a series of "prehistorical" novels set in Bronze Age Western Europe, which will make good use of her degree in anthropology. Visit her at www.sff.net/people/JDVinge/.